PRAISE FOR JOHN SAUL

The Manhattan Hunt Club
"Nonstop action keeps the book
moving at a brisk pace."
—*Library Journal*

"Thrilling . . . Packed with plot twists."
—*Booklist*

Nightshade
"[Saul] haunts his shadowy realm ingeniously and
persistently. . . . *Nightshade* may be his masterpiece."
—*Providence Journal*

"Gripping . . . Saul, and his unerring instincts to instill
fear, returns to tap into our deepest, most closely
guarded shadows and secrets."
—*Palo Alto Daily News*

The Right Hand of Evil
"[A] tale of evil that is both extreme and entertaining."
—*Chicago Tribune*

"[A] whopper of a nightmare tale . . . Dazzling . . .
Dizzying twists."
—*Publishers Weekly*

*Please turn the page
for more reviews. . . .*

By John Saul:

SUFFER THE CHILDREN***
PUNISH THE SINNERS***
CRY FOR THE STRANGERS***
COMES THE BLIND FURY***
WHEN THE WIND BLOWS***
THE GOD PROJECT**
NATHANIEL**
BRAINCHILD**
HELLFIRE**
THE UNWANTED**
THE UNLOVED**
CREATURE**
SECOND CHILD**
SLEEPWALK**
DARKNESS**
SHADOWS**
GUARDIAN*
THE HOMING*
BLACK LIGHTNING*
THE BLACKSTONE CHRONICLES:
      Part 1: AN EYE FOR AN EYE: THE DOLL*
      Part 2: TWIST OF FATE: THE LOCKET*
      Part 3: ASHES TO ASHES: THE DRAGON'S FLAME*
      Part 4: IN THE SHADOW OF EVIL:
          THE HANDKERCHIEF*
      Part 5: DAY OF RECKONING: THE STEREOSCOPE*
      Part 6: ASYLUM*
THE PRESENCE*
THE RIGHT HAND OF EVIL*
NIGHTSHADE*
THE MANHATTAN HUNT CLUB*

*Published by The Ballantine Publishing Group
**Published by Bantam Books
***Published by Dell Books

THE MANHATTAN HUNT CLUB

John Saul

BALLANTINE BOOKS • NEW YORK

This book contains an excerpt from the forthcoming hardcover edition of *Midnight Voices* by John Saul. This excerpt has been set for this edition only and may not reflect the final content of the forthcoming edition.

A Ballantine Book
Published by The Ballantine Publishing Group
Copyright © 2001 by John Saul
Excerpt from *Midnight Voices* by John Saul copyright © 2002 by John Saul

All rights reserved under International and Pan-American Copyright Conventions. Published in the United States by The Ballantine Publishing Group, a division of Random House, Inc., New York, and simultaneously in Canada by Random House of Canada Limited, Toronto.

Ballantine and colophon are registered trademarks of Random House, Inc.

www.ballantinebooks.com

ISBN 0-449-00652-2

Manufactured in the United States of America

First Hardcover Edition: August 2001
First Mass Market Edition: May 2002

10 9 8 7 6 5 4 3 2 1

For Ralph and Paulette
—with thanks for twenty-five
years of friendship

PROLOGUE

Time had finally lost its meaning.

Weeks could have passed. Or months.

Not days, though, for the memories of what his life had once been were fading into the fog that filled his mind. Not years, either, for the memories still had shape and texture and color and smell.

A tree.

Not just any tree, but the walnut tree behind the house in which he grew up. When he was little, the tree was huge, its lowest limbs branching off so far up the trunk that his daddy had to hold him up to touch them. When he got big enough, he climbed up the rough-barked trunk into its spreading canopy—even built a tree house once, where he could hide on a lazy summer afternoon. The sun filtered through the dome of leaves, and the whole world seemed to glow with the faintest tinge of pale green.

In the cypress hedge that surrounded the yard, hundreds of sparrows roosted at sunset, their rustling almost inaudible until his dog—a little black mutt named Cinder—went racing up and down, shattering the quiet with her high-pitched yap. The birds would explode from the hedge in a rush that sounded like wind and looked like a swirl of autumn leaves. The sparrows would wheel in the sky, etched against its darkening blue, and slowly settle back to the hedge, only to be flushed again a moment later.

Those were the memories that were still brightest in his

mind, for they were the oldest, and though he himself wasn't old, his mind was already playing the tricks of the aged. Why could he clearly remember that tree from nearly twenty years ago, but barely recall the last room he'd lived in?

Was it because he didn't want to remember that room?

As he paused in the gloom that surrounded him now, vague outlines re-created themselves in his mind. A tiny space almost filled by a single sagging bed, a metal table with a chipped enameled surface. The stairs leading to it reeked of piss, partially masked by the stink of stale cigarette smoke. Not that he'd worried much about it—he had lived in rooms like that before. Then one day he left the room and never went back. He didn't care—he couldn't pay the rent anyway, and the bastard landlord who lived in the crummy apartment in the basement probably would have changed the locks in a couple of days.

Not much to remember after that.

He'd wandered around the streets for a while, and that hadn't been too bad. At least he didn't have to waste any money on rent. But then it started getting cold, and once or twice he'd gone to one of the shelters. Not the one out on the island—what the fuck was the name of it? Like some department store from a long time ago.

Wards. That was it—Wards Island.

He hadn't been about to go out there. Not that he figured it would be any worse than the places he'd seen since he followed Big Ted down into Grand Central.

They'd been hanging around the food joints on the lower level when a couple of transit cops started looking at them funny. "Come on," Big Ted muttered, and he'd followed him to the platform down by Track 42.

On the other side of the track there was a weird jumble of walls and pipes and ladders. Half the walls seemed to be falling down, and most of the ladders didn't look like they led anywhere. Big Ted jumped off the platform, crossed the track, and scaled a ladder on the opposite side. He hesitated, then heard someone yelling, and didn't wait to find out what they wanted. He quickly followed Ted across the track and up the ladder and was just able to keep up as the other man ducked through a door.

Ted led him through a couple of rooms, then climbed up on some pipes and started working his way into the darkness. He still heard shouting behind them, and it drove him on, following Big Ted.

At first it was kind of fun—sort of like an adventure. He figured he'd hang with Big Ted for a couple of days, then maybe go somewhere else. Maybe even get out of the city. But a couple of days later it started snowing, and at least it was warm down in the tunnels.

Well, at least it wasn't freezing cold down there.

If you were careful, you could use the men's room around the corner from the Oyster Bar, if you didn't stay too long and the transit cops weren't feeling too mean. But after he barely got away when they busted Big Ted, he spent more time in the tunnels than upstairs.

He got used to it. It wasn't nearly as dark as it seemed at first. There were more lights than he'd thought, and after a while he even grew accustomed to the noise. "Like the gentle rolling of ocean surf," Annie Thompson had called it in her gentle drawl that two years on the streets of New York hadn't hardened. "Puts you to sleep just like you were on the beach at Hilton Head." He didn't believe she'd ever lived in Hilton Head, but then, she probably wouldn't have believed he'd grown up in California. It didn't matter.

All that mattered was that they were both still alive.

Or what passed for alive. Most of the time there wasn't much difference between night and day, unless you were under one of the grates that opened up into a park or something, and for the last couple of days—maybe even a week—he'd been staying away from the grates.

The grates, and the subway stations, and the train stations, and the culverts, and the mouths of the tunnels. None of it was safe anymore.

None of it.

Not any friends anymore, either.

A few days ago, maybe a week, he'd had friends. Annie Thompson, and Ike, and that girl—the one whose name he couldn't remember. Didn't matter no more anyway, once they started coming after him.

"They."

The thing was, he didn't know who "they" were. Up until the craziness started, he'd thought "they" were his friends.

But then one day when he left the tunnels, he snatched a purse. It was real easy—he'd watched Big Ted do it lots of times. The woman he'd snatched it from hadn't even tried to hang on to it.

She didn't even yell for help.

A couple of hours later, still on the outside, he ran into Annie Thompson. She'd been right there in the subway station where he made the snatch, and saw it all. But instead of asking him how much money he'd gotten or to split it with her, which he might even have done, she told him off. "You crazy? What did you want to do that for?" She kept on talking, but he didn't listen—he was too busy looking at a girl who'd just come out of the big church on Amsterdam Avenue, and wondering what it would be like to talk to her. Not touch her or anything like that. Just talk to her. So he'd pretty much ignored Annie until he ran into her later—he couldn't remember exactly when—and she'd warned him. "Better get out," she said. "You really think you could get away with that? Now they're comin' after you."

He hadn't believed her until the next time he tried to get to the surface through one of the subway stations and some of Ike's friends had shown him their knives.

He could tell by the look in their eyes they weren't kidding.

He'd been on the run ever since.

And he'd been going deeper and deeper, climbing down ladders whenever he found them, crawling through drainpipes he could barely fit into, creeping on his belly through slimy passages so tight that if they hadn't been slick with scum, he wouldn't have been able to make it at all.

Now he lay on a ledge above a passageway that was so dark, if he shut off his flashlight he couldn't see his hand in front of his eyes. The batteries were dying, and even if they hadn't been, he couldn't risk the dimming glow of the flashlight giving him away.

He heard something moving in the dark, then felt whatever it was skitter across his hand.

In the distance, a train rumbling.

In the darkness, a flash of red.

The rumbling of the train grew louder.

He shrank back against the wall behind him, instinctively holding his breath. The whole passage trembled as somewhere above him the train roared over. As the rumbling tremor faded away, the passage grew still.

He let himself relax.

He took a breath, and the fetid odor of decay filled his nostrils.

Again a glimmer of red, this time from the other direction.

Now he could see two spots of red, creeping along the floor like glowing insects. They came together and seemed confused for a moment. Then both glowing red spots began moving toward him.

He tried to squirm back deeper on the shelf, but the cold, dank hardness of solid concrete stopped him.

He lost sight of the glowing dots for a moment, then looked down.

They were both on his chest, close together.

He never heard the shots. Long before the reports of the exploding shells reached his ears, one of the bullets tore into his heart, while the other smashed his spine.

Even in that last split second before he died, he still didn't know why it had to happen.

He only knew there was no way to stop it.

CHAPTER 1

*K*ill him, Cindy Allen silently prayed. *Kill him, and let me know that this is over.*

Sensing her tension, Bill reached over and took her hand. "They'll lock him up forever," he said softly. "They'll lock him up and you'll never have to be afraid again."

Though she squeezed Bill's hand as if his words had comforted her, Cindy knew they weren't true. She would be afraid for the rest of her life.

Afraid to walk by herself in the streets—if she could ever walk again.

Afraid to look at the faces of strangers, fearful of what she would see in their eyes: pity and revulsion and embarrassment.

Afraid even to look at Bill, of seeing shades of those emotions in his eyes.

And all because of the man whose face now filled the screen of the television set at the foot of her bed.

She tried to put aside her anger and her fear for a moment, tried to look dispassionately at the face of Jeff Converse. It was a handsome face—she had to admit that. Clean-cut, even features.

Not the kind of face you'd expect to see on a monster. Indeed, nothing about Jeff Converse's pleasing appearance hinted at the cruelty that lay within. Not the dark, wavy hair, not the warm brown eyes, not the expression on his face. In the image on the television screen of the man she'd testified

6

against in court, Jeff Converse looked as frightened as Cindy Allen felt. Except that she knew her fear was real.

His was just another lie, like all the lies he'd told in court.

"What if the judge believes him?" she whispered, not quite aware that she'd spoken aloud.

"He won't believe him," Bill replied. "The jury didn't believe him, and neither will the judge. He'll give Converse everything he's got coming to him."

But he won't, Cindy thought. He might put Jeff Converse in jail, but he won't do to him what he did to me.

As the image of Jeff Converse vanished from the television screen, replaced by the smiling visage of the pretty blonde who anchored the morning news, Cindy looked away, her gaze shifting to the mirror over the dresser that she'd made Bill hang low on the wall so she could see herself as others saw her.

"It will be all right," Bill had said, trying to reassure her the first time she'd looked into the mirror after the bandages were removed. "I've talked to the doctor, and he says he can repair almost all the damage. It will just take time."

Time, and five surgeries, and more money than she and Bill earned in a year.

And even then, even if they found the money and she went through all the procedures, the plastic surgeon had explained to her, she wouldn't be well. Her features might once again bear some resemblance to the face that had been hers until that horrible night six months ago. But even if they could repair the scars on the outside—rebuild her crushed cheekbone and shattered jaw, repair the lower lip that had been nearly torn away when he'd slammed her face into the concrete, breaking five teeth in her lower jaw and four in her upper— they'd never be able to repair the scars on the inside. Even if they could find a way to mend the damage to her spine that had made it impossible for her to walk, they'd never be able to make her feel safe on the streets again.

That was what Jeff Converse had taken from her. She had

been on her way to meet Bill. It was late, but not that late. He'd had to work, and so had she, and they were going to meet for dinner at ten.

The subway was almost empty—only one seat was taken on the car she got on at Rector Street—and that passenger got off at Forty-second. Then she had the car to herself, which was just the way she liked it. Alone, she was able to concentrate on the IPO she was analyzing before making her final recommendation on Monday morning. By the time she got to 110th Street, she'd marked half a dozen sections to go over with Bill during dinner.

The station was nearly as deserted as Rector Street had been, and she barely noticed the solitary man standing on the platform, waiting for a downtown train.

She was just starting up the stairs when she felt the arm snake around her neck, felt the hand clamp over her mouth. She was yanked backward, then dragged down the deserted platform until they were at its northernmost end.

That's when her face was smashed the first time, slammed so hard into the tile wall that her nose shattered and blood started streaming down. Stunned, she had no strength to resist as the man shoved her to the platform and began tearing at her clothes. Finally, she started fighting back. She struggled to roll over so she was facing him, but he was too strong for her. He slammed her face into the concrete platform as though trying to break the head of a doll, and for a second she blacked out. When she came to an instant later, she was lying on her back, and though her eyes were already swelling and swimming with her own blood, she could see his face clearly.

The brown eyes looking down at her.

The shock of dark hair.

She lashed out, her fingernails raking his cheek as she found her voice and screamed. She tried to twist away from him, but something was wrong with her body—she couldn't move her legs.

She screamed again and again, and after what seemed an

eternity, during which she was certain she was about to die, help appeared.

Abruptly, the figure above her was pulled away, and a moment later she was surrounded by people. Two transit policemen asked her what had happened, but by then the agony was already overwhelming, and as she saw two more cops dragging the man away, she drifted into unconsciousness.

When she woke up again, she was in a hospital.

They brought her pictures of a dozen men when she was well enough.

She recognized him immediately.

She would never forget him.

"I want to be there," she said now, as another image of Jeff Converse appeared on the television screen. "When the judge sentences him, I want to be there."

"You don't have to, Cindy," Bill replied, but Cindy Allen was determined.

"I want to see him. I want to see the fear in his eyes." Without waiting for Bill to help her, she began working her broken body out of the bed and into the wheelchair that stood next to it. "He deserves to die," she said. "And the scariest part is, I wish I could watch them kill him."

Carolyn Randall felt the tension in her expensively decorated breakfast room as the newscaster finished her story on the sentencing of Jeff Converse. When Jeff's face first appeared on the screen, she'd instinctively reached for the remote control, but not quickly enough. The blond newscaster—who Carolyn was almost certain had been flirting with her husband at a Cancer Society benefit two weeks ago—had already spoken Jeff's name, and both Carolyn's husband and her stepdaughter had immediately turned to look.

"Why do you two insist on watching every report about this awful thing?" she demanded when the newscast cut to a commercial. "It's over. You've got to let it go."

"It's not over," Heather replied without hesitation, her

voice tinged with anger. "It won't be over until they let Jeff go."

" 'They,' as you put it, are not going to let him go unless he's innocent," Perry Randall said in a condescending tone, which Heather recognized as one he ordinarily reserved for dim witnesses who were ignorant of the facts. "And since he is not innocent, I don't think that is going to happen."

"You don't know—" Heather began, but her father cut her off before she could finish.

"I know the facts of the case," he reminded her. "I saw the police report after Converse was arrested, and though I re-cused myself from the case for obvious reasons, that does not mean I didn't review it carefully." He saw in the way his daughter's jaw set that his arguments would be no more per-suasive this morning than they had been on any other day since Jeff Converse had been apprehended at the scene of the assault on Cynthia Allen. His own stubborn streak now revealed itself. "I know how you feel, Heather, but if feel-ings were allowed to rule our courts, our prisons would be empty. There isn't a man on Rikers Island—or anywhere else, I suspect—who doesn't have a girlfriend who swears he's innocent."

"But Jeff is innocent!" Heather flared. "Daddy, you must know he's not capable of what he's accused of doing!"

Perry Randall's left eyebrow arched. "No, Heather, I really don't know him."

Heather felt she was choking on the stream of furious words rising in her throat, but held them in. What was the point of arguing with her father now? His mind was made up—had been made up since the moment she'd called him after Jeff's arrest.

She had called him in the hope—no, in the *certainty*—that he'd be able to talk to someone and straighten everything out. Now she realized she should have known better. Hadn't it been her father's cool, analytical responses to nearly every emotional issue that ever came up that had finally driven her mother away? Still, she hadn't been prepared for his response to her request for help:

"I want you to come home immediately," he'd told her. "The last thing I need right now—"

"*You* need?" she'd retorted. "Daddy, Jeff's in jail!"

"Which in my experience means he's undoubtedly done something to get himself there," her father replied. Then, in the face of her anguish, he'd softened. "I'll look into it in the morning. It's going to take some time for the precinct to book him, but there should be something in the office by tomorrow morning. I'll take a look—see what people are thinking. Then I'll see what I can do."

So Heather had come home.

Except the big apartment overlooking Central Park didn't feel like home anymore—hadn't felt like home since her mother had left a dozen years ago, when she was eleven.

"Left."

There was a nice euphemism. Now that she was twenty-three, Heather knew that "taken away" would better describe what had happened. She hadn't seen it herself, but over the years, she'd gotten a pretty good idea about what had happened. All she'd known at the time was that she'd come home from school as on any typical day and found her mother gone. "She just needs a good rest," they told her.

It turned out her mother was "resting" in a hospital.

Not a regular hospital, like Lenox Hill, over near Lexington, or the Manhattan Eye, Ear and Throat Hospital down on Sixty-fourth.

The one her mother was in looked more like a resort than a hospital and was out in the country. But it wasn't a resort. It was where her father had sent Charlotte Randall to stop her from drinking and taking pills.

At first her mother promised she'd come home soon. "It'll only be a little while, sweetheart," she said the first time

Heather visited. But her mother never came home again. "I just can't," she explained. "When you're older, you'll understand."

The divorce was quiet—her father had seen to that.

And her mother had left New York—her father had seen to that, too.

Charlotte was living in San Francisco now. When Heather turned eighteen, she'd flown out to see her, over her father's objections. Her mother was sober when Heather arrived that morning, but she had a glass of white wine with lunch. "Don't look at me that way, darling," she said as she took the first sip, her voice brittle, her smile too bright. "It's only one glass. It's not as if I'm an alcoholic." But it hadn't been only one glass; that had been merely the first. By dinner her mother didn't even try to deny it. "Why shouldn't I drink? I may live in San Francisco, but your father still controls my life."

"Why do you let him?" she'd asked.

Her mother only shook her head. "It's not that easy—when you're older, you'll understand." But all the trip to San Francisco accomplished was to destroy the illusions about her mother that Heather had nurtured during the years they'd been apart.

Now she did understand, as her mother had said she would. In some ways, her father controlled her just as much as he had controlled Charlotte. Heather was still living in the rambling apartment on Fifth Avenue, still going to school at Columbia.

Still being supported by her father, still living in his house. But she knew it would end when Jeff finished architecture school and they got married.

Then that terrible night had come when she'd waited for Jeff at his apartment but he hadn't returned. Finally, certain something must have happened to him, she'd started calling.

First the hospitals. St. Luke's, the clinic on Columbus, the Westside Medical Center.

And then the precinct station on West One hundredth Street.

"We got a Jeffrey Converse here," the desk sergeant told her, but refused to give her any of the details over the phone.

Heather thought it must be some terrible mistake, until she went down to the precinct house. Jeff, his face scratched, his clothes covered with blood, had looked at her helplessly through the bars of the single cell in the detectives' squad room. "I was trying to help a woman," he said. "I was just trying to help her."

And the nightmare had begun.

The nightmare that her father, the Assistant District Attorney, had done nothing to end. "There's nothing I can do," he told her the next day. "I've looked at the case, and the victim has made a positive identification. She's sure it was Jeff."

"There must be something—" Heather began, but was interrupted.

"My job is to prosecute people like Jeff Converse, not defend them. I'm sorry, but there's nothing I can do."

But Heather knew it was more than that. Her father didn't want to do anything for Jeff.

He'd never wanted her to date Jeff.

He certainly didn't want her to marry Jeff.

He did, however, want to be District Attorney, an ambition that might very well be satisfied in the next election. Unless, of course, something embarrassing happened—something like being on the wrong side of a much publicized case.

And because of the violence that had been committed against Cynthia Allen, Jeff's case had become very high-profile indeed. To Perry Randall, it was bad enough that his daughter had been dating Jeffrey Converse. To appear to be defending him was unthinkable.

"But he didn't do it," Heather whispered now. "I know he didn't do it." She might as well have said nothing at all, for her father had already turned his attention back to the newspaper.

*   *   *

Keith Converse reached for the knob of his truck's radio, but changed his mind before his fingers touched it. If he turned it on, he knew what would happen: his wife would pause in her prayers just long enough to give him a reproachful look, and even though she wouldn't say anything, her message would be loud and clear.

Don't you even care what happens to Jeff? the look would say as clearly as if she'd spoken aloud.

It wouldn't do any good to try to tell her how much he cared about their son. She'd made up her mind, and he had given up trying to argue with her months ago.

"It's God's will," she'd sighed when he first told her that Jeff had been arrested.

God's will.

Keith no longer knew how many times he'd heard that phrase in the last few years. It had become Mary's rationale for refusing to discuss every problem that came up between them.

He knew its origin, knew as well as she did where it had started. After all, they'd both gone to St. Mary's School, both grown up dutifully going to mass every Sunday at St. Barnabas Church.

When they were young, Mary had seemed just as relaxed about the Church as he was. But that began to change after the first night they made love, when Jeff was conceived. A thick blanket of Catholic guilt had fallen over Mary the moment she found out she was pregnant.

Keith assumed it would ease off as soon as they got married, and he'd seen to it that they did so right away. Eight months later, when Jeff was born, they told everyone he was premature, and since he'd been a small baby anyway, everyone accepted the lie.

Except Mary.

When she was withdrawn after Jeff was born, Keith hadn't been concerned. He thought it was because she was busy with the baby. But then Jeff was a toddler, and her withdrawn attitude only got worse. By the time Jeff was in school, they were making love no more than once a month, if you could even call it making love. Then it was more like once a year, and when Jeff was in high school, Keith had almost forgotten what sleeping with Mary was like. Still, in other ways she'd been a good wife to him. She'd kept their house immaculate, and taken good care of all of them. Yet every year, she seemed to withdraw even further into herself, spending more and more time praying.

And every time something bad happened, she said it was God's will.

Said they were being punished for having sinned.

That had hurt—hurt a lot. It was like saying they shouldn't have had Jeff.

Keith had wondered if he should have insisted they go to some kind of counseling. But the one time he suggested it, the only person Mary had been willing to talk to was their priest, and Keith hadn't seen how that would help. So he'd kept silent, concentrated on building up his contracting business, and hoped things would get better. When Jeff went off to college, Mary announced that she was leaving him.

"It's God's will," she'd told him. "We committed a terrible sin, but I've done my penance and God has forgiven me."

As usual, there hadn't been any discussion. Keith knew he might be able to argue with his suppliers, his subcontractors, and his customers, but he couldn't argue with Mary.

He couldn't argue with God's will.

So she moved out, and he rattled around in the little house in Bridgehampton that suddenly seemed way too big and way too empty, and tried to get used to having both his son and his wife gone.

It wasn't easy, but he got through it. Since Jeff had been arrested, though, it had gotten much worse.

When Jeff had first called him, Keith was certain it had to be a terrible mistake. Jeff had been a good kid—never even gotten into the kind of trouble most kids did. And then they'd arrested him, and charged him with things Keith knew his son couldn't possibly have done.

All through the fall, Keith's faith in Jeff had never wavered, even as he and Mary listened to the victim's testimony. He would pick Mary up and they'd go to the trial together. Keith knew the woman had to be mistaken, even though she sounded absolutely certain about what had happened.

Even though the victim pointed to Jeff in the courtroom and said, "That's the man who attacked me. I'll never forget that face as long as I live."

When the jury convicted Jeff, Keith had still been certain it was a mistake. He'd been sure it would be all right—the case would be appealed and Jeff would be released, and they would all go on with their lives.

But Jeff hadn't been released.

And Keith, despite himself, had started blaming Mary for what had happened.

Now, as the traffic on the Long Island Expressway came to a complete halt, he glanced at her.

"We're going to be late."

Mary sighed. "I suppose that's my fault, too."

Keith's fingers tightened on the steering wheel. "I didn't say it was your fault. Why do you have to take everything so personal?"

"Personal*ly*," Mary corrected.

Don't say anything, Keith told himself. *It won't matter if we're late anyway. It won't change anything.* But it would matter to Jeff. "I should've come in last night," he muttered. "I should have been there all along."

Mary Converse saw no point in responding to her husband's words. Indeed, she was weary of trying to talk to Keith at all. If he only had the same strength that she had—

She cut her thought short, knowing that Keith didn't share her faith, and never would. At first, like Keith, she assumed that her son was innocent, too. But since then, she'd come to grips with what had happened to Jeff. For a while she'd blamed herself, believing that if she and Keith hadn't sinned all those years ago, none of this would have happened.

Jeff wouldn't have gotten himself into trouble.

After he'd been convicted, she felt so guilty, she almost wished she could just die. But she'd talked it over with Father Noonan, who had explained that she wasn't responsible for anything Jeff had done, and that her role now was to let Jeff know she forgave him.

Forgave him, and loved him, just as God forgave and loved him.

In her faith, she'd been able to find peace and acceptance.

Keith, however, kept right on denying Jeff's guilt, insisting it had to be a mistake, utterly refusing to accept that all things are God's will. Deep in her heart, Mary knew better: Jeff had been conceived in sin, his soul corrupted from the very moment she had been weak enough to give in to Keith Converse's basest desires. The sins of the father were now being visited upon the son, and there was nothing she could do but accept it and pray—not only for her own soul, but for Jeff's as well.

Now, as the traffic jam evaporated as suddenly as it had started and they headed west on the Brooklyn-Queens Expressway, Mary's fingers began to move over the beads of her rosary as she once more began to pray.

God's will be done, she silently prayed. *God's will be done . . .*

CHAPTER 2

For Jeff Converse, mornings had taken on a terrible sameness. Each dawn that had broken over the last several months had brought with it a fleeting hope that he was finally awakening from the terrible nightmare his life had become. But as the comforting fingers of sleep released him from their touch, the hope that he was waking up from a bad dream always slipped away. The knot of fear that formed in his stomach when he'd been arrested pulled steadily tighter as he pondered the horrors the new day might bring.

At first he'd assumed it would be over within a few minutes—maybe an hour or two at the outside. As they locked him in the cell in the detectives' squad room at the police station on West One hundredth Street, he'd looked around with more curiosity than fear. After all, what had happened to him was obviously a mistake.

All he'd been trying to do was help the woman in the subway.

He had barely seen her at first—he'd been starting up the stairs from the platform when he heard something that made him pause.

If he'd just ignored it and kept going, if he'd paid no more attention to the muffled scream than he did to the car alarms that were always going off on the streets, he'd have been fine.

But a scream wasn't a car alarm, and without thinking about it, he had turned away from the staircase and started toward the far end of the platform.

There'd been no mistaking what he saw in the shadow-less glare of the fluorescent lights that filled the white-tiled subway station: a woman was sprawled out on the platform, facedown.

A man with his back to Jeff knelt next to her, tearing at the woman's clothes.

The idea of turning away from the scene never occurred to Jeff. Instead, he began running toward the kneeling man, yelling at the top of his lungs. Startled by the noise, the man glanced over his shoulder, then stood up. But as Jeff charged toward him, the man didn't turn to face him, made no move to defend himself. To Jeff's surprise, he leaped off the platform onto the subway tracks, vanishing into the darkness of the tunnel. By the time Jeff reached the woman, her attacker was gone. In the distance, Jeff could hear the rumble of an approaching train, but he ignored the sound, all his attention focused on the woman.

She was still lying facedown, and Jeff picked up her wrist, feeling for a pulse. As the artery beneath his fingers throbbed, he gently turned the woman over.

Her nose was crushed, her jaw was swelling, and her face was covered with blood. As the train roared into the subway and slowed to a stop, the woman's eyes opened. Her gaze fixed on him for a second, and then she suddenly seemed to come back to life. A scream erupted from her throat and the fingernails of one hand raked across his face. He grabbed her wrist, and her other hand came up, tearing at him. Jeff had no idea how long the struggle lasted—perhaps only a few seconds, maybe as much as half a minute. As he tried to pinion the thrashing woman beneath him, hands closed on his shoulders and he was jerked away.

"She's hurt," Jeff began. "Someone—" But before he could finish he was manhandled away from the woman and slammed facedown onto the subway platform.

His arms were jerked behind his back.

And his nightmare began.

As the handcuffs tightened around his wrists he heard someone say something about his not having to say anything.

They took him to the precinct house on West One hundredth Street.

Once again he was told that he had the right to remain silent, but since he knew that he'd only tried to help the woman in the subway station, it didn't occur to him to demand a lawyer before he recounted what had happened. He told them all of it—and kept telling them, even as he was processed into the system. By the time they'd taken away his watch, his class ring, his keys, and his wallet; by the time a computer had scanned his fingerprints and confirmed that he had no prior arrest record; by the time they finally sat him down in the detectives' squad room and asked him to once more describe exactly what had happened, he'd already told his story three or four times.

Even when they locked him in the holding cage in the squad room, he was certain it would soon be over. As soon as the woman from the subway station calmed down, she'd remember what had happened.

She would tell the police.

And that would be the end of it.

When they asked him if he wanted to call someone, he thought of his parents first, then changed his mind—with both of them far out on Long Island, what could they do? Besides, it was all a mistake, and why have them worry all night when by morning he'd be back home? Finally, he settled on Heather Randall, certain she would still be waiting for him at his apartment. But before he could even make the call, she arrived at the precinct.

"I'll have my father find out what's going on," she told him. "Don't worry—we'll get you out in an hour."

But they hadn't gotten him out. An hour later the police let him talk to Heather again, and she told him what was going on.

"The woman's in surgery, but the last thing she said was that you attacked her."

"But I didn't!" Jeff protested. "I was trying to help her!"

"Of course you were," Heather assured him. "And I'm sure when they show the woman pictures tomorrow, she'll know it wasn't you."

But when the police had shown the woman the photographs of a dozen men the next morning, she immediately placed a finger on the one of Jeff. Even though her face and jaws were heavily bandaged, she'd made it perfectly clear that he was the man who attacked her in the subway station.

So they'd taken him downtown.

The oddly detached feeling he experienced the night of his arrest gave way to real fear as he was processed into the Manhattan House of Detention.

Thinking about it later, he remembered most of that day as a blur. All he could recall was being moved through a maze of barred gates and climbing up two floors through a steep, narrow staircase that echoed with his own footsteps and with those of dozens of other people who were being moved slowly through the legal system.

There'd been an elevator, filled with the heavy, unmistakable smell of incense.

He remembered a holding area with cells containing the kind of disreputable-looking people whose gaze he had always avoided on the streets or subways. Now they were staring at him, calling out to him, demanding to know what he'd done.

He'd said nothing.

Finally, he was led down another stairwell and put into what looked like a cage on one of the landings. Perfectly square, the tiny chamber contained only a plastic molded chair.

He sat down.

He had no idea how long he waited—his watch was still in the envelope with everything else he'd had with him last night, and there were no clocks in sight.

At last, he was led into the courtroom, and the nightmare grew even more monstrous.

Though he was waiting in a different cage outside a different courtroom on this morning of his sentencing, in the Criminal Courts Building adjoining the Detention Center, the only apparent difference between them was the floor he was on. When he'd been arraigned and the charges against him were formally read—charges that ranged from assault to attempted rape and attempted murder—it had been on one of the lower floors. Back then, nearly half a year ago, his hopes had still been high. Cynthia Allen would recognize her mistake, he assumed, and the charges would be dropped. But the charges hadn't been dropped. Instead, he heard the cops who had arrested him, followed by two people from the subway that had pulled into the station right after he'd found her, and finally Cynthia Allen herself, all testify to what they thought they'd seen that night. As he sat listening to Cynthia Allen speak—sitting in the wheelchair she had been confined to since the attack, her face still misshapen, even after the first of her cosmetic surgeries—he realized he was going to be convicted.

Known that if he'd been sitting in the jury box instead of behind the defense table, he'd have believed every word she was saying.

"I saw him," she whispered, glancing toward him before turning back to the jury. "He was on top of me—he was trying to . . ." Her voice trailed off, and her silence was far more persuasive than any words she could have spoken.

Then it was his turn to testify. As he sat in the witness box wearing a shirt whose collar was now too large for his neck and a jacket that sagged on his gaunt body, he knew that the jury wasn't believing a word he said.

He'd seen the doubt in their eyes as he told them about the man who ran into the ink black tunnel, disappearing with the speed of a cockroach escaping from the light.

Through it all, his parents sat side by side in the first of the six rows of hard wooden benches—benches that reminded him of church pews—that were reserved for spectators. Every time he looked at them, they smiled encouragingly, as if they thought their own belief in his innocence would somehow be transferred to the jury. What they couldn't see— and he could—was Cindy Allen's family, sitting on the other side of the courtroom behind the prosecution table. His parents' smiles had been countered by their looks of pure hatred. Though his parents appeared shocked by his conviction, Jeff had felt only a numb sense that the verdict was inevitable, that his nightmare was never going to end.

Now, as he waited for the final phase of his trial to begin, he tried to summon up some shred of hope, but found nothing.

Where his body had once been full of energy, it now seemed exhausted. At twenty-three, he felt like an old man.

Where six months ago his life had stretched before him like a landscape with limitless horizons to explore, now all he could see ahead were endless days confined within the bars of a prison cell.

That morning, when he had looked in one of the worn pieces of polished metal that served as a mirror in the building known as the Tombs, he found himself staring for a long time at the pallor of his face, the gauntness of his neck and chest, and the dark rings of exhaustion around his eyes. *I look like what they think I am,* he'd thought. *I look like I belong in prison.*

The door leading to the courtroom opened then, and Sam Weisman appeared. In the months since his trial began, Jeff had learned to read more from his lawyer's posture and expression than from what he said. At sixty, Weisman's thick hair was snowy white, and his shoulders tended to sag as if carrying the weight of every case he had handled. "They're ready," he said, and though his tone was neutral, there was something in his stance that made Jeff wonder if, finally, something good might be about to happen.

"What's going on, Sam?" he asked as the correction officer unlocked the gate of the cage and swung the barred door open.

Weisman hesitated, as if weighing his response, but then simply shrugged. "I'm not sure," he said. "I've just got a feeling, you know?"

The brief flicker of hope faded as quickly as it had flared up. Sam Weisman had had a "feeling" when the jury stayed out for more than one day, and he'd had a "feeling" when they filed back into the jury box the following afternoon. The jury had found him guilty on every count he'd been charged with.

So much for Sam Weisman's "feelings."

Now, with the cuffs removed from his wrists, Jeff stepped through the door and into the courtroom, Sam Weisman right behind him.

Jeff felt suddenly disoriented. They were all there—the prosecutors at their table, Sam Weisman's assistant at the one next to it.

The same people sat on the spectators' benches—his parents behind the defense table, and Cynthia Allen's parents behind the prosecutor's. The same smattering of reporters who had covered the trial were in the rear, present now to witness the final act.

And Heather Randall was sitting by herself at the end of the bench his parents occupied, just as she had every day of the trial.

"Why don't you sit with my folks?" he'd asked when she visited him after the first long day in court. Heather had shrugged noncommittally, and the impenetrable look she always adopted when she was hiding something dropped over her face. He realized that he knew the answer to his own question. "Dad's blaming you, isn't he? He thinks that if it hadn't been for you, I would have stayed in Bridgehampton."

"Wouldn't you have?" she asked.

Jeff shook his head. "He might as well blame Mom—she's the one who made sure I went away to college."

"Easier to blame the summer people," Heather replied. "And God knows, as far as your father's concerned, that's all I'll ever be."

"He'll change his mind. When all this is over, he'll see."

And now, this morning, it *was* all over, but obviously Keith Converse had not changed his mind.

One thing in the courtroom was different today, though: except for the day she had testified, this was the first time Cynthia Allen was present. Looking diminished and help-less, she sat stoically in her wheelchair. Her husband stood behind her, his hands resting on her shoulders as if to shield her from any further harm. One of Cynthia's hands covered her husband's, the other was clasped by her father, who sat on the bench next to her chair. All three were staring at Jeff with such coldness that he shivered. Still, as he walked to the defense table, he held Cynthia's gaze, praying that even now she might remember what had really happened, might see in his eyes that he'd never intended to do anything but help her.

All he saw was her hatred of him.

He lowered himself into a worn wooden chair, only to rise again as the bailiff's voice began to drone and the door from the judge's chambers opened. A moment later, as Judge Otto Vandenberg settled himself behind the bench, Jeff sank back into his chair.

Vandenberg, a large, gray-haired man whose body seemed even more enormous in his black robes, began shuffling through the stack of papers that lay before him. Finally, he peered over his half glasses at Jeff. "Defendant rise," he said in a voice so low-pitched that people had to strain to hear it, yet carrying such authority that no one ever missed a word he uttered.

Jeff rose to his feet, Sam Weisman at his side.

"Do you have anything to say before I pass sentence?" he asked.

Jeff hesitated. Should he try one more time to convince

the judge that he was innocent? What good would it do? The jury had already decided. But there was one thing he had to say—one thing he'd never had a chance to say during the trial. He turned and once more met Cynthia Allen's gaze. "I'm sorry," he said softly. "I'm sorry I didn't get there a few minutes earlier, so maybe none of this would have had to happen to you at all." He held her gaze until she looked down into her lap. Then he turned back to face the judge once more.

Otto Vandenberg gave no sign that he'd heard Jeff's words.

"I've listened to all the testimony in this case, and I've read the recommendations of both the prosecution and the defense. While the crimes of which you've been convicted are very, very serious indeed, and certainly are not to be taken lightly, I have also chosen to take into account the fact that this case—as do so many—comes down to one person's word against another's. I also have to take into account that prior to this case you have been an exemplary citizen, and that none of your psychological evaluations indicate that you are anything other than a perfectly normal young man."

The flame of hope in Jeff flared up again.

"I therefore remand you to the custody of the Department of Correction for a term not to exceed one year, including time already served."

Seven months! He would be out in just seven more months—maybe even less!

"I was right!" Jeff heard Sam Weisman whispering exultantly. "I had a feeling, and I was right! He believed you, Jeff!"

But then he heard another voice, which rose furiously from the back of the courtroom.

The voice of Cynthia Allen's husband.

"A year?" he bellowed. "After what he did, you give him a year? I swear to God, I should kill him myself!"

Jeff whirled around to face the furious man.

"That's what you deserve," Bill Allen went on. "You

should be dead." Before anyone could react to his words, Bill Allen turned his wife's chair around and pushed it out of the courtroom.

"**W**hat do you mean, you don't want to do anything about it?" Keith Converse asked. Though his voice remained steady, the tension in his face betrayed the anger he was feeling at the sentence the judge had read moments ago.

"Keith, you have to calm down," Mary said, nervously eyeing the vein throbbing in Keith's forehead. "Losing your temper won't help."

Keith's eyes moved around the crowded conference room. Jeff sat at the end of a worn table with Sam Weisman flanking him on one side, Heather Randall on the other. Mary was sitting opposite their son, while a correction officer stood by the door, her expression utterly impassive. "Do you mind if I ask just what *is* going to help at this point?"

As if no one in the room was familiar with the case except himself, Keith Converse began reciting the events of the past few months. "First they arrest Jeff while he was trying to help that woman. Then, instead of letting him go and giving him a medal like they should have, they charge him with everything they can think of. Then they find him guilty, just because the same woman looks like she's half dead, and everyone feels sorry for her." He held up a hand against the protest he could see rising in Mary. "I'm not saying I'm not sorry for what happened to her. I am. But you know her being in that wheelchair influenced the jury, and now Jeff has to serve a year in jail for something he didn't do. And is the victim even happy that someone got convicted? Oh, no—her husband threatens to kill Jeff!" He shook his head in disgust, and his gaze settled on Sam Weisman. "You're supposed to be a lawyer—can't we charge him with something? He can't just threaten Jeff like that, can he?"

"He was upset, Dad," Jeff said before Weisman could answer. "He didn't mean it literally."

"Good God, will you listen to yourself?" Keith sighed, shaking his head. "I swear, sometimes I don't understand what makes you tick. You've been convicted of a felony, and it doesn't bother you that someone just threatened to kill you, too? Don't you have any idea what kind of spot you're in?"

Jeff's lips compressed. "I probably know what it means better than you do, Dad," he said. He unconsciously placed his hand over Heather's, his fingers tightening as his emotions threatened to erupt. "It's over, Dad—they found me guilty, and there's nothing that can be done about it. I was in the wrong place at the wrong time. All I want to do now is get through the next seven months, and then get on with my life."

"What life?" Keith asked, his shoulders slumping tiredly. "You really think they're going to take you back at Columbia after this?"

"Keith, don't," Mary pleaded. "We should be giving Jeff our support, not—" Her voice broke in the sob she'd managed to hold in check until then. "Oh, God," she whispered, turning from her husband to her son. "I'm sorry, Jeff. I promised myself that no matter what happened, I wasn't going to fall apart."

"It's okay, Mom," Jeff told her. "If I'm lucky, I might be out in five months." He forced a wry smile. "Hey, think of it as if I'm just taking a semester in Europe or something."

Heather snatched her hand away. "How can you joke about it? Do you have any idea what it's like out there? Daddy says—"

The mention of Perry Randall made Keith turn on her, his eyes smoldering. "Your 'daddy'? You really think any of us care what your 'daddy' has to say?" Heather recoiled from the angry words, but Keith plunged on, finally finding a target upon which he could vent the frustration and anger that had been building in him over the months since Jeff's arrest. "Did it ever occur to you that one word from your father would have ended all this months ago?"

"He couldn't—" Heather began, but Keith silenced her.

"They don't have to prosecute anything they don't want to! The worst crooks in this city are walking the streets because they're good buddies with guys like your father! You think I don't know why he didn't do something about this mess? It's because people like him don't think that what happens to people like us matters. So what if Jeff's life is ruined? He doesn't care!"

Heather's eyes blazed and she stood up. "If that's what you think—" she began, but cut her own words short. There'd been tension between her father and Jeff's for a long time—a tension that had only increased as she and Jeff had begun to fall in love. *"He's not our kind of people,"* her father told her over and over again. *"People like us marry other people like us—not the son of the handyman."* And she knew Keith's attitude was exactly the reverse—that he thought of her as nothing more than a society girl who would demand a standard of luxury Jeff would never be able to provide. She and Jeff had long since stopped trying to deal with either of their fathers on the subject, and now was certainly not the time to resurrect it.

She bent down and kissed Jeff. "I'd better go," she said, her voice dropping. "Maybe they'll let me come back later—"

Jeff reached toward her arm, but didn't quite touch it. "This isn't a hospital."

Their eyes met, then Heather's flicked toward Keith Converse for a moment. When he made no objection, she slowly sat back down. "I'm sorry," she said quietly. "I just thought my fath—"

"It's okay," Jeff cut in. His gaze shifted to his father. "Look, Dad, none of this is anybody's fault. It's not Heather's, it's not her father's, it's not mine. It's just something that happened. So let's just try to get through it, okay?" Keith Converse's jaw tightened, but he said nothing. "It could have been a lot worse—I could have gotten twenty years."

"And he can be out in five months with good behavior," Sam Weisman added.

"He shouldn't be in there at all," Keith insisted.

Jeff stood up and went to his father, felt the older man stiffen as he put his arms around him. "I'll be okay, Dad. I'll get through it, and so will you. But right now, there isn't anything you can do about it. You're just going to have to deal with the way things are."

Keith's arms came up and he embraced his son. "You be okay," he said, his voice rough with emotion. "Don't let 'em get to you, all right?"

"You bet, Dad."

Jeff held on to his father for another second or two, and then the correction officer led him away.

CHAPTER 3

Eve Harris was sorely tempted to ignore the buzzing of her intercom. The day, as always, had proved to be a couple of hours too short, and even though she tried her best to keep to her schedule, she had, as always, failed. First, the City Council meeting had gone on an hour longer than it should have, which wouldn't have been fatal, since she'd learned on the first day of her first term on the council that no meeting of that body would ever end on time. Too many egos wanted the last word.

It was the meetings with constituents that always wound up completely destroying the schedule, because while Eve had a natural ability to screen out the more pompous of her fellow councilmen's pontifications, she had no ability whatsoever either to end a meeting with one of New York City's masses of the disenfranchised or to deafen herself to their complaints. In her first two terms, she'd earned a reputation for having not only the most accessible office on the council, but the best ears as well.

When her constituents talked—no matter how inarticulately— Eve Harris listened. It had always been so, from her first days at P.S. 154 up on 126th Street in Harlem, where all the other kids seemed to bring their problems to her, right through graduation from Columbia University, where she'd finished magna cum laude with a double major in sociology and urban planning. Nothing had changed, even after she'd married Lincoln Cosgrove and moved into Linc's huge duplex on Riverside

Drive. She'd kept her job with the city, doing what she could to make life better for the poorest of its citizens, spending endless hours solving what problems she could, and just as many hours listening to problems for which there seemed to be no solutions.

But Eve Harris—who had refused even to consider hyphenating her name to include Linc's, let alone giving up her own—had always insisted there could be no insoluble problems in a city as complex as New York, no matter how unmanageable it might seem. It was simply a matter of finding the right minds, applying the minds to the problem, and implementing the solutions the minds came up with. Which was why, a year after Linc's heart simply stopped beating on a beach in Jamaica on the first day of the only vacation they'd ever taken, Eve had agreed to run for City Council. Using only her own money and refusing any donation of more than ten dollars, she had easily gotten more votes than all the rest of the candidates combined.

Ever since, the doors to her office had been open to all the people who had no other access to the power structure of their city. She rarely worked less than sixteen hours a day, and never took a day off. And every day, it seemed as though there were more problems to be addressed, and less time in which to address them.

The intercom buzzed a second time, and Eve punched the button that would allow her assistant to speak directly to her. "What is it, Tommy?"

"Channel 4," Tommy replied. "You'll want to see it."

Barely taking her eyes from the final revision of the speech she was due to give that evening, Eve switched on the television and flipped it to Channel 4. She recognized the face on the television screen—Cindy Allen, who had nearly been murdered in the 110th Street subway station last fall. But it wasn't Cindy who was speaking—it was her husband. "—might as well have just let him go! How is anyone supposed to feel safe on the streets when—"

Her eyes still on her speech, Eve Harris switched the TV off and punched the intercom button. "How much time did he get?" she asked with no preamble. After five years as her assistant, Tommy would know exactly what she meant.

"He'll be out in seven months, five if he behaves himself."

Eve sighed heavily—if Jeff Converse had been black instead of white, he'd have been lucky to get out in fifteen years. And starting tomorrow morning, the families and friends of half her constituents would start calling her office, demanding to know why their sons, lovers, and fathers were sitting in jail for years while the white boy only got a slap on the wrist.

And Eve knew she would have no answers.

It was just one more thing that wasn't fair.

One more thing she needed to work on.

Putting the speech aside, she picked up the phone and dialed the D.A.'s office. "What can you tell me about the Converse sentence?" she asked when Perry Randall came on the line. She listened to him speak for nearly five minutes, then shook her head. "What am I supposed to tell my people, Perry?" she asked. "If he was black, they'd have put him away for the rest of his life." She barely paused, knowing the prosecutor would have no answer. "Oh, I'm not blaming you. It's not your fault, is it?" She dropped the phone back on the hook, then stared at it, shaking her head. "That's the bitch of it," she muttered to herself. "Nothing is ever anybody's fault."

And that, she realized as she went back to work on her speech, was exactly why everything she did was so important.

By eight that evening the wind was whipping a cold rain through Foley Square and the park around City Hall, but Eve Harris didn't even think about hailing a cab, let alone using one of the city cars that was always at her disposal. Instead she headed for the subway station, her head lowered against the wind and rain, and scurried down the stairs along with a smattering of other people whose overload of work had kept them in their offices three hours past the time when everyone else had gone home. Not that looking for a cab or taking a city car would have helped—the cabs had all vanished into the black hole that sucked up every cab in the city within minutes after the first drops of rain began to fall, and taking a car would have made the trip up to the Waldorf-Astoria twice as long as the run on the subway. She dragged her MetroCard through the slot with a well-practiced swipe, pushed through the turnstile, and headed down to the platform to catch a train that would drop her off virtually under the hotel. As the train rattled to a halt, Eve glanced at her watch. She wouldn't get there in time for dinner, but that was all right—most of the people she would be talking about tonight wouldn't be getting any dinner, so why should she? But she knew she would arrive in plenty of time to be on the dais when Monsignor McGuire was ready to introduce her. So it would be all right. She stepped into the car, sank onto a vacant seat, and was about to read through her speech one last time when a rough voice spoke.

"You Miz Harris, ain't you?"

The woman was clinging to one of the poles in the middle of the car, perhaps to steady herself against its swaying as the train moved on, but more probably against the cheap red wine that had obviously been her dinner. The bottle—its neck sticking out of a crumpled and stained brown paper bag—was still clutched in her hand, and even as she gazed blearily at Eve through bloodshot eyes, she raised it to her lips, tipped it up, and sucked out another mouthful. As a few drops of the dark red fluid dribbled down her chin, she thrust the bottle toward Eve. "Want some?" she asked, her words half questioning, half challenging.

Eve felt the man next to her shifting in his seat, and didn't have to look at him to know he was adjusting his newspaper to block his view of the shabbily dressed woman who seemed to be carrying all her possessions in three layers of plastic garbage bags so ragged that tufts of dirty material were bursting through in half a dozen places. Behind the woman, Eve saw two other people edge away before the woman could focus her attention on them.

Eve hesitated only a moment, then met the woman's gaze straight on. "Actually, there's nothing I'd like better right now," she said. "But I'm on my way to make a speech, and I'm not sure I should." The woman seemed to weigh her words, turning them over in her mind as if seeking some hidden meaning. As the train began to slow for the Canal Street stop, the man next to Eve stood up and scuttled toward the door at the far end of the car, as if afraid of getting too close to the woman who was still clinging to the pole. As another man started edging toward the empty seat, Eve patted it and smiled at the woman. "Why don't you sit down?"

The woman's eyes widened slightly, then darted first to one side, then the other, as if she couldn't quite believe Eve was speaking to her. Half a dozen people were watching now, and the woman seemed about to bolt. "At least put your bag down for a minute. It looks heavy."

Finally, the woman made up her mind. Plumping herself down on the seat next to Eve, she placed her bag between her feet, keeping her hand on it as carefully as if it were a case of diamonds. "Most people look the other way," she said.

Eve folded up her speech, shoved it into the enormous leather shoulder bag she always carried, then groped around in the bag until her fingers found what she wanted. When her hand emerged, it was clutching a large, Hefty trash bag, one of the extra thick ones with drawstrings. "Maybe we ought to put your bag in this," she suggested. "It might be raining pretty hard when you get off."

"Might not get off till tomorrow morning," the woman countered truculently.

Eve shrugged. "According to the weather report, it might rain for days. Besides, isn't it always nice to have new luggage?"

Suddenly, the woman smiled, and let go of her bag long

enough to stick her hand at Eve. "I guess it's true what everyone says about you, Miz Harris. My name's Edna Fisk. But everybody calls me Eddie."

"Everybody calls me Eve," the councilwoman replied. "At least my friends do."

Through the next half-dozen stops, Eve Harris chatted amiably with Edna Fisk, who finished her bottle of wine during the course of the conversation, carefully recapped the empty bottle, and shoved it into her bag with her other belongings. "I'm not keeping it," she said, even though Eve hadn't questioned her. "I just hate litter. Soon's I get off the train, I'll put it in a trash barrel."

"I wish more people were like you," Eve observed. A moment later both women glared balefully at a man who left a crushed and greasy paper bag on his seat when he left the train at the next stop. "Some people are just slobs," Eve said, getting up to retrieve the bag, then sitting back down next to Edna. "You want to dump this, or shall I?"

"I'll take it," Edna said, shoving the greasy bag in after her empty wine bottle. Then she smiled shyly, a black gap showing where one of her front teeth once had been. "And if I can still have that new luggage, I'd sure appreciate it." By the time the train began slowing at Fifty-first Street, Eve had helped Edna Fisk get her worn bags inside the new one. "I guess what I heard was right," she said as Eve stood up and moved toward the door. "You're not much of a one for preaching."

Eve Harris's brows arched. "Oh, I preach, all right. I just like to reserve my preaching for those who need it." She hesitated, then said, "There are places you could go, you know. . . ." But when Edna Fisk's eyes clouded and she shook her head, Eve let her voice trail off. The train squealed to a stop and the doors slid open. "It was nice talking to you," she said as she stepped out. She headed toward the stairs, the doors of the car slid closed again and the train pulled away.

But as it passed, Eve looked up and saw Edna Fisk looking at her.

Looking at her, and smiling.

Twenty minutes later, as Eve stood on the dais of the ballroom in which the benefit for the Montrose Shelter for the Homeless was being held, she didn't need to even glance at the speech she'd written. "Tonight," she began, "a woman smiled at me. A woman named Edna Fisk. Let me tell you about her."

Half an hour later, as her speech ended to a wave of applause—and a flurry of checkbooks—Monsignor Terrence McGuire leaned over to whisper in her ear. "I have to tell you, Eve—you're full of more blarney than my father even thought of, and you've got more courage than anyone else I know. But all those people down in the subway aren't like your Edna Fisk—a lot of them are dangerous, and if you get hurt down there, you aren't going to be able to do Montrose House any good at all."

"I'm not going to get hurt," Eve assured him. "I've been riding the subways since I was a little girl, and nothing's ever happened."

"Well, you should consider yourself lucky," the elderly priest went on. "Terrible things happen down there. There was the woman who almost got killed up on the West Side last fall—"

"That wasn't one of my people," Eve Harris cut in. "As I recall, it was an architecture student at Columbia."

"It was not!" another voice cut in angrily. "Jeff didn't do it!"

The priest and the councilwoman turned to see a young woman standing behind them, next to Perry and Carolyn Randall.

"Heather . . ." Eve heard the Assistant District Attorney say warningly, but the young woman ignored him.

"It was someone else," she said. "Jeff was trying to help Cynthia Allen. The man who attacked her disappeared into the subway tunnel. Jeff said he looked like one of the homeless."

Perry Randall's hand tightened on the young woman's arm. "My daughter," he said to Eve, his lips forming a tight smile. "All she said was that she wanted to meet you." He turned to Heather. "This is Councilwoman Harris, Heather."

Eve offered Heather Randall her hand. "You know the young man?"

Heather nodded. "I'm going to marry him."

Eve's eyes flicked toward Perry Randall, and as she was searching for something to say, Randall himself rescued her.

"You can be sure we'll send you an invitation, Eve," he said, keeping his voice just light enough to take the edge off his words. "In the meantime, I think I'd like a drink. Terrific speech, Eve," he added. "You can count on me for ten thousand this year."

"And I'll hold you to it," Eve Harris assured him.

But as the crowd closed around her, Eve found herself watching Heather Randall as she moved toward the bar, and recalled her words: *"Jeff said he looked like one of the homeless."* One of the homeless . . . Why did everyone always want to blame the homeless? she wondered.

Why did the homeless always have to take the rap?

But Eve already knew the answer to her own question— the homeless took the rap because they had nobody to defend them.

So she would just have to work harder.

CHAPTER 4

JoAnna Gartner gazed at the man who lay on the bunk on the other side of the bars. Right now he looked utterly harmless. His hands—slim fingered, almost feminine—were folded over his chest, which was rising and falling in the slow and steady rhythm of sleep. His eyelids, barely twitching with the tic that kept them constantly blinking whenever he was awake, now hid the glowing flame of rage that made JoAnna want to shrink away from him whenever his gaze fell directly on her.

Jagger.

That was his name: Jagger. He had a first name, but she, along with everyone else at Rikers Island, never used it.

Nor did they use the nickname the other prisoners had given him, back when he had been in the general population.

The Dragger.

Jagger the Dragger.

She hadn't understood it at first; when she first heard it, she assumed he must be in the habit of dragging things out. A lot of the prisoners did that—filling the long hours of their sentences with even longer tales of why they didn't belong here at all, or dragging out their chores in the kitchen, or the laundry, or the dining room, in an effort to avoid going back to their cells. But that wasn't how Jagger had gotten the nickname. He'd come by it far more legitimately.

Initially, JoAnna hadn't believed the story. She assumed it was just one of the rumors that flowed through the cell blocks every day, getting more and more outlandish with every re-telling. But then she'd seen the photograph.

In the photo, a body was lying on a floor in the midst of a pool of blood that all but obliterated the worn-out carpet on which it lay. It was easy to see where all the blood had come from: the body was so badly mutilated that its gender was no longer distinguishable.

Its face was covered with makeup, put on so garishly that it looked like the work of a child.

The muscular arms of the corpse had been shoved through the sleeves of a woman's blouse—a blouse so small that the arms themselves had torn the sleeves to shreds. There was a skirt, too, partially wrapped around the corpse's waist.

"Jagger dressed him up in drag after he killed him," the person who showed JoAnna the photo explained. "Guess he wanted to pretend he was screwing a girl."

JoAnna's stomach heaved, and she dropped the photo as if merely touching it could somehow infect her with the insanity it depicted.

Right now, though, asleep in his cell, the Dragger looked perfectly harmless.

But she knew that he was not.

If he was, then Bobby Breen would still be alive. But Bobby Breen wasn't alive, because JoAnna herself had found his corpse yesterday, stuffed in a closet in the large kitchen where he and Jagger had both been working. Stripped naked, the genitals hacked away with the same jagged tin can lid that had been used to slit his throat, his cheeks and lips were stained a purplish red with grape juice, and an apron was tied around his waist as a makeshift skirt.

Jagger had not yet spoken a single word about what had been found in the closet. In fact, he hadn't said a word about anything.

"They want him downtown for evaluation," JoAnna had been told an hour ago, as her captain handed her the orders transferring Jagger from the prison to a hospital. "Don't know why they're bothering—if they want to know if he's crazy, all they have to do is ask me."

Or me, JoAnna had thought. But she hadn't said it. Instead she'd looked at the clock—it was after midnight, but nowhere near four A.M., when they usually woke up the prisoners that were being taken downtown. "Why now?"

The captain shrugged. "I figure they're just trying to make him disappear—get him out before anybody has a chance at him. Everybody liked Breen—everybody hates Jagger. So what are you gonna do?"

So now JoAnna Gartner stood in front of Jagger's cell on the second tier of the Central Punitive Unit.

"Time to go." Though her voice was low enough not to waken any of the prisoners who might be sleeping, Jagger's eyes snapped open. Sitting up, he locked his eyes on to hers, and, as always, JoAnna had to resist an overwhelming urge to step back from the burning fury that glowed inside the man.

"Stand up and turn around, back to the door, hands behind your back," she ordered.

Jagger's eyes flicked toward JoAnna's backup, Ruiz, who was standing a few yards away, silently using a video camera to capture every second of the prisoner's transfer. Saying not a word, Jagger obeyed. As he unfolded himself from the bunk, his six-foot-five-inch frame—bulked up to nearly 250 pounds of heavily tattooed muscles—loomed over JoAnna, and once again she had to resist the urge to back away from him.

Only when Jagger's hands were shackled behind him did JoAnna open the door. He started to turn around, but JoAnna reached out and grasped the chain between the manacles on his wrists, lifting his arms just enough to let him know how much it would hurt if she raised them any higher. "Let's just take this nice and slow," she told him.

With Ruiz keeping the camera trained on them, she steered Jagger out of the cell and down the steps to the main floor.

They paused at the pen just inside the entrance to the CPU while two more officers fitted Jagger with leg irons and waist chains and moved his hands to the front of his body, where they were locked to the waist chains. Then they began the slow progress toward the main entrance, waiting for each barred door to close behind them before the one in front opened.

It was twenty past midnight when they emerged from the building. A black van was already waiting, with a captain and an officer from the Emergency Services Unit ready to receive the prisoner.

Twenty minutes later the van pulled into a hospital emergency entrance. Four men in orderlies' uniforms were waiting with a gurney. Both officers got out, one glancing up and down the deserted sidewalk while the other unlocked the padlock on the back door of the van.

A minute later Jagger was out of the truck.

"Get on the gurney," one of the orderlies said.

When Jagger made no move to obey, one of the officers nudged him with the butt of the MP-5 cradled in his arms. "You heard the man."

His eyes smoldering, Jagger lay down on the gurney.

The orderlies strapped him tight.

With two of the orderlies at the front of the gurney and the other two at its rear, they moved Jagger quickly through the doors, down a hall, and into a waiting elevator.

The doors slid closed, but instead of pressing a button that would take the elevator up to the floors housing the patients, one of the orderlies slipped a key into a lock, turned it, and punched a button that sent the elevator down.

In the second subbasement, they emerged into a long hallway. The orderlies quickly pushed the gurney to the far end, through two dark rooms, and finally into a third, lit only by a single bulb hanging in a metal cage in the center of the ceiling.

At its far end was another door, covered in metal.

One of the orderlies produced a key and opened the door.

Beyond lay only darkness.

CHAPTER 5

If Jeff had slept at all, neither his body nor his mind had benefited from it. The thin pallet that separated him from the cold metal of the bunk felt no softer than the steel itself; his left hip was numb, his whole back felt sore, and his left shoulder ached from the weight it had borne through the long hours of the night. Every muscle in his body felt weaker now than when he'd lain down last night, as if he'd been running for hours instead of sleeping. His mind felt no better than his body, for as the endless minutes crept by, the terrible reality of what had happened to him only tightened its grip on his consciousness. At first his mind had refused to accept the truth, still clinging to some frayed shred of hope that even now that the trial and the sentencing were over, something would happen to free him from the surreal world in which he was trapped. But as the sounds of the night—the shouts and curses of angry prisoners, the clanging of barred doors as the night watch plodded through its routine—kept sleep at bay, hope had finally ebbed away, and the truth at last began to twist his mind as surely as the cold cell and hard bunk had wracked his body.

Maybe I should've just killed her, he told himself. At least then it would have been his word against a dead body's. Wouldn't that be something? Walk away from a murder instead of going to jail just for trying to help. Well, fuck it—the guys he'd met in jail were right: once they busted you, it was over. It didn't make any difference whether you'd done something or not—it was the cops against you, and the cops always won.

So he'd get through it. He'd do his time, and stay out of trouble, and get out as soon as he could. And then—

But he couldn't even think about it. All he could think about now was the yawning chasm that lay ahead. A chasm he was about to be thrown into, empty except for cell blocks, boredom, and constant fear.

As the clamor of voices and clanging cell doors rose around him, he sat up and pulled on his clothes—the same clothes he'd been wearing for a week, which Heather had brought him when she took the other clothes home.

The clothes she'd have been picking up today, except that today he was being moved to Rikers.

Numbly, his body functioning more by rote than by conscious decision, he began following the morning routine, until an hour later he was standing in front of one more in an endless series of locked doors. Two C.O.'s flanked him, but no other prisoners were in sight. Then the door opened and he stepped outside.

He was in the sally port between the Detention Center and the Criminal Courts Building. Though dawn hadn't yet quite begun to break, the darkness in the heavily gated courtyard was washed away by floodlights, and he could see the bridge connecting the two buildings spanning the courtyard two flights up. A bus sat near the door to the Courts Building, from which the last of this morning's first batch of prisoners from Rikers Island were being unloaded for their day in court. For the next several hours they would wait in the holding areas or the feeder pens, exactly as he had waited during the endless days of his trial. Just before going into the building, the last of the prisoners turned and stared at Jeff. Understanding exactly where Jeff was being taken this morning, he smiled and ran his tongue suggestively over his lips. With a wink at Jeff, the prisoner finally responded to the officer's nudge and disappeared through the door to the courthouse.

Sitting a few yards from the bus, with two more C.O.'s flanking it, was a windowless black Ford van. "Pretty fancy," one of the officers next to Jeff remarked, his lips twisting into a sarcastic smile. "Your very own limousine."

Jeff kept his mouth shut; he'd learned by now that when the guards made jokes, he wasn't included.

As the two guards from Detention escorted him toward the van, the other two opened its back door. Ducking his head, Jeff climbed inside, sliding onto the first bench he came to. Ahead of him was a heavy black-painted metal grille separating him from the next bench, which could only be accessed from the side door. Ahead of that was another grille, another bench, yet a third grille, and then the driver's compartment. As Jeff sat on the bench, his wrists still cuffed, the door slammed behind him and he heard a padlock drop against the back panel.

A minute later, one of the officers slid behind the wheel and the other climbed into the passenger seat.

Though it was barely visible through the three sets of thick mesh grilles and the windshield, Jeff saw the big gate ahead of the van swing open, and a moment later the truck passed through and turned right. A block later it turned left, then went straight ahead for three blocks. As it made another left turn, Jeff caught a glimpse of a sign.

Elizabeth Street.

In the last few minutes before dawn, the street was all but deserted of any traffic except a few lumbering trucks, and as the lights ahead turned green, the van began to accelerate. But several blocks later it began to slow again.

The driver turned right, and finally Jeff knew where they were going—straight ahead he could see the Williamsburg Bridge.

The light at Bowery turned green, and the van surged ahead as the officer behind the wheel once more hit the gas pedal.

As they were crossing Bowery, however, something crashed against the van, smashing into the sliding door on the passenger side. As the door caved in, the van itself skidded sideways and spun around. It sheared off a fire hydrant, then slammed into the front of a building on the west side of Bowery. Knocked off his seat by the first impact, Jeff bounced off the grille in front of him. A moment later his shoulder slammed into the side of the van, and as his back twisted a sharp pain shot from the injured shoulder down his arm.

Now a cacophony of shouting voices rose over the sound of water pouring down onto the wrecked van from the geyser of the broken hydrant, and then the back door was jerked open. "Out, fuckhead!" a rough voice commanded as the cage door opened.

His head spinning, and half blinded by the blood streaming from a cut on his forehead, Jeff stumbled out of the van.

He stood unsteadily on the street. Water from the hydrant was spraying everywhere, and a crowd of shabbily dressed people seemed to have materialized from out of nowhere. As people milled around, someone grabbed Jeff's arm and whispered urgently in his ear, "Don't talk—don't think—don't do nothin'! Just follow me, and maybe we can get you out of here!"

His brain as fogged with pain as his eyes were with blood from the still-streaming wound, Jeff didn't hesitate. Knowing only that for the first time in months he was free from the claustrophobic confines of barred cells, locked holding pens, and sealed transport vans, he sucked the cold predawn air into his lungs and shambled across the intersection toward the subway entrance that lay only a few yards away.

Only at the top of the stairs leading to the subterranean station below did he pause. Around him lay the shadows of the fading night. The geyser of water still shot into the air from the sheared-off hydrant. Below him lay the brilliantly lit, windowless crypt of the subway station.

If he ran, he could vanish into the darkness and quiet.

He could be alone, for the first time in months.

The darkness, the quiet, and, most of all, the air pulled at him, but just as he was about to take the first step, everything changed.

A siren, then another, shattered the silence. An instant later a third one wailed to life.

All of them were coming toward him, closing on the surrealistic scene before him.

Then it happened.

The van exploded, and as the fireball rose into the air, instinct took over. The mass of the subway entrance protecting him from flying debris, Jeff stumbled down the stairs into the station.

It all occurred in only a few seconds. The man who had pulled him from the van was already leaping over the turnstiles of the deserted station. Jeff followed, running down the next two flights of stairs and hitting the platform just as a downtown train ground to a stop. The doors opened and Jeff started toward it.

"You fuckin' crazy, man? Transit cops'll get you in five minutes flat!" the man he'd been following said. Pulling on Jeff's arm, he hurried toward the far end of the platform. "Come on," he yelled. "Quick, before another train comes!"

Jeff staggered after him, his mind still too numb to think clearly, but when they came to the end of the platform, he stopped short. There was nothing ahead except a blank wall.

He turned and looked back the other way. The train was just pulling away, its taillights quickly disappearing. There was only one other person on the platform: a derelict sitting on the floor, leaning against a pillar. He heard something next to him, and when he turned, the man he'd been following seemed to have disappeared. But then came the voice again:

"Move, damn it!"

At the same time, Jeff heard footsteps pounding down the stairs at the far end.

As they grew louder, he leaped down onto the tracks and raced into the tunnel.

The darkness swallowed him in an instant.

CHAPTER 6

Keith Converse was just getting out of the shower when the phone rang. Certain it was the foreman on the Leverette remodel—which was looking like it would run well over two million, easily making it the biggest job he'd ever done—he didn't even pause to grab a towel before dashing into the bedroom to snatch up the receiver before the machine downstairs picked up the call. "Yeah?"

"Mr. Converse? Mr. Keith Converse?"

The voice had a note of calculated calm that instantly put Keith on his guard, and as he equally carefully enunciated his reply, a chill of apprehension fell over him. "This is Keith Converse. Who is this?"

"My name is Mark Ralston. I'm a captain with Manhattan Detention Center. I'm sorry to have to tell you that there's been an accident . . ."

Still soaking wet, and now shivering, Keith sank onto the bed as Ralston told him about what had befallen the van carrying his son from the Tombs to Rikers Island.

"Are you telling me he's dead?" Keith interrupted, before Ralston had spoken the words. "You're telling me my son is dead?"

"There was an accident, Mr. Converse—" Captain Ralston began again, still intent on breaking the news as gently as possible. But once again Keith cut in.

"I'm coming down there. I want to know what happened, and somebody damn well better have some answers." He slammed the receiver down before Ralston could say anything more.

Dead? How could Jeff be dead? It wasn't possible!

Keith was still sitting numbly on the bed, his mind refusing to accept what he'd been told, when the phone rang again. This time he ignored it, and after the fourth ring it fell silent as the machine downstairs in the kitchen picked up.

Mary.

He had to tell Mary.

He reached for the phone, then hesitated. How could he tell her what had happened when he didn't even know himself? But he had to talk to her, had to tell her something. His hand closed on the receiver and his finger shook as he punched in the number. He was still trying to figure out what to say when her machine picked up and he heard her voice, its cheerful tone as false and forced as the note of hope he tried to leave in his message. "It's me, Babe," he began, unconsciously reverting to the endearment he'd used through all the years when he thought their marriage had a chance of survival, but had carefully avoided since the day she walked out on him. "Something's happened, and I have to go into the city to find out what's going on. . . ." His voice trailed off as he searched for something else to say. "There was some kind of accident, and Jeff—well—" Suddenly, the flood of emotions he'd held in check since hanging up on Captain Ralston overwhelmed him. His voice cracked and his eyes blurred with tears. "Look, I gotta get going—I gotta find out what happened. I'll call you later."

He went back to the bathroom, toweled himself off, and got dressed. He was out of the house five minutes later, into the Ford pickup that served not only as transportation, but as his mobile office as well, and out the driveway. Halfway to the expressway he swung into a McDonald's, ordered a McMuffin and coffee, then called his foreman while he inched the truck toward the pickup window. "I'm gonna be gone for the day. Anything you can't take care of?"

"What's going on?" Vic DiMarco asked. "You don't sound right."

"Not now," Keith said. "Just take care of things, okay? And if Mary calls you, just tell her I'll talk to her as soon as I know something."

"Why wouldn't she just call you?" DiMarco countered.

"Because I'm shutting this fucker off," Keith growled. "No one's going to be able to get hold of me for a while, so I just need you to take over for me." His voice took on a harsh edge. "You can do that, can't you? Isn't that why I hired you?"

DiMarco ignored Keith's angry tone. "You wanna tell me what's going on?"

"I'll tell you when I know," Keith snapped. Shutting the phone off as he finally came up to the window, he shoved some money at the gray-haired woman behind the counter and pulled the bag into the truck. Steering with one hand, he took the greasy sandwich out of the bag with the other. He was already chewing before he realized there was no way he could swallow even the first bite, let alone eat the whole thing. Dropping the sandwich back in the bag, he took a sip of the not quite hot enough coffee, washed down the bite of egg, sausage, and muffin, and had drained the cup by the time he steered the truck onto the expressway.

A now-familiar chill fell over Keith as he walked through the doors of Manhattan House. *Manhattan House,* he said silently to himself. *What were they trying to do, make people think it was a hotel instead of a jail?*

The first time he'd come to the building nearly half a year ago—and the first time he'd felt the strange chill to which he'd never become inured—it seemed part of a world he could barely comprehend. Except for a smattering of well-dressed people he assumed were lawyers, the people milling in the lobby were the kind that he'd seen only on television.

People who would have been arrested in Bridgehampton

for no other reason than the way they were dressed—if they'd ever appeared there at all.

The young ones all looked angry. Angry, and poor. The eyes that weren't glazed with drugs smoldered with fury, and when they glanced at him—which they rarely did—Keith knew that he looked as foreign to them as they did to him.

The older people—those his own age who were coming to see their children, just as he was coming to see his—looked only defeated. Most of them seemed as familiar with the jail and its procedures as he was with the building permit process in Suffolk County.

By his third visit, Keith had paid as little attention to the people in the lobby as they paid to him.

Today he didn't even have to think about the procedures—like any other habitué of the building, he automatically emptied his pockets, stepped through the metal detectors, and exchanged his driver's license for a visitor's badge. The officer who escorted him to Captain Mark Ralston's tiny office wore an expression as studiedly calm as Ralston's voice had been on the phone three hours ago. The office was painted the same sickly shade of greenish yellow that covered most of the walls in the building.

Ignoring the hand Ralston offered as he rose to his feet, Keith's angry gaze bored into the other man's eyes. "I want to know what happened."

Ralston's hand dropped to his side, and even though Keith Converse was still on his feet, he lowered himself back into the chair behind his desk. "I can tell you what happened," he said. "What I can't tell you is why it happened." He paused, and finally Keith sank onto the wooden chair that was the only piece of furniture in the room not covered with files or papers. He listened in silence as Ralston told him what he knew. "Two of our officers were on the way up to Rikers with your son when a car rammed their van. The van went over and caught on fire." Keith flinched, and Ralston's hands clenched into fists. "There was nothing that could be done, Mr. Converse. Two correction officers were trapped in the van, too. No one survived."

No one survived.

The words seemed to hang in the air, echoing and re-echoing off the walls of the room, battering at Keith's mind like a jackhammer. As the words sank in, the hope he'd been clinging to ever since Ralston called him faded away. "I want to see him," he said quietly. His eyes fixed on Ralston once again, but this time the captain saw only pain in them. "I want to see my son."

Ralston hesitated. He'd already seen the bodies of the two officers who had died in the burning van, and he wondered if Keith Converse would be strong enough to deal with what he would see when he looked at his son. But he knew that Keith Converse had no more choice than he himself had a few hours ago. Looking at the bodies—actually gazing upon the countenance of death—had been the only way Ralston could accept the reality of what had happened to his two men, and he knew it was no different for Keith Converse.

"He's at the Medical Examiner's office," Ralston finally said. He started to write down the address on the back of one of his cards, then changed his mind. "I'll take you there."

Twenty minutes later, Keith Converse steeled himself as the attendant pulled open the drawer containing his son's body. As the young man started to pull back the sheet, Keith almost changed his mind, almost turned away. Perhaps sensing his hesitation, the attendant looked at him, as if to ask whether he truly wanted to do this. Keith nodded. The attendant drew the sheet back.

A face—or what had once been a face—lay exposed to the bright fluorescent glare. The skin was burned away, the eyes nothing more than charred sockets.

The nose had been smashed flat, and broken teeth showed through a lipless grimace.

What remnants of clothing hadn't burned had been carefully picked away. To Keith, there was something obscene about the nakedness of the body, and he had to fight an urge to turn away from it. But he couldn't. He had to look at Jeff, had to see him one last time.

As the attendant finally dropped the sheet back over the inert form, Keith found himself making the sign of the cross for the first time in years, and uttering a silent prayer for his son's soul.

"I'm very sorry, Mr. Converse," Mark Ralston said softly as they started out of the morgue.

Keith didn't speak until they left the building. "I can't believe it," he said then. He sucked air deep into his lungs and blew it out hard, as if trying to expel not only the foul scent of formaldehyde that had hung in the air, but also the terrible image that was the last memory he would ever have of his son.

"I wish there was something I could say . . ." Ralston began. He groped for the right words for a moment, then gave up, knowing there was nothing he could say that would give Keith Converse any comfort.

Keith shook his head. "I'll be okay—I just need to get used to it." He took another deep breath, and this time a shudder shook his body. "And I gotta figure out how I'm gonna tell his mother."

"It's hard," Ralston said. "I just wish there was something I could do. . . ."

Keith looked up and fixed his gaze on the other man. "There was," he said. "There was something all of you could've done. You could've found out who really attacked Cynthia Allen." He jerked his head back toward the morgue. "Then my son would still be alive, wouldn't he?" His eyes locked onto Mark Ralston's. "Well, fuck you, Ralston. Fuck all of you." Turning around, he walked quickly away down the street.

Something had been gnawing at Keith, nibbling at the edge of his consciousness ever since he'd gotten back in the truck and started the long drive back out to Bridgehampton. Something about what he'd seen in the morgue.

About Jeff's body.

He hadn't wanted to remember that terrible sight at all, had hoped to blot it out of his consciousness. But no matter how hard he tried, it kept coming back. Coming back, jabbing at him.

Then, just as he was leaving the expressway, it came to him.

It wasn't something he'd seen at all—it was something he hadn't seen!

It was a tattoo—a small figure of a sun rising above a pyramid, which Jeff had let three of his friends talk him into getting during a spring break trip to the Caribbean two years ago. It had been etched into his skin, just inside his hip. "I wasn't really sure I wanted to do it at all," he'd explained when he finally showed it to his father. "So at least here no one can see it if I don't want them to. And if I really start hating it—or Heather hates it—I can have it removed with a laser."

Heather hadn't hated it, and as far as Keith knew, Jeff hadn't started hating it, either.

But the body he'd seen in the morgue hadn't had a tattoo.

Keith's heart was racing now, and he gripped the steering wheel tightly, his knuckles turning white as he slowed to a stop at the red light at the foot of the off ramp. He reached back into his memory, reluctantly pulling the image of Jeff's body into the forefront of his mind.

One of the only parts that hadn't been scorched was the groin. Like a tan line, he remembered thinking when the sheet had first been lifted and he'd seen horrible contrast between the badly burned skin above the waist and the less damaged skin lower down, where it had been protected by the heavy denim of his jeans.

There had been no tattoo.

And that meant—

No, I'm wrong, Keith told himself, refusing to let himself even complete the thought. *He must've gotten it taken off.*

But even if he had, wouldn't there have been a scar?

And there hadn't been a scar—not that he'd been able to see. And if there was no tattoo, and no scar, then—

Again he refused to let himself finish the thought, but as the light turned green and the car behind him began to honk, he just sat there, unable to do anything.

And the thought finished itself.

He's not dead.

If Jeff hadn't had the tattoo removed, then the body he'd seen in the morgue wasn't Jeff's.

His hands shaking, Keith picked up the cell phone, turned it on, then scrolled through its memory until Heather Randall's home phone number came up. He pressed the number, then waited nervously until the connection was made.

An answering machine picked up.

"It's Keith Converse," he said. "Call me as soon as you get this message, Heather. I've got to know if Jeff still had his tattoo. The one of the sun rising over a pyramid."

Leaving the number of his cell phone, he hung up.

This time, though, he didn't turn the cell phone off.

He left it on, and prayed for it to ring.

CHAPTER 7

Keith's phone started to ring less than a minute after he broke the connection with the answering machine in Perry Randall's apartment. Snatching it up and flipping it open, he pressed it to his ear and began speaking: "Heather? Tell me that Jeff hadn't had his tattoo removed."

But it wasn't Heather who replied, it was his wife. "His tattoo?" Mary said. "Keith, what are you talking about? What's happened?"

Keith ignored her question. "Mary? Where are you?"

"I'm at home," Mary began. "But—"

"Stay there," Keith told her. "I'll be over in ten minutes. I just got off the expressway."

Mary's voice rose, taking on a querulous edge. "Tell me now, Keith. I've been calling you for hours, but your phone—"

"My phone's been off," Keith said. "Just try to stay calm, Mary."

"I *am* calm," Mary said, her voice rising another notch. "But what do you expect, telling me—oh, there's another call coming in. Let me get rid of them and—"

"Take the other call, Mary. I'll be there by the time you get done." He snapped the phone closed before she could say anything else, and in two minutes less than the ten he'd promised, he slid his truck into an empty space in front of the art gallery on Hoquaquogue Road and was hurrying down the narrow path that led to Mary's little apartment. The open door framed his wife, whose face was ashen.

56

"He's dead!" she said. "And you didn't even tell me!" He reached out to put his arms around her, but she pulled away. "What happened?" she asked. "They said it was some kind of an accident."

"That's what they told me, too," Keith replied, reaching out again and gripping her shoulders. "They were taking him up to Rikers Island, and a couple of blocks before they got on the Williamsburg Bridge, a car hit the van. And the van caught fire." Keith felt Mary stiffen as she braced herself for his next words: "They couldn't get him out."

"God's retribution," Mary breathed. "It's God's—"

"It's not God's retribution!" Keith cut in. "God didn't have anything to do with it!" Mary recoiled as if he'd slapped her, but he ignored it, adding, "And there's something else, too. When I saw him—"

Mary drew back, her eyes wide. "You *saw* him?" she demanded. "What are you talking about?"

"I had to talk to them," he said. "I had to find out what happened and I—" He hesitated, then went on. "I had to see him for myself."

For the first time, Mary reached out and touched Keith, her fingers resting for a moment on his arm. "You should have taken me with you," she said. "I should have been with you."

Remembering the terrible visage he had forced himself to look upon—the charred flesh and ruined features—Keith shook his head. "No," he said, his voice rough as he struggled to control his emotions. "No one should have to see what I saw. But . . ." His voice trailed off. He'd been about to tell her about the tattoo and the doubt that it had created, but now he wondered if he should. If he told her and he was wrong— His thoughts were cut short by the ringing of his cell phone.

"I just heard what happened," Heather Randall said on the line, her voice shaking. "Daddy called me—he said it was some kind of accident, but—I can't—I just can't believe it—not Jeff! He—"

"Heather, listen to me," Keith cut in. "Do you remember Jeff's tattoo?"

"His tattoo?" she said, sounding dazed, as if she hadn't quite understood his words.

"The pyramid. The pyramid and the sun."

There was a moment of silence, as if she still hadn't understood, but then she said, "Of course I remember it."

As his wife regarded him with curiosity, Keith's pulse quickened, as it had in the truck a little while ago. "And he still had it?"

"Still had it?" Heather echoed, puzzled. "Of course he did. Why wouldn't he?"

Keith kept his voice carefully neutral. "People have them removed sometimes."

"Not Jeff. He loves his tattoo."

"And you're sure he still had it?" Keith pressed.

"Well, of course I'm sure," Heather replied. "I mean— Mr. Converse, what's going on? Why is Jeff's tattoo so important?"

Keith hesitated, part of him wanting to tell Heather about the idea that had taken root in his mind, but an equally strong part wanting to spare her from false hope if it turned out he was wrong. But the look on Mary's face told him it was already too late, and the words she spoke confirmed it.

"What is it, Keith?" Mary asked. "Why are you asking her about the tattoo?"

Keith hesitated, then told her: "I'm almost certain the body I saw this morning didn't have a tattoo."

"You mean it might not be Jeff?" Mary asked, immediately grasping what he was saying.

"I don't know," Keith said, still trying to protect both Mary and Heather, in case he was wrong.

"I want to see," Mary said. "I want to see for myself."

A little more than two hours later, Keith stood once more in the morgue, facing the drawer in which lay the body he had seen that morning. This time, though, Mary stood on one side of him and Heather Randall on the other.

"I have to see," Heather had told them when they'd found her waiting just inside the front door. As he had with Mary, Keith tried to dissuade her, and like Mary, Heather had insisted.

Now, as the drawer was pulled open, her fingers dug into the muscle of his left arm. The orderly—a different one than had been on duty that morning—pulled the sheet back, and Mary uttered a strangled sound of horror. She turned away, steadying herself against her husband as she struggled to fight back the wave of nausea that had risen inside her.

The orderly glanced questioningly at Keith. His own stomach knotted as he looked down again at the charred remains that had been pulled from the burning wreckage that morning.

His eyes fixed on the spot where there should have been a tattoo.

And all he saw was charred flesh.

CHAPTER 8

He wasn't crazy.

No matter what anyone said, Francis Jagger knew he wasn't crazy.

He'd had to kill the girl. He'd even tried to warn her. When they first met her, he warned her about Jimmy, how she needed to stay away from Jimmy.

But she hadn't.

Instead, she started acting real friendly toward Jimmy.

He'd warned Jimmy about her, too. Told him she was just like his mother.

Jimmy had just smiled at him, the way he always did. "Come on, Jag—you don't even remember your mother."

But he did remember his mother. He remembered how, when he was a little boy—before he even went to school—she started hanging around with someone. Ted, that was his name. And right from the first time he met Ted, he'd known what was going to happen.

"Don't worry, Francie," his mother kept telling him. "He's not going to take me away from you."

"Don't call me that! That's a girl's name!"

"No it's not. And even if it was, so what?" She'd picked him up and swung him in the air. "Aren't you pretty enough to be my little girl?"

The boy next door had heard her say that, and started calling him Francie, too. And then Francine.

He'd hated that.

And he would have stopped that boy from doing it, too, except that before he could decide exactly what to do, he'd come home one day and his mother was gone.

His mother, and Ted, and all their stuff.

He waited for her to come back, and tried not to cry, and ate the food he found in the refrigerator, and sat up all night so he'd be awake when she came back for him.

He waited all the next day, and the next night, too, but his mother hadn't come home.

Finally, a stranger had come and taken him away from his house and sent him to live with someone else.

There had been a lot of people he'd lived with, moving from one house to another, never staying in any of them long enough to feel like he belonged. By now, all the people who had taken him in for a few weeks—but never more than a few months—had run together in his mind. Even if someone had asked, he wouldn't have been able to put their faces together with their names.

The only person he really remembered—even wanted to remember—was Jimmy.

He'd met Jimmy three years ago, and right away he knew they were going to be friends. Part of it was Jimmy's smile— the way it made him feel inside. He hadn't felt anything like it since his mother left. He and Jimmy started hanging around together right away, getting drunk and doing some drugs. Jimmy didn't have a room, so Jagger let him come and stay with him. He'd even given him the bed, and started sleeping on the sofa himself. Jimmy told him the bed was big enough for both of them, and that almost wrecked everything. For a second he felt like killing Jimmy, but then got himself under control. "I ain't no fag," he said, his voice trembling with barely contained fury.

Jimmy's smile had faded away. "Hey, man, I never said you was. All I said was the bed was big enough. No big deal, okay?"

And it had been okay—it had been okay right up until they

met Cherie. "It's spelled the French way," she said right off, like he cared. "It means sweetheart." She smiled at Jimmy when she said that, and Jimmy smiled back at her.

That was when Jagger knew she was going to go away with Jimmy, just like his mother had gone away with Ted. But he hadn't let it happen. He'd known when they were planning it—known that whole day. The way they were looking at each other, and talking to each other when they thought he wasn't listening. But he'd known exactly what they were up to.

He'd even told Jimmy: "You're goin' away, aren't you? You're goin' away with her, just like my mom went away with Ted."

"What're you talkin' about, man?" Jimmy asked, but there was a look in his eyes that told Jagger he knew exactly what he was talking about. "Why'd I wanta go away with her? You're my bud, Jag. It's you and me!"

Jimmy had smiled at him, and Jagger had wanted to believe him—had wanted to believe him more than anything. But he hadn't, and that night, while they were smoking some dope that Cherie had picked up somewhere, he started seeing things really, really clearly.

He kept looking at Jimmy—looking at his eyes, and his slim body, and the way he smiled.

He started thinking how pretty he was.

Almost pretty enough to kiss.

He'd cut that thought out of his head. Where the fuck had it come from anyway? He wasn't a fag!

But the more he tried not to think about it, the more he kept thinking about it, even though he knew it was all wrong.

Jimmy was a guy, for Christ sake. He had a dick!

But if he didn't, and if he had boobs . . . boobs like Cherie's . . .

He sucked in another hit on the bong they were all sharing, and then things started getting kind of hazy. He couldn't remember what happened after that, except that he wanted to touch Jimmy. Wanted to touch him really bad.

But it was wrong—it was all wrong! He was a guy, just like all the rest of the guys.

But then he figured out how to make it right! All he had to do was fix things.

Fix Jimmy.

Cherie had fallen asleep, and now Jimmy was smiling at him again, smiling the way that made Jagger's stomach feel all queasy, and his balls start to ache, and his dick get hard.

"Come on," Jimmy whispered. "Come on, Jag—you're my bud. You know what you want. So come on and get it." He'd lain back on the floor then, and Jagger knew that Jimmy wanted him to do it.

Jimmy wanted him to fix it so they could be together.

The knife slid into Jimmy easily—just slipped through his shirt and between his ribs and into his heart. It didn't hurt Jimmy—Jagger never would have wanted to hurt him. Jimmy just looked sort of surprised for a second, and then he lay real still, stretched out on his back, his eyes fixed on him.

And he was still smiling at him, so Jagger knew it was okay.

He slid the knife into Cherie next. She didn't even wake up—she just lay there, but her boobs stopped moving like they had when she was breathing.

He undressed both of them, being really careful not to disturb Jimmy. Then he cut Cherie's boobs off, and carefully put them on Jimmy's chest.

Then came the worst part. He didn't want to touch Jimmy's dick—didn't even want to look at it. But he had to, in order to cut it off. It was a lot bigger than his own, and it seemed to take a long time to get it off. But finally he cut it free, and then everything was all right.

Jimmy didn't look like a guy anymore—he looked like a girl.

A pretty girl.

Exactly the kind of girl his mother would have wanted for him.

Taking off his own clothes, Jagger lay down next to Jimmy.

He stroked Jimmy's face with his finger, tracing his smile, brushing a lock of hair back from his forehead.

He kissed Jimmy, gently at first, then harder.

He pressed himself close to Jimmy, pressed their bodies together, rubbed himself against Jimmy's strong torso, until . . .

He couldn't remember anything after that—not until the police came.

He'd told them it wasn't his fault, that it was Jimmy and Cherie's fault. If Jimmy hadn't been planning to go away with Cherie—

But they'd locked him up anyway, locked him in jail.

Locked him up, and told him he'd never get out.

And that was where he'd stayed until they came for him the other night. He hadn't said a word when they took him out of his cell and put him in the van, but he listened, and he heard where they were taking him.

To a hospital.

He figured it must have something to do with Bobby Breen. Jagger had liked Bobby Breen almost as much as he'd liked Jimmy. And Bobby Breen had liked him, too. But something had happened to Bobby—something Jagger couldn't quite remember. They'd been together—real close together—in one of the little closets behind the kitchen where they both worked. Then something had started happening to Bobby. He'd started turning into a woman—a beautiful woman. Jagger had wanted to kiss the woman, to make love to her.

And she'd let him. She let him do everything he wanted to do.

She hadn't moved, hadn't tried to push him away.

She'd just lain there on the floor, very still, and for a long time after he'd loved her, he just looked at her. She was beautiful—even more beautiful than Bobby Breen had been. He didn't remember much after that. Some people asked him what he'd done, but he hadn't said anything, knowing that nobody was going to listen to him anyway.

They'd taken him to the hospital, but instead of putting him in a room, they brought him down into the basement.

That was when he began to think maybe something was wrong, and he'd finally spoken. "Where the fuck are we?" he demanded. "What's going on?"

But instead of answering him, one of the orderlies hit him—hit him hard enough to knock him out. The next thing he remembered was waking up in the room he was in now.

A room that didn't have any windows, and stunk of urine and shit and garbage. There were a couple of moldy mattresses on the floor and only one light—a naked bulb hanging from a wire in the ceiling.

The only door was locked from the outside.

Jagger didn't have any idea how long he'd been in the room—didn't have any idea what time it was, or what day it was, or even if it was night or day. Every now and then the same guys who'd taken him out of the hospital opened the door and gave him some food. Mostly it was stale bread, but sometimes there was some meat, and they usually gave him an old tin can filled with water to wash it down.

Every time they came, he asked them what was going on, but they never told him. "You'll find out," was all they ever said. "And when you find out, you're going to like it—you're going to like it a lot."

Now he could hear them coming again, hear their footsteps outside the door. He heard the key working in the lock, and heard the bolt slide back.

The door swung open, a man was shoved inside, and then the door was pulled closed again.

Pulled closed, and bolted.

Jagger looked at the man. He was young—maybe twenty-two or twenty-three.

Just about the same age Jimmy had been.

But he didn't have blue eyes like Jimmy's. He had brown eyes.

Brown, like his mother's.

And curly hair like his mother's, too.

And he looked scared.

"You got a name?" Jagger asked.

The man hesitated, then nodded. "Jeff."

"Jeff," Jagger repeated softly, almost to himself. Then he nodded. "I like that. I like that a lot."

CHAPTER 9

The silence between Mary and Keith during the drive back to Bridgehampton had none of the easy comfort that surrounds couples who have lived together for enough years so that each can sense the other's mood without a word being spoken. Rather, their silence was a gulf, a chasm that had widened over the years to the point that now, even with the tragedy that had mutually befallen them, they were unable to make any kind of connection.

Yet Mary felt she had to say something. Keith's pain was an almost palpable presence in the truck, and she knew that he didn't have the resource of faith to help him bear it alone. So at last, after having offered up every prayer she knew for the salvation of Jeff's soul, she turned her attention to the man who had been her husband for so many years. "I know how hard this is for you, Keith," she said softly, facing him directly. "But if you'll just let Him, the Lord will help you bear whatever burden He gives you." She bit her lip, knowing her next words would cause Keith pain, but knowing as well that they had to be spoken. "It's because of us," she said. "So many years ago, when I let you——" She fell silent, no longer willing even to speak the words out loud. "Well, you know what I'm talking about. It's our fault—all of it."

For a moment Keith made no reply at all, only glancing across at her and shaking his head sadly. "For God's sake, Mary," he sighed. "Why do you want to blame yourself? We didn't do anything wrong, no matter what Father Noonan says. And Jeff certainly didn't do anything wrong."

"If he didn't do anything—" Mary began, but Keith didn't let her finish.

"Don't give me any crap about the jury, or Cynthia Allen, or anything else," he growled. "Jeff didn't do a thing to that woman. No way." Finally looking straight at her, he said, "And that body in the morgue? That wasn't Jeff."

The words struck Mary like a punch in the stomach. Not Jeff? What was he talking about? But of course she understood—the pain of what had happened was too much for him to face. But to deny it—to try to pretend it hadn't happened—would only prolong the agony and make it worse when he finally had to accept it. Mary reached out and took her husband's hand in her own. "Keith, you were there—you saw him. It won't help to try to pretend—"

Keith jerked his hand away. "Pretend?" he cut in. "What are you talking about, pretend? I'm telling you, Mary—that wasn't Jeff we saw back there!"

Mary shrank back. "For Heaven's sake, what are you talking about? What are you saying?"

Keith took his eyes off the road long enough to throw her an angry glare. "I'm telling you that wasn't Jeff. When I was there this morning, that body was different."

Mary felt dizzy. Different? What was he talking about?

"The tattoo!" he said, his words coming in a harsh torrent. "Jeff had a tattoo, and that body didn't have one!"

"I know about Jeff's tattoo," Mary replied, trying to fathom what he was talking about. "But it was gone. It was—" She hesitated, shuddering as the image of Jeff's burned and disfigured body rose in her mind once more. "It was burned, Keith!" she finally managed to blurt. "That doesn't mean it wasn't there!"

"But it wasn't burned this morning," Keith shot back, his hands tightening on the steering wheel and his foot unconsciously pressing on the accelerator. "When I was there this morning, that part of that body wasn't burned." His voice rose. "And there was no tattoo, Mary! I'm telling you—"

"Look out!" Mary yelled as the truck threatened to smash into the back of the car ahead of them. "Will you calm down? Do you want to get us killed, too?"

Keith slowed the truck, then reached over to take Mary's hand. This time, though, it was she who pulled away, shrinking back against the door, moving as far from him as she could. "He's dead, Keith," she said, her voice trembling. "Jeff's dead, and you've got to face it."

"I don't have to face anything except the truth. And I'm telling you, that wasn't Jeff they showed us down there!"

An angry reply rose in Mary's throat, but she bit down on her lip—bit it hard, until the wave of anger ebbed away. When she spoke again, she kept her eyes straight ahead. "Take me home," she said. "Just take me home. I don't know what you're thinking, and I don't want to know."

"I'm thinking—" Keith began, but Mary cut him off.

"Our son died this morning," she told him. "I have to get used to that. I have to accept the burden that has been placed on me. I don't know how I can do it, but I have to. But I can't do it with you trying to pretend it didn't happen. So just drive me home, Keith. Just drive me home, and don't talk to me."

Another silence fell over them, and this time neither Mary nor Keith tried to break it.

CHAPTER 10

U ntil that day, Jeff hadn't realized he was afraid of the dark. But until that day, he had never before experienced true darkness, the kind of darkness that makes you wonder whether you'll ever see again, that wraps around you like a shroud, that suffocates you as much as blinds you. He had no idea where he was—no idea how long he'd been there. All he knew was that the single dim lightbulb that hung from the ceiling had become his lifeline to sanity.

He'd made a mistake—he understood that now. When the man who'd guided him down the stairs into the Bowery subway station jumped off the platform and dashed into the shadowy darkness of the tunnel itself, he should have stayed where he was—should have waited for the police who were only seconds behind him. But he hadn't been thinking—hadn't had time to think. And so he'd followed his instincts.

And the instincts that had leaped up from deep within the most primitive part of his brain were those of a wild animal that was being pursued. He'd turned and fled into the subway tunnel, suddenly less afraid of the man who had led him down the stairs than of the people racing toward him on the platform. He'd pounded down the tracks, desperately trying to keep up with the figure ahead of him—a fleeting form made visible for only an occasional second or two by one of the tiny bulbs that were the tunnel's only illumination. He'd almost crashed into the running man, unaware that the man had stopped.

Over the panting of his own breath and the pounding of his heart, he heard a sound.

A familiar rumbling sound that was getting steadily louder. In the distance, a light appeared.

"Off the tracks!" the man barked. "Now!"

Jeff started to step over the rail to his left, but the man grabbed his arm. "Here!"

Half guiding, half dragging him, the man led him up onto a narrow catwalk. He pulled Jeff after him into a shallow alcove in the tunnel's concrete wall.

The rumbling became a terrifying roar, and the spot of light grew into a beam that pierced the darkness of the tunnel. Jeff shrank back, pressing himself against the cold concrete.

The train shot by, so close that if he'd reached out, he could have touched the glass and metal monster roaring past. Swirling dust enveloped them, and as Jeff drew in a breath, he took in the dust and began choking and coughing. Automatically, he raised his hand, and the man next to him in the alcove caught it before it would have brushed against the speeding train. Suddenly, it was over, the roar of the train fading away as quickly as it had come. Still choking on the dust the train had stirred up, and trembling so badly his knees threatened to buckle beneath him, Jeff sagged against the wall until his coughing finally ceased.

"It's worst the first time," the man beside him said. "After a while you learn to hold your breath—that way the dust don't get to you so bad. Come on."

As surefootedly as if he were walking the streets on the surface, the man jumped back onto the tracks. Jeff followed, and a while later his companion ducked into a passageway leading off to the left, then led him up a ladder and through another series of passages, these filled with pipes.

Jeff had no idea how long they'd moved through the tunnels, nor how far they'd gone. There was no way to tell what time it might be, and he'd lost all sense of direction within seconds after he'd climbed the first ladder. All he knew was that if he didn't keep up with the man, he'd be hopelessly lost.

Lost somewhere under the city.

Lost in the darkness.

When he was so close to exhaustion that he wondered if he could go any farther, they came to a heavy, metal door. The man opened it and pushed him through. The door closed behind him with a hollow thud.

At first, the light inside the room had been so bright that its glare blinded Jeff. But a few seconds later, as his eyes adjusted, he realized he wasn't alone. There was another man in the room—a man a few years older than he.

A few years older, and a lot bigger, maybe four inches taller. The man outweighed him by at least fifty pounds, and none of the extra weight looked like fat.

Jeff recognized the orange jumpsuit as what the inmates at Rikers Island wore, once they'd been convicted. It was what he himself would have been wearing now, if not for the car that had crashed into the van.

"You got a name?" the man asked.

He hesitated, then nodded. "Jeff."

"Jeff," the man repeated softly, almost to himself. Then he nodded, too. "I like that. I like that a lot."

The man smiled at him, revealing a missing tooth. "I'm Jagger," he said. His smile faded as he looked at Jeff's clothes. "You ain't from the jail, are you?" he asked, his voice turning suspicious. " 'Cause if you think I'm goin' back, you better get a whole lotta help. I ain't goin' back."

Jeff shook his head quickly as he saw Jagger's right hand ball into a huge fist. "I'm not taking you anywhere. I don't even know where we are."

"Under the hospital," Jagger told him, sinking down onto the mattress that was the only thing in the room.

"The hospital?" Jeff asked. "What hospital?"

"The one they took me to."

"When was that?"

Jagger frowned, then shook his head, shrugging. "Don't know. Sometimes it's hard to think, you know?" His smile returned, and he patted the mattress next to him. "You want to sit down?"

Jeff hesitated, then shook his head as his hand closed on the knob of the door behind him.

Though the knob turned, the door was bolted.

Jagger uncoiled from the floor and took a step toward him. His voice dropped and took on a menacing edge: "You ain't leaving. I don't want you to leave."

Jeff thought he knew which hospital Jagger had said they were beneath. It had to be Bellevue. He'd heard stories about the place from people at the Tombs. "I'd rather be at Rikers," most of them said, shivering. "At least out there, everybody isn't crazy." But why had they taken Jagger to Bellevue? And why had he been at Rikers in the first place?

"I'm not going anywhere," he'd said as Jagger's hand tightened into a fist again. He moved away from the door, and Jagger's fist relaxed.

That had been an hour ago—or maybe two, or maybe even more. Jeff wasn't sure. He'd finally sat down on the floor, leaning against the wall. He thought he might have fallen asleep for a few minutes, but wasn't any more sure of that than of how long he'd been here. But when he opened his eyes, Jagger was sitting on the mattress, watching him. Jeff's muscles ached, and the cold of the concrete seemed to have sunk into his bones.

Then the light had gone off, and the terrible darkness closed around him.

Darkness, and silence.

A darkness so thick and heavy it felt like he was suffocating, and a silence so complete, it seemed he might never hear again.

A moment later, he'd felt something.

Something creeping toward him.

"Jagger?" he said, his voice sounding unnaturally loud in the darkness.

"Yeah," Jagger replied, his voice little more than a croak.

It sounded to Jeff as if he was still on the mattress on the other side of the room.

Then something skittered across his leg, and when he struck out at it, his hand hit something soft. There was a squeak as the object hit the wall a few feet away.

A rat!

Jeff jerked his legs up, then scrambled to his feet.

Then he heard something else.

It was a voice from the other side of the door.

"Get away from the door. Both of you sit on the mattress and don't move. You move, and the door closes and the light don't go back on. You got till I count to ten."

The man began counting, and for a moment Jeff was paralyzed. Where was the mattress? How was he supposed to find it? "Jagger," he whispered. "Where are you?"

"Over here," Jagger whispered back.

Jeff took a tentative step toward the other man's voice, then another. "Say something," he hissed into the blackness.

But instead of speaking, Jagger reached out in the darkness. His huge hand brushed against Jeff's leg, then closed on it. "It's okay," Jagger said. "I got you."

As the man outside finished counting, Jeff sank onto the mattress.

The door opened, a brilliant halogen beam cutting through the darkness, blinding Jeff as effectively as the darkness had a moment earlier.

"Welcome to the game," the voice said. "You win, you go free. You lose, you die."

Jeff heard the sound of something being set on the floor.

The halogen beam vanished, and the room was plunged back into blackness.

The bolt on the door slid back into place with a dull thump.

And then the light came back on.

Sitting next to the door was a large enamel bowl filled with something that looked like stew. The handles of two spoons protruded from the glutinous mass. Next to the bowl was a canteen.

Jagger got up and brought the bowl back to the mattress, setting it between them and offering Jeff a spoon.

Jeff shook his head.

Jagger shrugged and began to eat.

As he watched the other man consume the food, Jeff thought about the words that had been spoken in the darkness: *"You win, you go free. You lose, you die."*

His eyes shifted from Jagger to the single dim bulb that hung overhead.

You win, you go free. You lose, you die.

And if the light went off—

But Jeff knew what would happen if the light went off. The terrible suffocating darkness would close around him, and whatever lay hidden in the darkness would once more begin to creep toward him.

He repeated the words to himself again: *Welcome to the game. You win, you go free.*

You lose, you die.

CHAPTER 11

Keith Converse felt as if he hadn't slept at all. He'd spent the evening alone, which hadn't been a good idea. He'd consumed almost half a fifth of scotch—and not the good scotch he and Mary had always saved for company, either. It had been the cheap stuff that he kept on hand for the days when he felt he just needed a drink after work. The whiskey was raw enough that until last night he'd never been able to swallow more than one or two, and usually he wound up pouring what was left of the second drink down the drain. But last night nothing had gone down the drain. He'd just kept drinking, hoping that the alcohol would eventually take away the image of the burned body he'd seen that day.

The body that everyone had told him was his son's.

All evening, as he sat in his chair sipping whiskey and trying to forget what he'd seen, what Mary had said kept recurring to him: *"He's dead, Keith . . . Jeff's dead, and you've got to face it."*

But all he saw, no matter how much scotch he forced down his throat, was that patch of unburned skin, the patch that hadn't been charred this morning, but was burned so badly by afternoon that no tattoo could have been seen even if it were there.

Sometime after midnight, he forced himself to go to bed, but the patch of unmarked skin hung in his mind's eye as if it were somehow lit from within. The patch of skin where a tattoo should have been.

76

As the sun came up, Keith finally gave up on sleep and rose to try to clear his head with a cold shower, his doubts having congealed into an absolute certainty.

The body they'd shown him wasn't Jeff's.

Then what had happened?

Was it a mistake?

Could they have shown him the wrong body?

Was it possible there had been another burned body in the morgue? While the coffeemaker did its work, Keith went into the tiny alcove off the living room that served as his office and logged on to the Internet. He ran the search every way he could, checked the archives of every news agency in the area. In the last week, only three people in all of New York had died in a fire.

Jeff and the two correction officers.

So they hadn't showed him the wrong body.

Then what was going on?

He drank three cups of coffee, the argument raging inside his throbbing head. Mary had to be right—he was just refusing to face the reality of what had happened, grasping at any straw, no matter how weak it might be. *Face it,* he told himself over and over again. But no matter how hard he tried, a voice inside him kept insisting that something was wrong, that it hadn't been Jeff's body he'd seen in the morgue, no matter how impossible that seemed.

Back in his truck, and back on the expressway, he headed once more to the city. This time, though, he didn't go to the Medical Examiner's office. He headed instead to the Fifth Precinct station on Elizabeth Street.

He parked in a garage on the block north of the precinct house and walked south on a sidewalk that was already crowded at nine A.M. Twin green globes marked the station. Aside from that, it was a nondescript, not quite white building distinguished only by double front doors that had been painted a shade of blue so washed-out that Keith wondered if the bureaucrat who had chosen it had been color blind, or—more likely—the city had gotten a deal on a batch of paint no one else would buy. The blue doors stood open, though, and he stepped through a small foyer and pushed through an inner set of oak and glass doors, automatically looking around for the metal detectors that had stood just inside nearly every public building he'd been in since the morning after Jeff was arrested. But there were only several neutral-gray desks—only two of which were occupied—and a few patrolmen standing around talking. Around to the right he found the long, ornately carved oak counter that was the nerve center of the precinct.

The desk sergeant listened to his request, his face impassive. "Lemme get this straight," he said when Keith was done. "You want to see the report on that wreck yesterday morning, the one up at Delancey and Bowery?" When Keith nodded, the sergeant frowned. "How come?"

Keith was ready for the question. "It was my son that died," he said smoothly, giving no hint that he had any suspicions that it might not have been Jeff at all. "I just want to know what happened to him, that's all."

The desk sergeant's gaze shifted to a pair of patrolmen who were just heading out the door. "Hey, Ryan—didn't you and Hernandez catch that mess yesterday morning?"

The patrolman came over, and Keith introduced himself. "I just wondered exactly what happened. My son . . ." He let his voice trail off, leaving the last words unspoken.

"It was his kid that died," the desk sergeant offered, his voice finally taking on a note of sympathy. "You want to tell him what happened?"

Johnny Ryan shook his head. "Not that much to tell," he said. "By the time I got there, the van was already burning. Some old wreck of a car had slammed into it."

"What about the driver of the other car? Wasn't he hurt?" Keith asked.

Ryan shrugged. "If he was, it sure didn't slow him down

much. He was gone before anyone could even get a good look at him—but don't worry, we'll find him."

The other patrolman, whose name badge identified him as Enrico Hernandez, shook his head sourly. "Don't know how— the clunker'd been stolen off a lot out in Queens last night. We figure it was some kid out for a joyride, but without any witnesses . . ." He shrugged helplessly.

"But somebody *had* to have seen it," Keith pressed. "I mean, the middle of New York City—"

"You ever been over there at five-thirty in the morning? You could shoot a cannon down Bowery and not hit anything. Only people around at all were a couple of drunks, and neither one of 'em will say a thing. First one says he was poking around in a Dumpster, and the other was sound asleep. Said he didn't even wake up until the thing blew up." Then, remembering who he was talking to, he tried to backtrack. "I mean—"

"So nobody saw it all?" Keith asked.

"That doesn't mean we're not still looking," Hernandez said, a little too quickly. "Look, we want to know what happened just as bad as you do. It wasn't just your boy, you know. That guy killed two correction officers, too."

But a prisoner on his way to Rikers Island doesn't matter, Keith added silently to himself. "You guys happen to remember the names of the drunks?"

"One of 'em was Al Kelly," Johnny Ryan offered, obviously relieved to at least be able to offer something—no matter how insignificant—to the man whose son had died yesterday morning. "Kelly's almost always around that corner. He's got gray hair—really long. Maybe about an inch taller than you. He usually wears three or four sweaters and a coat, and if he isn't drunk by ten in the morning, you got the wrong guy." He glanced at Hernandez. "You remember the other guy?"

"Peterson, wasn't it? Something like that. Don't remember ever seeing him before, but that doesn't mean he won't still be around." He turned to the desk sergeant. "Any reason why he can't see the report?"

The sergeant shrugged. "Not that I know of." He pointed to one of the desks. "Ask Sayers. Just tell him what you want, and he'll find it."

Keith turned back to the two officers. "There going to be anything in it you haven't already told me?"

"Not much," Ryan sighed, shaking his head. "I wish there was—I really do. And a couple of the guys upstairs are on it, so maybe we'll still find the perp, you know?"

"They here?" Keith asked. "The guys upstairs?"

The desk sergeant glanced at the board on the far wall, then shook his head. "Maybe a half hour or so. You can wait over there." He tilted his head toward a bench that sat against the wainscoting—painted the same ugly shade of blue as the outside doors—then picked up a phone that had started ringing. "Fifth Precinct, Sergeant McCormick."

"Maybe I'll come back later," Keith said.

But as he left the precinct, he was pretty sure he wouldn't be back.

CHAPTER 12

The morning looked a lot warmer than it was, and Keith hunched his shoulders against the chill wind blowing down Elizabeth Street as he headed up toward Kenmare, which would run into Delancey at the corner of Bowery. Though he was only a couple of blocks from the collection of massive gray stone buildings that housed the city's government, he might as well have disappeared into another world. Elizabeth Street was lined on both sides with buildings of no more than four or five stories, with businesses operating on the sidewalk level and laundry hanging from lines strung between fire escapes on the floors above. Half the shops were grocery stores, though the Chinese fruits and vegetables they displayed were mostly unrecognizable to him. He had to thread his way through a milling throng of people who neither smiled nor nodded, let alone made any move to give way when there wasn't enough room for two people to pass. Once, a horn blasted as he stepped into the street to avoid a pack of hard-looking teenage boys with rings in their ears, lips, and noses, only to have one of those he was avoiding grab his arm and snatch him back onto the sidewalk an instant before the cab would have run him down.

"Watch it, man—you wanna get yourself killed?" the kid asked.

"Thanks," Keith said, but found himself talking to no one; the kid and his friends were already several yards away, and it was as if he no longer existed. Turning away from them, he bumped into a burly man slinging a barrel of garbage into a truck. As oblivious to him as the kids now were, the garbage man hardly glanced at him, going on with his work as if nothing had happened.

By the middle of the next block, Keith found himself doing his best to ignore the people around him, concentrating instead on the sidewalk directly ahead. Twice he made the mistake of waiting for a light to turn green at an intersection, and was nearly trampled by the crowd that ignored it. By the third block he discovered the trick everyone else already seemed to know—if you don't look at the cabs, they won't hit you. In fact, the cabbies didn't even bother to honk or curse at him, but let him cross with the same impunity they granted the city's natives.

At the corner of Kenmare, he turned right toward Bowery and Delancey—the intersection where the accident had taken place. He wasn't sure what he'd been expecting, but the vague sense of letdown—almost of disappointment—he felt at the corner's normality told him he must have been expecting something.

The bustling Asian community of Elizabeth Street suddenly gave way to restaurant equipment stores, except for one restaurant that seemed to be left over from an era when the neighborhood had been mostly Italian. Window after window displayed commercial mixers and kitchen equipment, bar glasses and furniture, and more kinds of lighting fixtures than Keith had even thought existed. It was almost devoid of people on the sidewalk, and there were no apartments above the businesses.

No windows from which some early rising resident might have seen what had happened yesterday morning.

It was just another impersonal city intersection, the cars heading east into Delancey and toward the Williamsburg Bridge waiting impatiently as the streams of traffic on Bowery flowed north and south.

No sign of the accident at all, except for the boarded-up windows of the restaurant supply house the van had careened into after the car struck it.

No sign that someone had died here only a little more than twenty-four hours ago.

This morning, with the sun shining incongruously on the spot where the black van had burned, it seemed almost impossible that it could have happened, and he stood for a moment on the southeast corner, trying to picture the scene from early yesterday morning. The van would have been coming from the west, heading toward the bridge. The car that hit it must have been going north on Bowery, and very fast—Keith had a pretty good idea how heavy a Ford van was, but could only guess how much force it would take to smash in the door of a reinforced van and knock it all the way across the street and into the building's windows. After it hit the van, the car's momentum would have carried it farther north, though the deflection of the crash should also have sent it skidding eastward.

He crossed the street, and twenty yards to the north found a wall that looked as if a car might have rubbed against it, leaving flecks of paint on the deeply gouged surface. His fingers unconsciously tracing the marks the careening car had left, he looked back toward where the van had burned.

"Man, it was somethin'," a slurring voice said.

Startled, Keith looked down to see a crumpled figure covered with enough ragged and filthy clothing that he was almost invisible, curled in the doorway of an empty store. He was peering blearily up at Keith through eyes so bloodshot their color was indistinguishable, and under the layer of grime that stained his skin, a vast network of ruined veins and scabrous sores spread over his features.

"Shoulda seen it, man—looked just like the fires of hell."

Keith's pulse quickened and he squatted down. "You were here yesterday morning?" he asked. "When the van burned?"

The man's lips twisted in a lopsided grimace, revealing the stumps of half a dozen broken teeth. "Where else am I gonna be?" His rheumy eyes fixed on Keith. "You got a couple'a bucks? I ain't ate in a while."

On any other day Keith would have walked away from the man, probably not even looked at him if he could have avoided it. In Bridgehampton, the man couldn't have stayed on the streets more than a few minutes before the police force—if you could really call Bill Chapin and his three deputies a force—would have hustled him onto a bus with a one-way ticket back to Manhattan. Certainly, he wouldn't have been allowed to roam the streets long enough for any of the town's wealthier citizens to have their weekend spoiled by stumbling across him.

But this wasn't an ordinary day, and Keith wasn't in the familiar confines of Bridgehampton, and instead of quickly standing up and walking away, he pulled his wallet out of his hip pocket.

It flipped open the same way it always did: to Jeff's graduation photo, taken almost a year ago.

Keith's stomach tightened as he gazed at the photograph. Taking out a five-dollar bill, he turned the wallet toward the man leaning against the building. "Did you see this person?" he asked. "Yesterday morning?"

The drunk peered at the photo. "Nah," he mumbled. "Who's that?"

"My son," Keith said. "He was—" He fell abruptly silent and flipped the wallet closed as the surrealism of the entire scene suddenly closed in on him. How had this happened? How could he explain to this man—this man whose own life had devolved down to sprawling in a doorway at ten o'clock in the morning—what he was doing here? Why would the man even listen, let alone care?

What was *he* even doing here?

Grasping at straws, just like Mary had said.

The drunk, his eyes glued to the five-dollar bill, said, "On-liest guy I saw was the one from the van."

Keith's pulse quickened. "The driver?"

The man shrugged. "Nah—who cares about him?" He frowned, then reached tentatively toward Keith's wallet. "Lemme see that pitcher again."

Keith reopened the wallet, but kept it just beyond the man's reach. The man leaned forward, squinting, and Keith winced as his breath—a combination of stale wine and tobacco—threatened to overwhelm him.

"I dunno," the man finally said. Keith moved the five dollar bill closer. "Maybe that coulda been him," the drunk went on. "But maybe not." Keith let him have the five. "They was over there—" He gestured vaguely in the direction of the fire hydrant. "—an' I was sittin' right here. An' I didn't get a real good look before they went down in the subway."

"The subway?" Keith echoed. "Who went into the subway?"

The man sighed as if explaining something to a child who wasn't paying proper attention. "I told you. The guy Scratch took outta the van." Something across the street seemed to catch the drunk's eye, and he struggled to his feet. "Gotta git to gittin'," he muttered, but Keith grabbed his arm as he started away.

"Scratch? Who's Scratch?"

The man's eyes widened, then darted once more across the street. "I dunno," he mumbled. "I dunno what you're talkin' about." Pulling his arm loose from Keith's grip, he started shambling down the street, one hand clutching at the collar of his filthy jacket while the other hand, which held the five-dollar bill, was plunged deep into his pocket. As he shuffled toward the corner, Keith scanned the street to see what had spooked the bum.

All he saw were three homeless people—a woman and two men—moving along the sidewalk, the woman pushing a shopping cart that seemed to be stuffed with nothing more than a bundle of rags. The little group, making their way slowly along the sidewalk with their heads down, looked far more pitiable than frightening. Keith shook his head to rid himself of the pathetic image, and also because of a twinge of guilt that he was going to do nothing to ease their plight.

The subway.

The man had said "Scratch" had taken someone from the van—someone who might have been Jeff?—to the subway.

At the corner he saw the sign, and the flight of stairs leading down into the subterranean station.

He started toward it.

Al Kelly glanced back over his shoulder. The man who'd given him the five dollars was headed the other way, but across the street, Louise and Harry were still coming. Al didn't know the guy with them, but it didn't matter—he looked like trouble. Looked like he didn't belong on the surface at all, in fact. Al shuddered, just thinking about the way some people lived. Okay, so he curled up in a doorway every now and then, or slept in the park over on Chrystie Street, at least when the weather was nice. But when it was bad, he slept indoors— went to one of the shelters, even if he did have to listen to some preaching or say he was going to try to clean up and find a job. But at least he still lived like a human being instead of some kind of rodent sneaking around in the sewers.

Of course, Louise had told him it wasn't that bad, not if you knew where to go, but he didn't have any desire at all to find out if she was telling the truth. No matter what happened— no matter how bad things got—he was going to stay on the surface.

He glanced over his shoulder again. Louise and Harry and the other guy had crossed the street now, and he was pretty sure he knew exactly what they wanted.

The five bucks the tourist had given him.

Shit!

He should've been more careful, should've palmed the

bill, or at least made sure no one was looking when he took it—the last thing you wanted was money in your pocket.

He turned onto Rivington Street, cut diagonally across, then ducked into Freeman Alley and headed toward the jog halfway up it. Maybe Louise and Harry wouldn't spot him, but even if they did, he might find a place to stash the money, at least until he could lose them and their friend. He quickened his pace, but the blister on the sore on his right foot was hurting real bad today, and he couldn't move quite fast enough. He was just coming up to the jog when Harry's hand closed on his shoulder and turned him around.

"Hey, Al—whatcha doin'?"

Al's eyes darted from Harry to the other man, then back to Harry. "Nothin'. Just lookin' for something to eat."

"Why don't ya buy something?" the other man asked. "You got the money, don't you?"

"I ain't got nothing," Al protested, but Harry's hand tightened on his shoulder.

"We saw you, Al," Harry said. "We saw you talkin' to that guy, and we saw him give you the money. So what were you talkin' about, Al?"

Al Kelly sighed heavily—no point trying to pretend he didn't have the money. They'd just go through his pockets, and probably beat him up for making them look for it. Pulling the five out, he handed it to Harry. "Okay, so you got it." He started to pull away, but the second man blocked his way.

"Harry asked you a question, Al. Ain't you gonna answer it?"

Al shrugged. "He was just askin' about somethin' I saw yesterday, that's all."

The man's eyes narrowed. "So what did you tell him?"

Al shrugged. "Nothin' much. Just about the guy goin' into the subway."

Harry's grip on Al's shoulder tightened, and the other man reached into his pocket. When his hand emerged a moment later, Al saw the blade of a knife.

"What did you want to do that for, Al?" Harry asked, sounding almost sad.

"What's the big deal?" Al protested. "He wasn't a cop—he was just some guy lookin' for his kid. I—"

But before he could say anything else, he felt a strange sensation in his belly, like somebody had punched him. He looked down, and sure enough—the other guy's fist was right up against his belly. But where was the knife?

The man jerked his arm and fist upward then, and Al Kelly knew where the knife was. It was deep in his gut, and now the blade was moving up, slashing through his flesh and organs.

A guttural sound bubbling up from his throat, Al tried to pull away, but it was far too late.

Harry held him upright as the knife slashed through his lungs and its point pierced his heart. Then, as the other man pulled the knife free of Al Kelly's lifeless body, Harry lowered it gently to the ground and propped it against a door.

A door that was painted a shade of red that almost matched the blood oozing from the wounds in Al Kelly's body.

Slipping the five-dollar bill into his own pocket, Harry and the other man quickly went back to the street where Louise was waiting for them.

Anyone looking into the alley would see nothing more than Al Kelly's feet, and assume he was just another drunk sleeping it off in solitude.

That's what they would have thought, unless they noticed he was sitting in a pool of his own blood.

Keith took the stairs down to the subway station two at a time, fishing in his pocket for money. He had no idea how much a subway token cost now—it had been twenty years since the last time he'd ridden one. He glanced around for the token booth but saw instead several machines that looked like some kind of ATM. Frowning, he went over to a machine, read the directions, pressed some buttons, then put five dollars in the slot. A few seconds later a plastic card popped out.

With the card in hand, he moved toward the turnstiles, then stopped.

What did he think he might find, out on the platform?

Did he believe Jeff might be down there waiting for him?

If it had even been Jeff that the old drunk on the sidewalk had seen. Chances are the man just made up the story, wanting the five dollars he'd been waving in front of him like a fly above a trout.

But the bum had seen someone getting out of the back of the van. And not just getting out, either—the drunk had said: *"The guy Scratch took outta the van."*

Not "got" out, or "let" out. "Took" out.

But after the fire, there'd been someone in the van—someone who burned to death.

Someone they'd told him was Jeff.

Or he was wrong, and the drunk was either confused or making up a story to get the money.

It all came back to the body in the Medical Examiner's office. If he was right, and the body wasn't Jeff's, then maybe the drunk was right, too. Maybe someone had let Jeff out of the van before it burned. But he had to know—had to know with absolute certainty whether the body was Jeff's or not. And now he realized there was a way—it had been staring him in the face all the time.

If they said the body was Jeff's, they would have to release it to him. He was Jeff's father, wasn't he? So when they were done with the autopsy, done with whatever examinations they were performing, they would release the body to him.

And then he could have his own tests done.

DNA tests.

Wheeling around, he went back up the stairs almost as fast as he'd gone down them, yelled at a cab that had stopped for the light at Bowery, and five minutes later was once more in the Medical Examiner's office.

"I want to claim a body," he told the woman at the reception counter. "My son's body."

Not so much as a flicker of sympathy—or even concern—passed over the woman's face. Instead she simply pulled out a form and pushed it across the counter to him.

Keith filled it out, turned it around, and pushed it back.

The woman glanced down at it, then looked up again, frowning. "You here for the Converse case?" she asked. "Jeffrey Converse?"

Keith nodded. "Is there a problem? I just want to arrange to have his body transferred to a funeral home whenever your office is done."

The woman turned to a computer terminal, tapped a few keys, and her frown deepened. "I'm afraid he's not here anymore."

"Not here?" Keith repeated, his head suddenly swimming. What was going on? How could the body not be here? But the woman on the other side of the counter was already telling him.

"It was released yesterday afternoon," she said.

"Released?" Keith echoed. "What are you talking about, released?"

The woman's eyes never left the computer terminal. "To a Mary Converse."

Keith's eyes narrowed angrily. "How could you do that? I'm his father, for Christ sake. How come nobody called me?"

The woman behind the counter shrugged helplessly. "Mrs. Converse was listed as his next of kin in all our records, sir. Either her, or a Keith Converse." She glanced at him almost disinterestedly. "I guess that would be you?"

"You guess right," Keith growled. "And you better get whoever authorized this down here right now." The woman's expression hardened, and Keith realized his mistake. "Look," he added, trying to mollify her. "I didn't really mean it the way it sounded. But he was my son! It just seems like—"

The woman softened slightly. "I'm sorry," she said, "but all the procedures were followed. If you like, I can tell you where the body was sent." Before Keith could answer, her efficient fingers tapped at the keyboard once more. "Ah, here it is." She copied down the address on a card and pushed it across the counter. "Vogler's," she said. "They're up on Sixth Street, I think. They picked up the body at—let me see—yes, here it is. Five twenty-three." She smiled brightly, as if having come up with the precise minute at which the body had left the Medical Examiner's should somehow mollify him.

Keith, though, was already out the door, and as soon as he was back on the sidewalk, he punched in Mary's number.

"What the hell are you doing?" he demanded. "You want to tell me what the hell is going on?"

Mary, understanding what must have happened, sighed heavily. "I should have called you, I suppose, but I just didn't want to get into another argument. And knowing how you feel—what you think—" She fell silent for a moment, then went on. "I decided to take care of it myself." Her voice took on the faintly superior tone that he knew meant she was about to wrap her religion around herself as a protective, and utterly impenetrable, shield. "He *was* my son, and no matter what he did, I have an obligation to him. There's going to be a memorial mass at St. Barnabas next week."

Keith frowned. Memorial mass? What was she talking about? If she was sure it was Jeff who had died, wasn't she going to have a funeral? But before he could ask the question, she answered it.

"I decided a funeral would just be too hard—too hard for everyone. And now that he's gone . . ."

Keith's anger smoldered as her voice trailed off. But even though she wouldn't do it herself, he had no trouble finishing her thought: *now that he's gone, I don't have to deal with him anymore.* "Where's the body?" he demanded. "Is it still at this Vogler place?"

There was another silence, then she said, "There isn't any body, Keith," her voice breaking. "I—I had him cremated. After what happened, I just couldn't stand the thought of—

well—" There was a short silence before she concluded, "It just seemed like the best thing to do, that's all."

But Keith was no longer listening.

Cremated.

The body—whoever it was—was gone, and gone with it was any possibility of proving whether it had been Jeff.

So all he had left were the words of the drunk.

And a subway station.

Wondering if he shouldn't go back home and just try to do as Mary wanted—try to accept what had happened—he started back toward the garage where he'd parked the car. But instead of going into the garage, he kept on walking.

Kept walking until he was back at the subway station on Delancey Street.

CHAPTER 13

By seven o'clock Eve Harris was almost four hours behind in her work. Not surprising, considering that she'd managed to fit two committee meetings into the day, along with lunch with the mayor and a carefully planned but apparently impromptu drop-in on Perry Randall—in which she'd succeeded in extracting the check he'd promised at last night's banquet. She was now wrapping up a meeting on Delancey Street, at Montrose House itself, where she'd been pleased to be able to deliver Perry Randall's check in person.

"By the way, did you hear about Al Kelly?" Sheila Hay asked as Eve was pulling on her coat. The councilwoman's brows rose questioningly, and Sheila unconsciously brushed a strand of her prematurely graying hair from her forehead as she pulled off her glasses and let them drop on their gold chain to rest on her ample bosom, as she did at the end of every meeting. "Louise and Harry found him in an alley this morning."

The words hung in the air: *"found him."*

Not "found his body," or even "found him *dead*."

Just "found him."

The rest was implied.

What kind of world are we living in? Eve wondered. What kind of world is it that we just assume that if someone was found, they were dead? But she knew what kind of world it was—it was the world she'd been dealing with all her life. "Did they say what happened to him?" she asked.

Sheila Hay shook her head as much in resignation as in sadness. "You know how these things go—unless there's someone around to make a fuss, who's going to ask?"

Again Eve knew exactly what the other woman meant without having it spelled out. "Did the police even take a look?"

Sheila rolled her eyes. "Sure—that's their job, isn't it? And I'll bet I can tell you exactly what the report says, too— 'assailant unknown.' There'll be enough gobbledy-gook to make it look like a report, and that'll be that." Her eyes met Eve's, and now Eve saw the sadness in them. "Who can even say they're wrong—it probably *was* some junkie looking for money, and how many thousands of those do we have? Like Al would have had any money. He didn't even have a place to live, for God's sake!"

"Louise and Harry didn't see anything?"

Sheila shrugged. "Come on, Eve. You know what they're like—even if they saw it happen, they wouldn't tell the police. Or me. Or you, either. They don't trust us."

"Is there a reason why they should?" Eve asked. Then, seeing the hurt in Sheila Hay's eyes, she quickly softened her words. "I don't mean you, Sheila. You know how it is—it's *us*. All of us. I mean, there they are, living like animals, and all they ever hear are promises. But they never see anything change! They—" She cut off her words as quickly as they'd come. "What am I telling you for? You know it all as well as I do."

Saying good-bye to Sheila, she considered going back to the office, then quickly changed her mind. Whatever messages were waiting for her could wait until tomorrow, and the two reports she had to review by tomorrow morning—one on the need for more public housing, the other on the failure of the public housing that already existed—were already in the ever-present leather bag she carried slung over her shoulder. Not that she needed to read them to know what was in them, since she was fairly certain that both reports contained far more lobbyists' arguments than actual facts. Indeed, she'd weighed the option of leaving them on her desk unread, but in the end the weight of her own conscience was far heavier, so she'd stuffed the two thick reports into her bag.

Two minutes later she was hurrying down the stairs to the subway station, barely looking around as she passed through the turnstile and descended to the platform. Though rush hour was over, there were still a few dozen people waiting for trains, and Eve moved toward the far end of the platform where the crowd was thinnest before reaching into her bag and pulling out one of the reports. She was just starting to leaf through it when she heard an insistent voice from farther down the platform.

"All I'm asking is if you were here yesterday morning!" The man sounded strident, almost angry. "A little after five."

"What's it to you?" another voice said, sounding even angrier than the first. "I got a right to be anywhere I want—"

Eve looked up from the report to see two men. One of them—a black man who could have been anywhere between forty and sixty—was wearing the uniform of the homeless: several layers of bulky clothes, all of them threadbare, none of them clean.

The other one—the one she'd heard first—looked like he had to be from out of town, though Eve couldn't have said exactly why. There was just something about his khaki pants, his denim shirt, and his work boots—or perhaps the unself-consciousness with which he wore them—that told her he didn't live in the city. And yet, for some reason, she thought she recognized him.

"I didn't say you didn't have a right to be here," she heard the out-of-towner saying. "I'm just asking—"

"You got no right!" the other man cut in, his voice rising.

Shoving the report back into her bag, Eve walked quickly down the platform to where the two men were standing. "Can I help you?" she asked.

The black man wheeled around, his eyes blazing, but the fire quickly died away, to be replaced by a look of uncertainty. "I got a right to be here," he said. "It's a public place, right? So I got a right to be here!"

"Of course you do," Eve said soothingly. "You have as much right to be here as anybody else."

"See?" the man said, turning to face the other man. "I told you! I got a right!"

"I'm not saying you don't," the other man said doggedly. "I'm just asking you to look at a picture." He was holding out a wallet, and Eve glanced at the photograph.

Suddenly, she knew why she recognized this man. She'd seen him on the news the day before yesterday, when they'd reported on the sentencing of Jeff Converse.

"You're his father," she said. "You're Jeff Converse's father."

Keith's brows rose. "You know my son?"

"I know he almost killed a girl, and I know he got sentenced to a year in jail for it." But then Eve's voice changed, some of the anger draining away. "And I heard he was killed in an accident yesterday morning." She hesitated, then said, "That must have been very difficult for you."

Keith's eyes narrowed. "What's really difficult is—" He cut himself short as he realized he was talking to a total stranger. "There's just a bunch of stuff I don't get, that's all."

Eve frowned. "I'm not sure I understand what you're saying."

"I'm not sure I do, either," Keith said grimly. "But one thing I'm finding out fast—so far it doesn't seem like there's one damn person in this city except me who cares if it really was my son that died yesterday morning."

Recalling Heather Randall insisting that Jeff Converse couldn't possibly have been guilty of the crime of which he'd been convicted, the councilwoman decided the reports in her bag would have to wait. She held out her hand. "I'm Eve Harris," she said. "Maybe we should talk."

Though he knew he'd been asleep—suspected he must have slept for several hours—Jeff felt as tired as if he'd been awake for days. The damp chill of the concrete walls and floor of the subterranean chamber had penetrated every muscle and bone in his body, and a bank of disorienting fog seemed to have settled on his brain.

Part of it was the simple fact that he no longer had any idea of what time it was. It was so long since he'd been allowed to wear a watch that he'd stopped missing it—in fact, he hadn't really needed a watch in jail. What use was a watch when everything happened according to someone else's schedule, and it didn't matter at all whether you kept track of time or not?

Someone told you when to get up.

Someone told you when to eat.

Someone told you where to go, and made sure you got there.

Someone even told you when to go to sleep, assuming you could sleep in jail at all.

But since he'd been locked in this windowless, featureless room, there was nothing to mark the passage of time except the occasional appearance of the man he'd made the mistake of following into the subway tunnel—a man whose name seemed to be Scratch. Even with the light on, as it had been recently, every real indicator of time had vanished.

Food appeared every now and then, always in the form of the same stewlike gruel he and Jagger had first been given. Usually there were two men with Scratch when he delivered the food, and the last time they'd appeared, Jeff had asked one of them what time it was.

"Animals don't care what time it is," the man retorted.

"I'm not an animal," Jeff shot back, "I'm a human being."

The man chuckled—a dark, hollow sound that carried far more menace than humor. "That's what you think."

The door had closed again, the bolt was thrown, and he and Jagger squatted down to share the bowl of the same gamy-tasting stew that was all they'd been given.

After he'd eaten—maybe an hour later, maybe two—he'd fallen asleep.

Now he was awake again, and his entire body ached, and his mind felt foggy.

And someone was watching him.

Jagger.

The first time it had happened, he'd woken up to find the big man hunkered down on the floor next to him, rocking slowly back and forth as he stared into his eyes.

Rocking, and humming something that sounded almost like a lullaby.

Jeff had rolled away and quickly sat up, automatically pulling his legs up against his chest.

Jagger's eyes had narrowed. "What the matter?" he asked. "You afraid of me?"

Jeff had hesitated, then shook his head, even though it was true. In fact, as Jagger's cold blue eyes continued to bore into him, it was all he could do not to draw still farther away.

Jagger had glanced toward the far corner and said, "There was a rat sniffin' around—figured you wouldn't want him climbin' all over you."

Jeff's skin crawled just thinking about it, and the fear induced by the man's intense gaze eased slightly. "Thanks," he said. "I guess I'm just jumpy."

Now Jeff could hear that lullaby again, and even with his eyes closed, he could feel Jagger watching him.

Then, before he could roll away, he heard the bolt on the door slide back with a clunk. Jagger's odd melody silenced.

A moment later the door opened.

Scratch came into the room, followed by two other men,

both dressed in the same kind of clothes Scratch himself wore: frayed and filthy pants, ragged shirts, and jackets so stained and greasy they could have been almost any color at all. One of the men had a tattered woolen scarf wrapped around his neck. The other wore a stocking cap with so many holes in it that great clumps of his unkempt hair were poking through.

"Well, I guess it's time," Scratch drawled. "You ready?"

Jeff and Jagger glanced at each other, then both of them peered suspiciously at Scratch. "Ready for what?" Jeff finally asked.

Scratch's lips curled into a twisted smile. "Ready to play." When neither Jeff nor Jagger spoke, Scratch snapped his fingers and one of the other men tossed a bundle toward the mattress.

Jagger's hands snatched it out of the air before it landed.

"Nice reflexes," Scratch observed. "They'll like that."

As Jagger began ripping the bundle open, Scratch said, "That's all you get. And remember the rules—get to the surface, you win. Otherwise, you lose."

Jeff's eyes narrowed suspiciously. "How do I win? The police are going to be looking for me."

Scratch shook his head. "No they're not—as far as they're concerned, you're dead." His eyes flicked toward Jagger. "Both of you are. So if you get out, nobody's going to be looking for either one of you." His cold smile gave way to a mocking grin. "*If* you get out." He jerked a thumb at the third man, who stepped forward, pulling his right hand from his jacket pocket.

The hand held a heavy pistol.

"It's a .45," Scratch explained. "And Billy here's a really good shot. So think of it as hide-and-go-seek, okay? After we leave, you count to a hundred real slow. If you do, you're on your own. But if you come through that door too soon, Billy'll have a good time blowin' a couple'a holes in you."

A few seconds later they were gone, but though the door

closed behind them, they didn't hear the familiar clunk of the bar. As Jeff went to the door and pressed his ear against it, Jagger finished tearing open the bundle. All he found inside were two flashlights and two sets of clothes as ragged as the ones Scratch and the others had been wearing, and even filthier. The smell that rose from them nauseated Jeff, but Jagger was already ripping off his orange coveralls. He tossed them in a corner and started pulling on the largest of the pants from the bundle, kicking the second set toward Jeff. "Don't matter how bad they stink," he said. "They ain't orange, and they don't say Rikers Island on 'em." He finished pulling on the filthy clothes, then picked up one of the flashlights and started toward the door.

"How do you know they won't shoot you as soon as you go out there?"

"Can't be any worse than sittin' here wondering what's going to happen," Jagger replied. He pulled the door open, hesitated a second, then stepped out into the darkness beyond.

Nothing happened.

"You coming?" he asked. "Because I ain't waiting."

Ripping off his own clothes, Jeff pulled on the ill-fitting pants and shirt that still lay on the floor, then picked up the second flashlight. He was about to turn it on, then thought better of it. If the batteries ran out in one, they'd need the other.

Moving through the door, he peered into the darkness that stretched away in both directions. "Which way?" he asked.

"Up," Jagger replied. "Except we haven't got a ladder."

From somewhere far off in the darkness to the right, they heard something.

It sounded like a shot, followed by a scream.

"Let's get the fuck out of here," Jagger said. Without waiting for a reply, he moved quickly into the blackness to the left.

A second later, before Jagger would disappear completely, Jeff followed.

CHAPTER 14

Keith and Eve Harris were sitting in a tavern—
Mike's, or Jimmy's, or something like that—at a
tiny table covered with a red-checkered tablecloth.
A real linen tablecloth with the stains to prove it. Every table
in the place was filled, and people were three deep at the bar
that ran the full length of the far wall. Curtains partially
blocked the view of the sidewalk outside, giving the illusion
that a steady stream of bodiless heads were drifting by. The
buzz of conversation was loud enough that Keith had to strain
to hear Eve Harris, but that same buzz gave them a degree of
privacy they might not have had at a quieter restaurant.

Keith's gaze had flipped back and forth between the woman
and her business card at least half a dozen times in the five
minutes since she'd led him into the tavern, ordered a glass
of merlot to his scotch on the rocks, and handed him her
card. "This is real?" he'd asked as he read the title beneath
her name.

"It's real," the waiter had said. "Nice to see you again, Ms.
Harris."

"Nice to see you, too, Justin. Everything going all right?"

"I'm still working, aren't I?" the waiter countered, then
turned to Keith. "If it weren't for Ms. Harris, I'd probably be
dead by now. You don't even want to know how I was living
before I met her. Be back in a minute with the drinks."

A minute was exactly what it had been, and in that minute
Eve Harris told him that she hadn't done much for the

waiter—she'd just gotten to know him when he was pan-handling in Foley Square, and after talking to him almost every day for a month, asked him what he wanted to do with his life. "He said he just wanted to get himself cleaned up enough to get a real job. So all I did was take him shopping. We got him new clothes and a haircut, and I rented him a room. Then I sent him in here to talk to Jimmy, and he's been working ever since." Then Justin reappeared with their drinks, and Eve Harris glared at him mischievously. "Of course, if he screws up, he'll be the best bartender living in a box on Foley Square."

"Don't worry, I'm not screwing up," Justin assured her, grinning.

Now that they were alone again, Keith said, "I don't get why you're even interested in this." He could feel Eve Harris studying him with as much concentration as he'd been studying her before answering.

She took a sip of her merlot, seemed to come to some kind of decision, then leaned forward in her chair. "I'm aware of who your son is, what he did, and what happened to him," she said. "But I'm also aware that Perry Randall's daughter doesn't think he was guilty, and was planning to marry him. What I don't understand is what you were doing in the subway, asking people if they'd seen your son. He's dead, isn't he?"

As briefly as he could, Keith told her what he'd seen at the Medical Examiner's office, and what the drunk over on Bowery had told him.

"And you believed him?" Eve asked.

"Why shouldn't I?" Keith challenged, a note of belliger-ence in his voice.

She shook her head almost sadly. "Mr. Converse, there are basically three kinds of people living on the streets of this city: the addicts, the crazies, and the houseless." She smiled thinly at the puzzled look on Keith's face. " 'House-less' is their term, not mine. Some of the people consider the streets their home, so they aren't homeless, at least according to them. Houseless, but not homeless. But a lot of the groups tend to overlap—most of the addicts and crazies are homeless, but not all the homeless are addicts or crazies." She tilted her head toward Justin, who was busily wiping down a table that had been momentarily vacated. "A lot of the homeless just need a break. But some of the rest of them . . ." She spread her hands in a gesture of helplessness. "I wish I could say they're all just down on their luck, but I've lived here too long and seen way too much. And I've learned that the addicts will tell you anything they think you might be willing to pay for." She fixed him with a look that told him she would know if he didn't tell her the exact truth. "So how much did you pay him?"

Keith felt utterly stupid. "Five dollars," he admitted.

"Tell me what he looked like. And be specific—shabby clothes and gray hair isn't going to cut it. That's half the derelicts I know."

Keith cast his mind back to when he'd talked to the drunk that morning, and began describing everything he remembered. When he was finished, Eve Harris nodded grimly.

"Al Kelly," she sighed. "Well, at least now I know what happened to him." She took a deep breath. "Mr. Converse, let me tell you a few things about this city . . ." She talked steadily, and when she was done, Keith's hands were clenched around his now empty glass.

"You're saying it was my fault Al Kelly died?" he asked, signaling Justin for a refill. "You're saying if I hadn't given him the five dollars, he wouldn't be dead?"

Eve shrugged. "Maybe, maybe not. But I do know better than to give money to addicts. Drunks and junkies—they're all the same—they'll lie, cheat, and steal to get what they want. And it sounds like you bought Al's lie for five dollars. Some other people saw the money change hands, and a few minutes later Al's dead. You add it up."

Now it was Keith who fell into a long silence. Out the window, it was starting to get dark, and cold-looking rain had begun to fall. The bar itself was so packed now that the waiter was barely able to get through with his drink. Keith pictured the subway platform again, and recalled the roar of the trains that streamed through the station every few minutes all through the long afternoon as he'd shown Jeff's photograph to anyone who would look. Most of the people—the well-dressed ones who had things to do and places to go—barely even glanced at the photo. Most of them turned their back on him, or refused to acknowledge his existence at all.

Only the bums—the ragged men and women who had nothing better to do—had been willing to talk to him.

And now Eve Harris was telling him that most of them would just as soon lie to him as tell him the truth.

Like Al Kelly had lied. And gotten killed for a lousy few bucks.

And even if Kelly hadn't lied, how was he supposed to find Jeff? he wondered. If his son had made it into the subway station, he could have gotten on any one of the trains and gone anywhere.

Maybe Eve Harris was right—maybe he should just give it up and go back home. But then he remembered there was still one more possibility. "Do you know a lot of them?" he asked. "The people on the streets?"

"Everybody in the city knows them," Eve replied. "I just take the time to talk to some of them." She smiled wryly. "I guess I sort of think of myself as their voice on the council— Lord knows they don't have another one, and if I don't stick up for them, no one will."

"So have you ever run into someone named Scratch?"

Eve shook her head. "I don't think so. Who is he?"

"The man Al Kelly said led my son down into the subway," he said.

"I suspect he's no more real than anything else Al Kelly told you he saw." She glanced at her watch, finished her merlot, and stood up. "I don't have any way of knowing whether your son was guilty or not, but I think I can understand how much you're hurting right now. So let me talk to a couple of people, and at least maybe we can find out if anyone else has ever heard of this 'Scratch' person. Call me tomorrow?"

Keith stood up. "Are you saying you believe me? That Jeff might be alive?"

"It doesn't matter what I believe," Eve said. "It's what you believe that's making you hurt. The only way you're going to stop hurting is by knowing for sure."

Then she was gone.

None of the men spoke; they didn't have to.

They all knew why they were there, what they had to do, what they were *going* to do. . . .

Silently, they stripped off the clothes they'd worn when they arrived, then just as silently began pulling on the clothes they would wear for the evening's adventure. First came the socks and gloves. The socks were thick to keep their feet warm inside the thin and flexible shoes they would wear. The gloves were thin, to allow their fingers maximum flexibility.

Both the socks and gloves were black.

Next came the insulated nylon coveralls, so the men would be protected against the chill of the tunnel.

Then the shoes and the smudges of makeup, as black as the gloves and the coveralls.

Only when they were completely dressed, when every inch of their skin was covered in a dull and nonreflective black material, did they begin equipping themselves.

Each of them carried a knife, strapped to the lower leg, where it could be easily reached from a crouch.

Most of the guns were Steyr Mannlichers, SSG-PI models, chosen for their combination of accuracy, a short barrel, and the option to add either a flash hider or a suppressor. Fully loaded and equipped with second generation rifle scopes that could take advantage of any available light or provide their own infrared illumination, the guns still weighed barely ten pounds.

A couple of the hunters carried far less complicated but usually just as effective M-14A1s, the favored sniper rifle of the Marines.

For communication, they carried Ericsson-GE two-way radios, though by now they rarely needed them.

As silently as he'd dressed, each man now nodded an acknowledgment that he was ready.

Only then did the leader—who looked no different from the others—unlock the heavy door set into the room's back wall. He swung the door open and stepped to one side. "I am Hawk," he said. Then, as each man passed, he whispered a code name. Tonight, all the names happened to be avian.

"Eagle."

"Falcon."

"Osprey."

"Harrier."

"Kite."

Beyond the heavy door, which the leader closed and locked behind him, was a wide tunnel filled with steam pipes. Dim lights—bare bulbs protected by heavy metal grilles—cast pools of illumination every hundred feet, and even the areas between the bulbs weren't quite dark. "Level Four, Second Sector," the leader said. "Teams of two. Eagle and Osprey. Falcon and Harrier. Kite with me."

The men quickly set off toward the north, darting from one shadowy area to the next, scurrying through the pools of light like cockroaches escaping into the shelter of darkness. Soon, they turned toward the west, and now the tunnel was narrower, its ceiling lower, its lights more distantly spaced. The men, though, were almost as familiar with the tunnels beneath the streets as they were with the streets themselves, and they slowed not at all as they moved deeper and deeper into the maze. So far they hadn't needed to speak at all, for each of them knew exactly where they were. The real challenge wouldn't come for another half hour, when they descended to a level none of them had visited before.

With luck, one member of the party would bag the trophy tonight.

More likely, tonight would be nothing more than reconnaissance, as it usually was whenever they began the exploration of a new territory. The teams would split up, each team mapping the passages they explored, searching the byways and shafts, familiarizing themselves with the terrain.

For many, the reconnaissance was nearly as satisfying as the bagging of the trophy itself, although in the end the kill would always be the ultimate prize.

"So how the fuck do we get out of here?"

Jeff could hear the fear behind Jagger's angry words—the same fear that had been burning away his own sense of hope.

Up!

That's all they had to do—get up to the surface. But as he tried to remember how he'd arrived at the airless room in the first place, tried to recall the twists and turns as he'd been led through the tunnels under the city, he realized it was impossible. He had no idea where they might be—no idea of how far he'd come from the subway station. Jagger had said they brought him down from the hospital, which Jeff assumed was Bellevue, but who knew how far from the hospital Jagger might have been taken?

What's more, he had no idea how deep beneath the city they might be.

Since the shot—and the scream that immediately followed it—had dictated the direction of their initial flight, they'd kept moving straight ahead. The tunnel, just tall enough so Jeff could walk upright, seemed to have been hacked out of the native rock itself. Pipes ran along the floor, large pipes that

Jeff was certain were water mains. He was also fairly certain that they must be moving either north or south, under one of the avenues.

Not Park—the commuter trains from Grand Central ran under Park.

Unless they were south of the station. The trains to the suburbs all ran north, didn't they? He wracked his brain, trying to remember. But there were so many trains running in and out of the city all day—not just from Grand Central, but from Penn Station as well.

And the subways.

How many were there?

Dozens.

And aside from the subway tunnels, how many others were there under the city?

Hundreds.

A dim memory came back to him, of a class he'd taken last fall. It seemed like another life—*had* been another life. Evenings with Heather Randall in his tiny apartment on 109th Street, just west of Broadway. A life that now seemed so far removed that even the memories seemed to belong to someone else. But then the memory of the class—a semester on urban infrastructure—came into sharper focus, and he could almost hear the professor's voice.

"No one really knows what's under the streets of Manhattan anymore. A lot of people know parts of it—there are maps of the water system, maps of the gas mains, and maps of the trains and the subway systems and the electrical grid. But there is no map of all of it."

As they'd followed the flashlight beam, which already seemed to be weakening, Jeff had tried to keep his eyes trained upward, looking for a shaft that would take them to the surface.

Now they'd found one. Directly above his head rose a narrow shaft with a rusting ladder anchored in rotting concrete.

"One of us goes up that shaft and sees where it leads," he said.

Jagger shook his head. "I ain't goin'. Could be anything up there."

"So what do you want to do, just keep walking? We're going to have to go up sooner or later."

Jagger peered up at the hole. "Doesn't look like it goes anywhere."

"It's got to go somewhere—if it doesn't, then why's it there?" He reached up and grasped the lowest rung of the ladder. "Give me a boost." As if he weighed no more than a child, Jagger raised him up until he was high enough to get a foot onto the bottom rung. "Shut off your light," he said as he switched on his own. "No use wasting the batteries."

"What if you don't come back?" Jagger asked.

"I'll be back," Jeff told him. "You think I want to be down here by myself? Just stay here and I'll be back in a couple of minutes."

He started climbing, creeping up the corroded ladder. Though he knew it had to be his imagination, the shaft seemed to be growing narrower, tightening around him until he felt he couldn't breathe. Panic welled up in him. If he got stuck—

You won't, he told himself.

But the higher he climbed, the worse the claustrophobia got. His skin was clammy now, his heart pounding, and his chest felt as if it were being squeezed by a boa constrictor.

Steeling himself against his rising panic, he kept climbing.

Then, above him, he sensed something.

Something was there, in the darkness above him.

He shined the light upward.

Two red eyes glinted.

It was a rat, no more than three feet above him!

He shied away from the rodent, his body jerking reflexively. His back slammed against the wall of the shaft behind him as one knee smashed into a rung of the ladder. The rat, baring its teeth and hissing at him, suddenly disappeared, and for a moment Jeff succumbed to the panic that had been building inside him since he'd begun climbing the shaft.

Where had it gone? Where could it have gone?

Down! It was coming down at him! He flashed the light around desperately, searching for the rat, but it had vanished. Then, as his panic subsided, he saw another passage going off to the side, three feet above his head. The hope that had been nearly extinguished by the claustrophobia and panic surged back, and he scrambled upward until he could see down the new passage.

Far in the distance he saw something that dissipated the terror of a moment before.

Light. Far away, barely visible, but utterly undeniable.

A way out.

CHAPTER 15

"Come on, Jinx, you know the rules. Move it along."

The girl barely glanced up from the greasy magazine she'd fished out of a trash barrel twenty minutes earlier. "What's the big deal? Is Mickey Mouse afraid I might pick his pocket?" She edged away as the patrolman moved closer. "Hey, come on, Paulie—what'd I ever do to you?"

Paul Hagen, who'd been working Times Square for most of his twenty-year career and was only now allowing himself to imagine a retirement that didn't begin by getting either shot or sliced up, couldn't remember how many Jinxes he'd seen over the years. And she was right—she hadn't ever done anything to him. And five years ago he probably wouldn't have bothered to speak to her unless he'd caught her with her hand in some tourist's pocket. But that was five years ago, and this was today, and Times Square wasn't what it used to be. In a lot of ways, Paul Hagen missed the old days, when Times Square was ground zero for all the people who couldn't survive anywhere else in the city, a place where they could make a life in their own way, hanging out with all the other losers. Hagen had learned to accept that part of it early on, the first couple of years he'd been patrolling the streets. There were two kinds of people in the world: regular people and scumbags.

He was a regular person.

Jinx, and everybody else who had wound up in Times Square with no visible means of support, no permanent address, no past, and no prospects, were scumbags. That was the way of the world. Scumbags hung out in Times Square, and everybody knew it. New Yorkers knew it. Tourists knew it. Whatever you wanted—whether it was a dime bag back in the sixties, or a quick line or an ounce of crack in the more recent past—you could get it in Times Square. A cheap drink, a dirty movie, a blow job from a drag queen—it had all been there, going on twenty-four hours a day, seven days a week. His job, at least as Hagen saw it, wasn't to put a stop to it, but to keep a semblance of order among the traders. Direct traffic, as it were. Maybe most of it was against the rules for the rest of the city, but Times Square had its own set of rules.

The tourists came to Times Square to see the kind of action they could never see back in Podunk, and if they got their pockets picked, or took home a case of venereal warts—hey, that was life in the big city. The city knew it, the tourists knew it, and everyone was happy.

But then everything changed.

Mickey Mouse came to town and turned Times Square into an urban Disneyland. Everybody said it was wonderful—that the city was safer than it had ever been. And Paul Hagen guessed that was probably true, at least for most people. But what about for people like Jinx? Where was she supposed to go now that he'd been told not to let her just hang out on the streets? The answer was easy—nobody gave a damn where she went, as long as they didn't have to see her. And his job, which had once been to make sure the Jinxes didn't do too much damage, was now to make sure that nobody even had to know she existed. So even though he didn't have anything against her, he didn't give her a break. "Come on," he said again. "You know the drill."

And Jinx did. She hadn't when she first arrived in the city three years ago from Altoona. Back then she'd just been trying to get away from her mom's boyfriend, who'd decided that even though she was only twelve, she was a lot sexier than her mother. And maybe she was. Her figure had sure been better than her mom's, which Elvin—what the fuck kind of name was Elvin?—had kept telling her while he pawed at her every night after her mom passed out. So she'd knocked Elvin out, hitting him over the head with one of her mom's empties, and split. She hitched about a hundred miles with an old guy who had pulled out his dick, but at least hadn't tried to make her do anything with it. She'd gotten away from him at a gas station near Milton, then caught a bus that brought her to New York. She hung around the bus station at first, sleeping in a chair and eating at the counter, and it had been the woman behind the counter—was her name Marge?—who gave Amber Janks her nickname. "You poor kid," she said after Amber told her the reason she'd left home. "You really got the wrong name, didn't you? Shoulda been Jinx instead of Janks."

Jinx it had been ever since, and now she no longer thought of herself as Amber Janks.

Amber Janks was dead, but Jinx was very much alive and taking care of herself.

Actually, it hadn't taken her long to figure out how. In the beginning a couple of men had said they wanted to take care of her, and Jinx believed them. At least until they tried to get her into bed. "Come on, baby," Jimmy Ramirez had told her. "We gonna make a fortune with that body, but you gotta know how to use it."

Elvin had already taught her how to use it, and Jinx had hated it, so when Jimmy started tearing her clothes off, she pretended to grope just long enough to get her hands on the knife he kept in his pocket. When she heard a couple of days later that Jimmy was dead, she wondered whether she'd killed him, then decided she didn't much care.

The other guy, who was maybe forty, hadn't been like Jimmy at all. He'd looked really nice, wearing jeans with a crease in them, and a plaid shirt. And he hadn't wanted to pimp for her, either. He said he just wanted to buy her lunch, and he bought her a few. But then, when they were in McDonald's, he put his hand on her leg, and she knew what that meant.

That time, she just got up and walked out. What was she

going to do, cut him with one of those crappy little plastic knives?

Then she met Tillie, and everything got better. Tillie had taken her home, or at least to the place Tillie called home, and within a couple of weeks Jinx thought of it as home, too. It was actually just a couple of big rooms, not far from Grand Central, and you got to it by going down to Track 42 in the station itself.

"Don't pay any attention to nothin'," Tillie had told her as they walked into the cavernous waiting room. "You don't look at people, they won't look at you. You don't talk, they won't talk. An' if you just keep walkin', the transit cops won't even bother you."

They moved through the waiting room and down a ramp, following a sign pointing to the tracks.

Finally, Tillie pulled open the door leading to Track 42 and started down the steps to the platform.

No trains stood on the tracks; no people were on the platforms.

The air smelled musty.

To the right were more platforms, more tracks.

To the left was a low wall, then beyond it a tangle of pipes and catwalks and ladders. From high above, a faint glimmer of daylight was filtering through a grating.

"That's the street up there," Tillie explained. "Where I *used* to live."

At the end of the platform was a sign warning people to go no farther, but Tillie ignored it, moving quickly down another ramp and onto the tracks themselves. Picking her way across Track 42, Tillie climbed over the low wall. When Jinx hesitated, Tillie urged her on.

"It's not so bad," she said. "You'll see."

At first Jinx was terrified, and she stayed close behind Tillie as they wound their way through what seemed to Jinx like nothing more than a jumble of tunnels and passages.

Then they'd come to Tillie's place.

The biggest of the rooms was about twenty feet square, and there was a rusty stove, a worn sofa, and a few chairs along with a battered table, and even a television set. "See?" Tillie told her. "Now, this isn't so bad, is it?"

"Does the TV work?" was all Jinx had been able to think of to ask.

Tillie had shrugged. "Nah, but it makes it kind of homey. And who knows?" she added with a grin that exposed a missing tooth. "Maybe we'll get cable someday!"

Half a dozen people had been living in the room, and when no one tried to get in bed with her that night, Jinx decided to stay. She'd lived there three years now, and Tillie and the others had taught her a lot. They showed her where the best Dumpsters were, the ones behind restaurants that threw away a lot of food. Some of them even wrapped up the food they were throwing away, just so people like Tillie—and now like Jinx—could take it home more easily.

She'd learned how to panhandle and tell the story about how someone stole her bus ticket and all she needed was thirty-four dollars to get back home. She never failed to marvel at how many people fell for that one. Of course, you had to be careful not to hit the same person twice with it, but even if you got caught, you could always disappear into the crowd, and pretty soon the person yelling at you just looked like another crazy.

She'd learned to pick pockets, too, and gotten so good at it that not even Paul Hagen could catch her. The trouble was, you couldn't just hang around Times Square anymore, and now here was Paulie, running her off the block for the third time in a week.

"So where'm I supposed to go?" she asked.

Paul Hagen just shrugged. "Hey, don't blame me—I'm just carrying out orders."

Jinx shrugged, too, and headed across Broadway, cursing just loudly enough so he'd hear it but not know what she was saying. She was just turning the corner onto Forty-third when

the person she'd been looking for suddenly appeared out of a
crowd of people hurrying to get to a theater before the curtain
went up at ten after eight.

"The hunt starts tomorrow," the person said softly, shoving
a thick envelope into Jinx's hands before vanishing back into
the crowd.

Resisting an urge to look back to see if Paulie Hagen had
seen her take the envelope, Jinx scurried across Broadway,
ducked into the subway, and was gone.

When Heather allowed herself a daydream, she and Jeff
were in his tiny apartment on the West Side. It was Sunday
morning, and she was wearing one of his old shirts, one that
was miles too big for her. That was all right; just wearing it
made her feel closer to Jeff. The Sunday *Times* was spread all
over the floor, and the sun was flooding through the window,
and if they ever got around to getting dressed, they'd go out,
maybe buy a bagel, and go over to Morningside Park and feed
the birds and the squirrels.

Like a movie—like one of those perfect little New York romance movies, where rain never fell unless the heroine wanted
to walk in it, and Central Park was as perfect for moonlit walks
as for muggings, and there wasn't a drunk or a crazy or a pan-
handler in sight, let alone a blizzard of trash wrapping itself
around your legs as the wind whistled in off the river.

But when she forced herself to face reality, it wasn't like
that at all. She was back in her father's apartment overlooking
Central Park, and it was dark outside, and Jeff was dead.

She wished she'd never gone down to the Medical Examiner's office. If she'd just ignored that telephone call, if she'd
just hung up on Keith Converse and stayed home—

If she hadn't actually seen the body.

Even now, as she lay half awake in the evening darkness,
she could see the terrible image of the ruined body in the
morgue, barely recognizable as human. The charred flesh, the
misshapen face, the—

The place where Jeff's tattoo had been.

How many times had she traced that tiny sun with her fingertip?

"It wasn't there," Keith had said. *"I'm telling you, this morning that part of his body wasn't burned, and the tattoo wasn't there!"*

Was that why she couldn't get past it, couldn't make herself believe that Jeff was really dead? Shouldn't she have felt a great void inside, a terrible emptiness where Jeff's love had always been? But she didn't feel that emptiness. Instead, she felt exactly as she had since she heard that Jeff was arrested: that it was all a terrible mistake, a nightmare they were all caught up in and from which they would soon awaken. It would be fall again, and Jeff would be waiting for her in their favorite little restaurant, and—

"Stop it!" The words erupted from Heather's throat in an anguished howl. Hugging herself against the chill inside her, she moved restlessly to the window of her bedroom and stared out into the gloom beyond the glass. If it was really only eight in the evening, why did she feel as exhausted as if it were three o'clock in the morning?

There was a knock at the door of the small sitting room that adjoined her bedroom, and a moment later her father appeared. "We thought we'd eat at Le Cirque. Would you like to join us?"

Le Cirque? *Le Cirque?* How could she even think about going to Le Cirque, or anywhere else, when all she wanted was to be with Jeff?

"What if it *was* a mistake?" Heather heard herself asking.

Her father seemed baffled by her question, but then his expression cleared and he shook his head. He moved toward her, reached out as if to embrace her, but when she drew away from his touch, his hands dropped back to his sides. "I know it's hard for you," he said. "But believe me, you'll get over this. In a few months—"

"In a few months I'll feel just as bad as I do right now, Daddy," she said. Then, at the look of anguish in his eyes, she relented. "Maybe I will feel better," she conceded. "But not right now. Why don't you and Carolyn just go on to dinner without me. I couldn't eat even if I went."

He hesitated, then kissed his daughter on the forehead. "I'll see you later then. If you want it, Dessie left some poached salmon in the refrigerator. Try to eat a little bit." He gave her shoulders a reassuring squeeze, then was gone.

But being alone only made Heather feel worse, as if the walls of the apartment were closing around her, suffocating her. A minute later she, too, left the building, heading down Fifth Avenue toward—

Where?

She didn't know.

"We'll know when we get there."

The voice that whispered in her mind was Jeff's. It was what he'd always said when he decided they should take an aimless ramble somewhere in the city on a Sunday afternoon. "But where are we going?" Heather would always ask. In her perfectly ordered life, she had always known exactly where she was going, and why she was going there. "Life should not be full of surprises," her father had always taught her. "One should be prepared to deal with the unexpected, but to search it out is a waste of time." Jeff, on the other hand, had always delighted in the unexpected, and always wanted to explore every unfamiliar thing he could find, be it a building, a block, or a whole neighborhood. When she asked him where he was going, and why, he would only grin and shrug his shoulders. "How should I know? We'll know when we get there." And now he was saying it again, if only in her memory.

Though she still didn't know where she was going, Heather felt a little better.

He'll show me, she decided. *He'll show me where to go, just like he always did.*

CHAPTER 16

Staring at the faint gleam of light far down the tunnel he'd discovered at the top of the shaft, Jeff felt a surge of hope that it would quickly guide them to the surface. Though his instincts urged him to run toward the light, to escape from the palpable blackness around him, he forced himself to wait until Jagger, too, had climbed the rusty rungs and emerged from the shaft like some subterranean creature creeping from its burrow. As Jagger hauled himself out of the shaft, Jeff started toward the light, his pulse racing. But when the two of them reached the source of the light, Jeff's hope was dashed: it wasn't coming from above, but from below.

Standing on opposite sides of the shaft, they gazed into its depths. Perhaps thirty feet down they could see the floor of another tunnel, and it was from there that the light emanated, seeping up the shaft—a beacon of hope as false as that of the signal lights pirates once placed on Caribbean beaches at night to draw ships onto the reefs. They peered down at the light for a long time, saying nothing.

Even had there been a ladder, neither of them would willingly have descended it. Finally, Jagger broke the silence: "We can't get out just by standing here."

Nodding, Jeff shined his light into the darkness that lay in both directions.

There was nothing, no hint as to what might lie beyond the blackness, nor how long it might be before they found another light. Out of this uncertainty, they remained close to

the light source, like moths hypnotized by a lightbulb, until
Jagger spun around and lunged into the darkness with a growl
that fell just short of being a howl of anguish. "We gotta get
out of here. Now!"

Jeff, now more terrified of being alone than of the dark,
stumbled after him. They moved as quickly as they could, still
using only one of the flashlights, until they came to an intersection with another tunnel, this one filled with what looked
to Jeff like electrical cables. Jagger had stopped abruptly.
"Which way?" he asked.

In every direction there was nothing more than the terrible
blackness. Jeff turned to his right. Jagger, not questioning his
decision, followed him as blindly as he'd followed Jagger a
little while ago.

The tunnel seemed to be narrowing, and though Jeff told
himself it had to be an illusion, he was starting to feel the terrible claustrophobia that had gripped him in the shaft.

The tunnel itself seemed to be crushing him, and he felt a
scream rising in his throat. But just as his howl was about to
erupt, Jagger's enormous hand closed on his shoulder, and
the solid grip somehow eased the sharp talons of panic that
had been sinking deep into his mind.

"Somethin' up ahead," Jagger whispered in his ear, his lips
so close that Jeff could feel the other man's breath.

"Where?" Jeff asked, matching Jagger's barely audible
tone.

Jagger's hand went over his mouth. "Sshhh . . ." he cautioned, clicking off his flashlight and plunging them into
blackness. The pounding of Jeff's heart sounded like drums
in his own ears, then Jagger whispered again. "Can't you
hear it?"

Jeff willed his heartbeat to slow, and very dimly it came
to him.

A whimpering sound, like an injured dog might make.

Jagger edged around Jeff. "Let me go first," he whispered.

They advanced carefully, Jagger flicking the light on just long enough to be certain he wasn't about to stumble into an unseen shaft.

The whimpering grew louder.

They came to yet another intersection, and now the whimpering was clear.

Not a dog.

A human.

It was coming from the left, and Jagger turned the light back on and played its beam into the darkness.

The whimpering fell silent.

At first there seemed to be nothing there but a pile of rubbish, a heap of filthy rags. Then the light glinted off a pair of eyes and an anguished moan came from the mound of rags.

Jagger inched forward with Jeff right behind him until they were standing over the rags. Jagger kicked one of them aside with the toe of his shoe.

A man's face, twisted into a mask of pure terror, peered up at them, his clawlike hands scratching at the floor of the tunnel as if he were trying to burrow into the cold concrete itself. As Jagger crouched down beside him, he cowered against the wall, clutching a ragged blanket to his belly. "Get away," he whispered. "Get away before they find you, too!"

"Who?" Jeff asked, crouching down and peering into the man's face. Though he'd thought at first that the man was much older, now he saw that he couldn't be more than twenty-two or twenty-three. His hair was tangled and matted, and his face was smeared with dirt and grease. "Before who can find us?"

The man's eyes rolled first one way and then the other, and for a moment Jeff thought he hadn't heard him. But then the man's jaw began working, and a dribble of blood ran down his chin. "Hunters," he whispered. "I thought I was safe. I thought I . . ." His voice trailed off and he lay against the wall, his chest heaving as he gasped for breath. Then, his words cracking like shards of glass, he said, "Can't get away. They said it was a game . . . said I could win. All I had to do was . . . was . . ."

He fell silent again, and Jeff heard something else. Another voice, softly echoing off the walls of the tunnel.

"Here—look at this. He went this way."

The man's eyes widened as he, too, heard the voice, and once again he seemed to want to speak. His body went rigid and a strangled gurgle came from his lips. Then, abruptly, he relaxed. His hands, still clutching at the rags, fell away from his belly.

The blood oozing from the hole in the man's stomach glistened crimson in the beam of the flashlight.

As the sound of voices grew closer, Jeff and Jagger plunged back into the darkness.

It was the kind of evening that was perfect for walking. The icy chill of winter had given way to spring, and there was a faint scent of new flowers drifting from the park. It was the kind of evening, in fact, that had often enticed Jeff and Heather out for one of their hours-long rambles, Jeff soaking up the architecture while Heather regaled him with stories of what it was like growing up as a poor little rich girl in the heart of Manhattan. Perhaps it was the perfect weather that kept Heather walking that evening.

Or perhaps it was the fact that there wasn't any place she wanted to be.

Certainly, she did not want to be anywhere near her father!

Pain—pain and anger—boiled up inside her as she remembered what he'd said after he gave her the news that Jeff had died. He'd put his arms around her and spoken words that, even in her anger, she assumed he must have thought were comforting: "I know you're upset, sweetheart, but you'll get over it. There will be other men, and in the long run I think you'll come to understand that this has saved you from a lot of grief."

And tonight he'd asked her to go to Le Cirque! Had he really thought she'd be able to sit in a restaurant where she not only knew most of the customers, but would have to put up with them acting as if nothing were wrong? After all, most of the people she'd grown up with had made it perfectly clear what they thought of Jeff Converse. "He'll never really understand you, darling," Jessica van Rensellier had told her a couple of years ago. "Fine for a summer romance, of course, but he's just not someone you could get serious about, is he? I mean, isn't his father one of those men who take care of our houses?"

For the last year, Heather had gotten the impression that Jessica and the rest of the people she'd grown up with were trying to avoid her, and she discovered she didn't mind—the people she was meeting through Jeff were a lot more interesting than the Le Cirque crowd had ever been. Carolyn was even worse than the people who had once been her friends. She had managed to not even mention Jeff's name in the last two days.

So Heather kept walking, heading away from the East Side, where she was all too likely to run into someone she knew from high school, someone coming home from a Junior League or DAR meeting. She wandered toward the West Side, but not until she found herself on Broadway, three short blocks from Jeff's building, did she realize exactly where she'd taken herself.

She almost turned away, almost hailed a cab to take her back home, when she paused, recalling Jeff's words as he'd told her where they were going: *"We'll know when we get there."*

Had he been leading her tonight? Was that why she'd walked all the way across town and fifty blocks north? She shook her head hard, as if to rid herself of the thought, then flushed as a passerby gave her a funny look and turned away—the same kind of look she sometimes gave one of the crazy people on the streets.

But they actually think they hear voices, she reassured herself. *I'm only remembering what Jeff always said.*

Yet even knowing it was only her recollection, Heather didn't raise her hand to hail a cab, though half a dozen of them were prowling the street, starved for fares, thanks to the perfect weather. Instead she gave in to an urge to walk the final three blocks and see the dark windows of Jeff's apartment.

Except that tonight his windows weren't dark, and as she gazed up at them a few minutes later—as she always had when she knew Jeff was waiting for her—she saw him standing just as he had always stood, looking down at her. Her heart skipped a beat. It couldn't be! It wasn't possible! Jeff was dead! Confused, knowing what she'd seen was impossible, she glanced around as if in search of someone who might have been playing tricks on her.

When she finally trusted herself to look back up at the window, the figure was gone.

But the window was still lit.

Who could it be?

The super? The moment the thought came to her, she knew that had to be the explanation. She could almost see the building superintendent, Wally Crosley—"Crawly Wally," Jeff had always called him—creeping around Jeff's apartment, helping himself to whatever he thought might be worth something. Her hand went into her purse and she felt for the keys she hadn't used in so long. They were still there. A few seconds later she was climbing the half-dozen steps to the building's door. She let herself in.

When she came to the third floor landing, she hesitated. What if it wasn't the super? she wondered. What if it was someone else?

She glanced down the hallway toward the back of the building. A light showed under the door across from Jeff's, which meant that Tommy Adams was home. She considered ringing his bell before she rang Jeff's. At least then she wouldn't have to face Crosley alone.

Heather was just reaching for Tommy's buzzer when Jeff's own door opened. But it wasn't Wally Crosley who stood there.

It was Keith Converse, and it seemed to Heather that he'd been drinking. His face was flushed, and his eyes didn't look quite focused. "It was you," he said. Then, to clarify, he added: "Down in the street just now."

Heather nodded. "I—I was just out walking."

Keith's brows lifted. "All the way over here from Fifth?"

Part of Heather wanted to leave. She'd heard about how Jeff's father could get when he was drinking, and if he started blaming her for what had happened to Jeff—

"I don't know why I got up and went to the window," he said. "I was just sitting in Jeff's chair, trying to think, and . . ." His voice trailed off, but then he pulled the door open wider. "Something just made me go look. Maybe I was looking for Jeff."

Heather's eyes blurred with tears. "I know," she whispered. "When I went out tonight, I didn't even know where I was going. He always told me we'd know where we were going when we got there." She shook her head, as her hand tightened on the key she was still holding. "But he's not here. He's . . ." Her voice trailed off, too, as she found herself unable to speak the words.

"He's not, Heather," Keith said quietly. She looked up at him, started to speak, was about to argue with him, but he held up his hand, silencing her. "Just listen to me, all right? No one else will. Everyone else thinks I'm nuts. But I talked to a man this morning. A man who saw Jeff yesterday." Heather frowned, said nothing, but didn't turn away. "He saw Jeff get out of the van after the crash."

Heather's breath caught in her throat, and when Keith held the door still wider, she stepped through it.

Eve Harris automatically glanced at her watch as she crossed Columbus Circle and saw the black car with official license plates already sitting in front of the Trump International. There were people you kept waiting and people you didn't, even if you were on the City Council. Carey Atkinson and Arch Cranston were two of the people you didn't. Chief of Police Atkinson and Deputy Police Commissioner Cranston, whose mostly ceremonial job had been bought with some of the largest soft-money political contributions in the history of the city, definitely ranked as people she should be on time for. So it was nine P.M. on the dot—exactly the time they'd arranged—when she walked through the front door, turned left, and entered the foyer outside the restaurant.

"I can show you right in, Ms. Harris," the maitre d' said, tipping his head just enough to be respectful without sinking into servility. "The gentlemen are already here." Even though she wasn't late, Eve made a silent bet with herself that Cranston would make a stupid remark about the unpunctuality of women. Smiling, she followed the maitre d' through the second set of doors into the restaurant—an elegantly simple room, and expensive enough that there was no need to crowd the tables close together. All the tables offered a degree of privacy unknown in most of the city's restaurants, but the headwaiter led her to a table at the rear of the room—away from the windows that Atkinson considered a security risk, and from the doors that admitted a blast of wind every time they were opened. Eve was more than willing to give up the view of Central Park to escape the draft, and, like the men, she preferred the privacy of the area behind the bar.

"That's what I love about you," Arch Cranston said, leaning over to kiss Eve's cheek and ignoring her attempt to turn her head away. "You're always on time—not like other women!"

Eve silently credited her mental gambling account with a five dollar win. "Flattery will get you everywhere, Arch," she replied, covering her annoyance at his cliché with one of her own. Arch, dependably, had no clue he was being mocked, but Carey Atkinson winked at her as they all sat down.

"So what's it going to be?" Atkinson asked as he signaled the waiter. "Are we going to pretend to be civilized and make small talk, or shall we get right to it?"

"I've never pretended to be civilized," Eve replied. "That's how I keep my seat. But I hear all kinds of things, and right now I'm hearing some very strange things about the young man who died in the Corrections transport van yesterday morning."

The two men glanced at each other, and while Cranston shifted uneasily in his seat, Atkinson leaned forward and asked, "Just what is it you're hearing, Eve?"

She could see by their expressions that they knew exactly what she was talking about, but she'd been in politics long enough to know when a charade needed to be played out. "I happened to run into Jeff Converse's father this afternoon," she said. "It seems he doesn't believe his son is dead."

Atkinson visibly relaxed. "Keith Converse seems to have been getting around today. How did he get to your office?"

"He didn't. I met him in the subway." As briefly as she could, Eve told them what had happened. When she was finished, neither Arch Cranston or Carey Atkinson said anything, and as the silence lengthened, Eve went on: "I also heard that the man he talked to—whose name was Al Kelly— is dead. Stabbed in an alley, apparently so he could be relieved of the five dollars Mr. Converse gave him for telling him about the wreck."

"So Al Kelly was the drunk?" Arch Cranston said.

"Al Kelly had a drinking problem, yes," Eve replied. "Many of the homeless do." Her eyes fixed on Carey Atkinson. "I'm assuming your department won't be able to find out who killed Al Kelly?"

Atkinson shrugged, spreading his hands helplessly. "You know as well as I do that we don't have the manpower to investigate every derelict who gets himself killed in this city."

"You'd find the manpower if you cared as much about the problems of the homeless as I do." Eve shifted her gaze to

Arch Cranston. "Which brings us around to the other reason we're here tonight, doesn't it? I didn't see you at the benefit for Montrose House last night." Her eyes flicked back to the police chief. "I didn't *expect* to see you."

Cranston reached into the inside pocket of his jacket and pulled out a thick envelope, which Eve eyed warily. "It's for Monsignor McGuire."

"Then send it to him," Eve said, making no move at all to pick up the envelope. "What I'm more concerned about is the way the department is hassling our people." Her eyes went back to the police chief. "How is it that you don't have the manpower to find out who kills homeless people, but you always have the manpower to run them off the streets?"

Atkinson shook his head impatiently. "There aren't that many of them—" he began, but Eve didn't let him finish.

"There are probably fifty thousand people living either on or under the streets of this city, and you know it."

Atkinson shook his head doggedly. "There aren't more than a tenth that number."

Eve didn't bother to respond. Both of them were aware of the fact that he knew better. The waiter arrived to take their order, and when he left, she returned to the subject of Jeff Converse. "I told the father I'd look into it," she said. "Obviously, I'm not going to be able to talk to Al Kelly to ask him what he saw myself, so I'm asking you two—is it possible that what Al Kelly told Mr. Converse could have happened? If I tell him you're positive his son is dead, is he going to be able to prove me wrong?"

Atkinson shook his head. "Converse made enough of a stink at the M.E.'s office that I heard about it, and I also heard from Wilkerson, the captain over at the Fifth Precinct. Mr. Converse was in there this morning, too, wanting to see the report on the accident."

"And he saw it?" Eve asked.

Atkinson shook his head. "In the end, he decided he didn't have to. He talked to the officers who caught the call."

"Then that's it?" Eve asked.

"That's it," Arch Cranston assured her. "If Converse actually comes back to you, you can tell him there was no mistake—his son died in the fire." He shook his head with the exaggerated sadness that comes so naturally to politicians. "A terrible thing—no matter what the boy did, I wouldn't wish that kind of death on him."

Eve Harris raised her brow but said nothing about Arch Cranston's transparent insincerity. Instead, she returned to the subject, and the name Keith Converse had mentioned.

"There was also a man called Scratch. According to Keith Converse, this Scratch led his son into the subway." She pinned Atkinson to his chair with her dark eyes. "It would seem to me that if he exists, someone at least ought to talk to him. Do I need to talk to Wilkerson about that myself?"

Atkinson sighed heavily. "No, Eve. I'll have someone call the Fifth in the morning—hell, maybe I'll even do it tonight. But if this guy lives in the tunnels, don't count on my men finding him."

This time Eve made no attempt to keep the mocking gleam from showing in her eyes. "Oh, heavens no, Carey. I certainly wouldn't expect New York's Finest to risk their lives down in those terrible tunnels. After all, they might get beaten up by a gang of rampaging homeless single mothers, wielding their fatherless babies! Wouldn't want New York's Finest to have to risk their lives against that, would we?"

Carey Atkinson chose to ignore her words, but Arch Cranston, his eyes flicking around the room in order to gauge the number of people who might have heard Eve's outburst, did not.

"Come on, Eve," he said, loudly enough for the woman listening from the next table to hear it as clearly as she'd heard Eve Harris. "Give Carey a break. You know what kind of people live in the tunnels. Hell, you probably know better than any of us. And you know what it's like down there."

Eve's lips smiled, but her eyes did not. "We all know what

it's like down there," she said. "And we all know what goes on. But sometimes I think I'm the only one in this whole city who actually wants to do something about it. The rest of you just want to—" She cut herself short, knowing she was starting to sound like a broken record. Besides, each person at the table knew perfectly well what the others wanted.

They also knew that people in their positions never discussed their true desires in public.

The truth, always, was reserved for intimate conversations in the most private of settings.

And that was a rule that even Eve Harris believed in keeping.

CHAPTER 17

Heather Randall stood at the window of Jeff's apartment, where Keith had been standing when she arrived half an hour ago. On the corner below, kitty-corner from the drugstore, she saw Jeff's favorite Chinese restaurant, where she had often found him sitting in the front booth, shoulders hunched in concentration as he pored over a textbook. Now she forced that memory away and turned from the window.

The room was exactly as it had been the night of Jeff's arrest. The last project he'd been working on—a design for a small office–cum–guest house for one of her father's neighbors in the Hamptons—was still pinned to the drafting board that covered the small room's only table. Her finger absently traced one of the graceful lines of the unfinished drawing—a line that managed to echo the architecture of the main house without imitating it.

The drawing, like the room itself, felt suspended in time, waiting for Jeff to come back.

But that was absurd—Jeff wasn't coming back, despite the strange story his father had just told her. Yet even as she tried once more to reject Keith Converse's fantasy, she imagined Jeff saying, *We'll know when we get there.*

Her eyes wandered over the room. Every object in it, from the posters on the walls that depicted Jeff's favorite buildings to the shelves of books ranging from architecture through poetry to zoology, were as familiar to her as the things in her

131

own bedroom on Fifth Avenue. More familiar, in a way, for despite the cramped dimensions and worn-out furnishings of the tiny room, she had always felt more at home here than in the cavernous apartment in which she'd grown up. "I love this place," she said, almost as much to herself as to Keith. He was straddling a battered wooden chair she and Jeff had found at a flea market on one of their Sunday walks. At five dollars, it had been too good a bargain to pass up. Jeff had just begun refinishing it when he was arrested. Now his father's arms rested on its sanded oak back, and he watched her in a way that reminded her of Jeff. "How long are you going to keep it?" she asked, her eyes sweeping the room once more.

"It's not mine to keep or give up," Keith replied. "It's Jeff's. All I'm doing is paying the rent till he comes back."

Heather moved back to the window, hugging herself in unconscious defense against the chill that suddenly wrapped itself around her. "You're so sure he's coming back?"

"If he was dead, I'd know it. He's my son. If something happened to him, I'd feel it. And I don't feel it." Though she still had her back to him, she could feel his eyes boring into her. "You don't feel it, either," he went on. "That's why you came here tonight."

Heather spun around, her eyes glistening. "I don't know why I came here tonight," she began. "I just—I was—" But then the truth of his words hit her, and her tears dried up. "You're right," she said, her voice steady now. "I don't feel like he's dead. So what do we do?"

"We find out what happened," Keith replied. "And we find him."

Heather dropped onto the chair opposite Keith. "Do you have any idea what you're saying?" she asked.

Keith's eyes narrowed and she saw his jaw set exactly the same way Jeff's did when he'd made up his mind about something. "What is it with all you people?" he demanded. "How come everyone in this city thinks they know every goddamn thing there is to know, and the rest of us don't know jack shit? Pardon my French, but if all you're gonna do is patronize me—"

"Patronize you!" Heather cut in. "When have I ever patronized you or anybody else?"

"All you people—"

"All 'us people'? What's this got to do with 'us people'? This is about Jeff, remember? And I'm not trying to act like I know everything about anything! All I know is that you don't just go out and find someone in New York City. Especially if they don't want to be found."

A flicker of uncertainty tempered the anger in Keith's expression. "What do you mean, not want to be found? Why wouldn't he—"

Heather was back on her feet. "He was going to prison, remember? So even if you're right, and he got out of that van, where was he going to go? The police? All they'd do is send him back to jail."

"But he didn't do anything, goddamn it!"

Now Heather's eyes were blazing as angrily as Keith's. "And who cares about that, except you and me? No one. So tell me—even if we can find Jeff, what are we going to do?" She turned back to the window and gazed into the night. At the corner, a shabbily dressed woman was maneuvering a small wire shopping cart down the stairs to one of the entrances to the 110th Street station. She did it with as much care as if it contained boxes packed with crystal and china instead of a jumbled mass of filthy clothes and blankets. The old woman paused, turned around, and looked up, almost as if she felt Heather watching her. She seemed to look right at the window for a moment, just as Heather had looked up at Keith a little while ago. Then the woman turned away and continued down into the subway.

As Heather's eyes remained fastened on the subway entrance, something flickered at the edge of her mind— something Keith had said earlier, as he was telling her what happened that morning. As she continued to stare at the subway entrance, it came to her.

She whirled around and said, "I'll bet no one ever even talked to them!"

Keith looked up at her in confusion. What was she talking about?

"The homeless people!" Heather said, her excitement growing as the idea gripped her mind. "The people who live in the subway stations and the train stations. What if one of them saw what happened to Cindy Allen that night?"

"The police must have talked to them . . ." Keith began, but his words died away as he remembered what he'd heard at the Fifth Precinct that very morning: *"They're all addicts and crazies . . . you can't believe a word they say."*

Heather's voice trembled with excitement. "The police— the whole city—hardly even admit they exist! Daddy says the police won't even go into the tunnels where most of them live. He says it's way too dangerous. Keith, what if no one ever even *asked* any of them? Let's try!"

He was going to die.

Jeff wasn't certain how long he'd known—wasn't certain even if there had been a moment when that terrible knowledge had crept into his mind, taken root, and begun to grow. It was like a disease, a cancer that had established an invisible beachhead on a single cell, then slowly reproduced, spread out, so that by the time it was big enough to be noticed, the tumor had a firm grip on the body. By now, however, the sure knowledge of his coming death was always in his thoughts.

The batteries in Jagger's flashlight had already died, though he still clutched it tightly in his hand, as if somehow he might transfer some of the energy from his body into the useless cells. Jeff's light was now the only weapon they had against the darkness. Every time he turned it on, the beam looked weaker. Soon it would completely die away.

Jeff tried to avoid that thought, but it kept coming back, and each time it did, it was harder to ignore. He knew what would happen when the light finally went out: they would have to feel their way along, keeping their fingers in contact with the walls as much to keep their balance as to guide them. But how long could they do that? How long would it be before they stumbled into one of the shafts that led downward, and plunged to an even deeper darkness?

Maybe, when the light finally died, he would find it better simply to sit down, rest against the wall, and wait until his soul slipped from the darkness of the tunnels into the final oblivion of death. By then, death might even be welcome. He began to imagine that the light he'd read about—the light people saw at the far end of the long tunnel that led toward death, the brilliant light that shone down out of eternity—was starting to become visible, offering a release from the darkness in which he was spending these final hours.

"There it is again," he heard Jagger whisper.

The words penetrated Jeff's mind slowly, pushing through the fog of exhaustion, hunger, and hopelessness.

How long ago had Jagger started leading? An hour? Two hours? Ten minutes?

When Jagger had first grabbed him in the darkness, jerking him to a stop, muttering about a glimmer of light up ahead, Jeff willed himself to see whatever his companion had seen. But he didn't see a thing, and when Jagger quickened his pace, certain that something had flickered in the darkness just ahead, Jeff had to struggle to keep up.

"Feel it?" Jagger whispered a little later. "We're getting close to something." Then, a second later: "There! Up ahead! See it?" But despite the certainty in Jagger's voice, Jeff had still seen nothing. He'd followed anyway, letting Jagger lead them toward the hallucinatory beacon. What did it matter where they went? They were lost in the labyrinth, and he was already sure that every passage would ultimately lead to the same place.

Death.

Now, finally seeing a tiny light himself, he wondered if it truly was a flickering beacon in the blackness, or the dying spark of his own mortality, glimmering in the darkness of his soul.

No, he told himself. *I'm not going to die. Not yet. I'm going to live. I'm going to live, and I'm going to get out, and I'm going to be free.*

Steeling himself, he fixed his eyes on the faint light. . . .

Creeper peered through the night scope just long enough to confirm that the two figures were still moving through the murky green fog that filled the scope's narrow field. Satisfied, he let the instrument drop down to dangle from the strap around his neck. He didn't need it. This part of the maze of tunnels was as familiar to him as the backyard of the house where he'd grown up.

The herders had done their job well tonight—the two men were exactly where they were supposed to be. In another few minutes, Creeper knew, it would be time for him to take over.

Even through the scope, he'd been able to tell that these two were a little different from the others.

Maybe it was just because there were two of them this time. Always before, there had only been one, and by the time Creeper "found" him, the man was usually in such bad shape that he almost had to carry him to the camp. Usually they were talking to themselves. Once, the herders had let someone stay in the blackness so long that by the time Creeper got to him he'd gone crazy, babbling about monsters and demons. Creeper had done his job and gotten him to camp, but the man had screamed so long into the night that finally Willie hadn't been able to stand it anymore and had made him shut up.

The next morning, Creeper had to go find a couple of herders and have them take the guy up to the surface before he started to stink. They'd dumped him on the tracks up by Riverside Park, and after the first train came through, there was no way anybody would figure out what had really happened to him.

But these two still looked strong.

Too strong?

For the first time, Creeper wondered if maybe he should have brought someone else along. But that was always dangerous—last time he'd done that, the quarry had bolted the instant it saw two men, disappearing into the darkness and forcing the herders to start all over again.

He flicked his light one last time, letting it shine for just a fraction of a second, then went into the next phase of the operation.

Moving into a cross tunnel—a long-abandoned railroad tunnel lit only by a faint orange glow from a hundred yards farther down—he ran along the remains of the tracks until he came to a small alcove. A cut-off barrel stood in one corner, beneath a shaft that rose straight up fifteen or twenty feet before opening into yet another tunnel. In the barrel glowed the remains of the fire Creeper had kept going for the last four hours. Now he fed it with some old magazines one of the runners had brought down, poking at it with a stick to stir it up. The embers nibbled at the fuel for a few seconds, then flames leaped up and the warmth of the fire began to spread through the alcove, the light spilling out into the tunnel growing brighter.

Creeper sat down, crossed his legs and waited.

He heard them before he saw them.

Heard their steps on the concrete floor, heard their indistinct whispering as they tried to figure out what they were seeing.

Heard them trying to decide whether it was safe to come toward the light.

Creeper stood up, stepped out of the alcove, and turned on his own flashlight. A brilliant halogen beam sliced through the gloom and picked the two men out of the darkness, blinding them.

"Stop right there," Creeper barked, his words echoing through the tunnel. "One more step and you're dead."

CHAPTER 18

I n the cold, bright glare of the subway station, Heather Randall could clearly see how worn Keith Converse looked. His face seemed to have aged ten years since the day before, when she'd seen him in the oddly similar brightness of the morgue. The gentler light in Jeff's apartment had softened the creases that were etched not only in his forehead but in his cheeks and jowls as well. The crinkles around his eyes had deepened into crow's-feet, as if all the worry, anger, and frustration that he'd managed to bottle up through the months leading up to Jeff's trial had now broken through.

The platform was deserted except for a solitary man who had apparently just gotten off a train that was now roaring into the tunnel on its way farther uptown. There was no sign at all of the woman Heather had seen from Jeff's window. The lone passenger vanished up the stairs, the sound of his footsteps fading into silence along with the rumbling of the train.

"She must have gotten on that train," Keith muttered.

But even as he spoke, Heather pointed toward the far end of the platform. "Down there!"

For a second Keith saw nothing, then a flicker of movement caught his eye. It was the woman.

She wasn't on the platform, but on the track itself, backing slowly away from the bright light of the station, painstakingly pulling her cart behind her.

"What's she doing?" Keith asked. "Where's she going?"

Heather was already running along the platform. "Ma'am?"

she called out, her voice reverberating on the tiles, echoing back through the empty station, almost drowning out Heather's next words: "We just want to talk to you for a minute!"

The woman's eyes widened, but instead of pausing, she moved a little faster, stumbling and almost collapsing onto the gravel beneath the tracks before she caught herself.

Now Keith was running, too, and twenty feet before Heather reached the end of the platform he sprinted past her. "Wait!" he called. "Stop!" But when he came to the end of the platform, the old woman had vanished into the darkness.

Suddenly, all the emotions churning inside Keith erupted in a single desperate howl.

"JEFF!"

Then once more, even louder: "JEFF . . ."

His son's name, twisted and contorted with Keith's own anguished frustration, resounded off the concrete walls of the subway tunnel, coming back again and again, mutating into something that sounded almost like laughter, taunting him, mocking him. The terrible sound finally died away with one last echo that, like the old woman, was lost to the blackness of the tunnel.

Turning away from the dark maw, Keith headed back toward Heather, his shoulders slumped, his step slowed. Then, his desperate cry into the darkness having faded away, he heard something.

Faint—so faint as to be barely audible—he thought he heard a single word drift out of the darkness:

"Dad . . ."

It was a whisper that died away so quickly, Keith wasn't sure he heard it at all, but when he turned to look at Heather, her eyes were wide and her face had gone pale.

"You heard it, didn't you?" he whispered, almost afraid to ask the question.

Time stopped as he waited for Heather to reply. Just when he thought he could stand the silence no longer, she said, "I heard . . . something, but I'm not sure what."

Three more times, Keith called out Jeff's name, and after each shout died slowly away, they waited to hear a response.

There was none.

Though it seemed impossible, the light was even worse than the darkness.

The brilliant halogen beam felt like a knife that had been jabbed directly into his brain, a searing brightness that was physically painful. When it first lashed out of the darkness, he had been shocked into absolute stillness—that same instinctive motionlessness wild animals use as their first defense against a predator. An instant later, though, instinct had given way to reason and he braced himself for the shot he was certain would follow the light. When it didn't come and he heard a voice ordering him not to move, he raised a hand to shield his eyes from the light.

"I said freeze, motherfucker." The voice reverberated off the walls of the tunnel, echoing back at them from behind.

The shot didn't come, but from somewhere above them, there was a muted rumbling as a subway train passed in another tunnel.

"Who are you?" the voice demanded as the sound of the train died away.

Jeff glanced over at Jagger, who was standing beside him, squinting tightly as he attempted to pierce the glare, his huge hands clenched into fists.

"We're just trying to find our way out," Jeff called back, not quite answering the question.

The light began to move closer, the brilliance of its beam holding them at bay as effectively as if it had been a shotgun.

Then, as suddenly as the light went on, it blinked off, and Jeff was plunged into yet a new kind of blindness. Now a black circle hung directly in front of his eyes, a circle that moved wherever his eyes moved, blotting out everything behind it. The halogen beam had burned into his retinas, leaving behind a negative image of the light that was no longer there.

"Can't see much, can you?" the voice taunted, so close now that Jeff shrank back. "Fuck with me, and I'll make sure you never see anything again. Got it?"

Jeff opened his mouth, ready to agree to anything that might push back the shroud of darkness that had fallen over him once again. But before he could speak, he heard a sound, drifting out of the darkness, then flitting away again so quickly he thought he must have imagined it.

But no! There it was again.

A memory rose unbidden from his mind, a memory from when he was a little boy, no more than four or maybe five. He'd been outside after supper one night, chasing fireflies, not paying any attention to where he was going. When the last firefly had finally vanished, flitting away from his grasping hands, he'd realized he was lost. A wave of terror washed over him, and he looked around frantically in the darkness, trying to see where he was. Then, just as he was about to start sobbing, he'd heard a voice.

His father's voice.

Calling out to him in the darkness.

It had been his father's voice that led him home that night.

Now, in the terrible blackness of the tunnel, he was hearing that voice again.

"DAD!" The single word burst from his throat before he even thought about it.

A flash of brilliance slashed into his eyes, and an instant later a fist sank deep into his gut.

The light went out again.

"I said don't fuck with me," the unseen man grunted as Jeff dropped to his knees, clutching his gut. "So I'm gonna ask you once more—you got it, asshole?"

"I—I got it," Jeff managed to mutter.

Jagger, meanwhile, hadn't spoken. The man said to him: "Make up your mind, big boy—behave yourself, or start wandering around in the dark all alone. Even guys like you get afraid of the dark. So I'm asking you for the last time—you got it?"

"I got it," Jagger replied, but Jeff could hear the fury in his voice.

"So here's what's gonna happen," the voice said. "I'm gonna turn the light back on, and you guys are gonna walk ahead of me. Not far—maybe a hundred yards. I got a nest down there. When we get there, I'll decide."

The light flashed back on, and the invisible man circled around until he was behind them. Now the beam of light slashed through the blackness of the tunnels, and as Jeff's eyes recovered from their blindness, he got a clear look at where he was for the first time since he'd left the subway platform.

The tunnel was lined with cracked and rotting concrete, so old that whatever care had been put into its original finish had long since worn away. The remaining uneven surface was streaked with black grime. Small stalactites had formed where seeping water had leached lime out of the concrete. The remains of a rusting railroad track ran along the floor of the tunnel, but sections of the rails were gone completely, while others were missing all their spikes. The ties were so badly rotted that the few remaining spikes looked like they could be pulled loose with a single yank. Here and there on the ceiling were the remains of rudimentary light fixtures, but not only had the bulbs long since disappeared, even the bases had been broken. The only sign of the electricity that had once powered them was a couple of dangling wires, their ends stripped of insulation.

"Up there," the man behind them said as they came abreast of an alcove. Jeff, followed by Jagger, scrambled up onto the small platform.

Though it was nothing but a dying fire in a trash barrel, the guttering blaze seemed as welcome to Jeff as a Yule log burning on the hearth of a New England inn on Christmas Eve.

The halogen beam suddenly vanished, momentarily blinding Jeff once again. When his vision cleared, the man who only moments ago had threatened to kill him stood revealed by the flickering firelight. Thin to the point of emaciation, his eyes were sunk deep into their sockets and his complexion was pasty. There was a feral quality to his face. Though he wasn't more than five feet six and couldn't have weighed more than 140 pounds, he didn't look the least bit intimidated by Jagger, let alone him.

And he couldn't have been more than twenty years old.

"You kill me, and you'll never get out of here," he said.

Jagger seemed to consider his options for a moment, then his eyes swept the alcove. "You got any food?"

The scrawny man nodded. "You like track rabbit?"

"I like whatever you got," Jagger growled. "So where is it?"

The man tilted his head toward the corner. "Behind the barrel." He smiled, revealing a row of broken teeth. "Got three today—guess I musta known you were coming." He moved around the barrel, picked up a dented and charred coffee can, and handed it to Jagger. "You want to clean 'em?"

Jagger looked down into the can and made a choking noise as it clattered to the floor. It rolled toward the tracks and its contents spilled out.

Three dead rats, their heads crushed and matted with blood, lay on the filthy concrete.

The scrawny man's grin widened as Jeff backed away. "What's the matter? You don't like rabbit?" Pulling a knife from his pocket, he opened its blade, squatted down, and picked up one of the rats. The tip of the knife disappeared into the rat's belly. With a quick flick of his wrist, the man slit the rodent's hide all the way up to its mouth. He dropped the knife and the fingers of one hand disappeared under the creature's skin. A moment later he jerked the skin loose so it hung, inside out, from the rat's feet. Using the knife, he cut the feet and tail away and tossed the skin out onto the tracks.

Immediately, another rat scurried out of the shadows, snatched the bloody skin and disappeared.

The man disemboweled the carcass, dropped it into the coffee can, then went to work on the next one. In a few more minutes the job was finished—all three of the rats had been skinned and cleaned, the discarded skins and guts disappearing almost as soon as they hit the tracks.

"They're not so bad, once you get used to them," the man said as he laid a rusty piece of grating over the barrel. He set the coffee can on it. "Tastes like chicken." He glanced from Jeff to Jagger, then back to Jeff. "You don't have to eat it. Nobody does when they first come down here. But like I said, you get used to it." His cold, broken-toothed grin once more flashed across his face. "After a while, you get used to everything down here."

CHAPTER 19

The night seemed to have grown darker when Heather and Keith emerged from the subway station. A few cabs were cruising on Broadway and a smattering of people dotted the sidewalks, but as they started up the long block toward Jeff's building, the noise of the traffic on Broadway died away, and the street was unusually deserted.

As they came to Jeff's building, Keith turned to face Heather. "This is all nuts, isn't it? I mean, what are we doing, following crazy old women down into the subway?"

Heather looked up at him. Though she hadn't seen a strong resemblance between Jeff and Keith until earlier that night, in the apartment, now, in the glow of the streetlight and the shadows that lay over his features, she clearly recognized the son in the father. Maybe it was something in his voice, or his posture, or even the line of his jaw, but whatever it was, she suddenly felt she was standing with Jeff himself, hearing all the uncertainty in his voice when he'd talked about the future, about the pain he was going to inflict on his father when he finally told Keith that he had no intention of going back to Bridgehampton when he finished school.

That pain, Heather knew, would have been nowhere near as terrible as the pain she could see Keith suffering right now.

"I'd better go home, and you should get some sleep," she said. She started to turn away, but Keith reached out and took her arm.

"Tell me I'm not nuts," he said softly. "Tell me I'm right."

"I don't know if you're right," Heather said. "But I know we heard something. I'm not sure what it was—it doesn't seem possible it could have been Jeff, but—" She gently pulled herself loose from his grip. "If you're crazy, then I guess I am, too." She started quickly back toward Broadway, but then turned to face him again, and this time met his eyes directly. "Tomorrow," she said. "We'll start looking again tomorrow."

"I'll wait for you," he said.

This time Heather didn't look back, but could feel Keith's eyes on her as she hurried down 109th Street toward the lights and noise of Broadway.

"Spare change?"

The phrase was so familiar to Heather that she almost didn't hear it at all, but as she raised her hand to signal to the cab that was still two blocks up Broadway, she heard it again.

"Come on, lady—don'cha even have a quarter?"

Still waving at the cab, Heather glanced at the source of the voice out of the corner of her eye. A boy, maybe ten years old, certainly no older. He was dressed in the typical clothing of the homeless: pants that were little more than rags and a grubby shirt whose tails were hanging out in back. His skin was pale and his unkempt blond hair hung in a tangle over his forehead.

It was his eyes that shocked her. They weren't those of a ten-year-old at all.

They were more like the eyes of an animal.

As he looked up at her, she could see them flicking first in one direction, then another, scanning the street for unseen danger.

She glanced at her watch. It was nearly midnight. What was he doing there? Was he a runaway?

She thought of the old woman she'd seen disappearing into the darkness of the tunnels.

The woman who probably had no more family than this boy.

The woman who had finally grown so fearful she wouldn't even speak to someone like her, preferring to disappear into the darkness and filth that lay beneath the streets.

She reflected that in a few more years, maybe even months, that's what this boy might be like.

As the cab pulled up, Heather burrowed deep into her purse until her fingers closed on a bill. Pulling it out—not even looking at it—she offered it to the boy. As he snatched the bill out of her hand like a squirrel snatching a nut from an old man in Central Park, Heather got in the cab. She pulled the door shut and gave the driver her address.

Why did I do that? she wondered as the cab pulled away. *Giving them money only encourages them.*

She twisted around to peer out the back window, but the boy was gone.

By the time she got home, she knew exactly why she'd given money to the boy.

He was no longer just another one of the faceless mass of homeless people who lived all around her.

Now he was someone—if she could ever find him again—who might be able to help her.

Help her, and help Keith.

Help them find Jeff.

"Time to go," Creeper said.

Jeff had been dozing fitfully, resting his back against the hard concrete. His stomach, which had been churning violently against the meal Creeper served them, was only now starting to settle down, and what little sleep he'd gotten had done nothing to ease the soreness in his muscles. A small groan escaped his lips as he unfolded his legs, which he had drawn up to his chest in an almost fetal position.

Jagger's huge hand closed on his own. "Gonna be okay, buddy," he said, pulling Jeff to his feet. The fire in the barrel had burned low, and the corners of the alcove had disappeared back into darkness. Jagger's eyes darted toward Creeper, who was already on the abandoned tracks, then he nodded toward his other hand. In the fading glow of the firelight, Jeff could see that he held a large railroad spike, the tapered end clutched in Jagger's fist, the head forming a heavy club with a hooked end. Jagger tilted his head toward Creeper. "Soon's we get somewhere where we can see a way out—"

He spoke in the lowest whisper possible, but it didn't seem to matter.

"You're gonna need that thing for track rabbit," Creeper said, not even bothering to glance in their direction. "Whack me with it, and you'll never get outta here." He started down the track, moving in the opposite direction from which they'd come.

Jagger watched him suspiciously. "Maybe we don't need him at all."

Jeff tried to see into the tunnel from which they'd arrived. If anything, the blackness seemed to have deepened. It was only a trick of his mind, he realized—the few short hours he'd spent in the glow of the firelight had deepened his reluctance to return to the pitch-darkness of the tunnels.

He switched on his flashlight, but the bulb barely lit at all, and rapidly dimmed to a small glowing pinpoint.

He remembered the voice—his father's voice?—drifting out of the blackness. *Nothing more than a hallucination.*

But then he thought of the very real voices they'd heard, and the shot.

"Better go with Creeper," he finally said. "At least he's got a light."

Jagger's eyes narrowed. "I could take that away from him."

"Even if you do, what do we do when the battery runs out?"

"Maybe we'd have found a way out of here by then."

"And maybe we wouldn't," Jeff replied. He jumped down onto the tracks. "You coming?"

Jagger still hesitated, but finally nodded. "I'm with you."

Creeper was already a dozen yards ahead of them, and as they started after him, he glanced back over his shoulder. "I'm shuttin' off the light," he said. "Just keep following me." The bright beam of the halogen torch went out, and as the blackness closed around Jeff, sharp-taloned fingers of panic began to rip at his nerves. He tried to move through the darkness, tripped over a rail, yelped with pain as his ankle twisted, then instinctively threw out a hand to steady himself. By pure luck his hand found the wall and he didn't fall. Instantly, the flashlight came back on.

"Fuckin' idiot," Creeper said. "Just keep touchin' the wall and you'll be okay."

The light went back out, and Jeff could hear him moving again.

A few seconds later the light flashed on again, then almost immediately went out yet again. Ahead of them Jeff could hear Creeper's footsteps echoing, and even before the light went on again, he knew the other man was moving much faster than he and Jagger.

"Fucker's tryin' to lose us," Jagger muttered the next time the light came on and they discovered they'd fallen nearly fifty yards behind.

"He can't lose us if we don't let him," Jeff said. Reaching out with his right hand, he felt the rough concrete of the wall. Somehow, just touching the wall steadied the vertigo induced by the darkness, and he stepped up his pace, ignoring the burning in his injured ankle.

The next time the light flicked on, Creeper was once again only a few yards ahead of them.

A few yards farther on, Creeper stopped and waited for them to catch up.

"How far are we going?" Jeff asked.

"No farther," Creeper told him. "Now we go up." He shined his light on the wall of the tunnel. There was another alcove here—far smaller than the one where they'd eaten and rested—but in this alcove, iron steps had been mounted in the concrete to form a ladder into a narrow shaft that led straight up. "There's another tunnel up above. Water mains." Without another word, he started scrambling up the ladder.

With no other choice than being left in the darkness, Jeff and Jagger followed.

After walking another ten minutes—or maybe half an hour, or even an hour—they'd climbed two more ladders and were in a third tunnel.

Far ahead, Jeff saw light.

Not the flickering, bobbing movement of flashlights, but the steady glow of electric lights mounted on the tunnel's wall.

Creeper, putting the halogen light out for the last time, picked up his pace. The throbbing in Jeff's ankle seemed to ease as a goal finally came into sight. They were in a utility tunnel—cables, pipes, and conduits ran along both walls and hung from the ceiling. Ahead, Jeff could see the first of a series of dim bulbs, each encased in glass and protected by a heavy metal cage, mounted in the ceiling.

As they came to the first one, Creeper stopped and turned to face them. "Welcome to the condos," he said with the same grin he'd offered them hours ago, when he showed them their dinner. "Manhattan's cheapest housing, all utilities included." He stepped through a door in the wall.

Jeff and Jagger hesitated. Jagger glanced at the door, then shifted his gaze to the dimly lit tunnel that stretched ahead of them. "I think maybe we oughta keep goin'."

Jeff, too, eyed the lights strung along the tunnel like lamps over a pathway. Creeper's voice came from inside the door.

"We got company."

"Anyone we know?" It was a woman's voice, and Jeff thought he heard a note of humor in it.

"Not me. Found 'em two flights down."

"Well, bring 'em on in—lucky they didn't die down there. And we got plenty of food—real food, not that track rabbit some people eat."

Creeper reappeared at the door, and along with him came a scent that filled Jeff's nostrils, started his mouth watering and sent pangs of hunger twisting through his belly.

Stew.

Not the thin, flavorless stew that was all they'd been fed when they'd been locked in the room somewhere down in the utter darkness below. This smelled like the stew his mother used to make, pungent with herbs.

"You guys coming in or not?" Creeper asked.

It was the aroma of the stew that ended whatever doubts Jeff might have had. As he stepped through the door, he saw the last thing he would have expected to find in this place.

CHAPTER 20

Whatever Jeff expected as he stepped through the door, it wasn't this. Not that he saw anything extraordinary—in fact, the objects that filled the chamber were utterly ordinary.

A stove—the back burner of which held the pot from which came the mouthwatering aroma of beef stew.

A refrigerator—its avocado green finish chipped, and parts of the worn-out gasket around its door missing. As if to prove it wasn't a mirage, it rattled to life at that moment, its compressor clattering grumpily before settling into a steady hum.

A table—a real table, with a Formica top and tubular metal legs, almost identical to the one in his own apartment. And around the table, half a dozen mismatched chairs. A couple of them were made of badly scarred oak, their finish all but worn off. The others, originally upholstered in various kinds of vinyl, were now mostly covered with duct tape.

Against the wall opposite the stove was the kind of sofa Jeff had seen many times on the streets of his neighborhood, dragged onto the street for the garbage men to haul away. This one looked to be of about the same vintage as the refrigerator. Its cheap pine frame was carved in an ugly Mediterranean style, and though the crushed-velvet upholstery was stained and torn, a bit of its original gold color still showed.

There were two easy chairs, one a recliner that was extended as far as its broken leg rest would allow. The damage didn't seem to bother the man sprawled out on it, sleeping noisily.

There were pictures on the windowless walls, but like everything else in the room, they looked as if they'd been cast off—some because the broken frames' contents weren't worth reframing, others because what they depicted could only have looked good in the tourist traps where they'd originally been sold. But all of them had one thing in common: they displayed some sort of landscape, as if the pictures were serving as windows to an imagined world on the surface. One showed a meadow in springtime with deer feeding on its lush grass. Another depicted a sylvan wood, foliage ablaze in autumnal glory, with a preternatural shaft of light piercing the forest's canopy as if God Himself were smiling down from the unseen sky.

In contrast to the fanciful pictures, the drab reality of the room was revealed by two old and crooked floor lamps, both in need of shades.

Most surprising was a television set, droning softly in the corner, tuned to CNN.

"You like my place?"

Jeff tore his eyes away from the TV screen.

The woman who was smiling at him looked to be in her sixties. Only a little more than five feet tall and heavy, her body was made to appear even larger than it was by the bulk of the clothes she wore. Her skirt was a paisley pattern in brilliant shades of scarlet, purple, and green. The bottom two inches dragged on the floor, causing the hem to be frayed and blackened with grime. Her blouse of deep burgundy velvet had rusty-looking streaks running through it, and a large, greasy-looking stain covered one side of her ample bosom. At least a dozen bracelets in as many styles jangled on her forearms, and countless necklaces and chains hung from her neck.

Her face was thickly coated with makeup that was caked in the deep crevices of her cheeks, and a bloodred shade of lipstick highlighted the wrinkles in her lips. A copper-colored wig couldn't quite contain the wisps of gray hair that curled over her forehead.

A tattered black shawl missing most of its fringe hung over her shoulders and trailed down below her waist. "Not bad, eh?" she asked, waving in an expansive gesture that took in the entire room. The long ash of her cigarette fell to the floor as she sucked in an enormous lungful of smoke.

"If the smoke don't get me, the cancer will," she cackled, her eyes twinkling as she gave Jeff a gap-toothed smile. Her gaze shifted from Jeff to Jagger, and her smile—along with the twinkle in her eye—faded. She stabbed her cigarette in his direction. "Don't remember invitin' you in."

Jagger's hand tightened on the rusty railroad spike.

"It's okay, Tillie," Creeper said quickly. "They won't be staying long."

"They won't stay at all if I say so," the woman retorted, her eyes still fixed on Jagger.

"Come on, Tillie," Creeper wheedled. "Didn't you just say they could have something to eat?"

"That was before I saw 'em," Tillie snapped back. Her cigarette jabbed at Jagger again. "Now I've seen him, I don't want him. So get him out of here."

Jeff could feel the tension building in Jagger.

"Maybe I don't want to leave," the big man growled.

Tillie's eyes narrowed and she pursed her lips, smearing her lipstick even more. "I guess you can eat," she said. "Then we'll see." Her eyes shifted back to Jeff, and she jerked her head toward an opening in the far wall. "There's a place you can wash up back there," she said. "Just make sure you put the lid back on the can if you use it. Don't like to stink up the place."

With Jagger right behind him, Jeff made his way through the gap in the wall.

"What is this place?" Jagger muttered as he gazed around.

On a battered table sat a chipped enameled pan—exactly like one Jeff's family had used on the camping trips they'd taken when he was a little boy—and matching pitcher. A towel, not terribly dirty, hung from a bar that had been precariously mounted in the concrete of the wall.

A naked lightbulb, hanging from a cord strung along the ceiling, filled the room with light.

On the wall above the table hung a cracked mirror, and for the first time since he'd left his cell in the Tombs, Jeff was able to see his own reflection. As he gazed at the image reflected in the glass, he barely recognized himself.

His skin was streaked with grease and grime, and his hair hung lank, heavy with its own oil.

His eyes were bloodshot, and dark circles had formed beneath them.

His forehead had broken out with pimples, and a cut on his chin—a cut he hadn't even known was there—looked like it was starting to fester.

Still staring at his own image, Jeff finally answered Jagger's question. "It's their home," he said. "This is where they live."

In the mirror, Jeff could see Jagger glancing speculatively around. In yet another chamber beyond the one in which they stood, he could see a few mattresses scattered on the floor—one of them even seemed to have box springs under it, and all of them had blankets.

Blankets and sheets.

The exhaustion Jeff had been holding at bay as they'd made their way through the darkness of the tunnels until they'd stumbled across Creeper suddenly overwhelmed him, and all he wanted to do was disappear into that next room and collapse onto one of the beds.

"And now it's where we live," Jagger said. Then he winked at Jeff. "Beats the hell out of Rikers, huh?"

Jeff said nothing, looking in the mirror once more.

But what he saw was no longer a reflection of himself.

What he saw was a derelict.

The kind of person he'd long ago learned to simply ignore.

Or even turn away from, as if to deny their very existence.

Malcolm Baldridge, who had been known simply as "Baldridge" for so many years that few people except himself even remembered he had a first name, reached deep in his pocket for the single key that was never kept on the large ring that hung inside his private pantry.

His innate obsession with detail, the obsession that made him perfect for his job, caused him to check the door for any sign of tampering. As always, there was none. He slipped the key into the lock, turned it, pushed the door open, then closed it behind him before turning on the lights. One of the tubes in the overhead fixtures flickered a few times before settling in to join the others in flooding the room with a bright white light—a light that Baldridge had insisted be matched to that of sunlight.

It was a matter of aesthetics, and aesthetics were important to Baldridge.

Indeed, his sense of aesthetics was another of his prime qualifications for his job.

Before he did anything else besides pull on a pair of the thin latex gloves he always wore when he worked in this room, he went to one of the supply closets, took a replacement tube from the stock on the top shelf, and replaced the offending tube in the overhead fixture.

No sense being needlessly distracted from his work if the faulty tube began flickering again.

Then he set to work.

As always, the carcass was precisely where the team left it on nights when the hunt was successful: laid out on a gurney in the walk-in refrigerator. The refrigerator had been expensive, and the renovations required for its installation even more so, but Baldridge had insisted on it. "The odor can sometimes become offensive," he'd explained, "and far more quickly than you might think." Also in accordance with Baldridge's precise instructions, nothing at all had been done to the carcass. "Restoration is my job," he'd explained. "It's best left to experts." Baldridge's own expertise was unquestionable. He'd apprenticed under his uncle, who was still working up in New Hampshire, and gained further training in a funeral home in California, moving to New York at the same time his employer in California moved across the border to Arizona in hopes of escaping prosecution for certain irregularities, only a few of which had taken place in Baldridge's area of the operation.

Baldridge had been in his present position for nearly five years, and though few people ever saw the results of his work, he was content. Tonight he whistled softly as he removed the blankets that had been wrapped around the carcass to make it easier to transport from the site of the kill to the refrigerator.

Wheeling the gurney out of the refrigerator, he removed one tattered layer of blanketing after another, appreciating— not for the first time—the supple layer of latex that prevented him from soiling his fingers on the filthy material that always covered the carcasses. He carefully placed the blankets in a bag that would be removed to the incinerator before he left for the night, then turned his attention to the carcass itself.

A buck, perhaps twenty-five years old—certainly no older than thirty.

The carcass was in fair condition. Most of the teeth were intact, though the hide was defaced with three tattoos. One depicted a serpent, which was coiled around the left bicep, and another proclaimed love for *Mother* in ornate, Old English–style letters across the left breast. The third, looking exactly like a meat stamp, was stenciled across the right buttock, and identified the posterior to be US GRADE-A PRIME.

The blond hair was limp and greasy, but at least it wasn't matted into the kind of dreadlocks Baldridge found not only unsightly, but almost impossible to work with.

The carcass was clad in the usual array of clothing, and although all of Baldridge's aesthetic instincts told him to cut it away and dispose of it in the same manner as the blankets, he instead carefully removed it, piece by piece, and transferred it to another bag, which was destined for the laundry. After the clothes were washed and pressed, Baldridge himself would make the decision if they could be used in the final presentation. If it was only a matter of replacing a few buttons, or resewing a hem, he would perform the repairs himself. If the damage or wear proved too extensive, however, he would take them to a discreet seamstress just off Seventh Avenue down in the Thirties and have them copied.

Finally, the carcass lay naked on the gurney, and it was time to transfer it to the worktable. He slid the carcass onto the table and began preparing for the real work.

His knives, all honed razor sharp, were kept in a velvet-lined drawer that slid out from beneath the worktable's granite surface.

He placed several large cardboard cartons—manufactured for the ice cream trade, but perfect for Baldridge's use—in a specially constructed trough running completely around the edges of the table's surface.

Using a digital camera, Baldridge photographed the carcass from every angle, then took careful note of all the pertinent measurements: not merely the girth of the breast, waist, and hips, though these were noted to within a quarter of an inch, but also the upper arms, lower arms, thighs, and calves.

Finally satisfied, he turned the carcass over so it lay face-down, and carefully made an incision from just behind the crown of the head all the way down to the base of the spine. Then, using a variety of knives—most of which were of his own design—he began working the hide away from the carcass, his fingers wielding the knives quickly but expertly, never penetrating the hide but leaving nearly nothing of either the fatty tissue or the muscle that separated the hide from the bones and soft tissues.

The back was relatively easy—flat planes, a broad expanse of hide, and plenty of room to work. Peeling the hide away from the back of the skull was just as easy, though it had taken Baldridge several months to master the ears, the trick being to cut deeply enough so that no incision would show in the final product. After that it was relatively simple to peel everything away except the lips and nostrils. The eyelids simply lifted off once the membranes around the eye sockets themselves were cut away. The nostrils and lips were merely a repeat of the ears—cut deeply enough inside those orifices so the loose edges would disappear completely when the re-mounting process was finished.

Once the hide was completely removed from the skull and face, it was nothing more than a careful stripping process, no more difficult than removing opera-length gloves from the arms or panty hose from the legs. A little care around the anus—more around the genitals—but that was really more for Baldridge's own sense of pride in his work than out of ne-cessity, since those areas would not be visible in the end product.

When the hide, still in a single, nearly unblemished piece, was finally separated from the carcass, Baldridge inspected it once more, noting with a certain degree of satisfaction that the only repair that would be necessary was the small hole in the forehead where the bullet had entered. His own work had left not even the tiniest of cuts or nicks. He then transferred the hide to the first of the vats in the row of tanning tanks that lined the opposite wall, and turned his attention to the re-mainder of the carcass.

Baldridge worked even more quickly now, for most of what still lay on the worktable was nothing more than garbage. Within twenty minutes all the muscles, organs, ligaments, and other soft tissue had been stripped away from the skeleton and deposited in the large ice cream cartons. Finally, he pulled the head away from the spine, carefully using one of his favorite knives to separate vertebrae from brain.

Abandoning the skeleton for a moment, he opened the glass top of a large box—seven feet long and two feet wide—that appeared to rest directly on the floor against the back wall. The box's bottom was covered with a coarse screen, and it was upon this screen that Baldridge laid the skeleton. Closing the top of the box, he peered down through the glass until he saw the first of the ants scurry up through the mesh, confirm what they'd found, and hurry back down to communicate their discovery to the rest of the huge colony that lived beneath the floor of the laboratory. Satisfied that the formicans had busily begun their work and that by morning they would have eaten the cartilage away while leaving the bones intact, he turned his full attention to the skull.

Though he knew it was perfectly permissible to cut the skull open with a surgical saw, once again his sense of aesthetics stopped him. Though no trace of this surgery would show in the end, he himself would know the imperfection was there, and it would bother him. Thus, even though it would take him at least a full extra hour, he set to work, cutting the brain away through the foramen magnum, using a variety of knives, spoons, and scrapers to clean as much of the tissue away from the bone as possible.

The tongue and eyeballs joined the brain matter in one of the handy ice cream cartons.

After Baldridge had examined the bullet hole in the forehead and determined that the damage to the bone itself was minimal, the skull was placed in its own ant box. It, too, would be ready by morning.

The hide, however, would require several days of preparation.

Only then, when both skeleton and hide were perfectly preserved, would Baldridge begin his true work. When he was done, the man who had died in the tunnels that night would undoubtedly look better than he'd ever looked before.

By the time Baldridge left the workroom an hour later, nothing remained of the waste materials: the full ice cream cartons had been placed in the incinerator, and even the small bit of residue left when the fires had burned out had been washed down the drain.

The granite tabletop was spotless, as was the drainage trough.

The gurney had been scrubbed down and disinfected, the latex gloves consumed by the fire that destroyed the waste tissues.

Taking the bag containing the worn-out fluorescent light with him, Baldridge inspected his workroom one last time.

All was as it should be.

In a few more days, tonight's trophy would be ready for display.

And tomorrow, another hunt would begin.

CHAPTER 21

It wasn't pleasure—it was the absence of pain that Jeff noticed most when he awoke.

He wasn't cold.

He wasn't in pitch-darkness.

He wasn't aching in every part of his body.

At first he thought the softness of the mattress beneath him and the warmth of the blanket that covered him couldn't possibly be real. For one brief moment he dared to imagine that when he opened his eyes, he'd be back in his apartment on West 109th Street. Heather would be scrambling eggs on the stove in his tiny kitchenette, and the morning sun would just be brightening his bedroom. In a few minutes he'd be out running in Riverside Park.

Then he opened his eyes.

He lay still, staring up at the bulb that hung from the ceiling. No, its glare was nothing at all like the delicate colors of dawn outside his bedroom window. Finally, he raised his hand to shield his eyes from it.

Next he became aware of a low rumble—a rumble that grew steadily until the whole room was vibrating around him. After it faded away and silence once again fell over the room, he sat up, the sheet and blanket falling away from his body. Only then did he notice Jagger sitting on the bed opposite him, watching him. As the big man's eyes moved over his torso, Jeff reached for the sheet and started to pull it back up again.

"What you think—I'm some kinda fairy?" Jagger growled.

Jeff shook his head. "You just surprised me." He looked around, spotting his clothes—obviously washed and neatly folded—in a pile on the floor next to the bed. He glanced back up at Jagger. "You do that?"

"I'm not a maid, either," Jagger said.

"Then who—"

"Who cares?" Jagger asked. "All I know is I'm hungry, and I smell food. You gonna get dressed, or wander around naked?" Heaving himself to his feet, Jagger moved through the makeshift bathroom into the living area beyond.

Left alone, Jeff flopped back down on the soft mattress. He lay there a short while before realizing that the part of his fantasy concerning scrambled eggs was more than just a dream, for he could actually smell them. And he could smell bacon frying, too. Throwing off the covers, he pulled on his clothes, then followed Jagger, pausing only long enough to throw some water on his face and to use one of the large cans to relieve himself. Then he went through the door leading into the main room.

There were half a dozen people in the room. Tillie was standing at the stove, a large spatula in her hand. A young woman, no more than eighteen years old, was sitting on the sagging sofa, nursing a baby. Around the table were three men, somewhere between thirty and fifty. One of them, who was sitting, looked drunk, and the other two had the glazed look of habitual drug users and were on their feet, each holding a knife as they eyed Jagger, who was clutching the railroad spike in his right hand.

Cowering near the door that led to the tunnel outside the room was a frightened girl who appeared to Jeff to be about fifteen, maybe even younger.

"Maybe it ain't him," Jeff heard the drunk man say, his words slurring. "Maybe Jinx is wrong."

"I'm not wrong," the girl near the door said. She was clutching a sheet of paper in her hand. "Why don't you look yourself?" Her eyes shifted to Jeff. "Shit! They're both here!"

As Jeff watched, Jagger took a step toward one of the men with the knives, but they both tensed, and Jagger restrained himself, his eyes darting from one to the other.

Jinx's eyes widened. "He'll kill you!"

"Jag?" Jeff asked. "What's going on?"

Jagger's eyes didn't leave the two knife-wielding men as he spoke. "She says she got some kind of paper with my picture on it, and these guys are sayin' we gotta leave."

Jeff's gaze shifted from Jagger to Jinx.

"A picture? What kind of picture?" He started toward her, but stopped as Jinx shrank back against the wall, and one of the junkies spoke.

"You touch her and your guts'll be on the floor before you even know what happened."

Jeff held his hands up in a gesture of peace. "Hey, let's just take it easy, okay? Nobody's going to hurt anybody. I'm just trying to figure out what's going on, that's all."

"You gotta get 'em out of here, Tillie," Jinx said. "You know—"

"I know this is my place, and I decide what's gonna happen here," Tillie cut in. Her eyes bored into Jinx as if daring the girl to challenge her. "And you keep in mind that I can kick you out, too, young lady."

For a moment Jinx looked as if she might try to argue with Tillie, but then deflated like a leaking balloon. "All's I want you to do is just look," she said, her voice taking on a wheedling note.

Tillie pursed her lips and she seemed about to refuse, but then put the spatula down and took the paper from Jinx's hand. Unrolling it, she studied it for a moment, her eyes flicking between the paper and both Jagger and Jeff.

"You boys want to tell me why you were in jail?" she asked.

Jagger's eyes narrowed. "I didn't do nothin'."

Tillie's eyes shifted to Jeff, and he could see that she hadn't believed Jagger.

"I was convicted of attempted murder," he said.

Tillie's eyes narrowed. "Did you do it, or not?"

Jeff shrugged. "It doesn't make any difference. I was charged with it, I was convicted of it, and I was in jail for it."

"How long they give you?"

"A year."

Tillie's brows lifted in apparent disbelief, but her gaze shifted back to Jagger. "How 'bout you?"

"Life," Jagger said.

"For?" Tillie's eyes never left Jagger as the question hung in the air.

Jagger seemed to ponder the statement for a long time, then he frowned. "They said I killed a couple people. And they said I killed a guy in jail, too. But I don't remember. I don't remember killin' nobody."

Tillie looked back at the paper she'd taken from Jinx, then passed it to Jeff. Though it was badly creased and smeared with dirt, he could see it clearly enough.

There were two photographs, one of Jagger, the other of himself. Beneath them there was a brief description of the charges that each of them had been convicted of. Below that were printed four words:

THE HUNT IS ON

"You can have some breakfast," Tillie said. "After that, you're gonna have to leave."

"How can they call themselves 'New York's finest'?" Heather Randall asked, spitting the last three words out as if they'd left a nasty taste in her mouth. "If they're too afraid of the people who live in the tunnels even to go in, how can they call themselves police, let alone anyone's 'finest'?"

Eve Harris leaned back in her chair, took off the half glasses she used for reading, and pressed her fingers against her temples in a vain attempt to stave off the headache that was starting to creep up out of her sinuses. She almost wished she'd refused to see the two people who were now sitting angrily in the chairs on the other side of her desk. Heather Randall was perched on the edge of her seat, while Keith Converse was leaning forward, his elbows on his knees, chin resting on folded hands as his eyes bored into hers. She knew he was silently challenging her to do something about the story he'd started telling her yesterday, and which had taken an even stranger turn this morning. She'd intended simply to have her assistant give Keith Converse the message that she'd been unable to find out anything about a man called Scratch, and be done with it. But when he'd shown up at her office instead of merely calling—and brought Heather Randall with him—she changed her mind. Even Eve Harris did not readily turn away the daughter of the Assistant District Attorney, given that there might well be a time when she would want a favor from him.

Sighing, she stopped massaging her temples and looked first at Heather, then at Keith. "I can understand your frustration. In fact, I can empathize with it. Lord knows, the police haven't always been my best friends over the years. But on the other hand, I'm not sure you understand fully what they're up against."

"A bunch of homeless people," Keith told her, "who they seem to think are all drunks, junkies, or nutcases." He smiled grimly. "And that's a quote from someone at the Fifth Precinct, a guy named—"

"I don't even want to know," the councilwoman cut in. "It doesn't make any difference, since most of them would agree."

"Which means they wouldn't have bothered to talk to any of them when they were investigating what happened to Cynthia Allen, right?"

Eve Harris's expression became guarded. "I thought you were looking for your son, Mr. Converse. If you're really after a retrial—"

"We're just trying to find out what's happening," Heather broke in, seeing that they were on the verge of losing Eve Harris entirely. "I know we heard something in the subway station last night. I can't swear it was Jeff—I suppose it might have been anybody. But Keith is sure the body they showed us wasn't Jeff's, and no matter what Cindy Allen says, I'll never believe that Jeff was trying to do anything but help her that night." She shook her head. "Maybe we're wrong— we probably are—but we have to try to find out. And all we know is what Al Kelly told Keith."

Eve's brows lifted and she looked at Keith. "You remembered his name."

"Why wouldn't I?" he countered.

"Most people don't," Eve replied. "To most people, the homeless don't have any identity at all—it's easier to ignore people if you know nothing about them. As long as you don't know the facts, you can assume anything you want— whatever condition they're in, it must be their own fault." Her eyes shifted to Heather. "That's why people won't even look them in the eye—you look in someone's eyes, and you might see things you don't want to know. So it's easier just not to look." When Heather didn't disagree, Eve abruptly shifted gears. "Why are you coming to me?" she asked. "Why not go to your father?"

Heather's demeanor clouded. "As far as my father is concerned, Jeff is—" Her voice caught and she couldn't bring herself to utter the word. Then she started over again. "My father doesn't believe in reopening cases. He thinks it's a waste of time. And when I called Jeff's lawyer this morning, he said he'd tried to talk to a few people in the subway station, but they wouldn't talk to him. He thinks we're wasting our time, too."

Keith, who had been watching Eve carefully as Heather spoke, stood up.

"I think we're wasting our time here, too," he said. He turned to Eve. "Look, Ms. Harris, whether you help us or not, we're going to talk to the people who live in the tunnels. I'll go into them myself if I have to. Yesterday you seemed like someone who'd help me. If you're not going to, just say so."

As Heather stood up, too, Eve Harris made her decision. "I didn't say I wasn't going to help you," she said, looking at her calendar. "I'm meeting someone at one o'clock this afternoon. If you can meet me at Riverside Park at one-thirty, I'll see what I can do. I can't promise you anything—these people can be very . . . well, let's just say they can be very skittish. And understandably so. But at least I can introduce you to someone who knows a lot about what goes on in the tunnels." She held up a cautionary hand at the excitement she saw burning in Keith's eyes. "But that's all I can do. I'll be just south of the marina, and I'll try to make the introduction. After that, you're on your own. Deal?"

"Deal," Keith replied.

"Then I'll see you at one-thirty."

Jagger's eyes fixed malevolently on Tillie. "If we don't wanna go, I don't see any way you're gonna make us." The muscles in his neck, shoulders, and arms were bunched into hard masses, and though he was still sitting at the table where he and Jeff had sat down to eat, he looked coiled tight, as if ready to spring. Standing at her stove like a general at a command post, Tillie appeared totally unaffected either by Jagger's demeanor or his words.

"This is my place," she said. "I decide who can stay and who can't."

"What do you mean, your place?" Jagger challenged. "This ain't nobody's place. It's nothin' but a fuckin' hole, for Christ sake. You don't own it, and if we want to stay here, that's how it's going to be."

"Maybe I better explain to you how things work down here," Tillie replied, still seemingly unmoved by the menace in Jagger's voice. "You know what a family is?" She paused, waiting for Jagger to reply, but he met her words with silence. Her eyes, sunk deep in fleshy sockets, narrowed. "I asked you a question. You got a hearing problem?"

Jagger half rose from his chair. "Fuck you, old woman."

"Take it easy," Jeff cautioned, putting a hand on Jagger's forearm. The girl called Jinx was still standing near the door opening out onto the tracks, looking as if she might bolt at any second. The two junkies were eyeing Jagger balefully as they kept the knives steadily moving in their hands, flicking first one way, then another, like the tongues of snakes readying to strike.

"You guys take it easy, too," Tillie said, her eyes shifting from Jagger to the two addicts. "Lester, didn't I explain the rules to you and Eddie before I let you join?"

One of the men lowered his knife, but didn't put it away. "I know the rules," he growled. "And so does Eddie. But this guy gives me the creeps."

"So cut him up somewhere else," Tillie said. Her eyes shifted to Eddie. "You got about two more seconds, Eddie."

For a moment Jeff wasn't certain if the man named Eddie had even heard Tillie, but then he snapped his switchblade closed and slid it into his pocket.

"Come on, Lester," Eddie said. "Let's go see if we can find Gonzales."

"Just don't bring it back here," Tillie told them. "You understand?"

Though neither of them spoke, Lester nodded, and a moment later they were gone, disappearing through the door without a word to anyone.

"So now that the muscle's gone, who's gonna back you up?" Jagger asked, dropping back onto his chair.

"They'll be back," Tillie told him. "And even if they don't come back, there'll be plenty of other people around." Jagger's lips twisted into a contemptuous sneer, but Tillie only shrugged. "You think you're pretty tough, don't you?"

Now it was Jagger who shrugged. He said nothing, but tilted his head slightly, as though the question wasn't worth answering.

Looking almost sad, as if she felt genuinely sorry for Jagger, Tillie scooped a huge serving of scrambled eggs out of the skillet, added half a dozen slices of bacon to the plate, and set it down in front of Jagger.

Jagger eyed the food suspiciously. "Thought you wanted us out of here."

"I told you that you could eat first," Tillie said. "I don't send anyone away hungry. You can get enough of starving outside." She fixed another plate and set it in front of Jeff, then filled a chipped mug with thick-looking coffee from a pot on the stove's back burner. After that, as Jeff and Jagger began to eat, Tillie dropped onto a chair next to the drunk and put the mug into his hands. She had to shove it back when he pushed it away. "Swear to God, Fritz—it ain't any worse'n the Sterno you drink."

"Come on, Tillie," Fritz whined. "This stuff tastes like shit!"

"Maybe it tastes like shit, but at least it won't kill you," Tillie retorted. Her gaze shifted to Jinx, who still hadn't moved from her spot by the door. "Sit down and have something to eat. These guys aren't gonna hurt you. Are you?" she added, glancing at Jeff and Jagger.

Jagger looked up from his plate and seemed about to speak, but Jeff didn't give him a chance. "We're not going to hurt anybody," he said, smiling at Jinx.

Her fear appearing to ease, Jinx went to the stove, put what was left of the eggs and bacon on a plate, and warily took the seat next to Tillie.

"Robby get to school okay?" Tillie asked.

Jinx nodded. "But he didn't want to go. He says some of the other kids are picking on him."

"Why would anyone want to pick on Robby?" Tillie asked. "He's a good kid."

"Clothes," Jinx told her. "He says the other kids tell him he looks like he's homeless."

"Assholes," the woman on the sofa said bitterly. The baby had fallen asleep in her arms, and now she laid him gently on the sofa, got up, and poured the last of the coffee into a tin mug. "Why can't they just leave him alone?"

"Who's Robby?" Jeff asked.

Nobody spoke, and everyone in the room except Jagger, Jeff, and the sleeping baby glanced at Tillie.

"Just a kid," she said. "He's about eight. Been living here for a while now."

"He lives here?" Jeff echoed. "A little boy?"

Tillie rolled her eyes. "What kind of dummy are you? Why shouldn't a little boy live here?"

"Do his parents live here, too?"

Jinx and the mother of the baby exchanged a quick glance. "I don't think you ought to tell him. If they get out—"

"They aren't getting out," Tillie said. "Did you ever hear of any of them getting out?"

"No, but—"

"No buts," Tillie cut in, and looked directly at Jeff. "They told you, didn't they? About the game?"

Jagger finished eating and pushed his plate aside. Jeff felt him tense, and again placed a restraining hand on the big man's arm. "They told us if we get out, we'll be free. They said all we had to do was get to the surface—"

"Doesn't matter what they said," Tillie interrupted. "They're going to kill you. That's why you're down here."

Jeff felt his stomach clench. "But why?" he demanded. "Why would anyone want to kill us? Who are they?"

Tillie's eyes bored into Jeff. "How would I know? Nobody sees them. Nobody even hears them. But we all know about them. And once they've made up their minds, that's it."

"But if we get out, they'll leave us alone?"

Tillie shrugged. "That's what they say. But I never heard of anybody getting out once the hunt's started." Her eyes flicked from Jeff to Jagger. " 'Course, I don't ever remember them hunting two at a time, either. Maybe if you stick together, you can do it."

Jagger abruptly leaned forward, his fingers closing on Tillie's wrist. "But what if we don't go anywhere?" he asked, his voice low and menacing. "What if we just stay here?"

If Tillie was frightened at all, she showed no sign of it. "I told you before—this is my place, and I decide who lives here. I got rules, and everybody has to live by them. Robby has to go to school, and Lorena here has to take care of her baby, and everybody has to look out for everybody else. We're not too far down yet, and I figure Robby and Lorena and Jinx still have a pretty good chance of moving back to the surface someday. That's why I don't let anybody in here that's going to mess things up—I want my kids to go up, not down." Her eyes fixed balefully on Jagger. "People like you don't go up," she said. "They only go down." Her eyes shifted back to Jeff. "That's the thing about the tunnels. When people first come in, they think it's only going to be for a little while— maybe a few hours, maybe just for the night. That's how I got here. I got tired of getting run out of Grand Central for sleeping on the benches—back before they took all the benches out. I'd been watching people go down the tracks, so one night I tried it myself. First good night's sleep I'd had in months. So I started going back. I had a little nest for a while, up in the pipes. And I'd go out every day. But then they started running us out of the station. So I started looking around, and after a while I found this." Her eyes roamed over the dank concrete of the windowless walls, and suddenly she grinned. "I figured the rent was right, and it was deep enough in so the cops wouldn't bother me." She jerked a thumb at Fritz, who seemed to have dozed off. "And once I found this one, it got a whole lot better. When Fritz isn't drinking, there's not much he can't do. He's the one who figured out how to tap into the electricity, and the cable, and even the water pipes. One of these days, I'll bet he even figures out how to bust us into the sewer."

"If his liver doesn't bust first," Jinx muttered.

Tillie glared at the girl, who fell silent. She turned back to Jeff. "Everybody thinks there's nothing but bums down here," she said. "And I'm not going to try to tell you there aren't a lot of those. But there's all kinds of other people, too. Like Jinx here, who had to get away from her stepfather." She tilted her head toward Lorena, who was once again nursing her baby. "She was pregnant, and her husband beat on her. And Robby's folks just left him."

"Left him?" Jeff echoed, now finished eating.

Tillie nodded. "They got on a bus, and told him to wait at the station. But they never came back. Jinx found him on a bench, just waiting, and brought him back here."

"Why didn't she take him to—well, to a shelter or something?"

"You ever been to one of those places? All they'd have done is put Robby into the system, and God only knows what would have happened to him. At least here he knows he's got a family that loves him. Up there . . ." She shook her head. "What am I even talking for? Everyone thinks it's so great up there, and I guess if you got money, maybe it is. But if you don't . . ." Her voice trailed off. "Things aren't so bad down here, at least not right here. Soon as the baby gets old enough, Lorena'll be getting a job, and I figure in a couple of years she'll be back on the surface. And one of these days Jinx is going to go back to school—"

"High school sucks," Jinx said.

"Being stupid sucks worse," Tillie informed her. She turned her attention back to Jeff and Jagger. "I don't know what you two did or didn't do. All I know is what's on that piece of paper. So I don't mind givin' you some breakfast, but that's it—I don't want you messin' with my family, and you sure ain't gonna be here when the hunters find you."

"So what are we supposed to do?" Jagger demanded.

Tillie stood up and began clearing away the empty plates. "That's not my problem. That's your problem."

"Maybe it *is* your problem," Jagger growled. "Maybe I'm gonna make it your problem."

Tillie shook her head. "Blacky?" she called out.

Instantly, the door opened and a man even larger than Jagger stepped inside. Behind him were two other men, neither much smaller than Blacky himself.

All of them carried knives, and they looked as though they knew exactly how to use them.

"These two were just leaving," Tillie said, nodding toward Jeff and Jagger. "Want to walk them to the corner?"

Blacky grinned. "No problem. No problem at all."

Almost before Jeff and Jagger knew what had happened, the two men were behind them, and Jeff felt the tip of a knife against the back of his neck. Raising his hands and getting to his feet, he started toward the door. But then he stopped, and even though Blacky once more jabbed the knife against his neck, he turned back to face Tillie. "What about our stuff?" he asked. "The flashlights and Jagger's spike?"

Tillie mulled it over. "Fair's fair, I guess—you had it when you came in, you can take it with you." After sending Jinx to retrieve their things from the other room, she turned back to Jeff. She seemed to think something over, then appeared to have come to some kind of decision. "One thing you might want to keep in mind—in the tunnels, the deeper you go, the crazier people get. So if you have a choice, go up. But don't plan on gettin' out. Once the hunters are after you, nobody ever gets out."

Jinx reappeared and wordlessly handed Jeff the flashlights and the rusty railroad spike. A moment later they left the room, the door swung closed behind them, and the brightness was gone.

All that remained was the darkness of the tunnels.

CHAPTER 22

Keith and Heather spent the entire morning downtown, moving from one public building to another, showing their identification and passing through the metal detectors so often that the process had become automatic. Everywhere they went, they met the same response—or, more accurately, the same lack of response.

To the city bureaucracy, it was as if the homeless problem had simply been solved. "Oh, there are still a few of them," they were told over and over again by blandly pleasant faces—both male and female—who sat behind bulletproof screens designed to keep them safe from the public they were employed to serve. "It's the strong economy, you know—anyone who wants to work can find a job. There just aren't as many as there used to be."

Or they heard: "The tunnels under the city? Are you nuts? You'd have to be crazy to live down there! I mean, there's no light, or water, or anything, is there?"

Eventually they gave up, grabbed hot dogs from one of the kiosks between the Municipal Building and Police Headquarters, then went down into the subway to head uptown.

"You know, they're right," Heather said as she glanced around the platform where they waited for a train. There was one person softly strumming a guitar, its case open in front of him, but everyone else seemed to have somewhere to go, something to do. "There really aren't as many of them as there used to be—a few years ago there were panhandlers everywhere. You couldn't get away from them."

A train rolled into the station, and they stepped into a half-empty car. As they sank down onto a bench, Keith said, "I think maybe I owe you an apology."

Heather's brows rose. "Me? Why?"

"Well, you know I wasn't too crazy about Jeff going out with you—"

"We weren't just going out," Heather cut in. "We were going to get married."

Keith sighed. "And it didn't matter what I thought, did it?"

Heather shook her head. "We'd made up our minds."

"Well, as it turns out, I guess Jeff was right, and I was wrong." His face flushed. "I guess that's what I wanted to apologize for—I thought you were just a spoiled rich girl. I even thought you might have been using Jeff as a way to piss off your father—a little rebellion before you settled down with a Park Avenue lawyer named Skip. But that's not it at all, is it?"

For the first time since Jeff had disappeared, Heather found herself smiling. "Daddy'd hate to hear you say that. To hear that maybe he failed after all the years of trying to spoil me . . ." She almost laughed, but her smile faded as she remembered where they were going, and why. "What if we don't find him?" she asked, her voice little more than a whisper.

Keith had no answer. The silence that fell over them wasn't broken until they emerged from the subway at Sherman Square and started west on Seventy-second toward the Hudson. The wind off the river put a snap in the air, and Heather buttoned up her light Burberry trench coat as they crossed West End Avenue. A quarter of a block farther they came to the foot of Riverside Drive. Directly ahead lay the entrance to the West Side Highway, and beyond the end of the ramp was the highway itself, a rush of traffic streaming in both directions. To the south lay one end of the huge new Trump development that stretched for nearly a mile along the river. To the north, Riverside Park stretched away into the distance, a belt of green that ran two and a half miles up to 125th Street.

"She said she'd be south of the marina," Heather said, ignoring the light and crossing Riverside Drive. "Come on."

Keith followed her into the park. She took them along a path that wound under the West Side Highway, and as they emerged at the top of a steep incline falling away to the river, Keith's eye caught some movement on the railroad tracks that he could glimpse to the south. There were several pairs of them, running under the highway and the park, only partially visible through the columns that supported the highway that covered them. Though there was a tall fence separating the tracks from the narrow strip of parkland between them and the river, the concrete wall behind the tracks was covered with graffiti.

"Those are the tracks from Penn Station," Heather told him. Two shabbily dressed men who were sitting at the base of one of the columns looked up at them. "And those must be two of the people who live in the tunnels." As if in confirmation, the two men lurched to their feet and walked along the tracks toward the mouth of the tunnel. Just before they disappeared from view, one of the men raised his left hand and extended its middle finger.

The gesture was enough to tell them how they could expect to be received by the locals.

They went down a steep ramp to the right. Halfway down Heather paused and pointed to a small tent that had been pitched on a level patch no more than fifteen feet off the path, separated from it by a metal railing. In front of the tent was a rickety-looking table holding a Coleman stove and a chipped enamel dishpan.

A woman clad in a long, mud-stained skirt and a much-mended man's flannel shirt was carefully sweeping the dirt in front of the tent.

Keith felt embarrassed even to watch her attempt at

housekeeping. The woman looked up as they passed, but when Heather smiled at her, she quickly turned away, pretending not to have seen them.

Fifty or so yards ahead they saw Eve Harris. She was sitting on a bench, talking to a woman wearing a paisley skirt, a purple blouse, and a tattered Navy pea jacket. As Keith and Heather approached, the councilwoman rose to her feet, but the woman with her eyed them suspiciously. "These are the people I was telling you about," Eve said to her, reaching out to take Heather's hand and draw her forward. "Heather Randall and Keith Converse. And this," she went on, turning to her companion, "is my good friend, Tillie." She glanced at her watch. "I've told Tillie what you want to talk to her about, and she says she'll listen. But there's no guarantee she can help you. Understood?"

"Understood," Keith agreed.

Apparently satisfied, Eve Harris leaned down, gave Tillie a hug, and kissed her on the cheek. "You take care of yourself now, hear?"

Tillie made a shooing gesture. "Don't you worry 'bout me," she said. "I been taking care of myself more years than I can count." But despite the gruffness of her words, she smiled, exposing a mouthful of ruined teeth. "You stay out of trouble, okay?"

"Don't worry about me," Eve assured her. "I can take care of myself as well as you can take care of yourself."

"Well, if that's the best you can do, you're in trouble. Now get on out of here and let me tend to these two." Tillie's smile vanished along with Eve Harris, and when she turned to survey Keith and Heather once again, her eyes were filled with suspicion. "She said you're lookin' for someone. Who?"

"My son," Keith said, sitting down on the bench beside her. "His name is Jeff Converse."

Tillie pursed her lips, then shook her head. "What makes you think he's in the tunnels?"

"A man named Al Kelly told me," Keith replied. "He saw him going in with a man called Scratch."

Tillie shook her head again. "I don't think so," she said. "No, I don't think I know a thing about either of them."

A girl wearing jeans and a flannel shirt appeared at Tillie's side. She eyed Keith and Heather closely. "They messin' with you, Tillie?"

Tillie shook her head. "It's okay—they're just looking for someone." She reached deep into an inside pocket of her pea jacket, and when her hand came back out, it was filled with money. She shoved it at the girl. "You take Robby shopping after school, okay? Get him what he needs so the other kids leave him alone." The girl took the money, peered at Keith and Heather one more time, then started away. "Jinx?" Tillie called out. The girl stopped and looked back. "You bring receipts, and change. And they better match, too." Rolling her eyes, Jinx darted away, and Tillie heaved herself to her feet. "Better be gettin'."

"But we just—" Heather began, but Tillie didn't let her finish.

"I told you everything I got to say. Miz Harris wanted me to talk to you, and I did. If I was you, I'd go on back to wherever you came from. There's things people like you don't know nothin' about, and never will. That's just the way it is." She turned away and started down the path.

As Heather watched her go, the faint hope that had been flickering inside her for the last few hours was almost extinguished. But when she turned to face Keith, his eyes were alive with excitement. "She knows something," he said, his voice low and intense. "She knows something, but she won't tell us."

"Why shouldn't she tell us?" Heather protested. "If she knows—"

"She's like the rest of them," Keith replied. "The men on the tracks and the woman in the tent. Didn't you hear her?

She said 'people like you.' That's what it's all about—they won't talk to us because we're not like them."

"Then what are we supposed to do?" Heather asked.

"*You* don't do anything," Keith said. "But I get a change of address."

Pushing her wire shopping cart, Tillie walked slowly along the paths of Riverside Park. She wasn't in a hurry—hadn't ever been in a hurry, really. Except when she was young. She'd been in a hurry then. Too much of a hurry. She was going to be an actress, and she'd come to New York when she was eighteen, right out of high school. She got a job as a waitress and started going to auditions, but nobody gave her more than a walk-on. But she kept trying, always certain that in just another year she'd finally get her break. At first it had been fun—she had friends who wanted to be actors and actresses, too, and some of them had actually gotten jobs. One of them was on a soap opera now—in fact, Tillie still saw him sometimes when he and his friends from the show ate picnic lunches in the park. Of course, she never spoke to him, and he'd never recognized her, and that was all right.

The trouble had started thirty years ago, when she was twenty-five. It hadn't seemed like trouble back then: all she'd done was fall in love with a man—not just dated him, but really fallen in love with him.

But he was married, and even though he kept promising to leave his wife, it seemed that every month he had another excuse why he couldn't. He made it up to her in other ways. He paid her rent, and gave her money every week—enough so she could quit her job as a waitress.

She still went to auditions, but most of the time she stayed at home, in case Tony called her or came over.

She stayed at home, and she drank.

Vodka, mostly, because it didn't taste like anything and Tony couldn't smell it on her breath. After a while she didn't go out much at all, and her other friends stopped calling her. But she had Tony, so it didn't matter.

Then one day Tony didn't call her, and when he didn't call her the next day, either, she called him. She must have called a hundred times, but his secretary wouldn't ever let her talk to Tony, so she started calling him at home.

After a while his wife had their phone number changed. That was when Tillie started hanging out in front of the building where he worked, waiting for him to come out. He kept telling her he didn't want to see her anymore, but she knew that wasn't true—that couldn't be true, because he'd always said they were going to get married someday.

When Tony's wife—her name was Angela—made Tony stop paying Tillie's rent and giving her money, Tillie went to see her. She was only going to talk to her, explain how Tony really loved her, not Angela. She only took the knife along to scare Angela with, but the more she talked to Angela, the madder she got, and when the police came, there was blood all over Tony's apartment, and the furniture was all torn up, and Angela claimed it was Tillie's fault.

Angela wasn't hurt—Tillie was bleeding even more than she was, and crying like it was the end of the world, so they'd sent her to a hospital for a while. When they let her out, she didn't have any place to stay, but it was the middle of summer, so that night she slept in Central Park.

The next day she stayed in the park and started talking to people. Pretty soon she made friends—even more friends than she'd had before Tony—and they taught her how to get along without much money. When winter came, she and her friends moved into Grand Central Station. At first Tillie thought she'd get another job, go back to waitressing or something, but as the months passed, she never quite got around to it, and finally she stopped thinking about it. Somewhere along the line—it didn't really matter when—she moved from Grand Central into the tunnels themselves, and the longer she lived under the city, the more she liked it. Of course, she still liked coming to the surface, but it didn't feel safe anymore; the city had changed so much in thirty years. When she was out on a day like today, she tried not to get too far away from her friends. Besides, today she had business to attend to, and as she shuffled along through the park, she kept an eye out for familiar faces.

When she came to Liz Hodges's tent, she left the shopping cart parked on the path, stooped to pass under the railing, and picked her way down to the level area that Liz always kept perfectly swept. Liz, always nervous, nearly jumped out of her skin when Tillie spoke a greeting. "Nobody but me," Tillie added quickly, and Liz's fluttering hand dropped from her throat to her skirt. She could barely meet Tillie's eye as she offered her a cup of coffee.

"I'm almost out, but Burt said he'd bring me some tomorrow."

"No thanks," Tillie replied, knowing that Burt, Liz's husband, wouldn't be likely to bring her anything, since he'd died three years ago. She dug into the inside pocket of her coat and pulled out some more of the money Eve Harris had given her. "Maybe this'll help you out," she said. Almost as an afterthought, she dug into another pocket and pulled out one of the handbills Jinx had brought home the other night. "Better keep an eye out for these two. If you see 'em, just tell any of the fellas. I don't expect they'll get this far though."

Liz nervously took the flyer and studied the two faces, then quickly handed the sheet of paper back to Tillie. "I don't know," she fretted. "I'll try, but you know me—when Burt's not here, I get frightened of my own shadow."

Tillie took the paper back, knowing that if she left it, Liz would worry for an hour over how she was going to get rid of it. She wouldn't dare set it down on her table, for fear that it would blow onto the ground, and she wouldn't be able to put it in her tent, either. Liz had a thing about any kind of litter at all, and having the flyer around her tiny campsite would drive her even crazier than she already was. "Well, don't you worry about it, Liz," Tillie said, automatically reaching out to give the other woman a reassuring squeeze on the arm. When Liz shied away from the contact, Tillie made her way back up to the path. As she retrieved her shopping cart, she saw Liz already busily sweeping away the footprints Tillie had left on the dirt around her tent. "Crazy," Tillie muttered, shaking her head sadly as she shuffled away.

Leaving the park, she headed over to Broadway. She recognized half a dozen people hanging around the subway entrance. Eddie was playing his clarinet, its case open at his feet. Tillie added twenty dollars to it and tucked one of the flyers in his pocket. Eddie winked at her but never missed a note, and Tillie moved on.

Blind Jimmy—whose eyesight was no worse than Tillie's—was just coming across the street, tapping along with his cane and clutching the arm of someone Tillie had never seen before. She moved her cart close to the curb, parking it next to a trash barrel, and listened as Jimmy ran his spiel: "I could sure use a cup of coffee, and maybe a Danish. I think there's a Starbucks in the next block. If you could just—"

But the mark—a man of about thirty, wearing a suit—was already walking away, and a second later Blind Jimmy was casting about for the next possibility. This time it was a woman of around forty, wearing a khaki trench coat. Blind Jimmy sidled up to her. "Is this Seventy-second Street?" he asked. Tillie couldn't hear the woman's response, but a second later she heard Jimmy's voice again. "If you could just help me get across, I'd sure be obliged." This time Jimmy had better luck—the woman gave him a dollar before going on her way. Blind Jimmy didn't wait for the light to turn green, but darted back across the street, which told Tillie he'd cadged enough money for a trip to the liquor store. He spotted her before he got to the sidewalk, and veered toward her. "Hey, Till? What's happenin'?"

"Hunt," Tillie said. She stuffed one of the flyers into Blind Jimmy's hand, along with a couple of bills.

"Ain't never seen one of 'em yet," Jimmy replied.

"Well, just keep your eye out."

"Always do," Jimmy cackled. "Al . . . ways . . . *do*!"

For the next two hours, Tillie walked down Broadway, giving a little money and one of the flyers to everyone she knew, and when the flyers were gone, she started back home. Most of the money Eve Harris had given her was still in her pocket, and she would dole it out slowly, making certain it did the most good. For the next week her family would eat well. The baby would have what it needed, and Robby would have new school clothes. A lot of other people in the tunnels would benefit, too; she would make sure of that.

Wherever she left some of the money, she left the flyer, too.

If this hunt was like the rest of them, it wouldn't last more than a night or two.

Three at the most.

That was the longest anyone had ever survived.

"**W**hat's that?" Jagger asked.

They were walking along railroad tracks, and though Jeff couldn't say why, he was almost certain they were moving south. He'd started counting his steps, too, so he was fairly sure they were about three-quarters of a mile from Tillie's place. They'd taken the first passage they'd come to that led away from Tillie's area and had enough light so they could see. A little while later they'd come to the tunnel they were in now, which had to be a railroad tunnel rather than one of the subways, since it had no third rail. It had been dead quiet, except for their own footsteps and the sound of their breathing.

Now, though, a faint rumbling could be heard.

A rumbling that got louder as they paused to listen.

"Train," Jeff said. He glanced around, searching for a way out of the tunnel, but there was none. In both directions the track simply stretched endlessly away, and there wasn't even a catwalk along the walls. He searched his memory, trying to remember the last time he'd seen one of the alcoves that were sunk into the walls at regular intervals.

Two hundred yards?

Three hundred?

The rumble grew louder. Far in the distance he thought he could make out a dim glow.

Jagger had seen it, too, and as the rumble grew into a roar and the glow began to brighten, he turned and started back the way they'd come.

"No!" Jeff shouted. "The other way! We have to go toward it!"

Jagger hesitated, turning back. "Are you nuts? We don't know what's up there!"

"I haven't seen an alcove for a while, so there should be one not too far ahead." The roar kept building, and then the glow began lighting up the wall to their right. Just before the engine swung so its headlight was aimed directly at them, he thought he saw what he was looking for. "Come on!" he yelled, starting to run into the stream of white light pouring out of the halogen headlight. He hurtled himself directly at the onrushing train, the roar so loud now that he couldn't hear if Jagger responded, and he couldn't risk looking back for fear of tripping over one of the ties. Though he was almost certain it had to be an illusion, the train seemed to be coming even faster now. He tried to keep his eyes on the ground ahead of him, tried to keep his stride perfectly controlled. His instincts screamed at him to run as fast as he could, to use every ounce of his energy to escape the oncoming juggernaut, but he didn't dare. If he increased his stride even a couple of inches, he'd miss one of the ties, lose his footing, and sprawl onto the tracks.

Where was the alcove? What if he'd already passed it?

He had to look up, had to search for it.

The roar was deafening now, and he could feel the floor of the tunnel trembling under the weight of the locomotive. Shielding his eyes with his right hand, he glanced up.

There! Just a few more strides ahead—

And then, as he dropped his hand to his side, his eyes met the oncoming beam of brilliant light and everything around him washed away in a tide of white. Rendered blind, he missed his stride, and a second later the fear of a moment ago became reality as his toe caught on one of the ties. He threw his hands out to break his fall, scraping them across rough wood, then into sharp gravel. His face hit next, and he felt a burning sensation as the skin of his cheek was torn away.

He tried to regain his feet, but with his eyes still blinded by the stab of light, he stumbled and started to fall again.

Stupid!

How could he have been so stupid? He should have gone the other way, followed Jagger. He might have been wrong about how far back the last alcove was. Maybe it hadn't been two hundred yards at all.

But it didn't matter, because the train was almost on him now. Its horn blared and the high-pitched scream of metal ripping against metal pierced his ears as the engineer tried to brake.

Then, just as he was about to go down, he felt something grab him from behind. He was lifted off his feet and almost hurled off the tracks, landing directly in the alcove he'd been trying to reach. A moment later he was crushed against its back wall as Jagger, too, pressed inside. His wind knocked out by Jagger smashing into him, he struggled to breathe as the train—its horn still blaring but its brakes now released—roared by.

By the time Jeff finally caught his breath, it was over. The last of the cars rattled past, and the roar of the locomotive, already muffled by the length of the train, began to fade away. The light on the end of the last car diminished quickly and then was gone.

Still pressed against him, Jagger finally spoke. "You okay?"

Jeff managed to nod, and the big man stepped back enough to give him some room, but not so much that he would fall if his legs failed to support him. Jagger's hands remained on Jeff's shoulders, and Jeff slowly tested his body. His legs seemed to be okay, though his right knee hurt so badly he was amazed that he had no memory of it slamming into something as he fell. The palms of both hands were stinging, and his right cheek was burning badly where he'd scraped the skin from it. But he was alive, and the rumble of the train was quickly dwindling away. "I'm all right," he managed to say. Jagger stepped back out onto the tracks. Jeff followed, his legs trembling so badly he had to steady himself against the tunnel's wall. "I thought you went the other way," he said, his voice shaking almost as badly as his legs.

"I was gonna, but I figured maybe you knew what you were talkin' about," Jagger replied. "Looks like maybe if I hadn't . . ." His voice trailed off, but Jeff knew exactly what his next words would have been.

"I owe you," he said. "Big time."

In the deep gloom of the tunnel, Jagger grinned. "So figure out how to get us out of here, college boy," he said. "You do that, we'll call it even." He glanced in the direction from which the train had come, then back the way it had gone. "Any idea which way we should go?"

Jeff nodded. "I think so. But first tell me if I'm right that before it hit the brakes, that train was speeding up."

Jagger frowned, then nodded. "So what?"

"If we both thought it was speeding up, that means it was coming from one of the stations, right?"

Jagger shrugged. "I guess."

"Don't most of the trains leave the city heading north?"

"How the fuck should I know?" Jagger growled.

Jeff ignored the question. "Because if they do, then at least we know which way we're going." He pointed in the direction the train had gone. Its rumble had almost completely faded away. "If that train was heading out, that way's gotta be north. Pretty soon it'll be running along the river. The tracks come out around Seventy-second Street—we might just be able to walk right out of this tunnel."

They headed in the direction Jeff thought was north, and this time he took careful note of how many paces he took before they came to the next alcove.

One hundred eighty-four.

"I never would've made it," Jagger said softly, and Jeff realized that both of them had been trying to measure the distance. "I guess maybe I owe you one, too."

They kept walking, moving steadily, until they came to the cross passage they'd used earlier.

Neither of them were tempted to turn into it.

A few hundred yards later, Jagger grabbed hold of Jeff's shoulder. "Holy shit," he breathed. "Would you look at that?"

For a second Jeff didn't trust his vision—it had to be a hallucination. But as they took a few more steps, he realized it wasn't a trick of his eye.

There was light ahead.

Daylight.

CHAPTER 23

The familiar beep of the answering machine in Jeff's apartment signaling a message waiting was so unexpected that both Keith and Heather stopped short at the door. Their eyes locked on the machine, the same thought crashing into both their heads.

Jeff!

He'd gotten out of the tunnels and was calling for help and—

And both of them hesitated before they'd taken more than a single step toward the machine. Why would Jeff call here? He couldn't know they were looking for him, let alone that his father was staying in his apartment. The red light continued to blink and the beep sounded again.

"No one knows I'm here," Keith said.

Where a moment ago both of them had been eager to listen to the message, they were now reluctant. Why would anyone call here?

"Probably my foreman," Keith said, but the lack of conviction in his voice told Heather he didn't really believe it. Finally, Heather went over and pressed the button.

"One new message," the impersonal voice of the machine intoned.

"Keith? Are you there? If you're there, you pick the phone up right now!" It was Mary's voice, and the edge on it told Keith his wife was on the verge of hysteria. There was a barely perceptible pause, and then she went on. "I know you're staying there—Vic DiMarco says he hasn't seen you since day before yesterday. You have to be at Jeff's. I don't see how you can stand it, with all his things around you—" She abruptly cut off her own words and Keith could almost hear her struggling to regain control of herself. Then she started over: "There's going to be a memorial mass for Jeff tomorrow. I was going to hold it out here at St. Barnabas, but then—well, I started thinking about how much Jeff loved the city, and how many friends he has there, and how much he loved St. Patrick's. So the mass is going to be there. At one o'clock tomorrow afternoon. I tried to call Heather, but she's not home. I'll keep trying. . . ." Her voice trailed off, and now Keith had the distinct impression she was trying to think of more to say, if for no other reason than to avoid hanging up the telephone. Finally, she spoke again, and now her voice had a flat, defeated quality. "If you get this, please call me back, Keith."

There was a click, and then the computer-generated voice spoke again: "1:52 P.M."

As the machine fell silent, neither Keith nor Heather said anything. Keith reached out and pressed the button that activated the outgoing message on the machine, and Jeff's voice emerged from the tinny speaker. "Hi! You know what to do, so go ahead and do it. I'll call you back as soon as I can!"

They both listened to the message, then Keith shook his head. "I can't erase it. We kept it on all through the trial because we were sure he was coming home. And I'm still sure."

Heather chewed at her lower lip. "What about the memorial tomorrow?"

"What about it?" Keith asked, a note of stubbornness creeping into his voice that told Heather what he was thinking as clearly as any words could have.

"We have to go," Heather said.

"But he's not dead!" Keith's voice began to rise. "What are we supposed to do, sit there acting like he's dead when we don't believe it?"

"I think we need to be there anyway," Heather replied. "If neither one of us goes, how will it look? Everyone else thinks that Jeff is dead, and if we don't go to the mass—"

"I don't give a damn what anyone thinks," Keith cut in. "Going to that mass is like admitting he's dead. I'm damned if—"

Suddenly, all Heather's tension erupted in pure anger. "Why doesn't anyone matter except you?" she demanded. "Don't you care about how anyone but you feels? And it's not admitting he's dead!"

"The hell it isn't!" Keith shot back. "It's not just a mass—it's a funeral mass. It's praying for the dead."

Heather hardly let him finish. "Then don't say the prayers for the dead! Pray that we find him—pray that he's all right—pray for any damn thing you want!" Her eyes fixed on him. "And call Mary. Don't be the same kind of asshole my dad is to my mother!" Shocked by her own outburst, Heather clapped a hand over her mouth for a second, then shook her head almost violently. "I'm sorry," she whispered. "I shouldn't have said that. I mean—"

But now it was Keith shaking his head. "It's okay," he told her, his own anger draining away as quickly as hers. "You're right—no matter what problems Mary and I have, she shouldn't have to go through all this alone." For the first time since they'd come into Jeff's apartment, he smiled. "Actually, one of the main things we fought about was you—Mary always thought you were the best thing that ever happened to Jeff, and as I'm sure you know, I didn't agree. So I guess it turns out I was wrong about that." He picked up the phone and dialed Mary's number. "It's me," he said when she picked up. "You're right—I'm at Jeff's. I'm—well, if I told you what I'm doing, you'd only think I was crazier than you already do."

"You're right," Mary replied. "I don't want to know." There was a short silence. "Just be at the mass tomorrow, all right?"

Before Keith could reply, the phone went dead in his hand.

*   *   *

"I still say it can't be this easy," Jeff said. The patch of daylight had been growing steadily, and now it seemed to be drawing them out of the grim shadows of the railroad tunnel like a magnet.

"Why not?" Jagger demanded, his eyes fixed on the expanse of blue sky ahead. "All they said was we had to get out—that if we could get out we'd be free." He took another step toward the bright beacon, but Jeff's fingers closed on his arm, holding him back.

"It can't be that easy," he said. "They're not going to just let us walk out." Now he had an uneasy feeling that they weren't actually alone in the shadows, that somewhere in the darkness, someone was watching them. He glanced around, but his eyes had already been blinded by the brilliant daylight ahead, and in contrast, the shadows behind him were an impenetrable pitch-black.

If there were people behind them—and he thought he could almost feel them now—he and Jagger would be framed in perfect silhouette against the bright backdrop of the sky. He moved off the center of the track like a creature of the darkness reacting to the dangers of daylight.

But Jagger was already moving toward the light again. Not wanting to lose his companion, Jeff followed him. After another eighty paces or so they could see the mouth of the tunnel. Though there was still a roof over the tracks and a solid concrete wall to the east, the west side of the tracks was open to the Hudson River. To the north they could see the George Washington Bridge, and across the river the wooded bluffs of New Jersey.

"Holy fuck," Jagger whispered. "Will you look at that? We did it, man! We're out!"

Jeff recognized where they were. The southernmost end of Riverside Park was just above them. From what he could remember from the long walks he and Heather had taken through the park a lifetime ago, a high fence separated the tracks from the park itself. It was designed to keep people away from the tracks, and out of the tunnels. A fence that now served to hold them in. But the fence was hardly insurmountable. It wasn't as if they were on Rikers Island, where the prison buildings were surrounded by two fences and a no-man's-land filled with razor wire. Here, there was only a single obstacle, maybe eight or nine feet high. A few strands of barbed wire ran along its top, but he remembered watching a couple of kids slither over the fence one day to retrieve a model airplane that had lost power at the wrong moment. Though one of the kids' mothers had yelled bloody murder at her son, the boy ignored her, scaling the fence with the ease of a chimpanzee climbing the wall of an old cage in the Central Park Zoo. If those two boys could do it, so could he and Jagger.

Yet even as he told himself escape was possible, an instinct told him that something was wrong, that it couldn't be as easy as it looked. From the moment he had tried to help Cynthia Allen on that subway platform, nothing in his life had been easy.

They moved forward again, but Jagger seemed to have been infected by the same unease, and instead of rushing toward daylight, he also moved ahead more cautiously.

The view of the Hudson broadened, and they could smell fresh air from the river. Jeff drew it deep into his lungs, reveling in its sweetness. As the crisp air flushed some of the staleness of the tunnels out of his system, his sense of danger began to diminish.

Perhaps, after all, they were about to escape.

But escape to what? Even if they got out of the tunnels, the police would be searching for them. For him, at least. The guards taking him to Rikers surely would have witnessed his escape.

Unless . . .

What if both the driver and the guard riding shotgun had died when the van exploded?

But even if that happened, the police would have found the van's open back door. And they wouldn't have found his body. They'd know he escaped, and they'd be looking for him.

On the surface, away from the terrible darkness and claustrophobia of the maze that lay beneath the city, at least he'd have a chance. "Maybe we can do it," he whispered, not really meaning to speak out loud.

"Sure we can," Jagger replied. He threw his arm around Jeff's shoulders. "Over that fence, and we're outta here. Come on."

Moving forward, they edged closer and closer to the point where the west wall of the tunnel would end. Ten feet from their goal, Jeff cast one backward glance into the darkness—the darkness he hoped never to see again. "Okay," he said. "Let's go."

Quickening their pace, they emerged from the shadows into the late afternoon sunshine. The fence was right where Jeff remembered it. And on the other side, he saw the softball field, where he'd played a couple of times in pickup games.

Maybe thirty-five yards to the fence—fifty at most.

And then he heard a voice, low and menacing.

Mocking.

"Too bad, boys. Wrong exit."

Jeff spun around to see five derelicts indolently watching them. Their hair was shaggy and unkempt. They wore grease-stained shirts and pants and had moth-eaten knit caps on their heads.

One was sitting on the ground, leaning against a rock. Two more were lounging against the wall of the tunnel itself. Another pair were sitting in faded canvas director's chairs, one of which was missing an arm.

The man who had spoken was holding a gun—an ugly snub-nosed revolver—and pointing it at Jeff. The other four had their hands concealed in jacket pockets, and Jeff was certain that another gun was concealed in every one.

Instinctively, he looked the other way, only to see three more men, dressed as shabbily as the rest, and looking just as menacing.

The softball field was empty, and he and Jagger were shielded from the view of any chance passerby. There was no one in sight except the eight homeless men.

Silently, Jeff and Jagger turned away from the fence and retraced their steps.

A few seconds later the darkness of the tunnel closed around them again.

CHAPTER 24

Something wasn't right with Jinx. Tillie could feel it, the way she could feel it whenever one of her clan was chewing on a problem. But she wasn't about to say anything—not yet, anyway. That was why most of the kids in the tunnels were there—too much yammering from folks who didn't give a damn about them and shouldn't have even had them in the first place. And with a lot of them—including Jinx, Tillie knew—it wasn't just yammering they'd finally run away from. For many, it was a lot worse than that. Not that she ever asked them questions—better just to let them be, listen to them when they felt like talking, and not push them to open up. So instead of demanding that Jinx tell her what was wrong, she went about her business, adding the contents of the bag of groceries she'd found on the table after meeting Eve Harris in the park to the kettle of soup simmering on the back burner. She didn't know who'd left the groceries—it could have been any one of the dozens of people who'd dropped in for a meal over the last few weeks. The groceries certainly weren't what she would have called Class A, which only showed up every now and then, since the wholesale markets were all the way downtown and not much of their goods ever made it this far north. No, this stuff looked like it had come from one of the restaurants—not a real greasy spoon, but not The Four Seasons, either. Maybe one of the places along Amsterdam Avenue. There were some potatoes—barely even beginning to get soft—and a bunch of carrots that had just started to go limp. Some meat, too—and pretty good stuff—a half-eaten filet wrapped up in tinfoil that Tillie suspected had been rescued from a trash barrel down the street from wherever the steak had come from, along with a few uncooked pieces of beef and lamb that were starting to smell. Starting to smell was a long way from inedible, though, and Tillie cut the meat into bite-sized chunks and added them to the soup. By the time the vegetables went in as well, the thin soup was rapidly turning into a pretty good-smelling stew. Nobody would even notice the track rabbit that had been the only meat in the pot before this windfall arrived. After giving the kettle a stir and putting the lid back on, she turned to look at Jinx, who was sitting at the kitchen table, idly leafing through a dog-eared copy of a movie magazine.

"Gonna be a movie star?"

Jinx rolled her eyes. "Yeah, right. The day after I graduate from Columbia."

"You could do that," Tillie said, dropping into the chair opposite her.

"Sure. All I'd have to do is walk in, right?"

"So maybe you'd have to do that test—the one where you get a high school diploma."

"And then take a bunch of other tests, like the SATs, and then figure out how to pay for it. You know how much it costs?"

Tillie shrugged. "Never gave it much thought."

"It's, like, thirty thousand dollars. And that's for, like, one year. Where'm I going to get that kind of money?"

"Work?"

Jinx shrugged. "Where'm I gonna get a job that pays that good?"

Tillie pursed her lips. "So is that what's buggin' you?"

Jinx shook her head, but didn't get up and walk away. That told Tillie she just wanted a little push. "So what is it? A guy?" Jinx started to shake her head, but her blush gave her away. "Aha!" Tillie grinned, exposing the gap in her teeth.

"So who is it?" But even as she asked the question, Tillie remembered the way Jinx had been looking at Jeff Converse that morning, and her grin faded. "Not that guy they're huntin'."

Jinx's expression tightened. "Why not?"

"You know damn well why not—they only hunt the bad ones."

"Well, he didn't look bad," Jinx said. "The big one was scary, but the other one—Jeff—he looked nice."

"Attila the Hun probably looked nice, too."

"Who?"

"Jeez," Tillie sighed. "You really did quit school, didn't you?"

Her eyes turning stormy, Jinx stood up. "And I can quit here, too! I don't have to hang around here, you know. If all you're going to do is bug me—"

"Now that's enough!" Tillie cut in. "You're too smart a girl to be talkin' that way, and I'm just tellin' you what you already know, anyhow. If he hadn't done something really bad, he wouldn't be down here. He ain't like us, and you know it!"

"I don't know anything!" Jinx retorted. "I'm just a dumb runaway, right?" Before Tillie could reply, Jinx grabbed her jacket—one that Tillie had found for her at the Salvation Army two weeks ago—and stormed out.

Jinx made her way through the tunnels easily, following a route she knew as well as the streets on the surface. Twenty minutes later she emerged into Riverside Park and started toward Seventy-second Street. Liz Hodges was sitting on a tiny camp stool outside her tent, but right now Jinx didn't feel like talking to Liz or anybody else. Leaving the park, she headed east on Seventy-second, then ducked down into the subway station on Broadway. Paying no attention to the transit cop who was leaning against the wall, she jumped over the turnstile and skipped down the stairs to the platform, oblivious to the cop's shouting. Coming to the platform just as the doors to an uptown train were starting to close, she wiggled on and perched nervously on the edge of a seat until the train had pulled out of the station—and out of the reach of the transit cop. *Damn Tillie! How does she always know when something's wrong? Sometimes it's like she can look right into my head.* Except that Tillie was only partly right—it wasn't just that Jinx had thought Jeff Converse was cute. There was something else, too.

He just didn't seem like the kind of guy the hunters would be going after.

He wasn't at all like the other guy—the one named Jagger. She hadn't liked that one at all. There was something about the way he looked at her that made her shudder. He'd killed someone, and it had been a woman.

But not Jeff. Jinx had seen a gentleness in Jeff's eyes. And yet everyone knew the men the hunters went after deserved to die—that was the whole thing about the hunt, wasn't it? The hunters were just getting rid of people who should have been executed anyway.

The train slowed to a stop at 110th Street, and Jinx found herself staring at the very spot where Bobby Gomez had mugged a woman last fall. She still wished she hadn't been hanging with Bobby that night, and after she saw what he did to the woman, she did her best to avoid him. He'd said he was just going to grab her purse. That wasn't what it had looked like to Jinx.

It had looked like he was trying to kill the woman, and he'd only stopped beating on her when she called out that someone was coming. She and Bobby disappeared into the tunnel so quickly that she hadn't even been able to tell if it was a cop who was coming down the platform. Not that it mattered—the main thing was that they'd gotten away, and Bobby hadn't actually killed the woman.

From then on Jinx stayed as far away from Bobby as she could, and when she heard he'd disappeared a few days ago, all she felt was relief—one less thing to worry about. But instinctively she still avoided the 110th Street station as much as she could.

Getting off at 116th Street, she emerged from the station on Broadway and crossed the street to the Columbia University campus. Columbia had become one of her favorite places in the city from the moment she'd stumbled across it two years ago. She could wander along its paths for hours, fantasizing about going to classes in its ornate brick buildings. Once, she almost snuck into the back of a lecture hall, but she lost her nerve at the last minute, certain that everyone would know right away that she didn't belong there and throw her out. But they couldn't throw her off the campus.

She was about to pass through the big gate onto the campus itself when she stopped. A few yards down the sidewalk a man was pushing a wheelchair in which sat a young woman.

The woman looked oddly familiar.

And she seemed to be looking back at her.

As the man pushed the woman closer, Jinx suddenly knew. It was the woman from the subway—the woman Bobby Gomez had mugged last fall!

Turning away at once, Jinx hurried through the gates and walked quickly toward the enormous quadrangle in the center of the campus, not daring to look back. If the woman recognized her and called the police—

Wanting to be as far away from the neighborhood as possible, Jinx veered off to the south, broke into a run, and kept going until she exited the campus at 114th Street. She kept going south, so freaked by seeing the woman that she skipped the nearby 110th Street station and disappeared back into the subway at 103rd.

Only when the train had rumbled off into the darkness of the tunnels did she feel really safe again.

*   *   *

The gnawing in Jeff's stomach told him the day had passed, so he knew that even if they found a place where they could peer out of the tunnels, the sight of daylight that had buoyed his spirits earlier would have faded into the semidarkness of a New York night. When the hunger in his belly had first begun to stir hours earlier, he'd simply ignored it—lunch was a meal he never minded missing, and before he was arrested, he'd almost given up eating it at all. But in prison, eating had become something to break up the dull monotony of the days, and though his palate had never grown fond of jail cuisine, apparently his stomach had. The small pangs of hunger he'd experienced a few hours ago had become far more insistent.

As he and Jagger retreated back into the darkness—their eyes still fixed on the tantalizing sunlight that remained out of reach—he'd been certain that they'd quickly find another way out.

There had to be hundreds of escape routes—surely they could find a storm drain emptying into the river, or a shaft leading up to a manhole in a street.

In his memory he could see dozens of gratings in the streets, in the sidewalks, in the parks—all of them leading into the maze of passageways beneath the city. Surely they'd quickly find one. It wasn't possible they were all guarded.

Was it?

Before they'd turned away from the last drop of daylight, they tried to develop a strategy. It seemed simple at the time: the hunters—whoever they were—knew they were on the West Side. So they would start working their way east. Somewhere, they would find an unguarded escape route to the surface.

They'd started east, following the plan, but after an hour, perhaps two, they lost their bearings.

At first it hadn't been too difficult to keep track of their direction—the passages seemed to be laid out on a grid that mirrored the grid of the streets above. They stayed away from the darkest areas and tried to keep to the upper levels, heeding Tillie's words about the increasing craziness of the people who lived in the lower depths. But at certain crossroads their way was blocked by knots of hard-eyed men in gangs large enough to intimidate even Jagger. The fifth time it happened, Jeff was certain that the men weren't simply blocking escape routes, but instead were steering them in a particular direction. They were being herded like cattle.

With the way up blocked, they'd finally had no choice but to burrow deeper, and it had now been hours since Jeff had had any real idea of their location, much less a plan for how to escape.

The tunnels were all starting to look alike—the one they were currently in was lined with pipes and lit every hundred yards or so by a bulb just bright enough to allow them to make their way, but dim enough to leave them deep in darkness most of the time.

Suddenly, Jagger's strong fingers closed around his arm. "Somethin' ahead," the big man whispered softly, so that no echo of his words would betray their presence.

Jeff peered into the darkness and saw what Jagger meant.

A faint, orange glow.

A campfire, perhaps.

They remained where they were, frozen in the darkness, searching the gloom for any movement, straining to catch any sound.

All was quiet.

"Stay here," Jagger whispered. "I'll go see."

"We'll both go," Jeff whispered back. Before Jagger could argue with him, he pulled free from the other man's grip and began creeping toward the glow. It was emanating from the same kind of opening in the tunnel's concrete wall that led to the chambers in which Tillie and her family dwelt.

But how many rooms might there be?

And what kind of people were sheltered there?

When the opening in the wall was only five yards away, they paused again, listening to the faint crackling sounds of burning wood.

Still no voices.

They moved closer, then Jagger darted ahead, crossing in front of the doorway and pressing himself against the wall on the other side.

Jeff started to follow but Jagger raised his hand to signal him to stay where he was. As Jagger's hand rose, a shadow filled the door and a gruff voice said, "Lester? That you?"

Jeff flattened himself against the wall, too late. A form stepped out into the tunnel, and the beam of a flashlight blinded Jeff.

"Who are y—" the voice began, but was cut off in a strangled yelp as Jagger's arm snaked around the man's neck and jerked him backward. As the flashlight dropped from the man's hand and clattered to the tunnel's concrete floor, Jagger forced the man back through the door from which he'd just emerged. Jeff snatched up the flashlight and followed.

It was a small chamber, lit only by the flickering light of a fire burning in a barrel so rusted that large areas of the metal had corroded all the way through. There was some kind of shaft in the ceiling of the chamber, which acted as a chimney, and the draft from the open door was just enough to keep the room from filling with the fire's black smoke. A battered plastic crate served as the only furniture. Filthy blankets piled in one corner appeared to be the man's bed, and an old kettle hanging from a makeshift tripod could be put over the fire barrel for cooking. The pot was steaming, and Jeff assumed the man had just pulled the tripod away from the fire. The smell from the kettle, however, was nowhere near as savory as that produced by Tillie's stove.

Jagger released the man with a shove that hurled him against the wall. He collapsed to the floor and huddled there.

Pulling his knees to his chest, he peered fearfully up at them. His eyes flicked furtively from one to the other, but every few seconds they came to rest on a spot behind them. Jeff turned to see what was capturing the man's interest. In the corner was a large black plastic bag out of which spilled the kind of tattered clothing so many of the city's homeless carried around with them.

"It's mine," the man said, his voice trembling with apparent fear. "Nothing in it. But it's mine—you can't have it."

Jagger's eyes narrowed. "See what's in it," he told Jeff, his eyes fixing on the man.

"No!" the man shrieked. In a lurch, he scuttled across the floor and wrapped his arms protectively around the bag. "You can't have it. It's my treasure!"

"Gotta be somethin' in there, the way he's bawlin'," Jagger said. Reaching down, he peeled the man's arms away from the bag and pulled him away. "Take a look," he told Jeff again.

Jeff hesitated, but the look in Jagger's eyes told him it would be useless to argue. Crouching down, he began sorting through the contents of the bag. A few clothes dropped to the floor, and the man, pinned to the wall by nothing more than Jagger's right arm, whimpered as if he'd been jabbed with a knife. More clothes came out of the bag, and then, hidden beneath them, he found what the man must have been referring to as his "treasure."

Purses.

There were half a dozen of them, mostly the type of small leather clutch bags that women of a certain age carried in the evening. Purses with no straps for their owners to hang on to if someone tried to snatch them out of their hands.

"Mine!" the man howled as they tumbled out on to the floor. "I found them!" His eyes filled with tears and a sob rose in his throat as Jeff started going through the purses.

In the third purse, Jeff found a cellular phone. For a moment all he could do was stare at it, but as he realized what it might mean, his hand began to tremble. He took it from the purse slowly, as if it might vanish before his eyes like a mirage of water in the desert.

Dead, he thought. *The battery has to be dead.*

He flipped it open and pressed the power button. To his amazement, the screen lit up.

The battery meter showed one bar.

The signal strength meter showed nothing at all.

Turning the phone off, he flipped it closed, but instead of putting it in his pocket, he just stared at it.

With the phone, they might just find a way to get help. If they could reach some place where they could get a signal . . .

If the battery didn't die . . .

Part of him wanted to leave right now, to start crawling through the maze of tunnels again, searching for a place where a cellular signal could get through.

A subway station? He was almost certain he remembered hearing someone complain about how weak the signal was in the stations, but if there was any signal at all . . .

But even as the urge to start hunting for some place to use the phone grew in him, another part of his mind told him not to do anything foolish.

They were tired and hungry, and had no idea what time it might be.

If he tried to use the phone and got no answer, he might wind up wasting whatever juice the battery still held.

Better to wait.

When he was rested, fed, and could think clearly, he would figure out how best to use the phone. The man whimpered as Jeff slipped it into his pocket, but he didn't care. Obviously, the man had stolen it, and just as obviously, he hadn't been using it. He was probably crazy enough that he didn't even know what it was for.

He looked into the man's eyes.

"We're going to stay here tonight," he said quietly. "We're

going to eat with you, sleep for a while, and then we're going to leave. We're not going to hurt you." Jeff's voice seemed to soothe the man, and he nodded, wiping his nose with his sleeve. "Let him go, Jagger," Jeff said. "He's not going to hurt anyone."

It was hours later.

They'd eaten their fill of whatever was in the kettle—it hadn't tasted very good, but as far as Jagger was concerned, it was better than the food at Rikers.

Jagger had slept for an hour while Jeff stayed up keeping watch, then Jagger took his place. The guy who lived in the room slept, too. He'd never told them his name—he acted like it was some kind of secret—but Jagger didn't care. He didn't like the guy.

It was the way he looked at Jeff.

He could tell the guy liked Jeff.

Wanted Jeff to stay with him.

Wanted Jeff to be his friend, the way he was Jeff's friend.

But that wasn't going to happen. As soon as Jeff woke up, they were going to leave, and then it would be just the two of them again.

Jagger didn't know whether they were going to be able to use the phone. But if Jeff wanted to try, then it was okay with him—Jeff was pretty smart, and if he thought it would work, it probably would. After all, he'd almost gotten them out over by Riverside Park. If it hadn't been for those guys, they'd already be free.

Free, and looking for a place where they could live.

Once they found a place to live, he would figure out a way to make enough money to take care of them both. Just like he'd taken care of Jimmy before they'd put him in jail.

He stretched, and as his right leg straightened out, his foot touched the sleeping form of the crazy guy who lived there. The man rolled over and one of his arms flopped over Jeff.

As Jagger watched, he moved closer to Jeff, snuggling up against him just like—

Jagger cut the thought off. But he couldn't take his eyes off the man, and a moment later, when he thought he saw the guy pull Jeff even closer to him, he felt the first flashes of anger.

The guy was trying to take Jeff away from him!

But that wasn't going to happen.

His hand went to the heavy railroad spike nestled in the big pocket of his coat.

As the man seemed to squirm up against Jeff, Jagger's hand tightened on the spike.

After that, Jagger wasn't sure what happened. All he knew was that Jeff was suddenly awake, and the other guy was moaning and bleeding.

Bleeding from a big hole in his back.

Jeff was staring at him like he'd done something terrible.

"He was going to hurt you," Jagger said. "I couldn't let him hurt you, could I?"

"Jesus," Jeff breathed, "He wasn't— He—"

A spasm seized the man and blood spewed out of his mouth. Then the fit subsided, and a moment later he fell still.

Utterly still.

Jeff reached out, hesitated, then put his fingers on the artery in the man's neck.

Nothing.

He looked up at Jagger. "He's dead."

Jagger's eyes widened. He hadn't meant to kill the guy— he was almost sure of it. "He was gonna do something to you—" he began, but Jeff was already standing up.

"Let's just get out of here," he said quietly. Quickly, they picked up their things and started out of the room, but just before they passed through the door, Jeff turned and looked back. The man's open eyes seemed to be staring at him, glowing in the reflected firelight.

CHAPTER 25

"**Y**ou better get to gittin' or you're gonna be late for school."

Robby, carefully leaning forward so he wouldn't spill anything on his new shirt—a real new shirt, instead of a used one from the thrift shops—finished his bowl of cereal and eyed the chipped coffee mug in front of Tillie.

"Don't even think about it," Tillie said, not even bothering to look up from the two-day-old newspaper she was reading. "You want to stunt your growth?"

"Come on, Tillie," Robby begged. "Lots of the kids drink coffee. They bring it in thermoses and—"

"And you're not lots of kids," Tillie broke in, trying to fix Robby with a glare, but unable to resist winking at him instead. "Tell you what—one sip, and no more arguments? You go right off to school?"

Robby's eyes widened with disbelief. "Really?" he breathed.

Robby gazed at the mug reverently, almost certain someone would either snatch it away from him at the last second or hit him.

Or both.

Tillie could recall the night Jinx had first brought him to the co-op. He'd been so frightened that she stayed up all night, sitting next to his bed, holding his hand. For a long time, certain that he was going to find himself abandoned on the streets again, Robby had refused to go anywhere, and

when anyone went near him, he flinched as though anticipating a beating. Tillie began to suspect that his parents had
actually done him a favor by abandoning him. When school
had started, at first he refused to go. The only way Tillie could
convince him to take the risk was by promising that someone
from the co-op—someone he knew—would always be on the
sidewalk right outside the school. Half a dozen people had
taken turns that day, and finally the school called the police to
complain about the number of homeless people hanging
around. But Robby had survived the day, and gotten safely
back to the co-op, and soon it was enough if someone walked
him to within a block of the school and met him at the same
place afterward. Everyone in the co-op knew they risked her
wrath if Robby was left alone, even for a minute.

Slowly, very slowly, Robby was starting to trust people
again. Now, as he gazed warily at the steaming mug of coffee,
Tillie pushed it a little closer. "It's okay—it won't bite you.
But it's hot, and you might not like it."

Robby picked up the mug and held it to his lips. As the
liquid touched his tongue, his eyes snapped open and he put
the mug down so fast he almost slopped it down his front.
"Yuck! Who could drink that?"

"I guess not you," Tillie observed, retrieving the mug.
"Now get along with you—you're gonna be late. Jinx, do
something with the boy."

But Jinx, who was sitting across from Robby, wasn't listening. Her eyes were fastened on the torn and stained newspaper that was only partially flattened out on the table in front
of Tillie. Her eyes were focused, in particular, on a picture
that had a moment ago been covered by Tillie's mug.

It was a picture of Jeff Converse.

"Can I see that?" she asked, pulling the paper toward her
before Tillie could answer.

"*May* I see that," Tillie corrected, but Jinx hardly heard her
as she quickly scanned the article:

. . . DIED WHEN A STOLEN CAR RAMMED THE DEPARTMENT
OF CORRECTION VEHICLE IN WHICH HE WAS BEING
TRANSPORTED . . .

. . . SENTENCED YESTERDAY AFTER BEING CONVICTED OF
ATTEMPTED RAPE AND MURDER . . .

. . . THE VICTIM, CYNTHIA ALLEN, CONFINED TO A WHEEL-
CHAIR SINCE MR. CONVERSE'S ATTACK ON HER, HAD NO
COMMENT . . .

. . . APPREHENDED IN THE 110TH STREET MTA STATION . . .

The memory of the woman she'd seen last night suddenly
came back to Jinx.

The woman in a wheelchair.

The woman Bobby Gomez had been mugging when she'd
seen someone running toward them.

It had happened in the 110th Street station!

"This isn't right," she said, not realizing she was speaking
out loud. "He didn't do it. . . ."

"What do you mean, he didn't do it?" Tillie countered.
" 'Course he did it! If he didn't do it, how'd he get convicted?"

"But I was there," Jinx protested. "It was Bobby Gomez!"
She told Tillie what she could remember about that night, but
when she was done, Tillie shook her head.

"Just because Bobby Gomez tried to mug someone don't
mean this guy didn't do nothin'," she insisted, tapping Jeff's
picture with her finger. "Folks get mugged in the subway all
the time—I've seen it happen a dozen times."

"But it's 110th Street," Jinx insisted. "And last night I saw
the woman Bobby beat on—she was in a wheelchair!"

Tillie's expression hardened. "Now you listen to me, young
lady. You're only fifteen years old, and even if you were
right—which you're not—I still wouldn't let you have nothin'

to do with that man." Ignoring the storm brewing in Jinx's eyes, Tillie plunged ahead. "He's gonna be dead by this time tomorrow, and there's nothin' you can do to stop it. Once the hunters are on to someone, that's it! You want to be there when they find him? Now just get on with taking Robby to school, and forget about that guy—I never should've let him in here at all."

Knowing it was useless to argue with Tillie, Jinx shoved the paper back at her. But half an hour later, as she watched Robby walk down the tree-lined block on Seventy-eighth Street toward P.S. 87, she was still thinking about what she'd seen in the paper, and by the time Robby disappeared into the building, she knew what she was going to do.

Jeff couldn't get the image of the dead man out of his mind. Dead, vacant eyes staring at him.

What had happened back there in that tiny room buried deep in the tunnels? What had the man done that made Jagger attack him while he slept?

When Jeff woke up, the room had been illuminated only by the faint orange glow of the dying fire in the barrel, but his eyes—now more accustomed to the darkness beneath the city than the light of the surface—had fixed immediately on Jagger, who was staring down at him with such hatred that his first instinct had been to try to scuttle away. But even as he pressed back into the hard concrete of the wall, he realized that it was the other man—the man who hadn't even told them his name—upon whom Jagger's gaze was fixed.

It was as if Jagger were in some kind of trance. When Jeff had spoken to him, Jagger had barely reacted. He'd remained crouched down, slowly rocking back and forth on the balls of his feet, watching the man die. Only when the man's last rattling breath bubbled from his lips had Jagger looked at him.

The hatred in his eyes had died away, and Jeff saw something else.

Desire.

Jagger's hand had come up—a hand still covered with the blood of the man he'd just killed—and reached toward him. Just before his fingers would have touched his cheek, his hand dropped away.

Then Jagger's eyes cleared and he glanced around the room as if seeing it for the first time. When his eyes fell on the corpse at his feet, he looked puzzled, as if he didn't know what had happened.

"He was gonna do something to you."

But what? The man had been crazy, but he'd been far more terrified of them than they were of him. What had Jagger thought he was going to do? They'd just been lying there, and—

A memory stirred.

Something *had* disturbed his sleep. He'd been dreaming, and in the dream he was back in his apartment, in bed, and he could feel Heather beside him, curled around his back, nestled into him like two spoons in a drawer. Her arm had come around him as she snuggled closer, and—

—and he'd come awake when the man on whose floor he was sleeping grunted in sudden agony as the rusted rail spike sank into him.

Maybe it had been more than a dream of Heather's arm— maybe it was the man's arm wrapping around him that had cued the dream in the first place. And if it was . . .

He remembered again the strange look he'd seen in Jagger's eyes, and Jagger himself reaching out to touch him.

His reverie was interrupted by the sight of glowing light ahead. Not the orange flicker of one of the fires that seemed to burn everywhere in the tunnels, nor the glow of the work lights that illuminated some of the passages near the surface.

No, this was the bright light of the outside.

He picked up his pace, his pulse quickening as the shaft of light grew stronger. They found that the light came from a shaft leading up from the utility tunnel they'd been following ever since they left the body of the man Jagger had killed. Jeff had thought they were still at least a couple of levels below the street, but now he peered up the shaft and saw a large, rectangular grating through which he could make out some kind of wall rising toward the sky. They must not have been as far down as he'd thought. Since leaving the dead man, he'd become more and more disoriented.

"How we gonna get up there?" Jagger asked.

Jeff scanned the walls of the shaft, searching either for the metal rungs that were sunk into the concrete of some of the shafts they'd come across, or for the molded hand- and footholds that marked others. This shaft, though, seemed to be an unbroken expanse of smooth concrete stretching toward the tantalizing grating above. It was set at least fifteen feet above them—fifteen feet that might as well have been a hundred.

"We gotta find a ladder," Jagger said.

Jeff didn't bother to reply. Instead, he was studying the screen of the cell phone he'd found. Holding his breath, he pressed the power button.

The battery indicator still showed only one bar, but the reception indicator showed two. Even as he watched, it flickered to one.

Then back to two.

With shaking fingers he entered Heather Randall's phone number and pressed the Send button.

Her number rang.

Once.

Twice.

Three times.

"Be there," he whispered under his breath as the phone rang a fourth time. "Please be—" His words died on his lips as the phone clicked and he heard Heather's voice: "Hi—I'm really sorry I missed your call, but if you . . ."

The answering machine! The damned answering machine! He waited for the message to end, and finally heard the signal to start speaking.

"Heather? It's me! It's Jeff! Heather, listen carefully. I'm using a cell phone, and the batteries are about to run out. I'm in the tunnels—the ones under the streets—and people are hunting for me. I can't get out and—" He broke off again, knowing how crazy it must sound. Then, as the battery beeped a warning that it was on the verge of giving out, he spoke the only three words that came to his mind: "I love you."

Cutting the connection off, he looked once more at the flickering battery indicator.

Maybe he could get one more call in.

CHAPTER 26

Mary Converse looked at the old woman staring back at her from the mirror. Mary was only forty-one, but the woman she was looking at couldn't have been a day under fifty-five. Gray was showing in her hair—hair that seemed to have become thinner overnight. Her eyes were puffy from lack of sleep, and a cobweb of wrinkles spread out from their corners. Her complexion looked distinctly unhealthy, like that of a heavy smoker, even though she'd smoked her last cigarette the day she found out she was pregnant with Jeff.

Jeff.

The vision in the mirror shimmered as her eyes filled with tears.

How was she going to do it? How was she going to get through this day? How was she going to sit in St. Patrick's Cathedral and say good-bye to her only child?

Be strong, she told herself. *The Lord will never give you a load too heavy for you to bear.* But she'd already been on her knees most of the night, praying for Jeff's immortal soul, begging every saint she could think of to intervene with God on her son's behalf. Her fingers were stiff from counting the decades of the rosary, and her knees were so sore that she wasn't even sure she'd be able to genuflect as she entered the cathedral.

But still she'd kept praying, begging for a sign that Jeff's sins had been forgiven and that he'd died in a state of grace.

None had come.

Taking a deep breath, Mary turned on the tap, soaked a washcloth in cold water, and wiped away her tears. *God helps those who help themselves,* she reminded herself. Stripping off her bathrobe and nightgown, she turned the shower on full force—and ice cold—then took a deep breath and stepped in. The freezing spray made her gasp, but she resisted the temptation of hot water and began scrubbing away the exhaustion of her sleepless night. After two minutes she could stand it no longer. Shivering, she shut off the water, stepped out of the stall, and wrapped herself in a bath towel.

The face that looked back at her from the mirror looked a little better: at least her complexion wasn't quite as sallow. Half an hour later, her hair dried and arranged into a tight French twist, dressed in the same black suit she'd worn to her mother's funeral five years ago, she surveyed herself one last time. Maybe—with the help of God—she'd get through the day.

And then the phone rang.

The sound so startled her that she almost dropped her cup, barely avoiding having coffee splash down the front of her suit. She set the cup on the counter as the phone rang again, and as she reached for the receiver, glanced at the little screen displaying the caller's identification.

The number on the display meant nothing to her.

She glanced at the clock: not even seven-thirty yet. Why would someone she didn't know be calling her at this hour?

The phone rang a third time. She knew she shouldn't answer it—she'd gotten the phone with caller ID to combat a stream of crank calls during the trial.

The phone rang again, and then the answering machine picked it up. After she heard her own voice inform the caller that she couldn't come to the phone, another voice, badly garbled, began to speak.

A frantic voice, shouting into the machine.

". . . Mo—are you . . . it's me, Mo—"

Mary's hand jerked away from the phone as if she'd been

stung. But as the words sank in, an incoherent cry rose in her throat and she snatched up the receiver.

"Who is this?" she asked. Her voice rose. "Who are you?"

The phone at the other end crackled, cutting in and out, but between the gaps of silence, she heard a voice: "Mom, it . . . me . . . I . . . dead . . ."

"Jeff?" Mary breathed. "Jeff? Is that you?"

The other phone crackled a couple of more times, and she thought she heard the voice again. Then there was nothing but silence.

For almost a minute Mary kept the phone pressed to her ear, willing the voice at the other end to speak again, but the silence only dragged on, and finally she put the receiver back on the cradle. As the impossibility of what she'd heard slowly sank in, she tried to tell herself that it hadn't happened, that she'd only imagined she heard the words, only imagined she recognized the voice.

Almost against her own will, she picked up the receiver again and dialed *69. She pressed the phone against her ear, listening.

There was a click at the other end, and then a voice spoke.

An automated voice.

"This is your last call return service . . ." She listened to the recorded message, then pressed 1 to have the calling number dialed.

Another automated voice came on the line. "The cellular subscriber you are calling is either out of range or—"

Cutting the call short, she tried calling the number twice more; twice more the same message was repeated.

At eight o'clock, when she could no longer put off leaving for the city, Mary tried the number one last time.

Nothing.

It wasn't him, she told herself as she left the apartment. It couldn't have been.

But even as she silently repeated the words, she recalled the sound of Jeff's voice.

*   *   *

Carolyn Randall woke earlier than usual that morning, and her first impulse was to roll over and go back to sleep. She and Perry had been to a party the night before—a party where she had met three movie stars as well as her favorite fashion designer—and her head was pounding with a hangover that was far worse than she deserved. All right, maybe she had one extra drink last night, or even two, but she hadn't been drunk, no matter what Perry said. Through the headache that felt like a jackhammer pounding at her skull, she could still remember Perry's words when they'd finally tumbled into bed at two-thirty: *"I have no use for a wife who gets a reputation as a drunk, Carolyn. I can survive another divorce—but if your drinking costs me the nomination when Morgenthau finally retires, I'll not only get rid of you, but see to it that you don't get a nickel. So make up your mind—go along for the ride without the booze, or take the money and get out now."* She'd felt like spitting in his eye. He sure hadn't talked like that five years ago when he found out what sex with someone like her was like instead of that old society prune he'd been married to at the time. But she also wasn't about to take a hike right now. So she hadn't argued—instead she'd given him the kind of blow job that could fix any argument they might have, and insisted that she wasn't drunk. Which meant that this morning, no matter how much she wanted to, she couldn't go back to sleep. Since Perry hadn't awakened yet, she'd get up now, make sure the useless maid had his breakfast ready when he got up, and pretend she felt fine, just as she had pretended to enjoy having sex with him all this time. So instead of rolling over, she rolled out of bed, padded into her bathroom, and turned on the shower. Before stepping in, she peered into the mirror.

And didn't like what she saw.

The first hint of wrinkles was starting to show around her eyes, and she thought she could even see some of those terrible little lines women who smoke get on their lips. She'd better start talking to the wives of some of Perry's old friends—God knew, they'd all had enough work done that they would know the best plastic surgeons in Manhattan. Fifteen minutes later, just as Perry was starting to snort himself awake in that way she considered disgusting, she headed for the kitchen and the coffeemaker. She decided that as soon as she heard Perry cough up the load of phlegm that always accumulated in his throat overnight, she'd bring him a cup. He'd be so happy she'd thought about him that he'd forget all about last night.

She was passing the door to the library when she saw the blinking light on the answering machine on Perry's desk. She hesitated, frowning. The light hadn't been blinking last night when they came home, which meant that whoever called must have called very late, or very early this morning. Since nobody ever called her or Heather this early, she knew the message must be for Perry, and it must be urgent. If she picked up an important message and passed it on to him right away, he really would forget about last night's little tiff. She went to the machine and pressed the Replay button, not noticing that it was Heather's voice-mail light that was blinking, not Perry's.

The voice she heard cleared the last of the alcohol from her bloodstream and made her headache vanish. "Heather?" Jeff Converse's voice asked through a crackling of static. "It's m—"

Then there was a series of broken fragments of his voice:

"It's Je—, —Heather, list—, —cell phone—about to run out—, —under the streets—, —hunting for me. I can't get out, and—"

There was a long silence, then she heard three more words: "I love you."

The message ended with the machine's impersonal voice announcing the time it had been received: 7:18 A.M.

For a moment Carolyn hesitated, uncertain whether she should even tell Perry about the message—he had an absolute *thing* about listening to other people's messages. And besides, it couldn't possibly be from Jeff Converse. He was dead—she'd heard it on the news and even read it in the paper. It had to be some kind of cruel prank someone was playing on Heather.

She knew Heather would be upset by it, and if Heather got upset, then Perry would, too. And if he got upset, he might remember he was already mad at her about last night. Better to tell him and let him decide what to do.

Five minutes later Perry was standing beside her in the long Charvet robe she'd given him for Christmas last year, listening to the message. She watched his eyes narrow as the voice spoke his daughter's name. As the message went on, his complexion—never the kind of George Hamilton tan that Carolyn found really sexy on a man—turned deathly white. Then the color came back into his face, and the vein that always stood out on his forehead when he got angry started throbbing.

He was even angrier than Carolyn had thought he would be, and she braced herself for the tirade she was certain was about to crash down on her. But when the recording was over, he said nothing at all. Instead, he hit the Replay button and listened to it again, and then again.

"Well?" Carolyn finally asked, unable to control her anxiety any longer. "Do you think it really could be him?"

"Of course not," Perry snapped, his voice cold with fury. "Converse is dead, so obviously it's not him. It's just someone's idea of a sick joke. The question is, who did it? Because when I find out—"

"Well, if it's not Jeff, it doesn't matter, does it?" Carolyn cut in, hoping to find a quick way to soothe her husband before he turned on her. "Why don't we just erase it? There's no reason why Heather should even have to hear it!"

Perry didn't even glance at her. "Just fix me some coffee," he said. "I'll take care of this—and I'll find out who did it."

Carolyn wasn't tempted to argue with him, having long ago learned that even when Perry was wrong about something, he wasn't willing to lose an argument.

"It's what makes me a good D.A.," he'd once told her. "I don't give a damn whether the bastards are innocent or guilty. My job is to win my cases, and I nearly always do."

"But what if the person didn't do anything?" Carolyn had asked.

The contempt in Perry's eyes when he answered her had made her feel ashamed of even asking the question. "If they didn't do anything, they wouldn't have been arrested," he told her. "The police aren't fools, you know." And that had been the end of it. So now, as Perry continued glowering at the answering machine, Carolyn scuttled out of the room, closing the door behind her, anxious to be out of the line of fire.

As soon as she was gone, Perry Randall picked up the phone and dialed a number from memory.

"We've got a problem," he said. "And we need to solve it today."

Hanging up the phone, he erased the message for his daughter.

The endless night was over, but Keith felt as if he'd hardly slept. After Heather left, he'd alternated between sprawling on Jeff's Murphy bed and standing at the window, peering out into the not-quite-dark of New York City. The traffic thinned as the hour grew late, but there were always a few taxis still cruising along Broadway, and a scattering of bar-hopping night owls meandering down the sidewalk.

Twice, when the walls of the apartment seemed about to close in on him and suffocate him, he'd almost gone out himself.

Sometime around four-thirty he'd finally fallen into a fitful sleep, and now, as he rose four hours later, he knew he would get no more sleep that night.

And he knew what he was going to do.

First he rummaged around the apartment and found a phone book. He leafed through it until he found the heading for thrift shops and scribbled down the addresses of three of them that looked like they weren't far from the apartment. Then he picked up the phone and dialed Vic DiMarco.

"It's me," he said. "I need a big favor, and I don't need any questions."

"You don't even have to ask," DiMarco replied.

"I want you to go over to my house. There's a locked cabinet in my office—the key's in my desk, in the second drawer on the right, in a little box way in the back."

"Gotcha," DiMarco said. "What's in the cabinet?"

"A gun," Keith Converse said. "It's a .38 automatic. I want you to bring it to me."

CHAPTER 27

Jinx glared up at the closed door, willing it to open. Curtailing her urge to give it an angry kick, she turned away and retreated back to the steps where she'd been sitting off and on for the last two hours. She would have been sitting on them the whole time if Paul Hagen hadn't kept running her off.

That was pissing her off, too. The first time the cop had come by, she'd tried to explain to him that she was just waiting for the library to open.

"Yeah, right, Jinx," Hagen had said, rolling his eyes. "So what's the game now? Gonna start lifting from the old geezers in the reading room? Give me a break!"

Jinx had kept her temper in check. The last thing she needed right now was for Paulie Hagen to start hassling her. If he really got pissed off, he could keep her at the precinct for most of the day, filling out a bunch of forms and making her talk to the welfare people. So she just shrugged his sarcasm off and walked away, heading over toward Madison Avenue. She knew Paulie couldn't follow her that far, and since she hardly ever went to the East Side, most of the cops over there didn't know her. She was mad enough at Paulie that she'd picked a mark, bumped into him, and lifted his wallet so smoothly that all the sucker had done was mouth an apology to her while he kept on talking on his cell phone. Probably wouldn't notice his wallet was gone until he tried to pay for his lunch, and by then he wouldn't even remember that someone had bumped into him. That was the great thing about cell phones—they distracted people enough so that most of the time they thought they'd bumped into her instead of the other way around.

She kept drifting back to the library at the corner of Fifth and Forty-second, hoping they might open it early this morning, but knowing it wouldn't happen. She killed some of the time watching tourists taking pictures of each other with the lions that crouched in front of the building. Then she glanced through a *Daily News* that someone tossed into the trash can on the corner. Twice she had to cut across the street when she saw Hagen coming down the block from Bryant Park. Why couldn't he stay over in Times Square where he belonged?

At least now she wasn't the only one waiting—half a dozen people were standing around. A white-haired guy in a suit that looked even more ancient than he did kept checking his watch, and a nerdy guy was pacing back and forth, looking nervously down the street toward Bryant Park.

Flasher, Jinx thought.

When the man bolted like a jackrabbit just as Paulie Hagen reappeared, Jinx was sure she was right.

Just as Hagen spotted her and headed over to run her off the steps again, she heard the lock behind her click and the heavy metal door finally swing open. Giving in to what she knew was a childish impulse, Jinx stuck her tongue out at Hagen, then turned and dashed into the vast lobby of the library. Off to the left two women stood behind an information desk. As Jinx started toward them, one of the women looked up. Her smile faltered as she took in the shabbiness of Jinx's clothes, and for a second Jinx wondered if she was going to get kicked out of the public library. "Where would I go if I wanted to look something up in an old copy of the *New York Times*?" she asked.

"How old?" the woman countered. "We have them back to 1897."

"Just last fall," Jinx replied. "Maybe October?"

"Room 100," the woman said. She pointed to Jinx's right. "Down there, take the first left, and it's the last room on the right. They'll be in the microfiche filing cabinets."

Not exactly certain what the woman meant, Jinx made her way down the corridor, found the room, and went in. Several large blocks of filing cabinets occupied most of the space just inside the door, and beyond them Jinx could see a lot of tables supporting machines with large screens. The white-haired man in the moldy suit was sitting down in front of one of the machines, and Jinx watched carefully as he took a roll of film out of a box, put the reel on a spindle, then fed the film under some kind of roller.

If he could do it, so could she.

She headed for the filing drawers and saw they were labeled with dates. She found the ones for the previous fall in Cabinet 41, pulled it open, and stared at the row of film boxes, each one marked with a precise span of dates. Picking up three of the boxes, she closed the drawer and headed for one of the machines.

Taking the first reel out of its box, she put it on the spindle, fumbled with the leader for a few seconds, then managed to poke it under the roller and glass. When the end came out on the right side, she threaded it into what looked like some kind of take-up reel, then started fiddling with the controls. There was a knob on the right side, and when Jinx twisted it, the reel instantly rewound, leaving the leader flapping. She swore under her breath, rethreaded the leader, then carefully twisted the knob the other way. The film spun forward and stopped, and Jinx began fiddling with a focus wheel until the print cleared enough for her to read easily. But the print was displayed on the screen sideways, so she had to twist her neck painfully to read it. Just as her neck was starting to ache really badly, a hand appeared over her left shoulder, twisted a wheel she hadn't seen, and the page on the screen flipped ninety degrees.

"Thanks!" Jinx said, turning to see the old man in the worn

suit smiling at her. "I figured there had to be an easier way, but . . ." Her voice trailed off as she glanced toward a man behind the counter who was making no effort to hide his resentment that someone like her would even dare to come into his precious microfiche room.

"Don't worry about him," the old man said. "He doesn't like anybody." His eyes shifted to the screen in front of Jinx. "What are you looking for? Maybe I can help you find it."

Half an hour later, after the old man had shuffled back to his own reader, Jinx reread the report of the attack on Cynthia Allen and the arrest of Jeff Converse one last time. She'd recognized the photograph of the victim at first glance—it was the woman she'd seen in the subway station the night Bobby Gomez had almost killed her, and then again at Columbia.

And there was no question that the Jeff Converse who'd been arrested was the man she'd met in the co-op.

Which meant that every word she'd just read—and then reread three times—was wrong.

Jeff Converse hadn't attacked Cynthia Allen.

And he wasn't dead.

At least not yet.

Leaving the last of the articles still glowing on the screen, Jinx got up and quickly left the library.

CHAPTER 28

*I*t wasn't Jeff, Mary Converse told herself again as she emerged from Grand Central Station into an incongruously bright morning.

It couldn't have been Jeff.

Jeff is dead!

The words had become a mantra, her lips now forming them as unconsciously as they formed the words of the prayers she'd been reciting every day for as long as she could remember. Yet this was not the mantra of a prayer, for in prayer she had always found hope and solace.

Even though the words she'd heard on the telephone only a few hours ago should have made her heart swell and her spirit soar, the reality of two days ago was still fresh in her mind. Every time she recalled the words—the broken phrases uttered by a voice that tore at her heart—the pain only grew worse.

"... Mo—are you ... it's me, Mo—"

"Mom, it ... me ... I ... dead ..."

But she'd seen his body, seen her son lying in a drawer in the morgue.

She'd also heard her husband deny that the body was Jeff's. She hadn't believed Keith, of course—hadn't been willing even to accept the possibility that a mistake could have been made. He'd been in a guarded van on the way to Rikers Island—how could there have been any kind of mistake?

But as she strode across Forty-sixth Street toward Fifth

Avenue, and the broken voice kept echoing in her head, she suddenly stopped.

What if Keith was right and it had *all* been a mistake?

What if Jeff's arrest had been a mistake?

What if his trial had been a mistake?

What if his conviction had been a mistake?

But that wasn't possible—God wouldn't have allowed such injustice to occur.

". . . it's me, Mo—"

As she turned onto Fifth Avenue, the cacophony in her head—a jumble of echoing words and conflicting emotions—threatened to overwhelm her. By the time she passed through the massive doors of St. Patrick's Cathedral, every nerve in her body was on edge. She paused at the font, dipped her fingers in the water and genuflected, and the vast, quiet space of the cathedral began to calm her. Though there were people all around—tourists taking pictures, a scattering of penitents on their knees in the pews and in front of the shrines—the immense structure reduced their voices to a soothing murmur. The peace she had always found in church began to calm her nerves and still the chaos in her head.

The Lady Chapel.

That was where Father Benjamin had told her the mass would be held. *"It's at the far end of the cathedral—intimate, very beautiful."* As she walked down the long aisle on the left, past the display cases documenting the history of the cathedral, past the niches holding icons of the saints, her fragile sense of peace grew stronger and more certain, until finally the voice she'd heard on the telephone—the voice that couldn't possibly have been Jeff's—was silenced. As she passed the altar, the thunderous opening chords of Bach's D Minor Toccata and Fugue suddenly resounded through the cathedral, the tones so deep that she could feel them as much as hear them.

At last she came to the end of the aisle, turned left, and found the Lady Chapel opening before her like a tiny jewel box.

There were only twelve rows of pews, divided by a single aisle. The chapel was dominated by a large statue of the Holy Virgin, her face tilted slightly downward so her eyes seemed to focus on the pews themselves. The statue had been carved from white stone, and the altar beneath it was white as well.

The pews were empty, and for a moment Mary had a terrible feeling that something had gone wrong—that she'd told people the wrong time, or that perhaps she was in the wrong place. But then she glanced at her watch and understood.

She was nearly two hours early.

Should she leave? But if she did, where would she go?

She genuflected once more, then slipped into a pew and dropped to her knees, ignoring their painful protest.

She was dimly aware of the voices of a boys' choir somewhere behind her, resonating through the vast chamber of the cathedral. Clasping her hands before her, she gazed up into the eyes of the Virgin Mother.

Is this how you felt? she silently asked. *Is this the pain you felt when you watched your child die on the cross?*

Her eyes filled with tears, and the statue before her blurred. But as she continued to gaze into the face of the Mother of God, the image seemed to smile at her. It was a soft, gentle smile that finally dispelled the last of the torment that had gripped Mary ever since the phone rang early that morning, and now, as the voices of the singing boys soared in the background, another voice whispered in her head.

Believe . . .

Mary stiffened, her fingers tightening on her own hands until her skin was as pale as the stone of the statue upon which she gazed. Her vision cleared, and the face of the Virgin once more came into focus. Now her eyes seemed to be fastened directly on Mary Converse's own, and her smile held a cast of mystery.

Believe, the voice whispered inside her head. *Believe . . .*

As the voice once again fell silent, the last notes of the

choir died away, and a calm such as Mary had never before experienced washed over her.

Then, as if it were coming from somewhere far, far away, she heard another voice.

"It's me, Mom," the voice whispered.

Jeff's voice, unmistakable now.

"I'm not dead, Mom.

"I'm alive. I'm alive. . . ."

As Jeff's voice faded into silence, Mary rose from her knees and sank onto the pew. She gazed up into the placid face of the Virgin, studied the perfectly carved stone. The eyes no longer seemed to be staring directly into hers and the smile had lost its mystery, but the words she'd heard still rang in her head. Finally she answered them with words of her own.

"It's the sign I've been waiting for," she whispered to herself. "I do believe. . . ."

Rising to her feet, the pain in her knees and the exhaustion in her body forgotten, Mary Converse hurried back the way she'd come and burst through the doors of the cathedral. She raced down the steps and yanked open the door of the first cab she saw. "Broadway," she said. "The corner of 109th."

Tillie was starting to wonder if something had gone wrong. She'd been sitting in the park for almost an hour and a half—she'd asked half a dozen people what time it was, and even though three of them hadn't even acknowledged that she was there, let alone given her the time of day, the other three had all agreed that it was almost eleven. She was sure it was Saturday, too, and not only because there were more people than usual in the park, but because she'd checked the date on a paper a man on the next bench had been reading.

So if it was the right day, and the right time, then where was Miss Harris?

Tillie was sure she hadn't made a mistake—she wasn't half crazy, like Liz Hodges. Besides, it had only been yesterday that she'd seen Miss Harris, and she'd said to meet her right here—on the same bench—at nine-thirty. Tillie had made sure not to be late, too. Not because Miss Harris would have been mad at her—she never seemed to get mad at anyone— and not because of the money, either. Tillie made sure she wasn't late simply because she knew Miss Harris was a busy woman—even busier than most of the surface people seemed to be—and she just plain liked her. Being on time was the least she could do.

Until this morning, Miss Harris had never been late.

Still, Tillie was prepared to wait all day if she had to. It wasn't as if she had anything else that needed doing. Besides, it was a nice day, and there hadn't been many nice days since last fall, when it got too cold to be outside at all, and she'd have to retreat into the tunnels for the winter.

Like a bear going into hibernation, she thought to herself. Maybe that's what she'd turned into—an old bear that curls up for the winter. The thought left her chuckling out loud, but a young couple pushing a baby carriage gave her a look that made the laughter die on her lips. That was the one thing Tillie hated about living the way she did—she could always tell that most people thought she was crazy. She was won-dering if maybe she ought to have some fun with the couple by acting really crazy, but then she saw Jinx walking briskly down the path, a combative look on her face.

"You said the hunters only went after criminals," Jinx said, her voice tight, her eyes glittering with anger.

Tillie frowned. What was the girl talking about? "Well, of course they do."

"Not this time," Jinx said, her voice rising.

"You want to tell me what you're talkin' about, or you just want to stand there yellin'?"

"Jeff Converse," Jinx said. Her voice was still rising, and as Tillie recognized the name, she glanced around. Nobody seemed to have heard Jinx, at least not yet, but you didn't talk about the hunters on the surface—in fact, most people didn't talk about them at all. Tillie grabbed Jinx's arm. "Now you just calm down," she said, scanning the area in one final search for Eve Harris. With no sign of her, Tillie decided not to wait any longer and started walking toward the river, her hand still clamped on Jinx's arm, steering her along the path.

"Let go of me," Jinx complained, trying to shake Tillie's arm loose.

But Tillie held fast, and a few minutes later they had skirted around the baseball diamond that lay on the shelf above the river and pushed through a nearly invisible hole cut in the high fence separating the park from the railroad tracks. More than a score of men were scattered around the weed-choked area, wearing the numerous layers of clothing that marked them as homeless. Mostly they were sitting in groups of two or three, but a few were standing like sentries, their backs to the rotting concrete columns that supported the highway, almost like a parody of the guards at Buckingham Palace.

Tillie nodded to most of the men as she steered Jinx past them, even spoke a few words to two of the sentries. It wasn't until the gloom of the railway tunnel had swallowed them up that she spoke to Jinx again.

"Now you tell me," she said, her eyes fixed on the girl. "What are you talking about?"

"He didn't do it!" Jinx said, her voice quivering with anger.

"Who didn't do what?" Tillie demanded. "What are you talkin' about?"

"The guys that came to the co-op—the ones you kicked out yesterday morning?"

Tillie's expression darkened. "What about 'em?"

"I don't know about the big one, but the other one—Jeff Converse?—he didn't do anything."

"You said that to me this morning, but that's not what it said in the paper."

"I know what it said in the paper. I know what it said in all the papers, 'cause I went down to the library today and read them. And guess what? They're wrong! I told you, I was there. I saw what happened that night. That guy was trying to help her. It was Bobby Gomez who did it. He was muggin' her, and the other guy got off a train."

Tillie only shrugged. "Even if you're right, it don't make any difference now—the hunters are already after him. He's as good as dead."

"Not if he gets out."

"But he ain't gonna get out," Tillie countered. "None of 'em get out."

Jinx took a step back from Tillie. "None of 'em ever had any help."

"What are you—" But before she finished the question, Tillie understood what Jinx intended to do. She reached out to grab the girl, but Jinx was too fast for her. Darting out of Tillie's reach, she went deeper into the tunnel, quickly disappearing in darkness. "Jinx!" Tillie called out. There was no reply, and a few seconds later she watched the girl's dark shadow pass through the pool cast by one of the dim lights fastened high on the tunnel wall. "You come back here," Tillie hissed. "Even if you find them, all that'll happen is the hunters'll kill you, too!"

But Jinx was running now. Tillie could hear the sound of the girl's pounding feet blending with the fading echo of her own words.

A moment later even those sounds died away and the tunnel fell silent.

Perry Randall sat at the desk in his walnut-paneled library overlooking Central Park. His desk faced the window, and the curtains were wide open, allowing morning sunlight to flood the room. Had he paused to appreciate the view, he would have seen the profusion of color that momentarily filled the park as the spring flowers entered their full, brief glory.

But Perry Randall had not looked out the window—indeed, since he'd heard the message intended for Heather, he had been on the telephone. He'd called half a dozen people, and when no one had been able to provide him with an answer to his question, he'd instructed them to meet him at eleven o'clock that morning. "At the club," he told them. Though he was a member of four clubs scattered around Manhattan, including the Bar Association, the Metropolitan, and the Yale Club, everyone he called knew that he meant The 100 Club. Over a century old, to its members it was simply "the club," and to those outsiders who knew of it and hoped to become members it was "The Hundred."

To everyone else, it was entirely unknown.

The Hundred had been formed with a single purpose in mind: to provide a private retreat for the hundred most powerful people in the city with no regard whatsoever to gender, race, or religion. The petty snobberies and bigotries of the better-known clubs that were spread across the city were abjured by every member of The Hundred, at least when it came to fellow members. Far smaller than Perry Randall's other clubs, The Hundred still occupied the nineteenth-century brownstone at 100 West Fifty-third Street which had been built to house it, and little else had changed during the years since its creation. Since the membership would never expand, there had never been a need to move. Recognizing that the tides of power would inevitably shift over time, the charter of The Hundred provided that five percent of the membership be dropped every five years, and a new five percent elected. The policy ensured that there were never any senile old folks dozing away their days in the members' lounge, and that no matter what happened, the power brokers of the city— whoever they might be—would have a place to meet in complete privacy.

Today, if it somehow had been Jeff Converse's voice he'd heard on the telephone, Perry Randall was going to need that privacy to deal with the situation that had suddenly arisen. Obviously, someone had made a terrible mistake, and that mistake would have to be rectified. As the ornate, heirloom Seth

Thomas regulator on the wall softly chimed the half hour, Randall closed the file on his desk—a file that contained every scrap of information relating to Jeff Converse's case, every page of which he'd reviewed again that morning—and placed it in his briefcase. Though he'd found nothing in it that seemed relevant to today's problem, one couldn't be too careful.

As he rose from the desk, he couldn't help pausing at the window to gaze at the park spread out below. A park that was, thanks to him and his friends in The Hundred, a safe place to walk once more. Much in the city had changed in the years since Perry Randall had been elected to The Hundred. The crime rate had dropped dramatically. The murders and muggings that had been so commonplace only a decade ago had all but disappeared.

The subways—though he himself never rode them—had been cleaned up.

The panhandlers that had choked the sidewalks and train stations were all but gone.

Much of that had happened, Perry Randall knew, because of the policies he and the other members had developed in the privacy of the club. Unwritten rules for the city had been decided upon, and if the public had not had a hand in forming them, everyone had certainly benefited from their implementation. The city had changed for the better more quickly than even the members of the club could have hoped. But obviously, in the case of Jeff Converse, something had gone wrong.

He was just opening the hall closet to choose a coat when the door from the far wing opened and Heather appeared. They were both surprised, and Perry tried to think of something to say, but it was Heather who broke the uncomfortable silence.

"I don't believe it," she said, her voice strained with tension. "You're really going?"

The question confused him, but his years in the courtroom and at the negotiating table kept his features from showing it.

Had she heard the message on the answering machine? That was impossible—if she had, she would have come to him right away, insisting that he use every connection he had to find out if somehow Jeff might possibly still be alive. Besides, Carolyn had told him the new message light was flashing when she'd listened to the message, and he'd erased it himself right after he listened to it.

"Is it such a crime for your father to go to the club?" he asked, cocking his head in the manner that had always brought her running into his arms when she was a child.

Today she made no move to come any closer.

Then, as he noticed the simple black dress she was wearing, he understood. "Jeff's funeral?" he asked, injecting just the right amount of concern into the question. "I'm— well, I'm afraid I didn't know." He hesitated, then shifted down a gear. "Nobody told me," he added. If she felt any of the guilt he'd intended her to feel, she gave no sign of it, and it occurred to him—not for the first time—that if she set her mind to it, she could be nearly as good a lawyer as he.

"I didn't really think you'd want to go," Heather replied. "Given the way you treated Jeff—"

"I didn't *treat* Jeff any way at all," he cut in, for once letting his aggravation show. "All I was doing was my job. And despite my personal feelings, I made it a point to remove myself from Jeff's case completely. I built a firewall between me and that case, Heather, and you know it. Now, I can't help the way I feel, but you have to understand that I did nothing—nothing at all—to influence the trial. It was the jury who decided Jeff's guilt, not me. And I have to tell you that the way you keep holding it against me—"

"It's not just the trial, Daddy," Heather cut in. "It's everything. You always treated him like a servant, and—" Abruptly, she stopped and glanced at her watch. "What does it matter now anyway?" she asked. "I don't really want to talk about it anymore, and if I don't go, I'll be late."

Perry held the door open for her, and after hesitating a moment, she stepped through. "Where is the service?" Perry asked as they rode down in the elevator.

"St. Patrick's. It was Jeff's favorite church. He loved the surprise of it in the middle of midtown. He said it was some of the finest architecture in the city."

"If you like that sort of thing, I suppose it's good for its kind. But I'm afraid I've always found it a bit . . ." He paused, then shrugged. "Well, I suppose what I think doesn't really matter, does it?" Heather offered no reply, and neither of them spoke again until they were on the sidewalk. "Can I drop you?" he asked, nodding toward the black Lincoln Town Car waiting by the curb, its driver holding the door open for him.

She shook her head. "It's such a nice day, I think I'll walk."

As the car pulled away from the curb, Perry Randall realized that even though Jeff Converse was no longer a part of Heather's life and would never be a part of her life again, she still had not forgiven him for failing to leap to the boy's defense. As the Town Car settled into the stream of traffic moving down the avenue, he tried to relax in the knowledge that sooner or later Heather would have to forgive him and they would return to the nearly perfect relationship they'd had before she fell in love with Jeff Converse.

After all, the boy had been proven guilty beyond a reasonable doubt, and eventually Heather would realize that. Besides, as far as she was concerned, Jeff Converse was already dead.

And in a few more hours, he undoubtedly would be.

•

CHAPTER 29

"Why don't you just tell me, okay?" Jinx said, struggling not to turn away from the steely gaze of the man who was staring down at her with the hardest eyes she'd ever seen. She'd never had any trouble staring people down before, but this man, whom she'd never seen before and already hoped she'd never see again, was different. She wasn't sure how old he was; he could have been twenty, or could just as easily have been forty—maybe even forty-five. She'd found him in the Seventy-second Street subway station, lounging against the wall at the far end. She'd known right away he was one of the herders, even though he was doing his best to look like he didn't have anything better to do than hang out in the subway. But if he hadn't been a herder, he'd have been sprawled out on the platform, probably holding tight to the brown bag that sat between his feet—no wino Jinx had ever seen let the bottle leave his hand, much less sit unguarded on the floor while he was standing up. The knife had most clearly given him away. Jinx spotted it right off, clutched in his right hand, only partly hidden by the ragged denim vest that he wore over a dirty flannel shirt with torn-off sleeves. Once she pegged him as a herder, she'd walked right up to him and asked him if he'd seen the two guys in the hunt.

He'd just stared at her blankly, like he didn't know what she was talking about. She hadn't realized how big he was until she was right in front of him. Now he towered over her, the

238

thick muscles of his tattoo-covered biceps rippling every time he flexed them, which she knew he was doing just to impress her. Well, screw him—she'd been on the streets way too long to be impressed with big muscles and small brains. She held her ground and her gaze never wavered. "Come on, what's the big deal?"

The man's lips pulled back to reveal his rotting teeth, and his glazed eyes told her he'd gotten hold of some drugs not very long ago. She wondered if Lester and Eddie were dealing again—if they were, Tillie'd kick their asses out for sure. But if the man was stoned, he was a lot more dangerous than he'd be if he was straight, or just drunk. His eyes finally shifted away from hers and raked over her body.

Sizing her up.

She saw him glance down the platform, checking out the crowd, and she steeled herself, knowing that if he was really junked up, he might try to rape her right there. Ready to spring away if he made a move toward her, she tried once more. "Look—all I'm supposed to do is find out if they tried to get out through here. So what do I say? That you were too fucked up to see?" The man tensed, and for a second Jinx thought she might have gone too far. But a second later the gamble paid off.

"One joint," the man snarled. "All's I had was one fuckin' joint." But even as he spoke, his right hand moved to cover the barely scabbed tracks on the inside of his left arm.

"So what about it?" she asked. "Did you see 'em or not?"

"What the fuck business is it of yours?" the man countered, but the aggression in his voice had given way to a faint whine.

"You got your job, I got mine. So what's the big fuckin' deal?" Her confidence restored, Jinx's eyes locked onto the man again.

"I ain't seen 'em," he said, his eyes shifting to the subway tunnel as if he expected them to come walking out of the darkness. Jinx was about to turn away when the man said, "But I heard they tried to get out over by the river yesterday."

The whine in his voice was more prominent, and then Jinx understood. He was scared of her now. He didn't know who she was or who she might be working for. But he knew exactly what would happen to him if he fucked up—the hunters would turn on him, and instead of having an easy source of the cash he needed for whatever he was shooting, he'd be running in the tunnels himself. She turned back to face him again. Suddenly, he didn't look nearly as big as he had a few moments ago, and the hard, empty glaze in his eyes had given way to a nervousness that told Jinx the junk was starting to wear off. The sweat that broke out on his forehead confirmed it.

"Like I care what happened yesterday," she said, seizing the opportunity. "What they want to know is where they are now."

The last of the man's junkie confidence crumbled. "I don't know—I'm tellin' you, I don't know nothin'." Then, as if searching for something, anything, that might make Jinx say something good about him to whomever she was working for, he said, "They found Crazy Harry this morning."

Crazy Harry? Who was he? She had never heard of him, but she said nothing, certain that her silence would be enough to keep the man talking. Sure enough, he started up again. "He was in his room, down near where Shine's bunch hangs out. Someone cut him last night." His voice dropped. "The guy that told me said it looked like they jammed a railroad spike in him." The man's head shook from side to side as if he could hardly believe what he'd heard. "Who'd do a thing like that? Shit, Harry was crazy, but he never hurt no one. Why'd anyone want to cut him up?"

But Jinx had stopped listening.

A railroad spike. The guy with Jeff Converse—Jagger, that was his name—had carried a railroad spike.

"Where'd he live?" she asked.

"Who?" the man countered.

"Crazy Harry!" Jinx replied. "You said he lived down near Shine. Where's that?"

The man shook his head. "How do I know? Down below somewhere—down where all the crazies live."

"How do I get there?" Jinx asked.

Now the man's eyes changed again, turning suspicious. "Thought you just wanted to know about them guys the hunters are after."

He started to reach for her arm, but with instincts honed by years on the streets, Jinx spun away before his huge hand closed on her. Flipping him the bird, she darted toward the stairs and was halfway up to the surface before the man had even moved. By the time she got to the surface, she knew exactly where she would go next.

Sledge.

She'd known Sledge almost as long as she'd known Tillie, and if anyone would know where this guy called Shine lived, he would. Sledge talked to everyone, and everyone talked to him.

Emerging into the afternoon sunlight, she headed north, abandoning the tunnels, at least for a while.

The man called Sledge thought he was somewhere around seventy years old, though he wasn't quite sure and he didn't really care. His real name was Charles Price, but he hadn't used it for so long that if someone had spoken it, he probably wouldn't have responded at all. He'd grown up in West Virginia, and after a year in the coal mines had decided that there had to be more to life than breathing dust and dying young.

As it turned out, that wasn't quite true.

For a long time he drifted from one job to another, always managing to drink his way out of them. Finally the day came when there were no more jobs, and Sledge found himself on the streets. It wasn't much of a comedown, since the free flophouses and missions weren't much worse than the rooms he'd been paying for. Then one night someone tried to roll him in one of the missions—it was the third time—and Sledge decided he'd had it. That was when he started looking around for a better place to live, and discovered the tunnels.

He started out in a nest on one of the catwalks above the tracks under Grand Central, using the washrooms to clean up and doing some panhandling in the huge waiting room. But the transit cops kept giving him a hard time, and finally he migrated north. For a while he lived in a really weird place—a little forgotten subway station that he'd stumbled into one night when he was really drunk. He'd thought the walls were all paneled with wood, and it hadn't looked like any subway station he'd ever seen before. He'd passed out, of course, but when he awoke the next day it turned out he hadn't been hallucinating at all. There really was paneling on the walls, and a grand piano on the platform, and a crystal chandelier hanging from the ceiling. If he'd kept his mouth shut about it, he might still be living there, but he told too many people, and one night some people from the surface showed up, and the next time he tried to get in, it was all locked up. He'd heard it was part of some kind of museum now, but wasn't sure and didn't care.

He just moved farther north.

He lived under the park now, in a railroad tunnel that was hardly used at all anymore. He'd started out in one of the cubbyholes dug into the walls, but when someone moved out of one of the work bunkers, he moved in. He'd added some worn carpet, a little furniture he'd found on the sidewalks—thrown out even though it wasn't in half bad condition—and hung some pictures on the walls. He'd found a barrel to use for a cooking fire, and stuck it under one of the big grates above the tracks—right outside his bunker—so he had skylights and ventilation, and most of the time it wasn't bad at all. When it turned out he was a pretty decent cook—folks said he could make track rabbit taste just like the real thing—other people started showing up, sometimes with food, sometimes not. If they had food, Sledge threw it on the barbecue, and if they didn't, he shared whatever he had on the grill. Now there were seven chairs around the barrel, and it seemed like people were coming and going all the time. Somewhere along the line Sledge had quit drinking—he hadn't thought about it, couldn't even remember when it happened.

Now, he was on his third or fourth barbecue barrel and thinking it might be getting time to start looking for a new one. On a day like today, with a brilliant blue sky overhead—far brighter than the sky over West Virginia had ever been when he was a boy—and sunlight streaming through the grated skylight overhead, Sledge thought life had turned out pretty good after all. He had lots of friends, and his friends knew they could count on him. He was always home, his fire was always lit, and pretty much anyone was invited to sit down and have a bite to eat. When he saw Jinx coming down the tracks, his smile widened. "Hey, young lady, what's a nice girl like you doing in a place like this?" He flipped over a piece of chicken that looked to be done just about right, transferred it to one of the mismatched but not too badly chipped plates that someone had just washed, and held it out to her. "Just in time for some hot lunch."

Jinx took the plate, and when she told him she was trying to find out where Shine lived, his smile faded. "You don't want to be goin' anywhere near those folks."

"I'm lookin' for someone," Jinx replied.

"You're lookin' for trouble if you go lookin' for Shine. How come you want to find him?"

"It's not him—it's one of the guys the hunters are after."

The last of Sledge's smile faded. "You ain't messin' in that, are you?" He glanced around, but even though they seemed to be alone, he still dropped his voice. "Them guys the hunters go after are even worse'n Shine's crowd."

"But one of the guys they're after didn't do nothing," Jinx protested.

Sledge's brows arched. He'd never met anyone in the tunnels

who didn't have some kind of hard luck story about how they got there, and not one of them ever admitted it might be their own damned fault. With the young kids, there was probably some truth to their tales, but he figured the rest of them were just making up excuses. "Bet he told you that himself, didn't he?" Jinx shook her head and told him what had happened. "So what happened to this Bobby Gomez guy?" he asked when she was finished.

Jinx spread her hands dismissively. "Gone."

"Well, if I was you, that's what I'd be, too. Gone out of here, gettin' myself a job, and gettin' my ass back in school. And I sure wouldn't be messin' in nobody's business except my own, especially the hunters'."

"All's I was askin' was where Shine—"

"Don't you be pushin' me, young lady," Sledge said. "I ain't tellin' you nothin' at all, you hear?"

"I was just—" Jinx began again, but before she could say anything else, a new voice called out.

"Hey, Sledge. You hear about Crazy Harry?"

Jinx turned to see two men coming down the tracks. One of them was a Puerto Rican tagger who spent most of his time spraying murals on the walls of the tunnels. She didn't recognize the other man.

"What about him?" Sledge asked as the tagger dropped a bag on one of the chairs and started pulling out groceries.

"Got himself killed last night down under the Circle."

The men kept talking, but Jinx had already stopped listening. The Circle had to be Columbus Circle. All kinds of subways came together around there, which meant there were bound to be a lot of herders. If she was careful and asked the right questions . . .

As Sledge and the two other guys kept talking, Jinx finished her piece of chicken, left the empty plate on the table, and slipped away. She headed south down the tracks, then made her way through a maze of utility tunnels and passages until she came to a shaft Robby had found that came up behind a utility building in the park. Leaving the park, she headed to Cathedral Parkway and the MTA station.

As she rode south a few minutes later, she glanced around the car, sizing up the crowd for an easy lift. But it was the wrong time of day—rush hour was best, when the cars were so crowded that even if someone felt her trying to pick a wallet out of a pocket or a purse, they wouldn't be quite certain who'd done it. The arrival of a transit cop in the car put an end to her reconnaissance, and she settled onto a seat.

The cop, recognizing Jinx, decided to stay in the car, too.

As the train rattled through the tunnel and pulled into the station at 103rd Street, Jinx waited for the cop to get up and move toward the door.

He didn't.

At Ninety-sixth Street Jinx stood up, and so did the cop.

Neither of them got off.

At Seventy-second Street, Jinx got off the car, then got back on.

So did the cop.

Jinx moved to the next car, the cop following her.

From his own seat a few yards away, Keith Converse—on his way to the memorial mass at St. Patrick's—watched the interplay between the cop and the girl. As far as he could tell, the girl hadn't done anything wrong.

She didn't look like a prostitute, and she didn't look like a juvenile delinquent. She just looked . . .

Homeless.

Homeless, and vaguely familiar.

Or was it that she looked like so many other girls he'd seen in the city, not only here in the subway, but downtown as well? He must have seen dozens of girls who looked just like this one during the months when he'd visited Jeff in jail. A lot of them had been there for the same reason he was: visiting someone.

Sometimes, rarely, it was a brother or a father.

Far more often it was a boyfriend or a pimp.

The ones who weren't dressed in the miniskirts and tight blouses that were the uniform of the prostitute had usually been wearing the same kind of worn shirt and jeans the girl on the subway wore today. If not for the strange interplay between her and the transit cop, Keith might not have noticed her at all.

At first, he'd assumed that the cop was going to arrest her. But when nothing happened, and the cop simply countered every one of the girl's moves with one of his own, Keith began to suspect that the girl hadn't done anything at all.

That the cop was just hassling her.

Why? Simply because he could?

He began paying more attention, and by the Seventy-second Street stop, he was sure he was right. If the cop had been intending to arrest the girl, he would have done it by now.

When he glanced around the car and saw that no one else was paying any attention to what was going on, he told himself that the other people were right, that it was none of his business, and that he was probably wrong anyway—maybe the girl was a criminal and the cop knew her.

A criminal? he repeated to himself. *What am I thinking? She can't be more than fifteen, for God's sake!* He took a closer look at her and realized she didn't much resemble the dozens of other down-on-their-luck kids he'd seen. For one thing, her eyes didn't have the glazed look of a junkie, and there was nothing about her to suggest she was a prostitute.

And he was almost certain he'd seen her before.

Then it started to fall into place.

She'd gotten on at 110th Street, where he'd gotten on.

Only a block away from Riverside Park, where Eve Harris had introduced him to the homeless woman on the bench yesterday.

There'd been a girl there. A girl wearing a flannel shirt and jeans, who'd asked Tillie if he and Heather had been messin' with her. The homeless woman had given her money and told her to go away.

Preoccupied with Tillie, he hadn't paid attention to the girl. But now, studying her face, he was almost certain this was the same person.

When the girl moved to the next car and the cop immediately followed, Keith moved to the back of his own car so he could watch them through the windows. Though he'd intended to ride the train on down to Fiftieth Street, he got off at Columbus Circle, following the cop and the girl.

He walked toward the stairs, certain that the girl would hurry out of the station, but instead she stayed on the platform, moving across toward the uptown side, peering down the tracks as if looking for a train. The cop lounged against a pillar, his eyes still on the girl.

A few people milled around on the platform, some taking the stairs toward the surface, just as many coming down to the platform.

The girl seemed utterly disinterested in anything except the tracks. A couple of minutes later an uptown train came in. The doors opened and the girl stepped on.

So did the cop.

Keith glanced at his watch. He still had an hour before the mass was supposed to begin, plenty of time to walk over to Fifth and down to St. Patrick's, or even catch the next train down to Fiftieth. But if he headed back uptown . . .

The mass could happen without him, he decided. Right now it was more important to talk to the girl. He dashed toward the train, but was still a few yards away when the doors started to close. He broke into a sprint and was about to thrust his arm between the closing doors when the girl suddenly slipped back out onto the platform.

The doors finished closing and the train pulled away.

The girl flipped her middle finger at the cop, who was now glaring at her from the departing train and talking into his radio. Then she turned and almost bumped into Keith.

"Jeez!" she said. "Can'tcha watch where you're goin'?" She started to push past Keith, but he put out a hand and held her arm. Her eyes locked on his. "Don't fuck with me, mister," she warned.

"I just want to talk to you for a second," Keith said, speaking so fast his words almost ran together. "I saw you in the park yesterday. With a woman named Tillie?"

The girl frowned, then nodded. "Yeah. You were with a girl. Kinda young for you, isn't she?"

"She's not—" Keith began, then shrugged. "Way too young," he agreed. He reached into his pocket and dug out his wallet, flipping it open. The girl recoiled.

"Shit! You're not a cop, are you?"

"God no! I'm—look, just take a look at this picture and tell me if you've ever seen this guy, okay?"

"Why should I?"

Keith pulled out a five dollar bill. "Will this help?"

The girl hesitated, then took the five dollars and glanced at the photograph. Her eyes widened. "How come you know him?" she asked. "You don't look like one of them."

"One of who?"

The girl hesitated. "Tell me how you know him."

Keith took a deep breath. "I'm his father," he said. "The police told me he's dead, but I don't believe it. I've heard he's in the tunnels." His voice broke, pleading. "All I'm asking is if you've seen him."

Jinx looked up into Keith's face, marked with obvious signs of tension and worry.

She could see the same strong line in this man's jaw that she'd seen in Jeff Converse's yesterday morning. Scanning the platform without seeing anyone who looked like a herder, she finally nodded. "I've seen him," she said. "He's down here. They're after him."

Keith stared at her. "After him? You mean the police?"

Jinx shook her head. "The hunters. They—" Abruptly, she

fell silent. Two transit cops were coming down the stairs, taking them two at a time. "Shit," she muttered. "That asshole called his buddies." Whirling away from Keith, she dashed down a short flight of stairs. Keith followed her, only to see her take a second flight, deeper into the station. By the time he reached the lower platform, she seemed to have vanished, but a moment later he spotted her. She was on the tracks to the right of the platform, and as Keith watched, she headed toward the mouth of the tunnel. In the distance he could hear a train coming.

"Wait!" he shouted. "What's your name?"

For a second he wasn't sure she'd heard him, but then she turned. "Jinx!" she called. As the roar of the train grew louder, she darted into the tunnel. The cops arrived just as the train sped into the station. A few people got off and on. The doors closed again, and the train began moving, gathering speed as it lumbered into the same tunnel that had swallowed Jinx a moment ago.

"Which way'd she go?" one of the cops demanded. "The kid in the jeans and flannel shirt?"

Without even thinking about it, Keith shrugged. "Don't know," he said. "By the time I got down here, she was gone."

The cops grunted and headed back toward the stairs, but Keith stayed where he was, staring into the tunnel. The train had vanished, its rumble fading away.

What about Jinx? he wondered. Had the train crushed her as it raced down the tracks? No, if it had hit her, surely it would have stopped, so she must have survived, must somehow have gotten out of its way. His first impulse was to jump down onto the tracks himself and follow her into the darkness. Then he remembered how he was dressed.

And that the gun Vic DiMarco had brought in from Bridgehampton was still sitting on the drawing board in Jeff's apartment.

Swearing silently at himself for having agreed to go to the

mass in the first place, he climbed the stairs back to the upper platform, punching Heather's cell-phone number into his phone as he went. "Tell Mary I couldn't make it to the mass," he said through the static when Heather answered. "I—" He hesitated, then decided that Heather, at least, had the right to know what he was going to do. "I'm going home to change my clothes," he said. "Then I'm going to find Jeff."

Giving her no chance to argue, he cut the connection and jumped aboard an uptown train.

Heather had been at Fifty-ninth Street when she received Keith's call. Instead of crossing the street, she turned around and ran the seven short blocks back to her building. Less than five minutes after telling the doorman to get her a cab, she was back in the lobby, clutching a paper sack full of the items she thought she'd need—or at least what she had been able to grab in the two minutes she was inside the apartment. Getting into the back of the waiting cab, she gave the driver Jeff's address, then prayed she wouldn't be too late.

As usual, Perry Randall paused across the street from the 100 Club, taking a few seconds to admire the building. From the outside, of course, there was nothing to reveal the power of its members, power they wielded not only in New York City, but far beyond. They whispered into the ears of the chairmen of the huge financial conglomerates that had swallowed up the small banks that had once been the nation's— and the world's—banking system. They stood behind the heads of the oil cartels that controlled the energy industry and the media giants that controlled the communications empires.

The Hundred was composed of those whose faces might not often appear in newspapers or on television, but whose influence exceeded that of senators or presidents.

These were the people who gave politicians their instructions, subtly and politely.

Perry Randall remembered the first time he had stood

across the street from The Hundred, before crossing Fifty-third Street, mounting the short flight of limestone steps, and letting himself in the front door. No doorman stood in front of the building to greet members, open the door for them, or hail them a cab. He'd already known there wouldn't be a bell to ring or a knocker to lift, for the door to The Hundred—at least the outer door—was never locked.

That, at least, was the legend, and on that first day, he had found no reason to doubt it. Despite the momentous occasion, his nerves that evening had been as steady as they had been the week before, when a heavy, cream-colored envelope had arrived on his desk. His name and address were written on the face of the envelope by a calligrapher. He'd assumed it was a wedding invitation until he flipped the envelope over and saw the return address discreetly engraved on the flap:

100 WEST FIFTY-THIRD STREET

There had been no identification of the city—certainly no zip code—but Perry Randall knew there was no necessity for one.

None of these particular cream-colored envelopes had ever been sent beyond the confines of Manhattan, or entrusted to the postal service. And none ever would be.

The following Thursday night, he had arrived at The Hundred as an elected member.

There was nothing extraordinary about the building, really. It could have been almost anything—a private home, a consulate, even the office of a small law firm. The ground floor facade was dominated by two large Palladian windows, discreetly shuttered. Between them was a large door carved out of a single slab of mahogany.

No knocker.

No bell.

Simply the number 100 engraved on a perfectly polished, small silver plaque.

The Hundred neither wanted nor received any publicity.

The people who passed it on the street never gave it a second glance.

Today it looked as it always had, and its simple facade gave Perry Randall the same feeling that had filled him the first time he had studied its understated grace.

The proper people were in charge; the world was under perfect control.

Or, he reminded himself, it had been under perfect control until Jeff Converse had left a message on his answering machine that morning.

Taking a deep breath of the spring air, Randall strode across the street, mounted the steps, and pushed open the great mahogany door. He paused in the small foyer between the outer door and the inner door, allowing the first to swing closed before opening the mahogany-framed glass panel that led to the club's main lobby.

In keeping with the facade, the lobby could have been the entrance hall of any well-to-do Edwardian family home. It bore none of the pretensions of the Vanderbilt or Rockefeller monstrosities farther uptown, all of which boasted entry halls of such grand vulgarity that only their owners could have admired them. Here at The Hundred the main lobby contained a discreet desk behind which the club manager usually sat, a large closet in which the members hung their own coats, a board upon which each member's name appeared, along with a peg to designate him or her "In" or "Out," and a small board commemorating the handful of members who had died before failing to be reelected.

Perry Randall's deepest, most secret wish was that his name would one day be added to that list.

Hanging up his coat, he went directly into the members' reading room. The men he had telephoned that morning were all present.

Arch Cranston leaned against the mantel, swirling a brandy that Perry Randall knew would eventually be left somewhere in the club, untasted. If Cranston's mind would be dulled by anything, it wouldn't be alcohol, but he'd long ago discovered the advantage to be gained by inducing others to have a drink or two.

Carey Atkinson, whose outstanding work heading the police department seemed unimpeachable by anyone, was chatting with Monsignor Terrence McGuire, who was not only in charge of Montrose House, but kept files on far more than half of the Vatican's College of Cardinals as well. In the current pontiff's failing years, McGuire had devoted considerable time to discussions with The Hundred about which cardinal might best serve as the next head of the Catholic Church.

The others in the room were of less visible influence than Cranston, Atkinson, and McGuire, but were no less important to the functioning of the club.

When Perry Randall walked into the room, the level of conversation diminished. Approaching the group, he wasted no time with greetings or preambles.

"Jeff Converse has gotten his hands on a cellular phone," he said, his baleful eye falling on Cranston, who held a controlling interest in one of the largest of the wireless networks.

Arch Cranston didn't bother to respond directly. Instead he merely lifted an eyebrow. "Perhaps we should go downstairs."

Less than two minutes later the entire group had descended two staircases, taking them deep beneath the portion of the brownstone that the membership usually visited. At the bottom of the stairs there was another door, cut from the same slab of mahogany as the building's front door. But here, the three engraved numbers of the front door had been replaced with three letters:

M H C

Perry Randall rapped three times on the door, and in seconds it swung wide open. Malcolm Baldridge stepped back, and bowed.

As they filed through the door, each member of The Hundred's truly elite admired the new trophy that Baldridge had mounted on the wall.

The eyes were bright—far brighter than they'd ever been during life.

The cheeks were ruddy—the picture of good health.

The smile was far more genuine than any offered in the years before he met the men who were now gathered around him.

Perry Randall gazed up at the perfect example of the taxidermist's art that was exhibited in their latest specimen. "Excellent work, Baldridge," he said warmly.

The Manhattan Hunt Club was now in session.

CHAPTER 30

"What time you think it is?"

Jeff suspected the question was motivated only by Jagger's desire to break the silence they had fallen into, since the time of day was no longer relevant to either of them. Long ago, Jeff had stopped trying to estimate what hour of the day or night it might be. His stomach told him when it was time to eat, his mouth and throat when he needed water, and his muscles and brain when he needed rest. They'd all been complaining for the last . . . what? Hour? Maybe two? Five?

With an effort, Jeff banished his speculation, reminding himself that it didn't matter. All that mattered was that the emptiness in his stomach had turned into a gnawing hunger demanding to be fed, that his mouth and throat had become so dry he had difficulty swallowing, and that his muscles—deprived of both food and water—would soon rebel.

He had no idea where they were. After the cell phone had failed, he tried to keep track of where they were going, at least in relation to the shaft with the tantalizing rays of daylight shining down through it.

After the last bar of the cell phone's battery indicator had flickered away, along with the rest of the display on the screen, they had gone in search of something to use as a ladder. When they found a utility tunnel, Jagger thought they would find some kind of storeroom. "They gotta work down here, and they gotta have tools. And what are they gonna do—drag ladders

255

down every time they need one?" Jagger's grip on the rail-road spike—still stained with blood—tightened in anticipation of using it to pry open whatever lock might secure a door that Jeff didn't think they would find.

He hadn't bothered to argue that if the shaft they'd located all those hours ago existed to provide access to the tunnel, then surely any work crew using it would lower a ladder from the top to get down, rather than pushing one up from the bottom to get out. His own hope was that if they didn't find a ladder, they might find something else—a pole, or a discarded section of track—anything that might help them lift the grate and climb to the surface. Better to take some kind of action than to wander aimlessly through the gloom.

It happened that in their search for ladders they'd come to a railroad tunnel, a wide one, which Jeff was fairly sure ran under Park Avenue. Eventually the tunnel widened into the vast track yard of Grand Central Station. That was where they'd found the ladders. Bolted to the walls, they led up to a maze of catwalks, and above the catwalks they could see glimmers of daylight shining through grates far overhead.

At first the yawning space seemed to be devoid of people, and the two men felt cautiously hopeful as they moved to the foot of one of the ladders. But as they started climbing, Jeff in the lead, he'd become aware that the catwalk above him wasn't deserted at all. Two faces were peering down at him. Hard, unshaven faces—the same kind of faces he'd seen on the men loitering near the river when he and Jagger had emerged from the tunnels. Jeff paused on the ladder, and when one of the men looming above smiled down at him, he felt a flicker of hope once again.

Then the man opened his fly, and a moment later a hot, stinking yellow stream stung Jeff's eyes. If Jagger hadn't caught him, he would have fallen ten feet to the rock-covered ground at the ladder's foot. Raucous laughter from above burned in Jeff's ears as Jagger got them both safely off the ladder.

"Fuckers," Jagger muttered as Jeff wiped his stinging eyes with a filthy sleeve. Though Jagger's voice was low, it was choked with fury. "Just let me get my hands on one of 'em. . . ." His voice trailed off as he scanned the catwalks, and he shook his head. "Bastards are everywhere—what the fuck do they want? If they're gonna kill us, why don't they just go ahead and do it?"

Jeff knew the answer to that. "Because it's a game." He gazed up at the faces leering down at him. "They're not here to kill us—all they want to do is keep us here." He felt Jagger's hand tighten on his shoulder, and his own fist clenched as some of the other man's rage flowed into him. "But they can't be everywhere. Somewhere, there's a way out—there's got to be. So let's find it."

The sound of laughter followed them as they headed back the way they'd come, then chose a passage leading to the right. Jeff was right about their location, they were heading toward the East River. But soon they came to a fork in the passage, then another and another, and at some point he realized that he no longer knew in which direction they were headed.

In another few yards they might find the Lexington Avenue subway, or be back on the tracks beneath Park Avenue. As their bodies inexorably consumed their small reserves of food and water, all hope began to fade. Finally, minutes or hours later, they found an alcove in the tunnel just large enough for both of them to sprawl out in, and decided to rest.

Jeff fell asleep, and when he woke up, he felt Jagger's arm curled protectively around him. He remained perfectly still for a moment, but the ache in his back from lying on the hard concrete finally compelled him to move. That movement awakened Jagger, whose arm momentarily tightened around Jeff. But a second later the big man, too, had come fully awake, sitting up and pulling away from Jeff almost as if he were embarrassed that their bodies had come together, even in sleep. Now, as they both sat up and tried to stretch the chill and stiffness from their limbs, the same thought occurred to both of them, though it was Jagger who spoke it out loud.

"We don't find some food pretty soon, we're gonna starve to death." He stood up and spoke again without looking at Jeff. "Which way?"

"Left," Jeff said. "At least it's someplace we haven't been yet."

They set out along the tunnel, and a hundred or so paces farther on, they came to an intersection. Off to the right, barely visible, a shaft of something like daylight seemed to be glowing, and they started toward it.

As they came closer and the light grew brighter, they heard sounds from above.

Real sounds, the sounds of the city, not the dripping of water and rumbling of trains that were the constant background noise of the tunnels. Now they were hearing the sound of car horns and the drone of automobile engines. They reached the pool of light and looked upward.

A grate, and beyond that, a patch of brilliant blue sky.

And a ladder! An iron ladder, bolted securely to the concrete wall of the shaft, its lower end reaching within two feet of the tunnel's floor, its top appearing flush with the grate that was all that lay between them and freedom.

They gazed at the ladder as if it were the Holy Grail and might vanish before them if they tried to touch it. Finally, Jagger reached out, his hands grasping the vertical rails.

He jerked hard, testing the ladder.

It was as real and solid as it looked.

While Jeff waited below, Jagger started climbing toward the light.

Fritz Wyskowski hadn't been expecting anything to happen at all. When Blacky had come up to him early that morning, stuffed a bunch of money into his hand, and told him that all he had to do was keep an eye on the grate and make sure no one came out of it, Fritz figured the money would keep him drunk for a week at least. And it would have, too, if only he weren't going to have to use part of it in a couple of minutes. For a second he wished he'd just taken Blacky's money, waited until Blacky left, then started drinking right away. In fact, he might have done just that if Blacky hadn't explained to him what would happen if he fucked up. So he'd agreed to do everything that Blacky told him, and sat down on the side-walk, leaned back against the wall, and stuck his hat out in front of him just in case any of the suckers walking along the sidewalk decided to drop some change in it.

Around noon, he'd spent a couple of Blacky's bucks to buy a hot dog from the vendor on the corner, and while the guy— who insisted on being paid even before he pulled the wiener out of the kettle—slathered some mustard on the dog, along with some chopped onions, Fritz kept half an eye on the grate, just in case.

Nothing, of course, had happened, and as he'd sat back down and munched on the hot dog, he wondered how much longer he was expected to wait.

"You stay until I tell you it's okay," Blacky had said, but with his stomach as full of food as his pocket was of money, Fritz was feeling a lot more cocky than when he'd talked to Blacky that morning. The siren song of a fifth of Black Label— or even two—was filling his brain now, and maybe he'd just call it a day and head for the liquor store around the cor-ner. But then, as he was about to come to a decision, he heard something.

Something from beneath the grating.

Getting to his feet, he stepped over to the edge of the grate and looked down.

Someone was coming up. Fritz couldn't see what the guy looked like, and the guy wasn't looking up, but it didn't matter—he knew what Blacky had told him to do, and despite the fact that it was going to cost him half the money in his pocket, he knew he had to do it.

Pulling fifty dollars out of his pocket, he went over to the hot dog vendor, dropped the money on the counter of the cart, then picked up the steaming kettle. "Hey, motherfucker, what you think—" the vendor began, but Fritz ignored him.

Turning away, he stepped back to the grate, glanced down at the man who was now only five feet below, and upended the kettle.

A stream of scalding water, accompanied by a couple of dozen overcooked wieners, poured down onto the grating.

As an agonized howl erupted from the shaft below the grating, Fritz dropped the kettle and shambled off down the street as quickly as he could.

By the time the vendor got around his cart, it was all over, and as he picked up his kettle and watched Fritz disappear, he decided that the fifty dollars the bum had left on the counter was worth a lot more than the hassle it would take to report to the police what had happened. Leaving the few hot dogs that hadn't fallen through the grating where they were, the vendor stowed the kettle in the cart then began pushing the cart away.

If any of the pedestrians moving along the sidewalk had even noticed what happened, they gave no sign.

Better not to get involved . . .

His initial scream of agony ending in an abrupt grunt as he struck the floor at the foot of the ladder, Jagger moaned and writhed as he instinctively tried to rub away the pain of the scalding water. Had he been looking up and taken the water directly in the face, he undoubtedly would have been blinded—as it was, blisters were already starting to rise on his scalp and neck, and the skin of his face was turning a bright red. Dropping to his knees, Jeff pulled Jagger's hands away from his head.

"Don't rub it—you'll pull the skin off!"

Jagger tried to pull his hands loose, but Jeff held fast, and slowly, as the worst of the scalding agony eased, his struggles weakened. "Wh-What happened?" he finally stammered, gazing up at Jeff with eyes glazed by pain and dazed in confusion.

"Someone dumped a kettle of boiling water on you," Jeff told him. Seeing the wieners that had fallen through the grate along with the water, he added, "Looks like it must have come from a hot dog wagon." Jagger still looked dazed, and Jeff tried to pull the big man to his feet. "Can you walk?"

With Jeff steadying him, Jagger heaved himself up. For a moment it seemed his knees might buckle, but then he regained his balance. As Jeff started to lead him away from the shaft before anything else could cascade down on them, Jagger stopped, his fingers closing on Jeff's arm like a vise.

"The hot dogs," he said. "Pick 'em up." When Jeff hesitated, Jagger said, "Fuck, man—we can eat 'em!"

Jeff peered down at the wieners covered with the scum that made the floor beneath their feet slick. The thought of eating them made his gut tighten. But then a hunger pang hit him, and he knew Jagger was right. Filthy as they were, at least they were food, and with any luck at all, they'd find a dripping pipe that would at least allow them to wash the worst of the muck away. As Jagger steadied himself against the wall, Jeff began gathering up the hot dogs and stuffing them in the pockets of his jacket, which was almost as filthy as the food itself.

"How bad is it?" Jeff asked as they started back the way they'd come.

"Feels like my whole head's burning," Jagger muttered. "Where we going?"

"To find some water," Jeff replied, his voice grim. A few minutes later they were back at the shelved alcove in which they'd found shelter before. "Stay here," Jeff told Jagger as the big man eased himself into the cavernlike space. "I'll be back as soon as I can."

Jagger's hand closed on Jeff's wrist, his fingers digging

painfully into Jeff's flesh. "No . . ." he said, the word emerging from his lips more as a plea than an order.

Jeff gently loosened Jagger's fingers from his arm. "I've got to find water," he said. "If I can't find some, we'll never make it."

"We ain't gonna make it anyway," Jagger said, the usual truculence in his voice giving way now to a tone of defeat. "Fuckers are never gonna let us out. What the fuck did we ever do to them?"

"It doesn't matter what we did or didn't do," Jeff replied. "Don't you get it? It's just a game, Jagger. The whole thing's nothing but a game."

Jagger, his skin burning wherever the scalding water had touched it, gingerly reclined, resting awkwardly against the concrete wall. "So what are we gonna do?"

"We're going to win," Jeff said.

The two men's eyes met for a moment, then Jagger's gaze left Jeff's face and moved slowly down his body with an intensity Jeff could almost feel.

It was as if Jagger's eyes were touching him, stroking his skin, exploring every contour of his body.

Turning quickly away, Jeff slipped into the suddenly welcome darkness, but even as he moved down the tunnel, he could still feel Jagger's eyes on him. His skin crawled, a shudder shook his body, and he unconsciously hurried his step until the blackness hid him from Jagger's burning gaze.

CHAPTER 31

Mary Converse got out of a cab at the corner of Broadway and 109th, crossed the street and hurried down the block toward Jeff's building, looking up at the brick structure's grimy facade. She'd never liked the building, even though Jeff had insisted that it was perfect—close to Columbia, and in a safe neighborhood, at least by New York City standards. But the steep staircase and narrow, badly lit halls had given her the creeps. She'd always asked Jeff to come downstairs to let her in, and take her upstairs himself.

But now Jeff was gone, and . . .

And nothing, Mary told herself. *You came here for a reason, so get on with it!* Unconsciously squaring her shoulders, she mounted the steps, went into the vestibule, and pressed the button next to Jeff's name.

After a long wait, the buzzer sounded, and Mary pushed the inner door open and went inside. Nothing about the building had changed—the lights were still dim, the hallway narrow, the carpet threadbare, and a musty odor still hung in the air. She climbed the stairs to the third floor, went to the end of the hall, and knocked sharply at Jeff's door.

"If you think you're—" Keith was already saying as he opened the door, but his words died abruptly when he realized it wasn't Heather Randall. Taking a half step backward, he eyed Mary warily. "I—I thought you were at the mass," he began.

Mary shook her head. "There's not going to be a mass," she said. As Keith's brow knit into an uncertain frown, she reached toward the door. "May I come in?"

After hesitating a second, Keith nodded, pulled the door wide and stepped back. As Mary stepped inside and saw Keith in the full daylight flooding through the window, her eyes widened in shock.

His face was unshaven and his uncombed hair looked as if it hadn't been washed in three days. Then, seeing his blood-shot eyes, she thought she understood: he'd been drinking.

"I know how I look," he said. "And I know you think I'm crazy."

She recalled the words of the Virgin that had come to her. Believe . . .

"Maybe not," she said. "Or maybe I'm crazy, too."

Keith's frown deepened, and she could see the suspicion in his eyes. "What is it, Mary?" he asked. "Has something happened?"

"I—I'm not sure," Mary stammered. "I was praying, and—" She faltered, and then, her head bowed as if she were ashamed, told him everything that had happened, starting with the broken, static-filled phone call she'd gotten that morning and finishing with the strange experience in the cathedral. "Suddenly I couldn't do it," she finished. "I couldn't listen to the mass for him."

"You were right," he said. Taking his wife's chin gently in his hand, he tipped her face up so she was forced to look directly into his eyes. "I know where he is, Mary," he said. "He's in the tunnels. The tunnels under the city."

Mary gasped, but before she could say anything, Heather Randall burst through the front door. "You're still—" she began, then saw Mary and took in the ashen look on the older woman's face. "What is it?" she asked. "What's going on? Why aren't you at the—"

"Jeff called her," Keith told her. "She could barely hear him, and at first she didn't really believe it was him."

"But it was," Mary breathed, her voice so soft it was almost inaudible. "He's alive, Heather. He's still alive."

Instinctively, Heather put her arms around Mary, but even as she embraced Jeff's mother, her eyes met Keith's. "I'm going with you," she said. Keith was about to object, but she shook her head and released Mary from her embrace, taking a step backward, as if preparing to do battle. "Don't argue with me, Keith. Either I go with you or I'll go in by myself."

Mary's eyes flicked from Keith to Heather, then back to Keith. Until now, she'd rarely heard them exchange more than a word or two, and what words they'd spoken had involved only the barest civility. "Go where?" she asked, even as she took in the way her husband was dressed and recalled what he'd said about the tunnels. Heather's words quickly confirmed her thoughts.

"We think Jeff is in the tunnels under the city," she said. "I know it sounds crazy, but we heard something, and we've been talking to some people, and—"

"It's more than that, Heather," Keith said.

As she listened to him recount his conversation with Jinx, her heart began to race. "You're sure it was the same girl we saw with Tillie?"

Keith nodded. "I'm sure." He glanced at his watch. "And I know where she was twenty minutes ago. If I can find her . . ."

A strange sensation of cold had spread through Mary as she tried to follow the conversation between Heather and Keith, but the same words kept flowing through her mind: *He's not dead . . . Jeff's not dead. . . .* But then more words— Keith's and Heather's words—broke through.

". . . tunnels . . . hunters . . ."

". . . the girl we saw with Tillie . . ."

The coldness tightened its grip, and a wave of dizziness threatened to overwhelm her. *No!* she told herself. *Not now! Get a grip on yourself, and start doing what you can to help!* " 'Hunters,' " she finally said, determined not to give in to her roiling emotions. "What was she talking about?"

"I don't know," Keith said grimly. "But the only way I'm going to find out—or find Jeff—is by going in there myself."

Mary's first impulse was to argue with him. There had to be a better way! She opened her mouth, about to speak, but restrained herself. Hadn't she been doing nothing but arguing with Keith for the last three months? She steeled herself, not speaking until she was certain she could betray none of the fears she was feeling. "What can I do?" she asked.

Keith glanced at Heather, who was pulling clothes from the bag she'd brought with her, and realized it was senseless to argue with her. As Heather headed to the bathroom to peel off the dress she'd intended to wear to the mass, he shrugged at Mary. "I'm not sure," he began.

"Food," Mary said. "What have you got?" When Keith made no reply, she turned toward the door. "I'll get some sandwiches," she said. Then her eyes met Keith's. "You leave before I get back, and I swear I'll go in after you, too." She left without waiting for an answer.

Ten minutes later they were ready. Heather wore a pair of torn jeans and a baggy sweatshirt that made her look younger than she was and covered the grip of the gun she'd tucked into the waistband of her jeans. It was a 9mm HS 2000, a Croatian weapon with four different safety devices. She had three extra magazines stashed in her pockets. Keith checked over the Colt .38 Vic DiMarco had brought in from Bridgehampton, and Mary packed the sandwiches she'd bought at a deli on Broadway into the pockets of Keith's pea jacket, which he'd deliberately smeared with enough grease and dirt to make it look as if he'd extracted it from a Dumpster rather than bought it at a thrift shop that morning.

"How long will you be gone?" Mary asked after Heather left and Keith was at the door.

"As long as it takes," he replied. He started toward the stairs, then came back, pulled Mary close, and kissed her. "Love you," he whispered in her ear.

"Love you, too," she whispered back. She waited until they'd disappeared down the stairs, and as she closed the door, realized how deeply she'd meant the three words she just uttered. "Love you, too," she repeated, though there was no one there to hear her.

Five minutes later Keith and Heather were on the subway platform, and ten minutes after that they got off a train in Columbus Circle. At the far end of the platform he saw the men he'd encountered earlier—the men to whom he'd shown the photograph of Jeff. With Heather following him, he turned and went the other way, down the two flights of stairs to the lower platform. Two derelicts at the far end of the platform barely looked at them as they approached, and this time Keith didn't make the mistake of showing them the photo of Jeff.

"Lookin' for Jinx," he said. "You seen her?"

One of the men shrugged. "Not for a while." He nodded toward the tunnel into which Keith had seen the girl disappear earlier. "Last I saw her, she was headin' downtown. Unless a train hit her," he added, nothing in either his expression or his voice indicating that he cared if such a thing had happened.

Nodding curtly, Keith gazed up the tracks. There was no sign of a train coming.

Nor did he see any transit cops on the platform.

"Come on," he said to Heather. "Let's go find her."

Jumping off the platform, doing his best to look as if he'd done it hundreds of times before, he headed into the maw of the tunnel.

A moment later Heather leaped off the platform as well, and took a last look at the bright light of the white-tiled station.

Then she followed Keith into the darkness.

Eve Harris was running even later than usual. Like most Saturdays, she was as busy as on any weekday, but on Saturdays, no matter what else she did, she always made time for the person who mattered most in her life.

Eunice Harris still lived in the apartment in which she'd raised Eve, steadfastly refusing to move no matter how much Eve argued with her. "I know this neighborhood, and I know my neighbors," Eunice insisted every time Eve reminded her that it was one of the most dangerous areas in the city. "Every place is dangerous if you're a stranger, and everyone around here knows me. And they know you, too. Who'd want to hurt me?"

And she was right—everyone in the neighborhood did know her, and looked after her. But that didn't change the fact that the neighborhood wasn't getting any better, nor was Eunice Harris getting any younger. But every time Eve suggested that it might be time to think about moving, her mother only fixed her with the indomitable gaze that Eve herself often used in council meetings. "I've been taking care of myself for eighty years. I think I can manage for a few more."

Eve had been intending to raise the issue again this morning, but changed her mind after she got the call from Perry Randall, requesting—no, ordering—her to appear at a meeting that afternoon. He'd made no effort to conceal his anger, and though he hadn't told Eve what he was angry about, he made it clear that her attendance was not optional. So she'd juggled her schedule and called one of the downtown missions to notify them that she wasn't going to be there for an afternoon meeting after all. But she hadn't even considered dropping her mother off her schedule, despite the fact that her mother, as always, had seemed surprised to see her.

"Well, isn't this nice," Eunice said as she opened the triple-locked front door to let Eve in. "I wasn't expecting you at all!" Eve knew it wasn't true, but also knew it was her mother's way of letting her know that if she hadn't been able to come, there would have been no recriminations. She'd sat with her mother for almost two hours, doing her best to look as if she had nothing else on her mind. She hadn't fooled her mother for even a minute, and when she finally tried to take her leave, she found herself unable to avoid her mother's penetrating gaze. "Is there something you want to talk about, child?" the old woman asked. Eve shook her head, but her eyes involuntarily went to the picture of her daughter, which stood alone on the table next to her mother's favorite chair.

Eunice's gaze followed Eve's, and she thought she understood. "It never gets easier, does it?" she sighed. "I—"

Eve shook her head. "That's not it, Mama," she said. "It's not about Rachelle." But of course it was about Rachelle. In the end, everything in Eve's life was about Rachelle.

Eunice seemed to understand. "Some things a mother never gets over. If it had been you, I know I wouldn't ever have stopped hurting."

Eve hugged her mother, glancing one last time at the picture of Rachelle that stood on the table, then hurried out onto the street, turning toward the subway station.

The same subway station where her sixteen-year-old daughter had been attacked more than twenty years ago. Rachelle had been on her way back from visiting her grandmother that day, but she hadn't even made it onto the train.

Instead she'd been raped, beaten, and left for dead.

And unlike Cindy Allen, who had been attacked just two stations farther south and a few blocks west, Rachelle had died on the way to the hospital.

As she waited for the train, Eve gazed at the spot where it had happened, at the far end of the platform. Back then, the station's walls had been covered with graffiti, just like the train cars themselves, but everything had changed now. The graffiti was gone, and the station looked cleaner and brighter— and safer—than it had before. But it wasn't safe. None of them were, as Cindy Allen had found out.

It was no safer than it had been for Rachelle all those years ago.

The train rattled to a stop, and Eve Harris got on, glancing at her watch one more time. She was going to be late, but it didn't really matter. As the doors closed, her eyes remained on the spot where Rachelle had been raped, and the part of her that had never recovered from her daughter's brutal death throbbed with a pain that hadn't been eased by the passage of years, nor by any of the good works she had done to honor her daughter's memory.

The pain—the anger—burned as intensely today as on the day she'd looked down on her daughter's unrecognizably battered face and made a silent vow.

It won't end, she had sworn. *I'll do something. I'll do something to make it right.*

That was the moment when Eve Harris became the woman she was today, the moment when her life had irrevocably changed.

From that moment on, her life would exist only to serve her daughter's memory.

The train slowed to a stop and she got off. The usual knot of derelicts was clustered there, but instead of being sprawled out on the platform, they were all on their feet, peering into the darkness beyond the station's boundary. Veering away from the stairs, she strode down the platform. One of the men heard her footsteps, turned toward her, then nudged the man next to him. As the third man noticed her, too, they spread apart far enough to allow her to step through the gap.

"Miz Harris," one of the men said, his head bobbing respectfully.

Eve Harris nodded an acknowledgment of his greeting, but her eyes were searching the darkness for whatever had attracted their attention. Then she saw it—there was someone standing just off the tracks, close to the wall. A moment later she could make out a face peering out of the darkness.

A face that was young—but not as young as the man who had raped and killed Rachelle.

A face that fueled the hatred inside her.

A face that she recognized as soon as she saw it.

The face was pale with fear and exhaustion, but as Eve emerged from behind the group of men who surrounded her to look at him more closely, she saw a bright flash of hope light his eyes, and he took a lurching step closer.

Eve felt the men around her tense.

"Please," Jeff Converse said, lifting his hand as if to reach out toward her. "Help me—Call the police. . . ." His eyes darted among the hard faces around Eve. "They won't let me out. They—"

But Eve Harris had already turned away, stepping back through the gap from which she had just emerged. The men closed the gap the moment she passed through, and though she could hear Jeff Converse's cries as she started once more toward the stairs, she knew she would no longer have been able to see him if she had turned around again.

At the stairs, she paused, scanning the sparse crowd on the subway platform. There were perhaps thirty people waiting for trains, most alone, some in groups of two or three. Some were talking on cellular phones as they waited, some were reading, a few chatting with their friends. All of them must have heard Jeff Converse's pleading voice as he called out after her, but not one of them gave any sign of it.

Just as no one had heard Rachelle the night she cried out against the man who had raped and killed her.

Satisfied that at least some things in the city never changed, Eve continued on her way.

Minutes later she walked through the front door of the 100 Club. Thatcher, who seemed not to have moved from his post since the first time Eve's husband had brought her here ten years earlier, nodded respectfully.

"Downstairs," he murmured.

Eve descended the same two flights that Perry Randall had taken earlier that day.

She rapped twice, and Malcolm Baldridge immediately opened the door to The Manhattan Hunt Club. As she stepped through, the first thing she noticed was that the new trophy had been put on display. She recognized the man at once, for it hadn't been long since he'd made the mistake of trying to snatch the wallet from her purse as she waited for a subway train. It had taken her no time at all to find his name—or at least the name he went by in the tunnels—and the word had gone out.

It hadn't been much of a hunt, but it set an example.

Eve Harris was certain that when the next crime statistics came out, the incidence of purse-snatching and pickpocketing—like the incidence of every other crime she and the others would no longer tolerate—would show a significant drop.

"Excellent job, Mr. Baldridge," she commented as she gazed into the extraordinarily lifelike face.

"The members did an excellent job," Malcolm Baldridge respectfully replied. "There was very little damage."

Eve continued to the next room, where Perry Randall and the rest of the Hunt Club were waiting for her. She listened quietly as Randall told her about the message left on his answering machine that morning. When he was finished, his cold eyes fixed on Eve. "I warned you that something like this could happen, and you assured me that your people could see to it that none of them would ever get their hands on a cell phone. If he was able to call Heather, he undoubtedly called someone else. And if he called someone else, we have a problem."

Eve regarded Perry Randall with no more warmth than he was offering her. "There is no problem, Perry," she said. Her eyes drilled into each man in the room one by one: the Assistant District Attorney, the Deputy Police Commissioner, the Monsignor of the Church, the Judge of the Supreme Court of the State of New York, and the Chief of Police. "I just saw Jeff Converse trying to escape into the station at Fifty-third and

Lexington, but my people were there, doing their jobs. Now," she finished, her voice as cold as her eyes, "I suggest that it is time for you to do yours."

CHAPTER 32

When the woman first appeared, Jeff thought he must be hallucinating. He wasn't sure where he was, except in relation to the spot where he'd left Jagger.

Part of him had wanted to abandon Jagger, to disappear into the tunnels and never come back. Even now he felt a shiver go through him as he remembered the way Jagger sometimes looked at him. There was something about the man's gaze—

No! He was only imagining things.

Except that Jagger admitted he'd already killed two people—

Again Jeff turned away from the thought forming in his mind. Jagger had saved his life at least once, and no matter what he thought, he couldn't just take off by himself, leaving Jagger behind like a wounded animal.

Knowing he wouldn't, couldn't, just abandon Jagger, he'd kept careful track of every move he'd made, counting his paces, remembering every turn, every ladder. He'd done his best to avoid people, shrinking back into any alcove in the concrete tunnel walls, making himself invisible. After leaving Jagger, he'd gone deeper, clambering down the rusty rungs embedded in the walls of a shaft so narrow he'd barely been able to fit through. There were fewer people on the lower level, but one of the groups he glimpsed made his gut churn with a fear he'd never felt before. There were four of them, appearing out of the gloom like a pack of wolves, utterly silent. Something predatory about them told Jeff they were hunting; they moved with an animalistic furtiveness that momentarily paralyzed him, like a mouse freezes in terror before the flicking tongue of a coiled snake. As they came closer, he quelled his rising panic, backed away, and climbed the same ladder he'd descended only moments earlier. Peering downward into the near blackness below, he waited, his heart pounding. The four men slunk past the bottom of the shaft, none of them looking up.

A few minutes later he came to a subway tunnel and saw the brilliant white light of a station glowing from his right. He stayed where he was, listening, and heard the rumble of a train in the distance. The rumble grew louder, and he saw the headlight of an approaching train pierce the darkness and felt the track vibrate. Stepping back into the narrow passage from which he'd just emerged, he waited for the slowing train to pass, then edged closer to the station, concealed not only by the train, but by its shadow as well. Only when the train pulled out could he see the station's identification set in a mosaic inlaid in the wall: 53RD STREET.

Which station on Fifty-third? But what did it matter, really? If he could just get out, get help . . .

Help from whom? The police? As soon as he told them who he was, he'd be arrested. But if he lied, if he made up a name . . .

He raked the platform with his eyes, searching for any sign of the kind of men who had turned him away from every possible avenue of escape he'd stumbled upon before. Sure enough, there they were. Three of them, sprawled out at the end of the platform. He watched them for a few seconds, and when none of them were looking his way, he edged closer.

Then one of the men moved, his heading swiveling, and Jeff froze—too late. The surge of hope the mere presence of the station had instilled in him faded away as quickly as it had come as the three men rose to their feet and closed ranks, their eyes fixed on him. None of them spoke; none of them needed to.

The threat that hung before him was suddenly palpable.

That's when the unbelievable happened. A woman—a well-dressed woman—appeared between two of the men. She seemed to know them—Jeff was certain he saw two of them exchange a greeting with her.

She wasn't tall, but exuded an aura of authority, and she appeared utterly unafraid of the dangerous-looking men around her. Something about her looked familiar—he was sure he'd seen her before. And when she looked at him, he saw a flicker of recognition in her face.

Hope once more surged within him and he stepped toward her, raising his hand. "Please . . . help me—call the police. . . . They won't let me out. They—"

The woman's eyes locked on his. He knew she could hear him; he could see the comprehension written clearly on her face.

But she said nothing—made not even the slightest gesture toward him.

Instead, she turned away.

She wasn't going to help!

But that wasn't possible—the woman wasn't like the men around her. She wasn't one of them—couldn't possibly be!

He opened his mouth to speak—to cry out—to beg her to help him, but it was already too late. She was gone, as quickly as she'd appeared.

The men who had flanked her closed ranks.

He stood as if rooted to the ground, staring at the three men who blocked the way to the platform. They made no move toward him, nor any threatening gestures. Yet their message was clear: he would not be allowed to pass.

The low rumbling of an approaching train broke the moment, and when he saw his own shadow cast ahead of him by the fast-approaching beam of the train's headlight, he turned away, stumbling back toward the dark refuge of the passage from which he'd emerged. As the train rushed by, he slumped against the wall.

He'd failed.

He'd found no water to slake his thirst or ease the pain of Jagger's burns, let alone a means of escape from the vast prison in which they were held.

Unconsciously obeying the demands of his stomach, his hand went to the pocket of his jacket and his fingers closed around one of the hot dogs he'd rescued from the slime beneath the grating. He didn't look at the wiener—tried not to think what might have been in the muck from which he'd plucked it. Wiping it as clean as he could, he held his breath, put it in his mouth, and bit a piece off.

A foul taste filled his mouth, and his stomach contracted violently. He struggled against his erupting gorge, and when his mouth filled with bile and acid, he refused to spit it out. Instead he made himself chew up the single bite of food and force it down his throat. Then he tried to eat a second bite, but this time his stomach won and he dropped the rest of the hot dog back into his pocket.

He wasn't dead yet, and he wasn't beaten. If it truly was a game he'd been thrown into, then there had to be a way to win. And if there was a way, he'd find it. Turning his back on the false hope the station had offered, he started back to where he'd left Jagger, all the turns he'd taken—and the number of steps between each turn—firmly etched in his mind.

He was about halfway to the alcove, moving through a utility tunnel, when he saw it. He'd barely even been aware that his eyes were scanning the floor of the tunnel, and if the object hadn't been white, it might not have caught his eye at all.

A discarded coffee cup, the paper kind that was so thin you burned your fingers if you picked it up when it was freshly filled.

He paused.

Why was it standing upright?

Next to it was a crumpled piece of paper—the kind in which a sandwich might once have been wrapped.

If a workman had been eating his lunch here and just walked away . . .

Squatting, his fingers trembling, Jeff reached for the cup, silently praying that this hope, too, would not instantly be ground to dust. His fingers closed on the cup and he lifted it up.

Not empty!

He stared into it, gazing at the quarter cup of dark liquid as if it were pure gold, then raised the cup to his lips and let a little of the cold, bitter fluid flow through his lips.

His mouth welcomed it as if it were a perfect wine, aged to perfection.

He was about to drink again, but didn't.

Jagger was every bit as thirsty as he.

His own thirst cried out to him, begged him to drain the cup. What if he couldn't find the alcove again?

What if Jagger was gone?

Almost of its own volition, his hand raised the cup to his lips again, but just as the paper touched his lips, he recalled a train hurtling toward him, and Jagger throwing them both out of its path only an instant before he would have been crushed.

He lowered the cup.

Straightening, he saw a flicker of movement a few yards down the passage, back toward the subway tunnel from which he'd just retreated. He froze, his eyes scanning the tunnel. He knew his eyes had not deceived him—something, or *someone*—was there, concealed among the pipes, or hidden behind one of the pilasters that supported the low ceiling of the tunnel.

One of the men from the subway platform?

Or one of the skulking predators from the lower depths?

He listened, but heard only the sound of a faraway train, its roar muted to a faint whisper. He held perfectly still, holding his breath as he searched the darkness and listened to the silence.

Two choices: he could either attempt to slip away in the darkness, and risk being followed, or confront whatever lay hidden behind him, and directly face whatever danger awaited. But there was really no choice, for he knew he could never elude whatever was following him, that it would only keep its distance, stalking him until the moment it chose to attack.

"I know you're there," he said, his voice echoing loudly in the darkness as he started toward the place from which the brief movement had caught his eye. "You might as well show yourself."

For a moment nothing happened, but just as Jeff was about to move closer, a small figure stepped out from behind one of the pilasters.

"It's okay," a girl's voice said. "It's just me." The figure stepped forward, and enough light from one of the dim bulbs overhead fell on her face for Jeff to recognize her as the girl at Tillie's. "I've been looking for you," Jinx said. "I—" She faltered, then went on. "I know you didn't do anything to Cindy Allen."

The words hung in the air. What could Jinx possibly know about that? Jeff wondered. How did she even know Cindy Allen's name?

A trick. That was it—it had to be some kind of a trick.

"How do you know?" he asked, his voice cold.

"Because I was there that night," Jinx replied. Then, as Jeff listened mutely, she recounted to him everything that had happened that night in the 110th Street station.

Recounted it exactly as he remembered it himself.

When she finished, there was a long silence, which Jeff finally broke. "How did you find me?" he asked.

"The herders in the Fifty-third Street station. They told me which way you went."

"Herders?" Jeff echoed.

Jinx nodded. "They work for the hunters. It's their job to keep you in the tunnels until the hunters can track you down."

Jeff's eyes narrowed. "And what's your job?"

"Sort of a messenger. Sometimes I pick up the money the herders get paid with, and sometimes I pass it out. Sometimes I just spread the word that a hunt is on."

She made no move either to come closer or to run away, and Jeff could sense that she wasn't afraid of him, but was waiting to see what he would do. "Who are the hunters?" he finally asked.

"Men from outside," Jinx replied. "They're only supposed to hunt for criminals. But you didn't do anything."

"So you're not going to tell them you found me?"

Jinx shook her head. "I'm going to help you get out."

Heather flattened herself against the hard concrete, turned her head away, and instinctively clamped her eyes shut. But she could still hear the train thundering past no more than twelve inches from her face, feel the rush of filthy air. That was the first thing she'd noticed after she followed Keith Converse off the platform and into the subway tunnel itself—not the darkness that stretched ahead of her, but the fetid odor that seemed to seep directly into her pores. Though they'd been in the tunnels for only half an hour, she already felt saturated with grime. Her skin itched, her eyes stung, and though her sense of smell had finally become somewhat accustomed to the foul odors that permeated the tunnel, her stomach had not. It wasn't just the air that was making her nauseous, but the terror that tightened its grip on her as she proceeded in the tunnel.

The first time they had seen a train coming, she was certain she would die. There was only a single track, with concrete walls rising on both sides. As the beam of the train struck her, she froze like a deer caught in an automobile's headlights. If it hadn't been for Keith, she knew that in fact she would have died, right there, the hurtling subway train mangling her body in an instant. But she'd felt him tugging at her, and heard him yelling.

"There's a catwalk!" A moment later he picked her up, swung her onto the catwalk, and rolled onto it himself. As that first train rushed by, she lay quivering, and when it was over—so quickly it almost seemed it couldn't have happened at all—she lay there trembling, her breath coming in gasps. "You okay?" Keith asked as he gently drew her to her feet. She nodded, unwilling to admit how terrified she'd been until Keith grinned and said, "Then you're a better man than me— I thought I was going to mess my pants."

"Actually, I thought I was going to die," Heather admitted as they gingerly climbed off the catwalk and back onto the track.

Now, as the fourth train thundered by, Heather knew she wasn't going to die, at least not by being crushed by a subway car. Silently cursing her own cowardice, she forced herself to open her eyes and turn her head so she was looking directly at the speeding train. A wave of dizziness struck her, but she steeled herself against it, pressing even harder against the concrete. After the last car raced by, she jumped back down to the tracks and gazed after it, reading the identifying letter on the back of the last car: D.

Before the train had come thundering up behind them, they'd seen that the tunnel ahead spread wider, and more tracks were becoming visible. Now, as she watched the speeding train, it banked around to the left, and she knew exactly where they were.

Fifty-third Street.

A few paces farther and the two of them were in the far wider section of tunnel that provided the space for the trains to turn, and they began to see the glow of the station far ahead. But before they were close enough that the light spilling from the station would allow them to be seen emerging from the darkness, Keith stopped. Wordlessly, Heather followed his lead, and they stood silently for a moment. In the distance they could hear the faint sound of a train moving away from them, but that sound faded away and a silence fell over the tunnel. But still Keith neither moved nor spoke, and when Heather finally turned to him, he raised his arm and pointed. Then she saw them: two men at the near end of the platform, staring into the tunnel.

Staring, as if looking for something.

Or someone.

"Just like the guys at every other station I've been to," Keith whispered, leaning closer so he could speak directly into her ear. "Except all the others were acting like they were just hanging out. These guys are looking for something."

"Us?" Heather whispered back.

Keith shook his head. "How would they even know we're here?"

"Someone who saw us jump off the platform at Columbus Circle could have taken a train and told them. The trains are full of homeless people."

"Or they could be looking for Jinx," Keith suggested.

"Or Jeff."

Her words hung between them, and Keith said, "You want to know something, the best thing to do is go ask, right? Wait here."

He started forward. Heather, ignoring his last words, kept pace with him. When he stopped and turned as if to say something, she shook her head, and there was a look about her that told him it would be useless to argue. She said, "If there's any trouble—"

"If there's any trouble," Keith repeated, cutting her off, "you just stay down." He pulled the gun out of his waistband, showed it to her, then shoved it and the hand that held it deep into the outer pocket of his pea jacket.

Heather's own hand tightened on the grip of the pistol she'd taken from her father's gun cabinet, which was now deep in the folds of her own coat, a badly worn bomber jacket that she'd tried to convince Jeff to get rid of more than a year ago.

"Let me do the talking," Keith said. "Act like a junkie."

They moved forward, Keith letting his body slump into the defeated slouch of the derelicts he'd seen in the streets, parks, and subways over the past two days. Heather shuffled beside him, her head down, her hair hanging limply so her face was only partly visible. When they came to the platform, Keith climbed up, then pulled Heather after him. "Fuckin' bitch," he muttered. "I oughta—"

Heather jerked her arm loose. "Keep your fuckin' hands offa me, asshole." As she turned sullenly away from him, he shrugged helplessly to one of the two men, who gave him a gap-toothed grin and winked.

"Shit, man—whyn't you dump her?"

Keith spread his hands. "She'll be okay. Seen Jinx?"

The man's grin faded. "What you lookin' for her for?"

Keith's mind raced, then he remembered the wad of cash Tillie had shoved into the girl's hands yesterday. He jerked his head meaningfully toward Heather, whose back was still to him. "Heard she's got some money."

The gap-toothed man shook his head. "You crazy, mothafuck? You roll Jinx, you be dead. Hunters go after you soon's they finish off the fuckers they're after right now!"

Keith spat out the kind of profanity that never failed to grab the attention of his work construction crew. "Any idea where they are?"

The second man nodded farther down the track. "Heard they was down three, and three workin' east, the rest comin' this way. If you ain't herdin' I'd get my ass outta here."

"Shit," Keith said. He grabbed Heather, tugging at her arm until she turned around. "Time to go."

She acted like she wanted to pull away from him. "Fuck you—why don't ya just leave me alone!"

"Maybe I will, bitch!" Keith dropped her arm and started down the platform as an eastbound train pulled into the station. "Who the fuck needs you anyway?"

"Don't you leave me here!" Heather screamed, running to catch up to him just as he stepped onto one of the cars. The doors slid shut behind her, and Keith winked.

"You're good," he said as the train pulled out of the station. "For a second I thought you were actually trying to get away from me."

"I figured I could count on you not to let that happen. Come on."

They made their way back to the last car, and when the train pulled into the Seventh Avenue and Fifty-third Street station, they got off.

They were back on the tracks before the train had pulled away, scurrying into the darkness like rats into a sewer.

"He said the hunters were 'down three'—got any idea what that means?"

Heather nodded. "Jeff took a class in urban architecture last year. There are all kinds of tunnels under the city, and they go deep. 'Down three' must mean three levels down from here." She peered into the darkness. "But how do we get there?"

"If there's a way down, then we'll find it," Keith said. "Come on."

Perry Randall felt the familiar thrill run through him as he moved through the semidarkness of the utility tunnel. Behind him, Frisk McGuire—who, like the rest of The Hundred, never brought his honorific through the anonymous door on West Fifty-third, leaving Monsignor Terrence McGuire on the street outside—was on his left, while Carey Atkinson watched the right. The formation wasn't necessary yet, of course, for they weren't nearly deep enough to be in any real danger. Yet at the same time you couldn't be too careful—the jungle beneath the streets could be far more dangerous than the African bush. Only two years ago they'd lost one of their members when the tribe that lived on the lowest level of the tunnels had set up an ambush that even the best of the club's gamekeepers hadn't heard anything about.

But that was what made the hunt thrilling. It wasn't as if there was danger only to the prey—nothing like the hunting farm he'd visited in Zimbabwe, where the sense of adventure was primarily an illusion. Here, beneath the streets of the most civilized city in the world, the risks were as real for the hunters themselves as for the quarry they tracked. Indeed, Perry could still remember the first hunt, after he and Linc Cosgrove had organized the Manhattan Hunt Club within the walls of The Hundred. When Eve had told him what she wished the club to do, it was obvious she already had her husband's support, and that if Perry didn't agree to what she proposed, Linc would simply find another member who would. Linc, after all, had nothing to lose—the heart problems that killed him on the Jamaican beach a few months later had already been diagnosed.

"The man who raped and killed my daughter was released from prison today," Eve had said, her dark eyes smoldering, her voice ice cold. "My daughter is dead, and now he's a free man." Until that moment, Perry Randall hadn't been aware that Eve Harris had ever had a child, let alone that the child had been murdered. But Eve anticipated the question before Randall could voice it. "My daughter didn't count," she said. "I was just another unwed mother, and she was just another black girl with no father. If my daughter had been white, the bastard would have been executed." Her eyes moved over the white faces surrounding her, daring any of them to argue. They all looked uncomfortable, but none of them spoke. "But she was my child," Eve went on. "And now he's back on the streets, going on with his life." Her voice dropped another notch. "You know as well as I do that he's already looking for his next victim."

Still Perry Randall said nothing, and then it was Linc Cosgrove who spoke. "It's not just my wife's daughter," he said.

"It's the tenor of the times we live in. No one is being held accountable for their own actions. Everything is someone else's fault." He passed a photograph to Randall, and the Assistant District Attorney found himself looking at a man of about twenty-five, with narrow-set eyes, a weak chin, and a shock of dirty blond hair falling over a sloping forehead. The man's name was Leon Nelson. "I've read the transcript of his trial," he went on. "They didn't try him—they tried Eve's daughter instead. When they were through, they gave this man fifteen years." Linc Cosgrove's heavy brow arched and his voice took on an edge of sarcasm. "It was a murder, after all—they had to do *something*, didn't they? But the prisons are overcrowded, and apparently he has behaved himself. So he is now out, and, as Eve says, undoubtedly looking for his next victim."

Perry Randall's gaze shifted back to Eve, his unspoken question hanging in the air.

"I want justice," Eve said. "But not just for my daughter. I want justice for every powerless victim in this city." She'd outlined her proposal then, in the same dispassionate tones with which she now discussed whatever proposal lay before the City Council, to which she'd been elected three years after that first meeting. "I think of it as a club within the club," she'd said. "A club of fair-minded people who have the greater good of the city and its citizens at heart." What she proposed was not a lynch mob. Rather, it was an orderly system in which the worst elements of the city would be identified and dealt with. "Each of them will have a fair chance," Eve explained. "There will be a time limit—a statute of limitations, if you will. And should any of them prove themselves capable of finding their way out of the maze that exists under our city, then they shall have truly won their freedom. But it must be won—we have been giving too many people too much for too long. It's time people began earning their lives again."

Perry Randall had long understood that the coddling of the

criminal element had to stop, and that the established system was unlikely to correct its own dangerous drift.

That was why The 100 Club had originally been established: to allow for society's elite to do what was necessary in private, without the necessity of convincing a seemingly uneducable public to find the spine to do the right thing.

Thus was the Manhattan Hunt Club born.

He and Linc Cosgrove had selected the original members themselves, and he could still remember that night when he, Linc, Frisk McGuire, and Carey Atkinson had first gone into the tunnels in search of the man who had murdered Eve Harris's daughter. Eve herself had organized the people living in the tunnels, those who had become the gamekeepers for the hunt, funneling money to them in payment for their work.

Carey Atkinson's people had discovered where the killer was living, and some of Eve's people escorted him into the tunnels, explained to him what was about to happen, and why, and had given him certain provisions.

Then they released him.

What Perry hadn't expected was the excitement that had run through him as he and the others moved through the special door that had been cut through from The 100 Club's subbasement—now the headquarters of the Manhattan Hunt Club—and began exploring the tunnels. That first hunt lasted nearly a week, as he and his team began mapping the tunnels, learning where there were hidden passages, and which passages led to dead ends. Eventually, they had trapped their prey in a storm drain on the fourth level down, backed up against a grating that opened onto the Hudson. Perry himself had shot Nelson, placing the red dot of his laser sight in the precise center of the man's forehead as he was silhouetted against the grate. The thrill he had felt as he squeezed the trigger, and the satisfaction of seeing Nelson's body slump into the muck covering the bottom of the culvert, had been better even than the sexual gymnastics Carolyn had taught him.

The thrill of the hunt had never waned for Perry Randall, and as he began tonight's adventure, he felt more alive than he had in weeks. He'd been anticipating this moment for months. From the moment Jeff Converse was arrested, Perry knew that sooner or later the young man who thought he might someday marry his daughter would become part of the hunt.

After the sentencing—the mere slap on the wrist the judge had inflicted—he knew the time had come. When Eve Harris called him to convene a meeting of the special committee that she herself chaired, he was prepared. Of course, Eve herself was going to have to be disciplined; it was inexcusable that Converse had been allowed to get his hands on a cell phone. But that could be dealt with later, after the hunt was over.

After Jeff Converse had been placed among the other trophies that lined the walls of the Hunt Club.

With senses made sharper by the adrenaline flowing through his body, his fingers tightened on the strap that held his rifle to his back. The gun was one of the Steyr SSG-PIs, to which he'd fitted a day-night scope with an infrared beam.

As he came to a place where a locked door led from the utility tunnel into the Fifty-third Street subway tunnel, he reached into his pocket and took out one of the numerous keys that had been supplied to the members of the hunt by one of their own, whose public responsibilities included overseeing most of the city's utilities. Randall fumbled with the lock as the key stuck, but then it turned and the door opened.

He glanced to his left and saw nothing but the distant glow of the subway station.

To his right, barely visible in the distance, a couple of derelicts—a man and a woman, judging by their size—were shambling off into the darkness.

By the time the rest of Perry Randall's team had come through the door and relocked it, the two figures had vanished.

*   *   *

Heather Randall's fingers closed on Keith Converse's arm. when he turned to look at her, he could barely make out her finger pressed to her lips in warning. She leaned forward and whispered into his ear. "I heard something—like a door closing."

Keith frowned in the darkness. They'd passed a door only a few minutes ago. He'd tried the handle, anxious to get away from the subway tunnel, but it had been locked.

He couldn't recall seeing another.

But he *had* found a shaft, a narrow one, leading downward, with iron rungs embedded in its walls. Until Heather's whispered warning, he'd been undecided about whether to take the shaft or not. Now his mind was made up, and with no hesitation at all he climbed down into the darkness.

A second later, Heather followed.

And less than a minute after that, Perry Randall and his fellow hunters came to the top of the shaft.

After conferring among themselves, they, too, began climbing down the rungs of the ladder.

CHAPTER 33

Jagger gazed down at Jeff's face. His eyes were closed, but Jagger wasn't sure if he was really sleeping or just pretending to. It didn't make any difference, because all he was going to do was look at him.

He just liked watching Jeff sleep. Liked the way his lips curled up a little at the corner, like he was smiling. Liked the way his jawline was squared off, like some kind of movie star.

His eyes left Jeff's face and began moving down his body. For some reason—a reason that Jagger couldn't quite remember—Jeff didn't have any clothes on, and even though Jeff wasn't shivering or anything, Jagger was sure he must be cold.

Jagger himself was shivering.

Maybe if he just lay down next to Jeff and put their bodies close together—

Suddenly, Jagger didn't have any clothes on either, and his body was pressed close to Jeff—really close. Jeff's skin felt warm and soft, and Jagger let his finger trace the curve of the other man's hip. Jeff moved, pressing closer, and Jagger felt his groin start to stir.

And his hand, which only a second ago had been on Jeff's hip, was now—

Jagger jerked awake, the dream shattering. His hand was on his crotch and—

He jerked it away and looked around, terrified that Jeff had seen him, and knew what he'd been dreaming.

Realizing he was still alone in the alcove in which Jeff had left him, he relaxed.

It was just a dream, he told himself. *It didn't mean nothin'. Nothin' at all!*

Then, as he came fully awake, he began to wonder where Jeff was.

And how long he'd been asleep.

He hadn't intended to go to sleep—hadn't even thought he could, the way his face was hurting. And now it wasn't just his face, either. Now his whole body hurt, his muscles aching with the chill of the tunnel. With a grunt, he rolled over, and a searing pain ripped across his right cheek. Without thinking, he put his grimy fingers to his face, flinching at the stinging. His fingers automatically went to his mouth, and he tasted the saltiness of blood.

More gingerly, he began exploring the rest of his burns. The blisters on his scalp and head were much worse—the last time he'd touched them, he could barely feel them. Now they seemed to be everywhere, and even though he knew he shouldn't touch them, his fingers kept going to them anyway, poking and prodding at them until finally they started to burst. They were on his face, too, and not just on his right cheek, where they'd torn open from the concrete he was lying on. They were on his chin and the side of his nose, and his right eye was starting to hurt so bad he could hardly open it. He must have had his head turned to the right when the bastard dumped the boiling water on him, because the left side of his face actually seemed to be okay. But the rest of the burns were hurting so bad it was like his whole head was on fire, and—

And where the fuck was Jeff?

Dumped me, Jagger thought. *The motherfucker dumped me.*

It seemed hours since Jeff had left. At first, Jagger hadn't been worried at all—he trusted Jeff—trusted him almost as much as he'd trusted Jimmy before—

Well, before the bad thing had happened.

Anyway, he hadn't trusted anyone else like he'd trusted Jimmy until Jeff came along, and when Jeff said he wouldn't be gone very long, he had believed him. But now, with no idea how long he'd been asleep, and with the pain from his burns getting worse, he was starting to wonder. All Jeff was supposed to be doing was finding some water. How long could that take? It seemed like there'd been dripping pipes all over the place.

Unless something had happened to Jeff.

He thought of all the people they'd seen in the tunnels, all the men that had flashed knives at them and looked like they wouldn't even think about it before sticking blades in their chests.

What if Jeff had run into a couple of those guys, and without him there to protect him?

Shit! What kind of idiot was he, letting Jeff go off by himself? Jeff was really smart—a lot smarter than he was—but he wasn't very big, and without him to take care of Jeff—to watch his back—anything could have happened. Any one of those guys could have taken him out.

Jagger heaved himself painfully into a sitting position, his back resting against the end of the alcove. His throat was parched, and his stomach ached with hunger.

And Jeff had taken the wieners.

Motherfucker! Took all the food and just took off, leaving him to starve to death.

Jagger's fury began to burn with as much heat as the wounds on his head. That was what happened when you trusted people—they fucked you over. It had happened with his mother, who'd just taken off one day and left him in the crummy house they lived in with no food and no one to take care of him. He'd started screaming then, and somebody had finally heard him, but all that happened was they put him in the foster home.

Jagger felt like screaming right now, but he'd learned a

long time ago that screaming didn't do you any good at all. It just got you in more trouble. What you had to do was pretend you didn't care. Pretend nothing was wrong at all. Then, when you got a chance, you got even.

The anger inside him burned hotter, and Jagger's fist closed on the railroad spike that was his only weapon. He began grinding its point against the concrete surface on which he lay, honing it sharper with each stroke. And as he worked the metal of the spike, he began imagining the things he would do to Jeff if he ever found him again. And not just with the spike, either.

With his hands, too.

He imagined his hands closing around Jeff's throat. And Jeff's eyes—his beautiful, soft brown eyes—staring at him, begging him not to do it, to let go of him. But it wouldn't happen—he'd only squeeze tighter, and watch while Jeff's face turned red, and his eyes bugged out, and his arms started flailing around as he struggled to free himself. But he wouldn't free himself, because Jagger knew he was too strong.

And he'd never let go of Jeff, no matter how much he begged. He'd just hang on to him, holding him, until he finally stopped struggling. And after that, when he knew that Jeff would never go away from him again, he would go on holding him, cradling him in his arms, rocking him, just like his mama had rocked him when he was a little baby boy, back before she left him.

And then they'd be together, just the two of them, him and Jeff.

A sound, so faint he almost missed it, drifted out of the darkness, and Jagger froze, the spike suspended a fraction of an inch above the concrete shelf. His body tingled with tension as he strained to hear.

The sound came again.

Footsteps, somewhere in the distance.

Footsteps that were coming closer . . .

*   *   *

Jeff was getting more worried. When Jinx had first appeared out of the darkness, he'd felt a surge of hope, had been certain, in fact, that she must know of a way to escape the tunnels. But now he was starting to wonder. They were halfway back to the place where he'd left Jagger, when he stopped and turned to face her.

"Why do they do it?" he asked.

Jinx looked at him uncomprehendingly. "Why does who do what?"

"The herders. Isn't that what you called them? The men guarding the subway station?"

"Why does anybody do anything?" she countered. Then, before he could reply: "Money."

" 'Herders,' " Jeff repeated, more to himself than to Jinx. "It sounds like they're running cattle or something."

"Not cattle," Jinx replied. "Don't you get it? They're running game."

"That's all it is?" he asked, his voice reflecting his outrage. "A game?"

The girl fairly glared at him this time. "Not 'it'! You. You and that other guy. Don't you get it? You're not cattle—to the hunters, you're just game. Like rabbits, or deer, or anything else people hunt."

Jeff felt numb. "And the people down here really help them?"

"Why wouldn't they?" Jinx asked, shrugging. "People die down here all the time and nobody gives a shit. Half the time nobody even knows who the bodies are. So if someone wants to pay us just to keep someone else from gettin' out, what's the big deal?"

Jeff eyed her warily through the gloom. She couldn't have been more than fourteen or fifteen, but there was a hard edge to her that told him she'd been on the streets for a while. "So why shouldn't I think you're just another one of the herders?"

Jinx looked at him as if he were stupid. "They only use guys for that. Big guys. Like I could keep you from doing anything? Jeez!" Then, out of nowhere, she asked, "What's your dad look like?"

"My dad?" Jeff echoed. "What's my dad got to do with—" And then it came to him. So much had happened since Tillie had thrown them out of the rooms she called the co-op that he'd almost forgotten the faint voice he'd thought was calling his name. "I thought I heard him," he breathed, almost to himself. "But—" He cut himself short, studying Jinx carefully. What could she possibly know about his father?

"There was a guy in the subway station," she said, eyeing him almost truculently now. "The one at Columbus Circle. He showed me a picture of you."

"What did he look like?" Jeff asked, his pulse quickening even as he told himself it couldn't possibly have been his father. Why would his father even be looking for him? And if somebody had seen him running into the subway, it was a lot more likely it was the police showing his picture around than his father.

"I guess he was a little shorter than you," Jinx was saying. "Kind of good-looking—blue eyes and blond hair." She cocked her head, studying his face in the dim light. "He looked kinda like you, I guess, except for your hair and eyes. Except your eyes are shaped the same. Just a different color."

"What about the picture?" Jeff asked, struggling to keep his excitement under control.

"It was you. Looked like you were younger—like maybe in college or something."

Jeff's heart raced at the description of the picture his father always carried in his wallet. "What did he say?" he asked, no longer trying to keep his voice steady.

"He just wanted to know if I'd seen you," Jinx replied. "I was telling him about the hunters being after you when—" Now it was Jinx who faltered, but then she took a deep breath and finished. "Well, the transit cops came and I had to split. They don't like me much."

Jeff barely heard her. If his father was looking for him, then who else was? His mind was racing now, trying to sort it out. How had his father known where he was? Could it have been the cell phone? But if Heather got his message, or his mother heard him before the phone went dead—

But if his father knew he was still alive, wouldn't the cops know, too? "What about the regular police?" he asked. "Were they in the subway, too?"

Jinx rolled her eyes. "They only go in the subway if they want to go somewhere, and they won't go in the tunnels at all. Bunch of chickenshits, if you ask me."

Jinx suddenly froze, and when Jeff started to speak, she grabbed his arm and put her finger to her lips.

From somewhere off to the left, Jeff heard a sound.

Footsteps.

Footsteps that seemed to be coming closer.

He glanced around. A few yards farther along there was a narrow passage he'd made his way through shortly after he'd left Jagger. If he led Jinx through it, he'd have no choice but to take her to Jagger as well. If she were lying, and working for the hunters, he would have led them right to the man who had already saved his life at least once. But if he didn't go through it—if he went in another direction and couldn't find his way back . . .

Then he would have abandoned Jagger completely.

Making up his mind, he signaled Jinx to follow him and started toward the passage, moving carefully so his feet made no sound. They came to the passage, and Jeff slipped into it, Jinx right behind him. He moved as quickly as he could, but the passage seemed endless, and now he thought he could hear the footsteps again, moving faster.

Coming closer.

He came to the end of the passage, turned left, and pulled Jinx after him. Both of them instinctively pressed their backs against the wall, struggling to control their breath as they listened.

In the distance they once again heard the sound of footsteps.

A pause.

On the wall opposite the end of the passage, a brilliant red dot appeared.

It moved over the wall, back and forth, working steadily downward until it reached the floor.

Laser sight, Jeff thought. *He's got a laser sight on a night scope, and he's using the scope to look for me.*

The crimson dot vanished as suddenly as it had appeared, and then they heard the footsteps fading away.

As Jeff was about to move deeper into the tunnel, Jinx's hand closed on his arm, holding him back. "Listen," she whispered.

Once again Jinx's ears had proved better than his own. Off to the right, in the opposite direction from which he'd originally come, he heard the faint sound of water dripping.

A little more than fifty yards up the tunnel, they found it— water was steadily oozing from a crack in the ceiling, a drop forming and falling every second or two. His thirst suddenly overwhelming him, Jeff held his finger up to the drip, caught one, and put his damp finger into his mouth.

The water tasted clear and fresh, and he was seized with an almost overwhelming urge to put his mouth to the crack in the ceiling and try to suck the moisture out.

Instead he put the paper cup under the drip and forced himself to wait until the cup had filled.

He drank only enough to slake the terrible dryness in his mouth, then filled the cup once more.

"Aren't you going to drink it?" Jinx asked as Jeff started back down the passage, carrying the cup of water as carefully as if it were filled with gold or diamonds.

"Jagger needs it more than I do," he said. "After he's had a drink, I'll come back for more."

*   *   *

*T*hey weren't going to find Jeff.

Heather wasn't sure exactly when the thought first entered her head, but the deeper into the tunnels she and Keith ventured, the stronger its grip on her mind became.

She had no idea where they were. Though she'd done her best to keep track of every turn they'd made, every passage they'd crept through, every ladder they'd climbed or crumbling wall they'd scaled, she had long since lost any sense of direction. The semidarkness itself was disorienting, though it hadn't been too bad when they'd still been near the surface, when she'd actually been able to catch glimpses of daylight now and then. Even the few rays of afternoon sun that penetrated through the scattering of grates that appeared here and there over her head were enough to keep her from feeling utterly lost. But since they'd fled down the shaft after hearing the sound of a door closing—a sound that would have been perfectly ordinary on the surface, but had seemed alien to the strange world of the tunnels—she'd been struggling against a rising tide of fear that was now edging toward panic.

Stop it, she told herself. *We'll be all right. We will find Jeff, and we will get out.* But when Keith, leading her by half a step, stopped and put a hand out to keep her from moving forward, all the fears she had barely held in check nearly broke free. She might even have cried out if Keith hadn't clamped his hand over her mouth, then held his finger to his lips. Her heart pounding, she strained to hear whatever it was that had spooked him, and a moment later, when her pounding heart finally began to settle back into a normal rhythm, she heard it.

Footsteps.

Slow, irregular footsteps, as if whoever was making them was frightened of something.

Or stalking something?

The thought came to Heather out of nowhere, and she tried to banish it.

They were approaching a crossroads where the passage

they were following intersected with another. The dimly lit area ahead was empty, and she couldn't tell from which direction of the tunnel the footsteps were coming, but they were definitely getting closer. She was afraid that at any second whoever was approaching would appear around the corner, and then—

Keith's grip tightened on her arm, and when Heather turned to look at him, his eyes were boring straight into hers and his lips mouthed two words.

Two words that her rising panic made utterly incomprehensible until he spoke out loud a second later.

"Where's tha bottle?" Keith slurred. "Didn't lose it, didja?"

Then the words he'd mouthed came into perfect focus: *Play drunk!*

"Threw it away," Heather mumbled back. "Was empty anyway."

"Fuckin' bitch," Keith said, a little louder now, and moving unsteadily toward the cross tunnel that lay ahead. "Thought I tol' you not to drink it all."

Heather shuffled after him, her hair over her face.

A figure stepped out of the intersection then, turning to face them. Heather knew he wasn't one of the people who lived in the tunnels, for there was nothing about him that suggested that he was a drunk or a junkie, or any of the other down-on-their-luck people who had been exiled to the tunnels.

This man faced them with a demeanor of utter self-confidence and authority, an authority strengthened by the ugly rifle he cradled in his arms. Its hard metal surfaces gleamed even in the dim light of the overhead bulbs, and the magazine protruding from beneath its stock told Heather it was some kind of automatic. There was a telescopic sight mounted above the short barrel, and the ease with which the man held the gun told her he would have no trouble using it. He carried a small backpack and was clad entirely in black like a figure out of a movie. His face was so smudged with black makeup that his features were totally obscured. He seemed puzzled that he'd run into them.

"Hey!" Keith said, a goofy smile spreading across his features. "Got anything to drink?"

The man ignored the question. "What are you doing here?" he demanded, his voice every bit as imperious as his stance. "There's a hunt going on—you people are supposed to stay clear of this sector."

Keith raised his hands in mock horror. "Well, pardon me all ta hell. Nobody didn't tell us about no—" He wove slightly, leaning forward as if he couldn't quite make the man out. "Wha'd you say was goin' on?"

The man's expression darkened. "Never mind. Just get out of here." He jerked the muzzle of the rifle toward the far end of the passage they were in. "There's a shaft about three hundred yards farther along. It will take you up to the subway tunnel. After that, just find a station and get out." His lips twisted into an unpleasant smile. "And try not to get hit by a train—it messes up the tracks."

"Hey, anything you say," Keith slurred amiably. "Don't want no trouble . . ." He took Heather's arm and began steering her along, and she did her best to match his shambling stagger. "Jus' lookin' for a drink," he muttered as they started past the man. Then, just as he came abreast of the man, Keith appeared to stumble, bumping into him. The man, startled, instinctively pulled away, raising his gun as if to fend Keith off. In an instant, Keith's foot lashed out, his shoe catching the man in the dead center of his crotch.

Wracked by a spasm of agony so paralyzing that only a strangled sound escaped his throat, the man collapsed to the floor, his fingers reflexively tightening on the rifle as he went down. Even before he hit the ground, Keith had pulled his own gun from the waistband of his pants and lashed it across the man's temple. Shuddering, the man sprawled onto the floor. His whole body trembled for a second, then he lay still, blood oozing from the deep gash in his scalp.

Heather stared at the crumpled body in horror. "Is he . . . dead?"

"Doubt it," Keith muttered, already on his knees, rifling through the man's pockets. "He'll be asleep for a while though—it's not like in the movies, where they wake up two minutes later and start chasing people again." He took the man's wallet and put it in his own pocket, then pulled the backpack loose and handed it to Heather. Last of all, he took the man's braided nylon belt and used it to tie his wrists and ankles behind his back. "Just in case he wakes up," he said. Picking up the rifle, he stood and peered down both the intersecting corridors. There was nothing in the darkness, at least as far as he could see. He nodded in the direction in which the man had been moving. "Unless you've got a better idea, it seems like we ought to go wherever he was headed."

Heather gazed down at the unconscious man lying in the muck on the floor. "What if someone finds him?"

"Then they'll know it's not going to be quite as easy as they thought."

As he started down the passage, Heather fingered the backpack. "Shouldn't we see what's in here?"

"We will," Keith assured her. "But if any of this bastard's friends come along, I don't want to have to explain what I did." Turning away, he moved deeper into the tunnel, Heather following him.

The first rat had caught the scent of blood within a few seconds after Keith's gun had slashed through the fallen man's scalp, and by the time Keith and Heather had disappeared into the gloom, half a dozen of the creatures were slinking toward the unconscious body.

They approached it warily, knowing that this kind of animal could be dangerous, but as they crept closer and it failed to move, they became bolder.

Two of them slithered close enough to sniff at the blood, dipping their tongues into its warm saltiness.

Three more joined them.

Soon four more appeared out of the darkness, and another dropped down from a ledge where it had remained concealed from the moment the man had first arrived.

They began nibbling at the man's fingers first, and when he made no move to jerk away, moved quickly on to his arms and his face, his legs and his torso. Then, as the skin and flesh were torn away and the internal organs were exposed, the cockroaches and ants began to swarm out of the darkness to join in the feast.

By the time the man in the coal black clothes died, nearly a quarter of his body weight had been consumed by the voracious creatures of the darkness.

He was awake for the last few minutes of his ordeal.

Awake, but not screaming.

His vocal cords had already been eaten away.

CHAPTER 34

"**T**hat man is going to die, isn't he?"

Heather and Keith had been moving swiftly since leaving the fallen man lying unconscious in the muck, both of them silently keeping track of the turns they took, counting their steps. Keith had come to a halt a moment ago, pausing just outside one of the pools of light cast by the widely spaced bulbs in the low ceiling of the utilities tunnel. His body had fairly quivered with tension as he held up a finger to keep Heather from speaking, and both of them had strained to hear, searching for any noise that might betray the presence of another human being.

All they had heard were the faint scraping sounds of rats creeping along the concrete.

Satisfied that they were at least temporarily alone in the tunnel, he moved closer to the light, and while Heather dropped down to rest on a large pipe, Keith rifled through the backpack the man had been carrying. Only when Heather asked her question did he look up.

"He might," he said. "He would have killed us. As soon as we were past him, he was going to shoot us."

Though she heard the words clearly, Heather's mind rejected what Keith Converse had said. Why would the man have killed them? He didn't know them, had no idea who they were.

"It's why he didn't send us back the way we came," Keith explained, sensing Heather's uncertainty. "He wanted us close to him, close enough so he couldn't miss."

"You don't know that," Heather said, her voice low. "Why would he—"

"We saw him," Keith said. "We saw his face. As soon as he said we weren't supposed to be there, I knew what he was going to do."

"Then why didn't he just do it?" Heather demanded, and Keith could hear her desperation, her need to believe the man would have let them pass unharmed.

"Because he's a coward," Keith said. "What other kind of person would hunt for an unarmed man with an automatic rifle?" He glanced around at the tunnel stretching away in both directions. Save for the shadowy areas of darkness between the pools of light, there was no place to hide. He reached back into the bag and continued removing its contents.

Night vision goggles—not the cheap Russian variety he had seen in hunting magazines, but a fancy-looking setup whose price he couldn't even guess at.

A two-way radio, smaller than any cell phone he'd ever seen.

A canteen of water and a packet of food—the kind hikers carried with them, weighing almost nothing but packing a lot of energy.

A neatly coiled length of rope.

A pint of scotch—Chivas—which Keith suspected wasn't part of the standard issue of whatever group the kit's owner was a part.

And at the bottom, a small leather-bound book, like a diary. Though its color was indistinguishable in the darkness of the tunnel, the softness of its grain told Keith it was of the same quality as the goggles and the scotch. It bore an elegant monogram stamped in gold:

M H C

Below the monogram, in the same lettering, but in a smaller size, appeared the words:

Keith flipped the book open. It wasn't a diary, but rather, a kind of logbook, and as he scanned the first page, his blood ran cold. When he was finished, he wordlessly handed it to Heather. As she silently began to read, he tried to grasp everything that first page implied:

Quarry: Leon Nelson

Crime: Rape & Murder

Date of Extraction: 6/16/94

Dates of Hunt: 6/18/94–6/22/94

Hunting Party: Hawk   Falcon   Rattler
                         Mamba   Adder

Bagged By: Rattler

Time: 1:17 A.M.

Place: Level Three, Sector Four

Notes: Subject made numerous attempts to escape, none either unpredictable or imaginative. Herders reported finding him half drowned after attempting to hide in a storm drain during a downpour. Begging for mercy when Rattler shot him. Hoping for better game next time.

Heather read through the page twice, wishing she could find a reasonable explanation for what she was reading, but unable to ignore the cold, clinical directness of the log. Her heart racing, she flipped through the book until she came to the most recent entry.

The last of her doubt faded away as she read the words that had been so carefully written on the page.

In the space for identifying the "Quarry," Jeff's name was neatly inscribed.

The "Date of Extraction" was three days ago, the date that Jeff had supposedly died in the crash of the Correction Department transport van.

The "Dates of Hunt" entry was only partially filled in, with today's date as its opening.

The closing date was still blank.

The "Hunting Party" consisted of Adder, Mamba, Rattler, Viper, and Cobra.

"I wish you'd killed him," she said coldly. "But who are they? What kind of people would do such a thing? What kind of people could even think of such a thing?"

Keith held out the wallet he'd taken from the man's pants. "His name's Carey Atkinson," he said.

Heather's eyes widened with shock, and when she exchanged the logbook for the wallet, her hands were trembling. She stared at the driver's license for several long seconds, and when she spoke again, her voice was as unsteady as her hands.

"Keith, I know Carey Atkinson. He's a friend of my father's."

Keith frowned. "How good a friend?"

Heather took a deep breath, then she met Keith's gaze. "Very good," she whispered. "He's the Chief of Police."

Keith's lips compressed into a grim line. "I guess we know how they got Jeff out of the van."

As the truth of what Keith had just said sank in, Heather felt cold fury. "Could you have killed him?" she asked. "If you'd wanted to?"

Keith nodded. "If I'd known who he was and exactly what he was doing, I would have. I'd have broken his neck."

Heather took the gun out of her pocket and gazed at it. "Until just now I wasn't sure I'd actually be able to use this. But if we find the rest of those men . . ." Her voice trailed off.

"Let's just hope we find Jeff before they do," Keith said. He flipped through the book, then stopped. "Holy Jesus," he whispered.

"What?"

"Look." He held out the book. "Maps."

Heather took the book and studied the hand-drawn maps

carefully. There were eight pages of them, meticulously detailed, and as she moved back and forth from one page to another, the maze of passages and tunnels began to make some sense. Her finger touched a spot on the first map, pointing to where the men must have entered the labyrinth that lay beneath the streets.

A suspicion began to grow inside her. *He wouldn't do something like this. He couldn't!*

But she couldn't dispel the suspicion that had taken root in her mind.

Jagger froze, turning his attention away from the pain of his burns, focusing on the footsteps. When he'd first heard them, echoing so quietly that he almost failed to catch the sound at all, he was so sure it was Jeff returning that he'd nearly whispered to him. But an instinct deep within him had issued an alarm, and he stayed silent.

The approaching footsteps slowed, became more cautious.

Now he knew it wasn't Jeff.

Then who?

A hunter?

Maybe just a drunk.

It didn't matter. The important thing—the only thing that mattered—was that it wasn't Jeff.

He inched back, shrinking his huge frame deeper into the alcove, pressing against the end wall so hard his spine started to go numb.

As the footsteps came closer, he almost stopped breathing, concentrating every nerve in his body on the dark space beyond the alcove.

Whoever was approaching seemed to sense his presence as well, for whoever was hidden in the gloom paused after each step, as if to listen, to take stock.

Then the footsteps stopped altogether, and Jagger held his breath, afraid that even the air moving through his lungs might give him away.

The tense moment stretched, and when it finally ended, it wasn't a sound that broke it at all.

Instead, it was a tiny spot of brilliant red that crept into the edge of Jagger's vision like a drop of glowing blood oozing slowly through the filth that covered the rough concrete floor of the tunnel.

Or some sort of predator stalking its next meal.

As Jagger's eyes followed it, the crimson spot veered toward the wall opposite his lair and began climbing, moving back and forth, patrolling the wall like a soldier tacking across a battlefield. When it came to the ceiling, the spot abruptly vanished, but Jagger neither released his breath nor let himself relax.

The spot reappeared, now on the wall of the alcove directly opposite his face, no more than six feet away.

It began creeping downward, once again moving back and forth, and when it paused, Jagger was certain it had found him. But a second or two later it continued its progress until it reached the floor of the alcove. Instead of moving closer to him, however, it went the other way, edging closer and closer to the lip of the alcove's floor, until it disappeared, almost as if it had fallen over the edge.

His lungs burning, Jagger slowly began letting his breath escape, struggling against the urge to exhale in a sudden burst and gulp in a fresh supply of oxygen. He could sense the presence in the darkness now, feel it edging closer. Keeping his back pressed against the end wall, he twisted his head until his neck started to cramp, straining his eyes against the darkness and his ears against the silence.

The barrel of the rifle appeared first. It crept into the range of Jagger's vision and paused, as if the cold metal itself sensed danger. Then it began to move again, lengthening until Jagger could see the end of the weapon's telescopic sight and the hand that gripped its stock.

Still he didn't move, waiting until his instincts told him the moment had come.

The fingers of one hand closed tightly around the wide end of the railroad spike, while the fingers of the other flexed in the darkness, readying themselves.

The hunter's other hand appeared, its forefinger curled around the weapon's trigger, and Jagger knew this was his chance. He whipped one arm up, his fingers closing around the stock of the gun, and jerked it forward so fast that the hunter had no time even to release it from his grip. In almost the same movement, Jagger's other arm arced around, his hand wielding the point of the spike as if it were a stiletto, plunging it deep into the man's chest.

The gasp that escaped the man's lungs was his final breath, for the spike had already slashed through his heart before he even knew what had happened. His lifeless fingers slipped away from the rifle and he crumpled to the floor, leaving his weapon in the hands of his executioner.

The tunnel containing the alcove where he'd left Jagger was only a few yards ahead now, and Jeff froze, his arm coming up to stop Jinx, who was half a pace behind him.

A sound had stopped him, an expulsion of breath, as if someone had just taken a blow that knocked the wind out of him. But now, instead of hearing low moans of pain, or the gasping of someone struggling to regain his breath, all he heard was silence.

Jinx remained frozen beside him as they both listened, but the silence stretched on, and Jeff began to wonder if he'd really heard anything at all. He started forward again, moving more slowly than before, still sensing that something ahead had changed.

He came to the intersection of the two tunnels, with the alcove several paces in from where the passages met. He paused there, listening.

Nothing.

Finally, he stepped out of the shelter of the cross passage and turned toward the alcove.

A shaft of red light shot out of the darkness, and Jeff's heart leaped as he realized what it was.

The hunters had found Jagger, and now he himself was pinioned by the slim shaft of a rifle's laser sight. But instead of a shot, he heard a voice.

"I got one of 'em," Jagger said, his voice echoing off the hard concrete walls.

The shaft of red abruptly disappeared, and Jeff felt the tension drain from his body as Jagger appeared. "Jesus, Jag, I thought you were going to shoot me!"

"An' I was startin' to wonder if you were comin' back at all," the big man replied. A second later he was sucking the last drops of moisture out of the cup Jeff had brought him.

Jeff saw the crumpled figure of a man sprawled on the floor of the tunnel and moved closer, feeling oddly numb as he gazed at the dead man on the floor.

The man was dressed in black clothing and had a small pack strapped to his back. Jeff could see that he wasn't one of the normal denizens of the tunnels, if there was anything normal about the strange tribe of society's detritus that had accumulated beneath the streets. Clearly, this man was one of the hunters, and as he stared at the fallen figure, Jeff felt not even a twinge of remorse at what Jagger had done.

He knelt down and pulled the backpack loose, then began going through it.

There were a couple of sandwiches in a bag from a deli on Broadway, and a bottle of expensive spring water whose flavor wasn't quite as good as what came out of the city's taps but would certainly slake Jagger's burning thirst as well as his own. In addition to the food and water, he found a flashlight, a pair of night vision goggles, some kind of two-way radio, and a notebook. He turned on the flashlight and was just opening the notebook when Jinx swore softly.

"Jeez! It's that priest!"

Jeff, puzzled, shined the flashlight in the ashen face of Monsignor Terrence McGuire.

"It's the guy from that place on Delancey Street," Jinx went on. "You know—they'll give you a free meal if you let them preach to you awhile."

"You sure?" he asked.

But before Jinx could answer him, Jagger spoke up, his voice full of suspicion.

Suspicion, and menace.

"What's she doing here?" he asked, his eyes fixed on Jinx as his right hand tightened on the railroad spike, which was still stained with the priest's blood.

"She knows the tunnels," Jeff replied, still trying to digest this new information, and overlooking the menace in Jagger's voice. "She can help us get out."

Eve Harris hovered restlessly behind the small bar in the room deep beneath The 100 Club that served as the sole meeting place for the Manhattan Hunt Club. In fact, she had been responsible for the design of the room. It had been an empty storage chamber when she first saw it, the walls and floor constructed of the same cold, moldering concrete that made up the catacomb of tunnels beneath the streets. She'd seen the possibilities of the space at once, the huge beams supporting the concrete of the first basement reminding her of a hunting lodge, and as she chose the paneling, the carpet, and the furniture, she never wavered from the lodge motif. It was more elegant and urbane than one might find in Montana, but perfectly matched the sensibilities of the members of the Hunt Club. The fireplace had presented no difficulties at all, since there was already a chimney for the furnace directly overhead—the masons only needed to tap into it. Its mantelpiece, from a Victorian gamekeeper's lodge in Northumberland, fit the room perfectly, and the bar, replicating one she'd seen in a small pub outside of Ulster, complemented the fireplace perfectly as well.

After pouring herself two fingers of the ancient cognac that had been her husband's favorite, and returning the decanter to its place of honor in the exact center of the second shelf of the back bar, Eve Harris regarded the trophy above the fireplace. "Bastard," she murmured, raising her glass to Leon Nelson, though there was no one else in the room to hear her. Nelson's sightless eyes stared back at her, and as she gazed at the impassive expression on the face of the mounted head, she wondered if it was the same expression he'd had when he killed her daughter. For a moment she almost wished he were still alive, so she could have the pleasure of killing him the way he'd killed Rachelle, slowly and painfully. Her eyes roamed over the rest of the trophies, and as always happened when she was in this room, the heat of vengeance began to thaw the cold hatred that had filled her soul for so many years. And it wasn't over yet, she thought. The prisons were still filled with criminals whose rights the courts had somehow held to be more important than those of the people whose lives they had ruined.

As she poured herself another two fingers of cognac, this time leaving the decanter on the bar, she glanced nervously at her watch.

The hunters had been gone more than two hours, and it had been an hour since any of them had checked in.

That was unusual.

Even more unusual was her growing sense that something had gone wrong. Eve Harris had long since learned to trust her instincts. So she picked up the two-way radio—a specially designed unit not available to the general public— and began going through the five frequencies programmed into it, a single frequency dedicated to each of the hunters, which allowed all of them to communicate with her but not with each other. It was both part of the sport and an extra precaution—if any of the radios fell into the wrong hands, nothing any of the other hunters said could be overheard by the wrong people. When the first of the five frequencies was glowing brightly in the LED screen, she held the miniature radio close to her lips and pressed the button.

"Adder," she said softly. "Report, please."

* * *

Heather Randall and Keith Converse were moving slowly through a darkness that was almost complete. According to the maps they'd found sketched in Carey Atkinson's notebooks, they were in the second sector of Level 3. The darkness was almost complete, but using the night vision goggles, Keith could clearly see what lay ahead. Through the eyepieces, the tunnels seemed to be lit by a surrealistic green light that appeared to have no source at all. Heather, following him, was blinded by the darkness and finding her way only by keeping her right hand on Keith's shoulder. The vibration in her pocket startling her, her hand jerked away from Keith, and for a moment she felt a surge of panic as her only link to another person was broken. Then her fingers found Keith again, and his hand closed over hers.

"What happened?" he whispered.

She was about to answer when she felt the vibration again, but this time realized it was the tiny radio they'd found in Carey Atkinson's backpack. They'd thought it was a cell phone until they discovered it had only two buttons, one labeled PWR the other TLK. When they'd turned it on, the screen had glowed slightly. There was a single earpiece, the kind inserted directly into the ear canal. A tiny hole on the face of the instrument appeared to be the microphone. Keith concluded it was a radio of some kind, though he hadn't seen anything like it before.

They toyed with the idea of using it, but quickly rejected the notion, for that would betray to whomever it might contact that it was no longer in Atkinson's hands. Now, as it vibrated a third time, Heather whispered, "The radio—I think someone's trying to call Atkinson."

"Put in the earplug and hit the power button," Keith whispered back. "But don't say anything. Not a word."

Heather fumbled with the earplug for a moment, then carefully went over the surface of the radio with her fingers. The power button was on the right, the talk button on the left, but she pressed neither until she was certain she held the radio right side up. Then, her forefinger shaking, she pressed the button. There was a moment of silence before she heard a voice, with the crystal clarity of digital technology.

"Adder? Report, please."

Eve Harris listened to the static-free silence, willing Carey Atkinson's voice to reply to her. The radio had the best range of anything yet developed, but in the maze of concrete tunnels, even this system's range was severely limited. The five miles it could reach in open space with a direct line of sight was cut down to half a mile, at best, in the tunnels. That should have been sufficient, however, because the gamekeepers and herders knew to keep the quarry well within the perimeter of the hunting ground. Though reception might be fuzzy in certain areas, every sector of every level was within the radio's range, and unless one of the hunters strayed too far, she should never lose contact with any of them. And this connection sounded as if it was clear.

Clear, or not there at all.

"Adder?" she repeated, her voice taking on an urgent note as her sense that something had gone wrong grew stronger. "Report, please. Now!"

When she still heard nothing but silence, she switched frequencies. In less than a minute she had determined the locations of Perry Randall, Arch Cranston, and Otto Vandenberg, and assured herself that at least they were operating well within the hunting ground.

Monsignor McGuire, like Carey Atkinson, didn't respond; but the cleric's radio had at least emitted the static that was missing from Atkinson's. Finally, she switched back to the original frequency she'd entered. "Adder," she said one more time. "Do you read me?"

But no voice emerged from the tiny speaker in her own radio, and a moment later, certain something had gone wrong, she severed the connection.

*   *   *

Heather's hands were shaking so badly that she nearly dropped the tiny radio, and when she pulled the earplug loose, she made no attempt to wind the wire around the radio itself, but instead just stuffed the whole thing deep into her pocket. Keith reached out to find her, felt her shivering, and steadied her against himself. "What happened?" he asked. "What did you hear?"

"A voice," Heather breathed. "It was asking for 'Adder,' asking him to report. When I didn't answer, the radio went dead." She hesitated, and when she spoke again, her voice trembled and had a note of deep fear. "I was just going to take the plug out of my ear when the voice came back. . . ."

"And . . . ?" Keith prodded her gently.

"I recognized the voice, Keith," she whispered, barely audible. "I know it sounds crazy, but I'd swear it was Eve Harris!"

The name struck Keith like a body blow, and his first instinct was to find an explanation. Eve Harris was the one person who had tried to help him, tried to—

And then he understood.

She hadn't been trying to help him at all. She'd only wanted to find out what he was doing.

"I'll kill them," he said softly. "I swear, I'll kill every single one of them."

CHAPTER 35

Jeff shut off the tiny penlight that had been in Monsignor McGuire's small backpack and closed the cleric's notebook. At first he hardly believed what he'd read, but as he slowly turned the pages, he realized that every page bore out the strange story Jinx had told him. He even recognized the name listed on the page before the one that was headed with his own. Jeff knew that Tony Sanchez had been in the Tombs before he himself arrived there. They'd been in adjoining cells for a few days, and the night before Sanchez was to be transferred to Rikers Island, he'd been bragging about how good his lawyer was.

"You shoulda heard him, man," he'd crowed. "Made it sound like it was all the bitch's fault. Shit, man, time he was done, the assholes on the jury figured she musta cut herself up!"

"But they still sent you up, didn't they?" Jeff had asked.

Sanchez's grin had barely flickered. "What's a fuckin' year? I'll be out in six months."

But a week or so later someone had told him that Sanchez escaped from Rikers. "Don't know how—dogs tracked 'im to the bridge and that was it—like the fucker just vanished."

But according to the book Jeff was now holding, Sanchez hadn't vanished at all. He'd been "bagged" in something called Sector 1 of Level 2 at 11:32 P.M. on November twelfth.

The name of the victorious hunter was "Rattler."

A cold numbness had spread through him as he turned the

316

pages of the bizarre logbook, but coming to the hand-sketched maps that filled the last few pages of the book, the numbness was forgotten as he realized what he was holding—the key to the maze of tunnels. As he studied them, though, his hope began to fade, since he had no way of knowing where on the map he, Jagger, and Jinx were located. But on the final page of the section containing the maps, he thought he saw a pattern emerge. He looked more closely, struggling to remember once again the route he'd used when he went to search for water. Slowly—so slowly that at first he thought he was imagining it—the path in his memory began to emerge from the jumble of lines.

Each page mapped a small sector of a specific level, with lines representing tunnels and circles marking the places where shafts connected one level to another. He felt the heat of excitement as he recognized their exact location—even the alcove in which Jagger had hidden was marked on the map. His excitement growing, he turned back through the pages of maps, piecing them together, matching the shafts marked on one page to those on the next, linking ends of the tunnels in the margins of the page until slowly the entire area began to take shape in his mind. And as the fog of confusion that had lain over the labyrinth began to lift, another memory stirred in him—a memory of the class he'd taken in the last semester before he was arrested.

They had been discussing the problems peculiar to construction in the heart of the city, where every site was often surrounded on two or even three sides by other buildings that could not be damaged by either the demolition of the existing structure or the construction of the new building. One morning his class had left the campus to look at a block where the stores had been vacated and boarded up but the demolition crews had not yet begun their work.

Now Jeff tried to recall the details of a new skyscraper's construction schedule. And as it came back to him, so did the beginnings of a plan start to develop.

"It might work," he whispered.

"What might work?" Jagger growled.

"There might be a way to get out of here."

Jagger glowered down at the corpse of Monsignor McGuire. "Only if we can kill 'em all. Don't even know how many there are."

"Five, according to this book." Jeff looked at the crumpled body, and when he spoke, his voice was devoid of emotion. "Which means there are only four left." His eyes lingered on the lifeless figure, and he tried to summon up some sorrow or pity for the man. But the contents of the priest's logbook had drained him of any compassion. "You got him with just the spike. Now we've got a gun with a laser sight, and a night vision scope as well."

"And they got the same stuff, and there's four of 'em," Jagger argued.

"So what do you want to do, just wait here for them to find us?"

"Least that way we could pick 'em off one by one."

"If they all come," Jeff replied. "But if they're all working different areas, then we could wait here forever." His eyes fixed on the blisters that covered Jagger's forehead. Some of the broken ones were already turning septic, the wounds swelling and reddening. "And those burns have to be tended to. God only knows what's already gotten into them." As if to emphasize his words, some kind of flying insect landed on Jagger's face and began probing one of the wounds, as if searching either for food or a place to lay its eggs.

Jagger smashed it, crushing the insect and spreading a stain of blood and pus across his forehead.

"Jeff's right," Jinx said. "We've got to get out of here."

Jagger glowered at her. What the fuck did she know? he thought. She was just a kid . . . except not such a kid that she wasn't trying to move in on Jeff. Did she think he couldn't see how much she wanted Jeff? Well, it wouldn't happen—he'd see to that. Muttering a curse, Jagger heaved himself to his feet, then had to reach out and steady himself against the wall as a wave of dizziness broke over him. He eased himself back down on the concrete shelf that was the floor of the alcove.

"Can you walk?" Jeff asked.

Jagger's eyes, closed to narrow slits, were fixed on Jinx. "I can walk," he said. "And that ain't all I can do," he added.

"Try anything and I'll—" Jinx began with more bravado than she felt, but Jeff didn't let her finish.

"If you can walk, then you're going to do it," he said to Jagger, his voice grim. He gazed at the muck that covered the floor, and sniffed at the putrid air that filled the tunnel. "We've got one sandwich and the priest's canteen. When that's gone, you're going to get worse. So let's see if we can get out while you can still stay on your feet."

Jagger heaved himself upright once more, swayed for a moment, but then steadied. "Let's go."

With the maps in the priest's log firmly in his mind, and the rifle slung over his shoulder, Jeff moved off into the darkness, Jinx right behind him, Jagger behind her.

A shiver ran through Heather Randall that had nothing to do with the temperature. Indeed, the temperature in the tunnels never seemed to vary at all. It was as if the climate beneath the city had reached a strange equilibrium—always stale and humid. Most of the people they'd seen were alone, moving slowly along the passages. Their heads were invariably down, and though they might have been looking for something—a dropped coin or a scrap of food—there was an aura about them that told her they had long ago given up searching for anything.

Every now and then she and Keith had come upon an alcove that was occupied. The first time it happened, Heather had felt a sense of shock and outrage that anyone should have to live in a nest of rags hidden away in a world of eternal twilight.

The man in the alcove, though, had barely glanced at her before turning away, his hands more tightly clutching the bottle he was nursing.

Now they were standing in one of the pools of light while Keith studied the maps he'd found in the notebook. As he pondered the diagrams, Heather uneasily searched the shadowy darkness that lay beyond the dim glow of the light for any sign of danger.

A memory of something Jeff had once said suddenly came to her: *it's safer to be in the dark and peer into the light than the other way around.*

The thought had induced the shiver, and as the icy finger ran over her skin, she scanned the darkness again, wishing that she, like the man in the alcove and the rats she could hear scurrying along the floor, were in the darkness rather than the light.

"I think we're right here." Though he barely spoke above a whisper, Keith's voice echoed off the walls, startling Heather. His right forefinger was touching an intersection on the map, and as she studied it, she tried to remember the turns they'd made, the ladders they'd used. But it was all muddled in her mind, and besides . . .

"What good does it do?" She unconsciously spoke the question out loud, then added, "What does it matter where we are if we don't know where we're going?"

"According to this, most of their 'hunts' wind up on what they call Level Four. Near as I can figure, we're on Level Two." He tipped his head toward the darkness ahead. "There should be a shaft up there somewhere."

Wordlessly, Heather followed Keith deeper into the darkness, and as they moved from the pool of light into the concealing darkness, her anxiety eased.

They came to the shaft, and Keith shined his light into its depths. The walls were slick with slime, and some of the rungs embedded in the concrete had rusted completely through. "I'll go first," Keith said. "If they'll hold me, they'll hold you."

Heather gazed down into the black pit and shook her head. "I'll go first. We'll tie the rope around my waist so if a rung breaks . . ." Her voice died away, but Keith understood what she was saying. If he was above, at least she'd have a chance. If it was he who fell, there'd be no chance at all. His weight would probably just pull her in after him.

As she tested the knot a minute or so later, Heather peered into the inky well below. Then she crouched down and extended a leg, feeling for the lowest rung she could touch. As Keith held the line taut, she found a rung and eased her other foot down, while still supporting her weight on the lip of the shaft. "Ready?" she asked.

"Ready."

She shifted her weight from her elbows to her feet.

The rung held.

Her fingers closing onto the top rung, she lowered herself deeper into the shaft.

The next rung held, too, and the one after that.

She began moving more quickly, her confidence growing, Keith playing out the rope as quickly as she descended.

Then, so suddenly that she had no time to prepare herself, one of the rungs gave way beneath her, snapping away from the wall.

She felt herself falling, and a scream erupted from her throat, a visceral cry of terror cut suddenly off as the loop around her waist jerked upward, caught under her armpits, and snapped tight. She swung loose then, dangling in the darkness, until her hand found a rung and her fingers instinctively closed around it. Pulling herself close to the wall, Heather clutched the rung with both hands while her feet felt for another. Meanwhile, she gasped to catch the breath that the tightening rope had driven from her lungs.

A wave of dizziness came over her as she gazed down the

shaft, and for a moment she was afraid she might fall again. Then Keith's voice drifted down from above. "You okay?"

A groan was the only sound Heather could muster until the dizziness passed. Finding her voice, she said, "A rung broke, but I'm all right now."

She took a deep breath and cautiously continued down, but now tested each rung before trusting it with her weight.

One more broke away, and two bent but held. Then she was at the bottom. Untying the rope, she called to Keith, and he pulled it up. Then he lowered it again, this time with the backpack attached to the end.

Two more of the rungs gave way as Keith made his way down the ladder, and when he dropped out of the shaft, he looked up grimly. "We're not going to get back up there," he said, then grinned in the gloom. "But on the other hand, no one else is going to be able to come down, either." His gaze shifted to the tunnels, and he studied the maps for a moment. "That way," he decided.

Heather looked at the map, but could see nothing in it that hinted about which way to go. "Why?" she asked.

Keith shrugged. "To tell you the truth, I don't have a clue. But we can't stay here." With Heather following, he headed into the darkness.

They'd gone no more than a hundred yards when they found the body. At first Keith thought it was another of the derelicts who were everywhere in the tunnels, either asleep or passed out. But shining his flashlight full on the man, he saw the crimson stain that soaked the clothes, and when he knelt down to look more closely, he noted the deep gash that had been slashed into the dead man's chest.

He was checking the inside pockets of the man's jacket when Heather gasped. He looked up at her and saw that it wasn't the gaping wound at which she was staring, but the man's face.

"You know him, too." It was a statement, not a question.

"Monsignor McGuire," she said softly. "He—he runs a shelter for the homeless."

· But Keith wasn't listening. He was paging through the notebook again, turning to the page on which his son's name had been entered. He stared at the list of hunters. Adder, Mamba, Rattler, Viper, and Cobra. "This guy's another friend of your dad's, right?"

Heather nodded.

Keith looked at the list again, remembering the man he'd killed earlier.

Carey Atkinson.

Now here was Monsignor McGuire, with a hole torn in his chest.

Atkinson and McGuire.

Adder and Mamba?

He sensed Heather close behind him, felt her breath on the back of his neck as she, too, stared at the page of the open notebook.

And heard her gasp as she, too, made the connection.

"It can't be," she whispered. "My father can't be doing this."

But even as she said it, she knew that no matter how often she repeated the words, the seed that had taken root in her mind would continue to grow.

CHAPTER 36

The hunter called Viper had hardly moved for more than two hours. The activity of brushing bugs away from his face or striking out at any too-curious rats that approached had been sufficient to keep stiffness out of his joints and numbness from his muscles. But while his body had rested, his mind was humming, taking in every bit of sensory information, and analyzing it from every angle.

For Viper, the hours spent on the hunt were the best of his life, far more interesting, far more challenging, than the endless tedium of listening to lawyers debate the arcane trivia of law, precedent, and Supreme Court decisions. Viper had always known what was right and what was wrong. It was why he had become a lawyer in the first place. He hadn't gone to law school out of any interest in arguing cases, but out of the certain knowledge that he had a unique ability to determine right from wrong.

With that in mind, Otto Vandenberg had set out to be a judge, and by the time he was forty, his ambition had been fulfilled. But as the years had gone by, his own satisfaction in his judgments had first been diluted, and then washed completely away—by the steady trickle of decisions from the courts above him, limiting his discretion, establishing maximum sentences, even dictating immediate release for some of the leeches that he believed were sucking the life out of decent men and women.

But the Manhattan Hunt Club had changed all that, and

from his first moment in the tunnels, when Vandenberg had shed his judicial robes for hunter's black and the role of the Viper, he'd once again experienced the deep sense of fulfillment that came not only from exercising his perfect judgment, but from having his sentences carried out as well.

Today, two of his sentences were to be enacted, and it was his intention to bag at least one of the trophies himself. Thus, after studying the records of every one of the previous thirty-seven hunts, and tracing the routes the prey had used in their attempts to escape their stalkers, he had settled on this particular spot, a nearly invisible shelf, so well-hidden in the maze of pipes and conduits running through the utility tunnel that he could stay in almost perfect concealment, his senses alert, ready to strike like the snake from which his code name derived.

His weapon was prepared—a 7.62mm M-14A1 that he had acquired directly from a friend at the Pentagon, but to which he'd added a special laser sight himself. His backpack held four magazines for the rifle, each of which contained twenty rounds, but Vandenberg fully expected to come back with three of the magazines full and the one in the rifle less than half empty.

The sporting method of bagging the prey, after all, was with a single shot.

The rest of the magazine was nothing more than insurance.

His night scope lay beneath his right hand, ready if he heard the sound of approaching prey. And his ears would have no trouble distinguishing the sound of the quarry from the background noise that constantly drifted through the tunnel. Vandenberg had long ago learned to tell the scurrying sound of mice from that of rats, the sound of a leaking pipe from that of a derelict pissing on the wall, the moans of a dying man from those of one who was merely ill. He'd learned to sort out the scents as well, sniffing out the smell of an approaching human being as efficiently as a great white shark can catch the scent of blood from miles away.

Now, as he lay concealed, all his nerves suddenly went on full alert. He couldn't have said what it was that set his senses on edge; perhaps it was a whiff of an aroma, or a nearly subliminal sound—or perhaps it was nothing more than the perfectly honed instincts of a predator.

All he knew was that something was coming.

Gotta get rid of her, Jagger thought. Gotta get rid of her before she wrecks everything. He watched Jinx following Jeff through the tunnel. She was ahead of him, but not very far, and she was staying close to Jeff.

He knew why she was doing that—so she could smell him, take his scent deep into her lungs, just the way he had last night and the night before, when he'd watched over Jeff, making sure nothing bad happened to him while he slept. But since Jinx had shown up, he hadn't been able to get anywhere near close enough to Jeff to—

He cut that thought off. He just wanted to take care of Jeff, to protect him, so they could be friends—best friends.

His fist tightened on the railroad spike, and he edged closer.

Otto Vandenberg gazed through the eyepiece of his night scope.

Three people coming.

He recognized two of them immediately—he'd sentenced Jeff Converse only a few days ago, and Jagger just last year.

But the girl . . .

Who was the girl?

He focused the scope on her, searching his memory.

He had it—a street girl, someone he'd seen in court.

Young, and pretty. Or at least she'd have been pretty if you cleaned her up.

He kept the scope on her until she was so close he could see her features perfectly. If she were alone, if he had more time—

The hunt was far more important than any transient pleasure his body might enjoy, he reminded himself. Plenty of time for girls later . . .

The trio passed below him, and he shifted silently around, making up his mind.

Converse, or Jagger?

Perhaps both?

His nerves tingled as he set the night scope down and turned to the sniper rifle.

Something had changed.

Jeff could feel it. There was a sense of danger lurking nearby, so close it was palpable. But where?

They'd been moving steadily for almost a quarter of an hour, and their destination wasn't too much farther ahead. Stopping would only serve to alert whatever threat lay in the darkness that he had been discovered, so he kept moving, but increased his pace—not enough to betray his awareness, but enough to get them past the unseen danger more quickly.

Behind him, he sensed that Jinx could feel the danger, too.

And then he realized where the danger was emanating from.

It wasn't the herders at all.

Or the hunters.

No, the danger he was sensing was coming from much, much closer.

It was coming from Jagger.

Jagger was close enough behind Jinx that he could almost feel her. If he reached out, he could touch her, could put his fingers in her hair and yank her back, drag her away from Jeff, twist her neck until he heard the bones pop, then plunge the point of the spike into her flesh.

That would stop her.

That would keep her away from Jeff.

He edged closer, his right hand clutching the spike so tightly his whole arm was trembling.

*   *   *

Otto Vandenberg felt the hypnotic calm of the imminent kill fall over him. His hands were steady, his breathing slow and even. He could feel the calm, rhythmic throbbing of his heart, and began silently gauging the perfect moment, anticipating the instant when his finger would take advantage of the utter stillness of his body when neither his lungs nor his heart could throw his aim off by so much as a millimeter.

He'd made his decision as to which trophy he would take first, and the crosshairs of the night sight were fixed on the spot where the single bullet he would fire would be most lethal but do the least damage to the prize.

Why make Malcolm Baldridge's job any more difficult than it already was?

The moment came—that perfect confluence of lung and heart—and Otto Vandenberg slowly squeezed off the single round in the rifle's chamber.

The soft phut of the silenced shot was barely audible, even to the Viper's sharply honed ears.

Jagger's left hand came up, and he reached toward Jinx's hair, imagining its tangled strands in his fingers. His heart pounded as—

Jeff whirled around to see Jagger looming over Jinx, one of his hands reaching for her, the other clutching the railroad spike, which hovered dangerously above her. Without thinking, he lunged at Jinx, knocking her to the side just as Jagger made his move.

But then he saw a look of utter astonishment on Jagger's face.

Jagger felt as if he'd been struck by a sledgehammer.

He stumbled, tried to regain his balance, but something had gone wrong.

He couldn't feel anything.

He dropped the spike, and his huge body crumpled toward the ground.

What had happened?

As he sank onto the floor, and realized he could no longer move his legs, the truth came to him.

Not a sledgehammer at all.

A bullet.

A bullet had struck him in the back, and—

He looked at his chest and saw blood oozing through his shirt and jacket.

But his mind still refused to grasp the reality of what was happening to him. If he'd been shot, why didn't he feel it?

He tried to speak, but there was no air in his lungs, and when he tried to breathe in, he heard a gurgling sound from somewhere deep in his chest.

And then he heard nothing at all.

CHAPTER 37

Jeff had Monsignor McGuire's rifle already raised. When he saw Jagger fall, his first thought was that Jagger had tripped while lunging at Jinx. Then he saw the blood oozing from the wound in Jagger's chest, and was about to go to Jagger's side when Jinx shoved him against the wall. As she did, a bullet ricocheted off the opposite wall, a few yards away.

"It's one of them!" she whispered. "He's gonna get us!"

Jeff rose to his knees and raised the rifle again, jamming the stock against his shoulder as he fumbled with the safety. Peering through the scope, he saw nothing, but pulled the trigger anyway.

The rifle came to life, pouring a stream of lead into the far reaches of the tunnel and shattering the underground silence with its roar. The gun vibrating in his hands, Jeff sprayed the tunnel with bullets until the magazine was empty, its twenty rounds fired in less than a second. The chatter of exploding cartridges died suddenly away. He groped in the priest's backpack for another magazine, but Jinx was jerking at his arm.

"Let's get out of here," she whispered. "They'll all be here in a few minutes!" She darted away into the darkness.

Instead of following her, Jeff crouched down next to Jagger's unmoving form. "Jagger?" he said softly. "Hey, Jag . . ." His voice trailed off when he saw there would be no response. He reached down and took Jagger's wrist, feeling for a pulse.

Nothing.

For a long minute Jeff stayed where he was, hunkered down next to Jagger's body.

He thought of the onrushing train that would have crushed him if Jagger hadn't hurled him aside. And of the man they'd come across in the depths of the tunnels, the man Jagger had killed, certain he'd intended Jeff some kind of harm.

How could he leave Jagger here? He knew what would happen as soon as he was gone. First the rats would come, and then the flies and ants and cockroaches.

But what choice did he have? Even if he could have carried Jagger, where could he take him?

From somewhere in the shadows, he heard Jinx's voice. "Hurry! They'll find us!"

Still he lingered, and finally lay his fingers on Jagger's forehead. "Thanks," he whispered in the darkness. "You were my friend."

Picking up Jagger's railroad spike from the floor, Jeff gazed down at Jagger one last time. Then, staying low to the ground, he turned and hurried away.

Eve Harris pressed the transmit button on her radio over and over again, as if the mere repetition might bend the instrument to her will. Yet she knew the problem didn't lie with the radio, but with the hunt itself.

Something had gone wrong.

Now Viper wasn't responding to her call. Viper, whose preferred method of hunting was to lie in ambush, waiting for his prey to come to him. She'd spoken to him only a few minutes ago, and his voice had been clear over the static.

And now nothing.

She told herself that Vandenberg might have decided to change his position—to set up his ambush deeper in the tunnels, where the radio couldn't reach. But she knew better. Vandenberg was a coward at heart, and unless he'd been flushed from his blind, he'd stay where he was until the hunt was over, bagging the quarry if it came his way, but content to let others stalk the tunnels.

Cursing softly, she turned her attention back to the radio, changing it from one frequency to another, silently praying that at least one of the hunters would still be within range of the transmitter.

Or at least still be alive . . .

Keith recognized the sound as soon as it crashed against his ears, echoing and reechoing off the concrete walls until it faded away.

A semiautomatic rifle, firing at least twenty rounds.

Heather, who had been behind him only a moment ago, was now next to him, her fingers digging into his arm.

"Where did it come from?" she whispered, as if afraid to speak out loud in the sudden silence that followed the volley of shots.

"Ahead," Keith replied, his voice grim. "Come on."

Giving Heather no chance to argue, he set out at a dogtrot, moving quickly down the tunnel in the direction from which the blast of gunfire had come. Heather caught up with him, and less than a minute later they came to an intersection.

"Which way?" Heather gasped.

Raising the night goggles to his eyes, Keith scanned the tunnels in both directions. At first he saw nothing, but then, at the farthest reach of the goggles' range, he spotted something protruding from a kind of shelf high up on the tunnel's wall. Something that looked like—

"This way," he said. "Hurry."

He took off again, not at an easy trot this time, but as fast as he could run.

Behind him, Heather struggled to keep up.

Perry Randall pressed the transmitter button on his radio, silently praying he was still within the instrument's short range. "This is Rattler. Come in, Control. This is Rattler!" He released the button and strained his ears to find a voice hidden in the static that was all he could hear.

Nothing.

He swore silently, glanced at the glowing dial on his watch, then played the thin beam of his penlight over the map in the back of his log. He was in Sector 2 of the second level, and Viper should be working the next sector on the same level. If the herders had done their job, Jeff Converse and Francis Jagger shouldn't be too far away. If they were a level down, though, Randall knew it was possible that Mamba might get them before he could get his own shot.

Not that it would matter if one of the others got Jagger— Randall didn't give a damn about him. When he'd looked over Jagger's record during the Hunt Committee meeting, it had been obvious that Jagger would be easy prey—big, and stupid, like a rhinoceros, dangerous only if you got too close. Indeed, Randall suspected that Jagger had already been taken, and whoever had bagged him was on his way back to the club, the carcass marked and mapped, ready for the gamekeepers to collect and deliver to Malcolm Baldridge. But Perry Randall wanted Jeff Converse himself—had wanted him ever since the night Converse had been arrested in the subway station, crouched over his victim. Of course, Heather had kept insisting the boy was innocent right up until the day he was sentenced, but that hadn't surprised him. The boy had a certain charm that, though it hadn't fooled him for a moment, had certainly taken his daughter in. Not that it mattered anymore— the boy would be dead within the hour, and it would be his own personal pleasure to bag that particular specimen.

Except that right now Perry Randall had the distinct feeling that something odd was happening.

He pressed the transmitter again. "This is Rattler. Come in, Control. This is Rattler." He released the button, listening.

Still nothing.

As he was about to try one more time, the quiet of the tunnel was shattered by a blast of gunfire.

Not a single shot, but a burst from a semiautomatic rifle.

His nerves suddenly tingling with the excitement of the hunt, Randall jerked the tiny plug from his ear and listened for another burst from the rifle so he could be certain of the direction from which it came.

Putting on his night vision goggles, he peered through the greenish haze of amplified light.

Three rats, invisible only a moment ago, could now be seen scurrying along the tunnel's floor, searching for any kind of edible scrap. As Randall watched, two of them caught each other's scent, froze, found each other, and hurled themselves to the attack, each determined to drive the other from its territory. Randall felt a twinge of excitement as he watched the rodents tear at each other, and when one of them finally gave up and scuttled up the wall to disappear into a wide crack near the ceiling, he felt a sense of disappointment.

The fight should not have ended that way, with one of the combatants fleeing the battleground.

The loser should not have been allowed to escape.

The loser should have died.

And today, the losers *would* die. Flush with anticipation, Perry Randall turned his full attention back to the hunt.

He heard another sound, this time that of running feet, and whipped around with the speed of a striking rattlesnake, peering deep into the greenish haze.

Even with the help of the night vision goggles, he almost missed it.

Almost, but not quite, for Randall's eyes were every bit as sharp as his mind, and though the shape in the distance had disappeared almost before he was aware that it was there at all, he caught it.

A man had gone into the cross passage ahead of him.

A rush of adrenaline sent a tingle through his nerves as Perry Randall started after the vanished figure.

He was certain the hunt would soon be over.

CHAPTER 38

Jeff could hear footsteps pounding somewhere behind him, but didn't dare to pause long enough for a backward glance. If it was one of the hunters, he'd be a dead man as soon as he stopped. If he and Jinx were to have any chance of escaping, they had to keep going, zigzagging back and forth across the tunnel in a pattern that wouldn't give whoever was behind them an easy shot. Ahead, he saw a narrow passage leading to the left. Sprinting to attract Jinx's attention, he came to the branching passage, turned quickly into it, and grabbed Jinx as she followed him in. He clamped his hand over her mouth so she couldn't cry out, wrapped his free arm around her and pressed his lips close to her ear. "We'll stay here," he whispered. "If they don't hear us, we can get them before they get us."

When Jinx nodded that she understood, he released his grip on her. His heart pounding, Jeff quickly looked around. The passage he'd turned into was far narrower than the tunnel they'd just left, and one of its walls was covered with rank upon rank of electrical conduits. The only illumination came from the faint glow leaking into the passage's entrance from a utility light a few yards farther down the main tunnel. Pulling Monsignor McGuire's night scope out of the backpack, Jeff switched it on and peered into the passage's depth.

The narrow shaft appeared to come to a dead end no more than fifty yards ahead. As he was scanning the walls and ceiling for a means of escape, Jinx's hand closed on his arm.

"Listen!" she whispered. "They stopped."

Lowering the night scope, Jeff turned back around, his head moving as he strained to hear something—anything—in the sudden silence that had fallen over the tunnel. The sound of racing feet that they'd heard only a moment or two ago had indeed stopped.

The hush was broken by the faint rattle of an approaching subway train. But even as the sound grew louder and the concrete beneath his feet began to vibrate, the familiar noise remained oddly muted, and then Jeff realized why—the train was above them by at least one level, maybe even two.

Which meant that if they were going to escape, they would have to get closer to the surface. But how?

If there was no escape from the passage he'd ducked into, then they had no choice but to return to the tunnel from which they'd fled only a moment ago.

Dust from the trembling ceiling of the passage settled down on them as the train passed overhead, and then its sound died away.

Jeff listened to the ensuing silence, which seemed even more frightening than the pursuing footsteps had only a few moments before.

Now they were no longer being chased.

Now they were being stalked.

Heather Randall shuddered as she stared at the corpse that projected grotesquely from a shelf just below the tunnel's ceiling. From where she and Keith stood, they could see only the body's head, shoulders, and arms. The head, covered with a shock of gray hair matted with blood, was hanging downward at an angle impossible in life. She watched as a fresh drop of blood fell into the puddle on the floor beneath the corpse.

The arms hung straight down, the hands outstretched, almost as if reaching for the body's lost blood—or perhaps the rifle whose stock lay half submerged in the puddle.

Struggling to control the nausea rising in her belly, she instinctively reached out to grip Keith's hand. They edged around the pool of blood until they could see the other side of the corpse's head, and the wound that had caused the man's death.

It looked as if the man had tried to turn away from the fusillade that had been fired at him, but given what they'd heard, Heather knew he hadn't stood a chance; the bullet that killed him had ripped away the right half of his forehead, leaving the pulpy mass of his brain exposed. In the dim light of the tunnel, the whole scene seemed impossible—it was obvious the man had been setting up a well-equipped ambush. What had gone wrong?

"Hold this while I take a look," Keith said quietly, handing her the rifle they'd taken from Carey Atkinson's corpse.

As Keith pulled himself up to the shelf on which the body lay, Heather continued to stare at the corpse.

How had he ended up getting shot himself?

Then her eyes fell on the rifle. It was exactly like the one she now held in her own hands.

When they'd found Monsignor McGuire, he hadn't had a rifle.

"Here's his bag," Keith said, pulling a backpack exactly like Atkinson's off the shelf, then dropping back down to the floor. As he was about to open it, the hairs on the back of his neck stood on end. "I think someone's following us," he whispered so softly that his words died away in an instant. "Start walking, and don't look back."

Heather did as Keith instructed. Pausing only long enough to pick up the dead man's rifle, Keith quickly followed.

Perry Randall watched the two figures through his night vision goggles. The images were clear—a man and a woman—but not clear enough for him to identify. Yet despite the haziness in the greenish light, there was something familiar about both of them.

That sense of familiarity kept Randall from killing them.

Eve would never let it drop if he shot two of her precious herders. It would have been easy—the silencer on his M-14A1 was already in place, and all he needed to do was track the glowing red dot of the laser sight along the floor of the tunnel, then up the back of one of them.

The man first—the woman undoubtedly had slower reflexes and wouldn't even understand what had happened until it was too late.

All he had to do was place the laser's brilliant light on the back of the man's head, where it would glow like a ruby lit from within, then squeeze the trigger and replace the laser's dot with a gush of blood.

He could pick off the woman even before the man had fallen to the ground.

Still, it would be better to follow them a little longer.

As they moved deeper into the tunnel, Randall stole silently after them, moving like a wraith through the darkness, his tread giving off no sound. He paused when he came to the corpse hanging out of the alcove. He'd been almost certain who it was when he'd first seen it through the night vision goggles, but now he raised the head and gazed into the face. Even with the damage the bullet had done, he recognized Otto Vandenberg immediately.

The man and woman had taken his gun, along with his backpack, which would contain his logbook.

Putting on his goggles again, he peered into the darkness ahead. The two figures were still moving, walking quickly away from him. If they found a cross passage and got away . . .

If they got to the surface with Vandenberg's logbook . . .

Removing his night vision goggles, Perry Randall unslung his rifle, released the safety, and pressed the stock against his shoulder. Turning on the laser sight, he readied himself for the first shot. . . .

*   *   *

Heather tried to tell herself that the mass on the floor ahead of her couldn't be yet another corpse, but she knew it had to be. It wasn't just his utter stillness that told her the man was dead, or the unnatural sprawl of his limbs, or even the dark stain of blood on his chest.

It was the rat that was already nibbling at his face.

A choked sound of horror and revulsion escaped her throat, and she thought she would finally lose control of the nausea that still churned in her belly. A wave of dizziness made her lean against the wall to keep from falling.

As Keith Converse squatted down to examine the body on the floor, Heather—overwhelmed by the images of death she'd already seen that day—wanted to sink onto the floor herself, close her eyes, and try to put all of it out of her mind. But as her knees began to buckle under her, she saw it.

A red dot, creeping along the floor toward her.

An illusion.

It had to be an illusion.

She focused on the dot, willing it away.

But it crept closer, and it stirred a memory.

A memory of her father, teaching her how to use the guns he kept in the cabinet in the library.

"The laser sight is the best. At night, you can't miss. Just put the red dot on the ground in front of you, then start moving the gun until the dot is on the target.

"Then squeeze the trigger."

The dot moved closer, and Heather's hands tightened on the gun she was holding.

The gun that was just like one of her father's. . . .

Then her nausea—and terror—gave way to cold, pure rage.

Her fingers working quickly, she found the safety and released it.

She switched the rifle into automatic mode.

Raising the gun so the barrel was two feet above Keith Converse's head, she peered down the sight. In the distance, silhouetted against the dim light of one of the utility lamps in the ceiling, she could barely make out a figure.

Heather squeezed the trigger, then quickly moved the rifle barrel back and forth.

Just as her father had taught her. . . .

The red dot on the floor disappeared as the silence in the tunnel was shattered by the angry chatter of the automatic rifle. Keeping her finger tightly squeezed on the trigger, Heather emptied the contents of the magazine into the darkness, spraying the entire width of the tunnel with bullets. Even after the last cartridge was spent, she could still hear bullets screaming as they ricocheted away into the distance.

As silence once again fell, Keith stood up.

"Jesus," he whispered.

"He was going to kill us," Heather said, her voice dull. Her hands suddenly went limp, and the gun clattered to the floor. "He was going to kill us just the way he taught me."

Keith gazed at her steadily. "Who?" he asked, wanting the answer to come from her.

Heather's control finally gave way. "My father!" she cried out, the words resounding in the tunnel. "Don't you see? It was my father!" As the echo of her anguished words died away, she walked slowly into the darkness toward where he lay. Her father was sprawled on his back, a bloodstain spreading across his shirt. His eyes were open, and as she shined a flashlight into his face, he seemed to look up at her with an expression of surprise. Kneeling, she gazed into his empty eyes, then laid a hand on his cheek. "I'm sorry," she whispered. "I'm so sorry." But even as she said it, she knew she'd had no choice.

It was her father who had set the rules, not her, and a moment later she would have been the one who died by his hand.

"What have you done?" she said softly. "Oh, Daddy."

Leaving her father there in the dark, she started back toward Keith.

*   *   *

The rattle of the semiautomatic rifle finally died away, but neither Jeff nor Jinx moved, remaining pressed against the side of the passage they'd turned into.

Another sound came to them—the clatter of something heavy falling onto the concrete floor.

Jeff's mind raced, trying to decide what to do. Whoever was out there hadn't been firing at them—they would have heard bullets ricocheting off the walls and pipes if the gunman had been shooting in their direction.

So whoever it was had shot the other way.

But why?

At what?

But what did it matter? Within a second or two the hunter would realize his mistake, reload, and then—

Unless I shoot first.

So there it was.

The rifle they'd taken from Monsignor McGuire was slung over his shoulder, and now Jeff took it in his hands. Reloaded with a full magazine, it felt strange—heavy, cold, and dangerous.

There was nothing about the gun that hinted at any kind of genuine sport. Jeff had seen hunting rifles before—dozens of them, in fact. He'd even admired some of them, for their remarkable craftsmanship. Some of the best had seemed almost warm to the touch, so perfectly was the wood of their stocks polished. Many had been inlaid with gold or silver or mother-of-pearl, giving the guns the look of a work of art.

Those were the guns used for target shooting or hunting game.

The gun in his hand, though, was purely utilitarian, constructed of cold metal and hard rubber, every part designed to function perfectly.

It was almost as if the rifle's designer had known it could have only one possible use, and had refused to try to disguise that use with any kind of beauty at all.

Jeff tightened his grip on the rifle, then released the safety.

Was that all he had to do? Was there nothing more left than to step out into the tunnel, point the thing in the direction from which the gunfire had come, and pull the trigger?

He looked around, searching in the darkness one last time for another way out, but knew there was none.

It was time to face whoever awaited him in the tunnel.

"Stay here," he whispered. "It's me they want. They don't care about you."

"But—"

Jinx's words were abruptly cut off by an anguished cry:

"My father! Don't you see? It was my father!"

Jeff stiffened, the echo of the words resounding off the walls, thundering down the tunnels, only to be back a split second later.

"My father . . . my father . . . father . . ."

"Heather," he whispered. He pictured himself standing in the middle of the tunnel, emptying the gun into the darkness with the intent of killing whoever might be there.

And he *would* have killed someone.

He would have killed Heather.

Dropping the rifle, Jeff Converse stepped out into the tunnel.

Keith heard the sound of someone moving in the darkness just beyond the range of his vision. He reached for the rifle he'd retrieved from the pool of blood beneath Viper's corpse and raised it to his shoulder after releasing the safety and putting the firing mechanism on automatic.

He peered into the scope and saw the silhouette of a man against the utility light that glowed in the distance. His finger began to tighten on the trigger, but as the figure took another step, he hesitated.

"Jeff?" he whispered, the name barely audible.

But it was enough for Heather. She was already racing down the tunnel toward Jeff, calling his name. Keith's impulse was to drop the rifle and run after her, to be with her when she threw her arms around his son. But he changed his mind.

Better to let them have their moment.

Putting the rifle aside, he reached into the backpack he'd taken from Vandenberg and took out the radio. Turning it on and putting the tiny headphone in his ear, he heard a voice.

Eve Harris's voice.

"This is Control. Report, Viper."

Keith raised the radio to his lips and spoke slowly and distinctly. "This isn't Viper," he said. "This is Keith Converse, Ms. Harris. Viper is dead. So are Mamba and Adder and Rattler. Maybe you can still save Cobra, whoever he is."

Dropping the radio back into the backpack, Keith moved down the tunnel to join his son.

CHAPTER 39

Eve Harris glared furiously at the radio in her hand. It wasn't possible—Converse was trying to trick her! They couldn't all be dead—there was no way he could have beaten five perfectly armed men.

No—not five.

Only four.

Cobra—Arch Cranston—was still alive out there somewhere. So the two of them would finish the job the other four had botched.

Her eyes shifted from the radio to Malcolm Baldridge, who stood near the door to his private workroom. He was so still, she could almost mistake him for one of the trophies to which he'd so expertly applied his skills. "Get me a pack and a rifle!" she snapped.

Baldridge made no move until she took a step toward him, radiating fury, her eyes flashing dangerously.

"You can't—" Baldridge began, but she cut him off.

"Do what I tell you," she commanded, her voice low, but carrying enough danger to send Baldridge scurrying into the next room. While he was gone, she stripped off her street clothes and changed into a black jumpsuit that was only slightly too large for her. By the time she was dressed, Baldridge was back, carrying a backpack in one hand, a Steyr SSG-PI in the other.

"It has an infrared sight and—" Baldridge began, but Eve Harris didn't let him finish.

"I know what it has," she hissed, snatching the rifle from his hands and quickly checking it over. "And I know how to use it." She quickly rifled through the bag, replacing the radio with her own, setting its frequency to match Arch Cranston's. Finally, she put on a pair of night vision goggles, opened the door to the tunnel, and stepped through. As Baldridge closed and locked the door behind her, she switched the goggles on, the blackness of the tunnel giving way to a greenish glow. She moved her head slowly around, studying the tunnel in both directions.

Except for a large rat creeping along the wall to the left, the tunnel was empty. She reached into her backpack, groped until her fingers closed on the radio, then turned it on, pressed the transmit button, and whispered into the microphone.

"Cobra, this is Control. Come in."

When there was no response, she repeated her words, then swore under her breath as she dropped the radio into one of the pockets of her black jacket.

In her mind, she reviewed the maps of the tunnels the men had made over the years. The range of the radios was short, which meant that Converse was probably still closer to her than Arch Cranston, assuming Cranston was still alive. But could she assume that?

What if Converse was lying? What if Cranston was dead as well?

But Converse could just as easily have been lying about who was dead. Perhaps it was only Vandenberg! She picked up the radio again and quickly tried to reach the other members of the team.

Silence.

She swore again, then made up her mind. The last time he'd reported, Viper had been in Sector 3, on Level 2. Eve Harris visualized the map, and could picture Vandenberg's favorite ambush as clearly as if she were looking at a page in the back of his notebook. The radio back in her pocket and holding the Steyr, she set out.

*   *   *

"**W**hat's going on?" Heather asked as one after another the radios in the backpack came alive.

"She's trying to figure out if I was telling her the truth," Keith replied. He pulled McGuire's radio out just in time to hear Eve Harris's voice demanding a response. The voice was clearer than it had been only a few moments ago, when he'd spoken to her himself over Vandenberg's radio.

"I think she's in the tunnels," he said.

"Where?"

"Behind us," Jeff replied, his eyes still fastened on the map in the back of Perry Randall's notebook. "Look," he said, as Heather peered over his shoulder at the page that was illuminated by a flashlight. He placed a finger on a mark on the thickest line on a page headed LEVEL 1, SECTION 1. "I think that's where they come in." He flipped a couple of pages, and placed his finger on another spot. "And this is where we are."

"But how do we get out?" Heather asked.

"What about one of the subway stations?" Keith asked.

Jeff shook his head. "They've got guards at all of them."

"And we've got guns," Keith replied, his voice hard.

Jeff looked up at his father. "And if we start shooting in a subway station . . ." His voice trailed off, but there was no need to complete the thought. The rest of them knew as well as he did what would happen if they started firing automatic rifles in a subway station. In a couple of seconds a dozen people could be dead, and twice as many wounded. Jeff's finger moved to another spot on the map. "Here," he said. "I think we can get out here, if we can just make it that far."

The three people huddled around him stared at the spot he was indicating, and it was finally Jinx who said what everyone else was thinking. "There's nothing there—it doesn't show any shafts or passages or anything."

"Exactly," Jeff said. "That's just what we need—a place where there's nothing at all."

Closing the notebook, he picked up one of the guns and

bags and headed west, picturing what he'd seen only a week
before he'd been arrested.

Maybe, if they were lucky, it was still there. . . .

It's all right, Eve Harris told herself. *I'm just imagining it.*
But she wasn't imagining it—she wasn't imagining it at
all. The green light in the night vision goggles was definitely
getting dimmer.

Not a problem, at least not yet—there would be a flashlight
in the backpack! Slipping it off her shoulders, she zipped it
open and plunged her hands into its depth.

No flashlight!

But there had to be!

Now she opened the bag wide, searching it thoroughly,
peering into its depths with the goggles.

No flashlight, not in the main compartment or any of the
auxiliary pockets, either. Damn Baldridge! Why hadn't he
checked the pack?

Then she'd just have to do without light for a while. Slinging the pack and rifle back on her shoulders, she switched the
goggles off and pulled them away from her head. She waited
for her eyes to get used to the dark, but it was far blacker than
she'd thought it would be, and as the darkness closed around
her and her irises opened as wide as they would go, she felt
the first tendrils of fear reach out toward her.

It's all right, she repeated to herself. *I know exactly where I
am, and if I have to, I can get back without the goggles.* But
even as she silently reassured herself, she knew it wasn't
quite true. She knew the turns well enough—there had been
only three of them, and she hadn't changed levels at all. But
as the smothering darkness wrapped more tightly around her,
those first tendrils of fear began to coalesce into terror, and
she quickly replaced the goggles over her eyes and switched
them on.

For a moment the green fog seemed brilliant, and her fear
backed away. But a few seconds later, as her eyes reacted to

the sudden light, the green faded again, and her fear came rushing back.

Cranston, she thought. Call Cranston.

Groping in her pocket, she found the radio, pressed the transmitter, and whispered into the mike: "This is Control. Come in, Cobra! This is Control!" Three times more she tried calling; three times more she got no response.

Dropping the radio back in her pocket, she turned around and started quickly back the way she'd come. She hurried her step as the green light began to fade.

After what seemed an eon, she came to the last turn she'd made. She remembered clearly that she'd turned right, so now she turned left and gazed into the distance.

The tunnel seemed to stretch on forever, disappearing into the green haze.

But that was wrong—it hadn't been that long; she was sure of it. Had she turned the wrong way?

Spinning around, she looked in the other direction.

Again the tunnel seemed to stretch away into the fog.

The green glow was dimmer now, and she wasn't as certain of her bearings as she'd been only a moment ago. She turned again, searching for some clue as to which was the right direction, then turned once more.

But which way was she facing?

As the batteries continued to lose their strength, the green light faded, and Eve tore the goggles from her head in frustration. Losing her grip on them, she heard them clatter away into the darkness as once again the blackness closed around her.

But the men had always talked about light! Utility lights that gave them enough illumination so they didn't need the goggles most of the time.

Most of the time.

But not all of the time.

The goggles!

She had to find the goggles!

Dropping to her hands and knees, she felt around in the slime that covered the floor, searching. They couldn't have fallen far away—surely they weren't more than a few feet from her! She reached out, groping in the darkness, and a piece of broken glass slashed through the palm of her hand. Reflexively jerking her hand back, she automatically put it to her lips.

The taste of blood filled her mouth.

With the other hand, she groped at the wound, trying to determine how bad it was. She could feel blood running across her palm and down her wrist, and then her filthy fingers found the cut.

Two inches long at least, running across her palm. She had to bite back a scream of agony as her fingers traced the open wound, grinding the filth from the floor deep into the open gash.

Clenching her fist to stanch the flow of blood, she reached out in the darkness once more, this time with her left hand. But then she jerked it back before she could touch anything, terrified of what might happen to her if she slashed her other hand, too.

Getting unsteadily to her feet, Eve Harris took a tentative step, and bumped into a wall.

Panic welled in her, but she fought against it, bracing herself against the wall, willing her heart to stop pounding, battling against the panic that seemed to be strangling her and made it almost as impossible for her to breathe as it was for her to see.

Light, she thought. *I have to find light.*

But everywhere she looked, there was only the blackness.

The blackness, and the creatures that she could suddenly hear creeping through it.

Creeping toward her.

*   *   *

Jeff froze.

"What is it?" Heather asked from behind him. "What's wrong?"

He reached back, his fingers finding her wrist and closing on it. "Listen," he said.

A silence fell over the four of them, unbroken for a moment by anything except the dripping of water. Then they heard it. A great whumping sound, as if something heavy had been dropped from a great height.

Less than a minute later they heard it again: *whump!*

They were still in the utility tunnel, but they'd come to a cross passage, and it sounded like the noise was coming from straight ahead. But before they heard the sound again, another sound intruded on the quiet; this time, though, it was the familiar sound of a subway train.

The sound grew steadily louder, and they could feel the draft of the air being pushed ahead of the train coming down the cross passage. A moment later they saw the beam of the headlight cross ahead of them, and then the train itself thundered past the end of the passage, its lighted cars flashing like a strobe, the couplings rattling, the brakes squealing as it began to slow for a station.

Then the train was gone and silence once again descended. Just as he was about to start into the passage, a glimmer of red caught Jeff's eye, gone so quickly he wasn't certain it had been there at all. Yet every nerve in his body now seemed to be sending him a tingle of warning, and he stopped short, putting his hand back to block Heather. They were so close to their goal, but someone, he was sure, still lay between them and the one place where they might be able to escape the tunnels with no resistance from either the hunters, the herders, or the gamekeepers.

As the other three clustered close behind him, he whispered a warning so softly it was almost inaudible, but to his own ears he might as well have bellowed it into the darkness. "Someone's there. One of the hunters."

"We'll go," Keith replied as quietly as Jeff. "Heather and Jinx, stay here."

Both the girls opened their mouths as if to argue, but when Jeff shook his head and held a finger to his lips, they said nothing. "Stay here until we signal you," he told them.

While Heather and Jinx crouched in the darkness, Jeff and Keith crept noiselessly forward, edging closer and closer to the intersection with the subway tunnel ahead. Each of them carried a rifle, along with one of the backpacks taken from the fallen hunters. As they came to the junction, Jeff pressed against one of the walls, Keith against the opposite.

They waited, listening.

Nothing.

The seconds stretched into a minute, then two.

Still nothing.

Jeff was about to edge out into the subway tunnel when his father shook his head. Then, as Jeff watched, Keith shouted into the darkness:

"I'm coming for you, you bastard!" And as he shouted, he hurled the backpack he was carrying into the subway tunnel, dimly lit by the wide-spaced bulbs mounted high on the walls.

Arch Cranston—code name "Cobra"—had already snapped at the bait by the time he realized it was a trap. At the sound of the angry words, he raised his rifle to his shoulder, and he'd already locked the sight onto the object hurtling from the side tunnel and squeezed the trigger before he realized it wasn't the man he'd expected at all.

But it was too late, he was already committed. As he realized what was happening, the trap closed.

Before Keith's words had died away, they heard the chattering of a rifle, and the backpack was torn to shreds by the rain of lead slashing through it. The rifle was still chattering when Keith, holding the Steyr at waist level, stepped into the tunnel, pointing the rifle in the direction from which the other gun was firing and squeezing the trigger, spraying the tunnel with slugs.

As his bullets ricocheted off the walls and whined away into the distance, the other gun fell silent, followed by a small, gurgling groan.

"Got him," Jeff heard his father mutter. Turning away from the sight of the man he'd just killed, Keith said to him, "Let's get going."

Signaling to Heather and Jinx, Jeff waited only long enough for them to catch up before he plunged into the subway tunnel, turning in the opposite direction from the fallen man.

Eve Harris heard two blasts of gunfire and instinctively dropped to the floor of the tunnel. Favoring her injured right hand, she fell hard on her left, and felt a sharp pain slash up her arm and into her shoulder. Cursing, she rolled over, shrugged the backpack and rifle off her body, and managed to sit up.

Gingerly, she touched her left wrist. The pain was so bad, she knew it wasn't just sprained, but broken.

Out, she thought. *I've got to get out.*

Lurching to her feet, she started along the tunnel once again, feeling her way along the wall with her cut right hand, her left arm far too painful to use at all. Ahead of her, she saw a glimmer of light.

At first she thought it was an illusion, but a moment later she knew it wasn't—somewhere ahead, somewhere far in the distance, there was the dim glow of a light. The pain in her left arm forgotten, her right hand once more clenched into a protective fist, she began to run through the darkness toward the beacon of light. Her panic washed away and her heart raced with excitement as her eyes fastened on the guiding light.

Then, so suddenly she had no time to prepare for it, her

right foot connected not with the floor of the tunnel, but with nothing at all. As her leg dropped into an open shaft, her face crashed against its far edge, the concrete lip smashing the bridge of her nose. Screaming in agony, she dropped down the shaft, her body bouncing off its walls, her torn right hand spasmodically clutching for anything that might break her fall.

A second later she dropped out of the bottom of the shaft, smashing onto the concrete floor below.

She lay there a moment, stunned.

The pain coursed through every nerve in her body.

But she wasn't dead. Not dead, or even unconscious, for she could see—see clearly—by the light of a bulb that hung in a metal cage from the ceiling a few yards away.

She was going to be all right!

She lay still for another moment, catching her breath, forcing herself to overcome the agony that possessed her.

Then, at last, she tried to sit up.

And discovered that she couldn't.

Couldn't move her arms, or her legs.

It felt as if all her bones were broken.

She tried to scream, to call for help, but even her voice had deserted her.

Then, from somewhere in the distance, she heard something.

Footsteps.

Slow, shuffling footsteps, but definitely footsteps!

Someone was coming! Someone who would help her! Hope surged inside her once again. She wasn't going to die here—she was going to be all right.

The footsteps came steadily closer, and then she saw a face looming above her.

It was a man, squatting down beside her, peering at her. His grimy face was covered with stubble, his eyes were bloodshot. He leaned closer, and when he opened his mouth, his fetid breath poured over her like so much sewage. In response, her belly contracted with a great spasm of nausea, and vomit spewed from her mouth.

The man recoiled, staggering to his feet, wiping the flecks of vomit from his face with the filthy sleeve of his coat as he swore at her. A moment later he straightened and his foot lashed out, and she felt her ear split as the toe of his boot crashed into it. Then he was gone, shambling off into the darkness, muttering to himself.

As she struggled to clear her windpipe of her own vomit, Eve Harris saw the first of the rats creep out of the darkness, drawn from their lairs by the scent of fresh blood.

Her blood . . .

In vain, she tried to cry out.

But even if she had been able to make a sound, there was no one left to hear her.

They were heading north in the subway tunnel. Jeff was almost certain he knew where they were—under Broadway—and what he was looking for should be just ahead. And then, in the distance, he saw it.

A streak of light, so thin it was barely visible. He moved faster, broke into a trot, then a run. Behind him he could hear Heather and Jinx and his father, their feet pounding on the concrete floor of the subway tunnel. They were between the tracks, the third rail on the left, and as they ran, the streak of light grew brighter.

Far ahead he saw another light. Though it was just a pinpoint, he knew it was another subway train, racing toward them.

"We've gotta get off the track!" Jinx yelled.

But there was nowhere to go—no alcoves cut into the walls, not even a catwalk! But the streak of light was only a few dozen yards farther along. "Hurry," he yelled. "We can make it!" He ran faster, hurling himself along the tracks, racing straight toward the train.

He could hear it now, even feel on his face the rush of the air the train was pushing in front of it.

The rest of them were right behind him, and suddenly he was there.

A plywood panel, covering a hole in the subway tunnel's wall, fixed to the outside of the tunnel so insecurely that the streak of daylight was obvious now.

"No!" he heard Heather yell as she realized what he was going to do. But it was too late.

Jeff hurled himself at the sheet of plywood, launching his body over the electrified rail, his arms raised, his body twisting so he'd hit the wood with his shoulder. If it held, and he dropped back—

His body smashed against the plywood. The nails holding it to the concrete squealed . . . but held, and Jeff dropped to the subway bed, missing the deadly third rail by a fraction of an inch.

There was a blare from a horn, and then the scream of brakes. Jeff looked up to see the train still hurtling toward him, and for a moment he froze, caught in the juggernaut's headlight like a jackrabbit. Then another voice crashed through the cacophony.

"Down! Now!"

Instinctively obeying his father's voice, Jeff dropped face-down into the gravel, then heard his father's voice bellow out again.

"Fire!"

Over the roar of the onrushing train there was a blast of gunfire. Jeff shrank away from it, but it was over almost as soon as it began, and when the blasting guns fell silent, everything had changed.

Light, daylight, was pouring through the hole in the concrete that only a moment before had been covered by the now-shattered sheet of plywood. Jeff scrambled to his feet and, with his father on one side, Heather on the other, and Jinx shoving him from behind, hurtled through the opening in the subway tunnel's wall. Then they were all blinking in the brilliant sunlight and breathing in the fresh breeze that was flowing off the river a few blocks to the west. Behind them, the subway train shot past, gone as quickly as it had come. As its roar faded away, Jeff looked out at the great excavation that lay before him.

It had changed since the last time he'd seen it, months ago, when his class in urban construction had taken another tour of the huge site where half a dozen buildings had stood. It had been a vast pit filled with heavy equipment meant for burrowing deep into the earth beneath the city. By now the pit had bottomed out, and the pile drivers were at work—the pile drivers he'd heard from deep within the tunnels—driving huge pilings into the bedrock to anchor the foundation of the skyscraper that wouldn't be completed for another two years.

All around them there were wooden forms for the concrete that would soon begin to fill the pit, and as Jeff gazed at them, he realized that just a couple of weeks later—maybe even less—the opening he'd just come through would have been blocked off forever.

But it didn't matter. None of it mattered, for he was free—free of the Tombs and free of the tunnels and free of the certain death that was all that had awaited him a few hours ago.

Reaching out and pulling Heather close, Jeff drew the cool afternoon air deep into his lungs, then leaned down and put his lips close to Heather's ear. "What do you say we walk home?" he murmured. "I think I'd just as soon skip the subway."

FIVE YEARS LATER

Randall Converse's grip on his father's hand tightened as he gazed down the stairs. "Don't want to," he said, hanging back and tugging his father's arm.

Stepping away from the stream of people emerging from the subway onto Broadway, Jeff squatted down so his eyes were almost level with his son's. The four-year-old's features had taken on the stubborn, frowning expression that was a perfect replica of his grandfather's face when Keith had made up his mind and wasn't about to have it changed. "It's okay, Randy," Jeff said, doing his best to keep his voice from giving away his own nervousness about going into the subway. Years later he still felt a twinge of anxiety whenever he went beneath the streets of the city. On the trains and platforms, he constantly found himself glancing over his shoulder, scanning the faces of the homeless who rode the trains and panhandled in the stations when the transit cops weren't around. A suffocating feeling descended upon him when the trains took him into the tunnels, and sometimes he imagined he saw the faces of the herders peering out of the darkness. The claustrophobia lessened when he reached the brilliant light of the stations, but his anxiety only disappeared for good when he was back on the surface. He and Heather were both determined that their son would not fall prey to their own fears, even in the face of Jeff's parents' arguments. "Millions of people ride the trains every day," Jeff had insisted when his parents—for once united, if only on this one issue—had expressed their shock that he would consider taking Randy into the subways. "I'm not going to have him grow up being afraid to use them."

He could now see the same fear in Randy's eyes that he'd seen in his mother's when she'd begged him not to take her grandson into the tunnels. "There's nothing to be afraid of," he said, brushing a stray lock of curly brown hair off the boy's forehead. "This is just another train. You like the train that brings us into the city, don't you?"

Randy said nothing, but Jeff saw the fear in the boy's expression start to fade as curiosity replaced it. "And you want to see where I used to live before you were born, don't you?"

Randy nodded, but there was enough uncertainty in his eyes that Jeff lifted him up into his arms. "How about if I carry you?"

"No!" Randy instantly objected. "I'm not a baby!"

Setting the boy back on his feet, Jeff took his son's hand and together they started walking down into the subway station.

A familiar knot of anxiety began to form deep in Jeff's belly.

"Now, this isn't so bad, is it?" he asked as they settled onto a bench in a well-lit car a few minutes later.

Randy shook his head, but said nothing until the train moved from the station into the darkness of the tunnels. "What if it gets stuck?" Randy asked. "How do we get out? Do we have to walk?"

The thought of actually walking through the tunnels chilled Jeff to his core, but when he spoke, his voice was steady. "It won't get stuck," he reassured the boy. "And even if it does, someone will come and fix it."

As the train moved north, Jeff sensed that Randy was starting to relax. As the stations flashed by one after another, so did his memories of the days he'd spent trapped in the tunnels beneath the city.

But in the end, the nightmare he'd lived since he'd saved

Cynthia Allen's life in the station at 110th Street had finally ended. He and Heather had been married a month after his escape, and nine months to the day after the wedding, Randy had been born.

With that, everything in their lives had changed once more.

He finished architecture school and moved back to Bridge-hampton, since neither he nor Heather wanted to raise Randy in the city.

In the days following Jeff's escape from the tunnels, there had been remarkably little publicity about the unusual number of prominent people who had died in such a short period of time. Not a word of the real story appeared in the press, and Jeff and Heather knew exactly why: The Hundred had closed ranks, and the members' version had replaced the truth.

It seemed Perry Randall had been the victim of a mugger.

Carey Atkinson had committed suicide in the face of a failing marriage, mounting debts, and a looming scandal in the Police Department.

Monsignor Terrence McGuire had retreated to an isolated monastery in Tuscany.

Judge Otto Vandenberg had died of a stroke and Arch Cranston had succumbed to a heart attack a day later.

Eve Harris, however, had apparently simply vanished, and though for months afterward the media had indulged in endless—and ever more sensational—speculation as to what might have happened to her, even that story had eventually faded away.

The One Hundred, as anonymous as ever, silently filled the vacancies within their ranks.

The life of the city went on.

When the train reached 110th Street Jeff stood up and led his son to the platform. As they headed for the stairs to the surface, he glanced at the spot where Cindy Allen had been attacked.

The spot where the near destruction of his life had begun.

Nothing about that far corner of the station hinted at what

had happened there almost six years earlier. Perhaps it was that very anonymity that gave him pause. He was still gazing at the blank white tile of the far wall when his son tugged at his arm.

"What's wrong, Daddy?" the little boy piped.

His son's voice pulled Jeff back from the past and he smiled down at Randy. "Nothing," he assured him, swinging the boy up into his arms and starting quickly up the stairs. "Nothing at all."

The anxiety of being in the subway evaporating in the daylight, Jeff lowered his son to the sidewalk, but didn't let go of his hand as they waited for a break in traffic.

"You said you lived right by the subway," Randy said, looking around at the restaurants and shops that lined the street.

"Up there," Jeff replied, pointing to the back of the building where he could see the familiar window of his old apartment. "See? The brick building. I lived on the third floor."

Randy gazed solemnly up at the grimy structure. "I like our house better," he pronounced.

"So do I," Jeff agreed as the light changed and the sea of traffic finally parted, allowing them to cross. "I like it a lot better."

A couple of minutes later they came to the landing on the third floor, and Randy, recognizing the woman who stood in the apartment's open door, pulled loose from his father and ran toward her.

"Jinx!" he cried out, wrapping his arms around Jinx's neck as she lifted him up and planted a kiss on his forehead.

"Look at you! Almost grown up. Too big for a lollipop, right?"

"No!" Randy squealed. Wriggling back to the floor, he looked at his father. "Can I have one?" he pleaded.

"Just don't tell your mom," Jeff said, winking at the little boy. As Randy peeled the wrapping off the lollipop Jinx had produced from the pocket of her sweatshirt, Jeff glanced around the apartment. Even with his drafting table gone, it had the unmistakable look of students' quarters. The posters on the walls had changed, and the brick-and-board shelves he'd built were now filled with Jinx's textbooks instead of his own, but the paint was still peeling, the curtains hadn't been changed, and the carpet was even more worn than he remembered.

"Hey, be it ever so humble, there's no place like home," Jinx said, grinning as she read his thoughts. "In two more years, I graduate, and then I'm out of here." Her grin faded. "I didn't mean that the way it sounded. If you hadn't let me move in here—"

"You'd have found somewhere else to live," Jeff cut in, not letting her finish. "You could have stayed with Tillie."

Jinx shook her head. "I love Tillie, but if I'd stayed down there much longer . . ."

Her voice trailed off. They both remembered the rooms under the streets where Tillie still looked after her family. Most of the faces had changed. Robby had moved to the surface two years ago when the parents of one of his schoolmates found out where he was living and invited him to share their son's bedroom. It wasn't until they'd invited Tillie and Jinx for dinner and discussed the whole situation that Robby had finally agreed to try the surface again, and that had only been with the understanding that he could go back to Tillie any time he wanted to. He still went to visit Tillie at least once a week, and she emerged from her "co-op" every few months to have dinner with Robby's new family. But at the end of the evening, she always looked forward to getting back to the tunnels. "Too complicated up here," she insisted. "Too much to think about, too much to worry about."

"So?" Jeff asked Randy as the boy began licking his lollipop. "Sure you don't want to move in here?"

Randy shook his head. "It's ugly," he pronounced.

"Hey! Is that any way to talk about Jinx's house?"

"The boy's got good taste," Jinx said. "Let's go get lunch. I have two classes this afternoon, and then I've got to get to work."

"Still working both jobs?"

Jinx shrugged. "The way I figure it, I didn't work any jobs for so long that now I'm playing catch-up. By the time I graduate, I figure I'll be even, and then I can cut back to one job. And that one is going to pay more than waitressing."

Leaving the apartment, they went to the diner that had always been Jeff's favorite and found a table by the window so they could watch the activity on Broadway. The mix of people hadn't changed much since Jeff had lived in the neighborhood: mostly students with a lot of university faculty and staff mixed in. But there were others as well—tourists and shoppers and people just prowling the city.

And always the homeless.

An old woman—nearly indistinguishable from Tillie to a casual observer—pushed an overflowing shopping cart, and down the street three shabbily dressed men sat on the sidewalk, their backs resting against a wall, panhandling for change.

For a long moment both Jinx and Jeff gazed at them in silence, and it was finally Jeff who uttered the thought that was in both their heads.

"Do you suppose it's still going on?"

Seconds ticked by as Jinx said nothing, but at last she shook her head. "It was Ms. Harris," she said. "She was the one who passed out the money, and without the money, it never would have worked."

"Ever wonder what happened to her?"

Jinx's expression darkened. "I'm just glad she's gone."

Half an hour later Jeff and Randy were back in the subway station, waiting for a train to take them back downtown. "Who's Ms. Harris?" Randy asked, looking up at his father.

Jeff hesitated, then said, "Just someone we used to know, a long time ago."

"Was she a friend of Auntie Jinx's?"

A southbound train roared into the station. Jeff clutched tight to Randy's hand as the crowd of departing passengers swirled past them, then helped him step onto the train. "No," he said as the doors closed. "Ms. Harris wasn't a friend of Auntie Jinx's. She wasn't a friend of anyone's."

The train started to move and Jeff reached up with his free hand to grab the railing above his head. For a fleeting second, he saw someone peering at him through the window from the platform.

A woman, her face nearly lost in the folds of a ragged shawl.

He glimpsed her face for only a few fleeting seconds, and yet it terrified him. It was a face that looked as if it had been attacked. The skin was deeply scarred, the features distorted and twisted. It reminded him of the tunnels and the time he'd spent in them, seeing people who had been attacked by other people, or rats, or insects, or alcohol and drugs, or simply by life itself.

It was a face that was universal in the tunnels.

It was the eyes that he recognized.

They were the same eyes that had looked at him during the one moment when he'd thought a stranger might choose to help him.

And that person had turned away.

Now, as the train began to move, it was Jeff who turned away from Eve Harris. When his son asked him a moment later if he knew who the lady was, he just shook his head.

"No," he said. "She wasn't anybody. I don't think anybody was there at all."

AUTHOR'S NOTE

ABOUT THE PEOPLE LIVING
UNDER MANHATTAN

A full count of the people living beneath the streets of Manhattan is difficult to achieve for two simple reasons: The population is transient and most census officials do not wish to go into the tunnels. Estimates of their numbers vary wildly, from a few hundred, to a few thousand, to tens of thousands. Since Grand Central Station was restored and most of its public seating removed, the homeless have largely disappeared from that very public venue, though they can still be found making efforts to keep themselves clean in the rest rooms on the lower levels. Though many of the "nests" above the tracks have been cleaned out, this does not mean the people who inhabited those nests are no longer in the city; rather, they have simply burrowed deeper into the tunnels, beyond the reach of official New York.

To date, there is no complete and integrated map of the tunnel system beneath the city. Partial maps exist: the subway system, the water system, the various utility systems. But in addition to the tunnels and passageways and storm drains that are still in use, there are miles of abandoned tunnels that have been long forgotten. Forgotten, at any rate, by everyone except those who live in them.

Contrary to popular belief, not all the people who live beneath the streets are derelicts and drunks. Many of them are productive members of society, holding jobs and attending school, giving false surface addresses to whatever bureaucracies they come in contact with. Some families have chosen to live under the streets rather than having their children separated from them by government agencies. Many of these people do not consider themselves homeless, but only "houseless." They organize themselves into tribes and family groups and establish territorial claims beneath the city. It is said that the deeper people live beneath the city, the less frequently they visit the surface and the less likely it is that they will ever live on the surface again.

Many of our subterranean citizens suffer from mental illness and chemical dependencies that often make them incapable of taking advantage of the services that are provided for them. They drift through our lives, muttering softly to themselves or ranting at invisible enemies, until finally they disappear back underground.

Underground and out of our consciousness.

All of the characters and events in this book, on the surface and in the tunnels, are fictional. At least, I hope they are . . .

—J.S.

ACKNOWLEDGMENTS

Many, many people helped me in the preparation of this book, especially with regard to the New York City criminal justice system. My dear friend Elkan Abramowitz and his partner, Bill McGuire, connected me with all the right people and guided me through the various judicial departments of New York City, and Marvin Mitzner, Esq., put me in touch with the mayor's office. People from the district attorney's office, the police department, and the Department of Correction were all very cooperative in showing me their facilities, familiarizing me with their procedures, and answering my innumerable questions. From the district attorney's office, I particularly want to thank Constance Cucchiara, who spent a morning guiding me through the courtrooms at 100 Centre Street and solved the mystery of the missing twelfth floor. From the Midtown South Precinct, I am especially indebted to Adam D'Amico, who gave me a guided tour of the precinct house and instructed me in the procedures involved in booking a person into the judicial system. I owe a special thanks to Deborah Hamlor and Jo-Ona Danoise of the City of New York Department of Correction, who spent an entire day with me as I toured Rikers Island and the Manhattan Detention Complex. They not only provided me with mountains of information but were endlessly patient. Many thanks to both of you! Others who were generous with their time and information at Rikers Island were Bureau Captain Sheila Vaughan, Head of

Special Transportation Brian Riordan, and many other correction officers. Thank you for an enlightening experience and for your time and energy. John Scudiero, warden of the Manhattan Detention Complex, also took several hours to educate me about his facility and its relationship to the New York City courts and provided me with a tour from a prisoner's perspective. I also wish to thank the judges and bailiffs who seemed utterly unsurprised to see me appearing through the doors usually reserved for prisoners. Thanks, too, to Mayor Giuliani's office for connecting me with various precincts in Manhattan, and to the transit police, who didn't apprehend me as I endlessly poked around subway stations and Grand Central station, taking pictures, peering down tunnels, and generally behaving in what must have seemed a very suspicious manner.

MIDNIGHT VOICES

Coming in hardcover in June 2002.
Published by Ballantine Books.

PROLOGUE

T *here's nothing going on.
      Nobody's watching me.
      Nobody's following me.*
The words had become a mantra, one he repeated silently
over and over again, as if by simple repetition he could make
the phrases true.

The thing was, he wasn't absolutely certain they weren't
true. If something really was going on, he had no idea what it
might be, or why. Sure, he was a lawyer, and everybody supposedly hated lawyers, but that was really mostly a joke. Besides, all he'd ever practiced was real estate law, and even that
had been limited to little more than signing off on contracts
of sale, and putting together some boilerplate for leases. As
far as he knew, no one involved in any of the deals he'd put his
initials on had even been unhappy, let alone developed a grudge
against him.

Nor had he caught anyone watching him. Or at least he hadn't
caught anyone watching him any more than anybody watched
anybody else. Like right now, while he was running in Central Park. He watched the other runners, and they watched
him. Well, maybe it wasn't really watching—more like keeping an eye out to make sure he didn't run into anybody else, or

get run over by a biker or a skater, or some other jerk who was on the wrong path. No, it was more like just a feeling he got sometimes. Not all the time.

Just some of the time.

On the sidewalk sometimes.

Mostly in the park.

Which was really stupid, now that he thought about it. That was one of the main reasons people went to the park, wasn't it? People-watching? Half the benches in it were filled with people who didn't seem to have anything better to do than feed the pigeons and the squirrels and watch other people minding their own business. One day a couple of weeks ago his son had asked him who they were.

"Who are who?" he'd countered, not sure what the boy was talking about.

"The people on the benches," the ten-year-old boy had asked. "The ones who are always watching us."

The little boy's sister, two years older than her brother, had rolled her eyes. "They're not watching us. They're just feeding the squirrels."

Up until that day, he'd never really thought about it at all. Never really noticed it. But after that, it had started to seem like maybe his son was right. It seemed like there was always someone watching whatever he and the kids were doing.

Some old man in a suit that looked out of date.

An old lady wearing a hat and gloves no matter what the time or day.

A nanny letting her eyes drift from her charges for a moment.

Just the normal people who drifted in and out the park. Sometimes they smiled and nodded, but they seemed to smile and nod at anyone who passed, at anyone who paid them the slightest bit of attention.

They were just people, spending a few hours sitting in the park and watching life passing them by. Certainly, it was nothing personal.

But somehow they seemed to be everywhere. He'd told himself it was just that he'd become conscious of them. When he hadn't thought about them, he'd hardly noticed them at all, but now that his son had pointed them out, he was thinking about them all the time.

Within a week, it had spread beyond the park. He was starting to see them everywhere he went. When he took his son to the barbershop, or the whole family went out for dinner.

"You're imagining things," his wife had told him just a couple of days ago. "It's just an old woman eating by herself. Of course she's going to look around at whoever's in the restaurant. Don't you, when you're eating alone?"

She was right, and he knew she was right, but it hadn't done any good. If fact, every day it had gotten worse, until he'd gotten to the point where no matter where he was, or what he was doing, he felt eyes watching him.

More and more, he'd get that tingly feeling, and know that someone behind him was watching him. He'd try to ignore it, try to resist the urge to look back over his shoulder, but eventually the hair on the back of his neck would stand up, and the tingling would turn into a chill, and finally he'd turn around.

And nobody would be there.

Except that of course there would always be someone there; this was the middle of Manhattan, for God's sake. There was always at least one person there, no matter where he was: on the sidewalk, in the subway, at work, in a restaurant, in the park.

Then it went beyond the feeling of being watched. A couple of days ago he'd started feeling as if he were being followed.

He'd stopped trying to resist the urge to turn around, and by today it seemed as if he were glancing over his shoulder every few seconds.

When he'd walked home from work this afternoon, he'd kept looking into store windows, but it wasn't the merchandise he was looking at; it was the reflections in the glass.

The reflections of people swirling around him, some of them almost bumping into him, some of them excusing themselves as they pushed past, some of them just looking annoyed.

But no one was following him.

He was sure of it.

Except that he wasn't sure of it at all, and when he'd gotten home he'd been so jumpy he'd had a drink, which he practically never did. A glass of wine with dinner was about all he ever allowed himself. Finally he'd decided to go for a run—it wouldn't be dark for another half hour, and maybe if he got some exercise—some real exercise—he would finally shake the paranoia that seemed to be tightening its grip every day.

"Now?" his wife had asked. "It's almost dark!"

"I'll be fine," he'd insisted.

And he was. He'd entered the park at Seventy-seventh, and headed north until he came to the Bank Rock Bridge. He'd headed east across the bridge, then started jogging through the maze of paths from which the Ramble had gotten its name. The area was all but deserted, and as he started working his way south toward the Bow Bridge he finally began to feel the paranoia lift.

There was no one watching him.

No one following him.

Nothing was going on at all.

As the tension began draining out of his body, his pace slowed to an easy jog. Late afternoon was turning into dusk, and the benches were empty of people. Even the few runners that were still out were picking up their pace, anxious to get out of the park before darkness overtook them. Behind him, he could hear another runner pounding along the path, and he eased over to the right to make it easy for the other to pass. But then, just when the other runner should have flashed by him, the pounding footsteps suddenly slowed.

And the feeling of paranoia came rushing back.

What had happened?

Why had the other runner slowed?

Why hadn't he gone past?

Something was wrong. He started to twist around to glance back over his shoulder.

Too late.

An arm snaked around his neck, an arm covered with some kind of dark material. Before he could even react to it, the arm tightened. His hands came up to pull the arm free, his fingers sinking into the sleeve that covered it, but then he felt a hand on his head.

A hand that was pushing his head to the left, deep into the crook of his assailant's elbow.

The arm tightened; the pressure increased.

He gathered his strength, raised his arm to jam his elbows back into his attacker's abdomen and—

With a quick jerk, the man behind him snapped his neck, and as his spine broke every muscle in his body went limp.

A second later his wallet and watch—along with his attacker—were gone, and his corpse lay still in the rapidly gathering darkness.

CHAPTER 1

Caroline Evans's dream was not a nightmare, and as it began evaporating into the morning light, she tried to cling to it, wanting nothing more than to retreat into the warm, sweet bliss of sleep where the joy and rapture of the dream and the reality of her life were one and the same.

Even now she could feel Brad's arms around her, feel his warm breath on her cheek, feel his gentle fingers caressing her skin. But none of the sensations were as sharp and perfect as they had been a few moments ago, and her moan—a moan that had begun in anticipation of ecstasy but which had already devolved into nothing more than an expression of pain and frustration—drove the last vestiges of the dream from her consciousness.

The arms that a moment ago had held her in comfort were suddenly a constricting tangle of sheets, and the heat of his breath on her cheek faded into nothing more than the weak warmth of a few rays of sunlight that had managed to penetrate the blinds covering the bedroom window.

Only the fingers touching her back were real, but they were not those of her husband leading her into a morning of slow lovemaking, but of her eleven-year-old son prodding her to get out of bed.

"It's almost nine," Ryan complained. "I'm gonna' be late for practice!"

Caroline rolled over, the image of her husband rising in her memory as she gazed at her son.

So alike.

The same soft brown eyes, the same unruly shock of brown hair, the same perfectly chiseled features, though Ryan's had not yet quite emerged from the softness of boyhood into the perfectly defined angles and planes that always made everyone—men and women alike—look twice whenever Brad entered a room.

Had the person who killed him looked twice? Had he looked even once? Had he even cared? Probably not—all he'd wanted was Brad's wallet and watch, and he'd gone about it in the most efficient method possible, coming up behind Brad, slipping an arm around his neck, and then using his other hand to shove Brad's head hard to the left, ripping vertebrae apart and crushing his spinal cord.

Maybe she shouldn't have gone to the morgue that day, shouldn't have looked at Brad's body lying on the cold metal of the drawer, shouldn't have let herself see death in his face.

Caroline shuddered at the memory, struggling to banish it. But she could never rid herself of that last image she had of her husband, an image that would remain seared in her memory until the day she died.

There were plenty of other people who could have identified him at the morgue. Any one of the partners in his law firm could have done it, or any of their friends. But she had insisted on going herself, certain that it was a mistake, that it hadn't been Brad at all who'd been mugged in the park.

A terrible cold seized her as the memory of that evening last fall came over her. When Brad had gone out for his run around part of the lake and through the Ramble she'd worried that it was too dark. But he'd insisted that a good run might help him get over the jumpiness that had come over him the last couple of weeks. She'd been helping Laurie with her math homework and barely responded to Brad's quick kiss before he'd headed out.

Hardly even nodded an acknowledgment of what turned out to be his last words: "Love you."

Love you.

The words kept echoing through her mind six hours later when she'd gazed numbly down at the face that was so utterly expressionless as to be almost unrecognizable. *Love you . . . love you . . . love you . . .* "I love you, too," she'd whispered, her vision mercifully blurred by the tears in her eyes. But in the months that had passed since that night more than half a year ago, her tears had all but dried up. Sometimes they still came, sneaking up on her late at night when she was alone in bed, trying to fall asleep, trying to escape into the dream in which Brad was still alive, and neither the tears nor the anger were a part of her life.

Caroline wasn't quite sure when the anger had begun to creep up on her.

Not at the funeral, where she'd sat with her arms holding her children close. Maybe at the burial, where she'd stood clutching their hands in the fading afternoon light as if they, too, might disappear into the grave that had swallowed up her husband.

That was when she'd first realized that Brad must have known he'd be alone in total darkness by the time he finished his run around the lake. And both of them knew how dangerous the park was after dark. Why had he gone? Why had he risked it? But she knew the answer to those questions, too. Even if he'd thought about it, he'd have finished his run. That was one of the things she loved about him, that he always finished whatever he started.

Books he didn't like, but finished anyway.

Rocks that looked easy to climb, but turned out to be almost impossible to scale. Almost, but not quite.

"Well, why couldn't you have quit just once?" she'd whispered as she peered out into the darkness of that evening four days after he'd died. "Why couldn't you just once have said 'This is really stupid,' and turned around and come home?" But he hadn't, and she knew that even if the thought had occurred to him, he still would have finished what he set out to do. That was when anger had first begun to temper her grief, and though the anger brought guilt along with it, she also knew that it was the anger rather than the grief that had let her keep functioning during those first terrible weeks after her life had been torn apart. Now, more than half a year later, the anger was finally beginning to give way to something else, something she couldn't yet quite identify. The first shock of Brad's death was over. The turmoil of emotions—the first numbness brought on by the shock of his death, followed by the grief, then the anger—was finally starting to settle down. As each day had crept inexorably by, she had slowly begun to deal with the new reality of her life. She was by herself now, with two children to raise, and no matter how much she might sometimes wish she could just disappear into the same grave into which Brad now lay, she also knew she loved her children every bit as much as she had loved their father.

No matter how she felt, their lives would go on, and so would hers. So she'd gone back to work at the antique shop, and done her best to help her children begin healing from wounds the loss of their father had caused. There had been just enough money in their savings account to keep them afloat for a few months, but last week she had withdrawn the last of it, and next week the rent was due. Her financial resources had sunk even lower than those of her emotions.

"Mom?" she heard Laurie calling from the kitchen. "Is there any more maple syrup?"

Sitting up and untangling herself from the sheets—and the turmoil of her own emotions as well—Caroline shooed her son out of the room. "Go tell your sister to look on the second shelf in the pantry. There should be one more bottle. And you're not going to be late for baseball practice. I promise."

As Ryan skittered out of the room, already yelling to his sister, Caroline got out of bed, opened the blinds, and looked out at the day. As the smell of Laurie's waffles filled her nostrils and the brilliant light of a spring Saturday flooded the room, Caroline shook off the vestiges of last nights dream.

"We're going to be all right," she told herself.

She only wished she felt as certain as the words sounded.